GYPSUM

Chris Rellim

BEACON
PUBLISHING GROUP

For information, or to order additional copies, please contact:

Beacon Publishing Group
P.O. Box 41573 Charleston, S.C. 29423
800.817.8480| beaconpublishinggroup.com

Publisher's catalog available by request.

ISBN-13: 978-1-949472-79-0

ISBN-10: 1-949472-79-5

Published in 2019. New York, NY 10001.

First Edition. Printed in the USA.

DEDICATION

This novel is dedicated to my parents, Michael D. Miller and Robin C. Miller (née Trotter), for supporting me in my creative endeavors both as a child and as an adult. I will be forever grateful.

SPECIAL THANKS TO

Sara Miller for mustering the courage to listen to my ideas I intended to include in Gypsum as I wrote it. Your reactions and feedback convinced me I was on the right track with the construction of this novel.

CHAPTER ONE
Mr. Favelle, Realtor

A new house, a new beginning. A new adventure, a new journey. A fresh start. Those were a few mottos among a handful Steven Dobrowski trumpeted the past few weeks to his family and friends. He, his wife Keisha, and their three children— Jeffrey, Tiffany, and Brittany— packed up their belongings in their old house in North Haven, Indiana, and loaded them into the moving truck. They were moving to Whitmond, a city also in Indiana, which was about a three-hour drive northwest of Bloomington.

Their new house was two-and-a-half times the square footage of their old house. It had six bedrooms, three bathrooms, and a finished attic.

Not only was it considerably larger than their old house, it was significantly more aesthetically appealing, too, both inside and out.

Their new house was a cottage style home that rested on an embankment. The main level exterior was made of cultured stone; some were gray, others maroon. Some off-white stones were randomly interspersed among the other stones. The remaining levels of the house were sided with grey siding. Not a color Keisha particularly cared for, but that wasn't a deal breaker. The concrete front porch was L-shaped; it started slightly after the front door and wrapped around the side of the house. The house was decadent, sugary eye candy to the sweet-toothed Dobrowski's.

Now, Steven and Keisha purchased this house without viewing it in person. The owner of the house, Antonio Favelle, also a relator, created a virtual tour video of the house. That's all the Dobrowski's needed. They were not only ready for a new house, but also desperate for one, since Steven recently accepted a position as a marketing analyst at an advertising agency.

The new house would also help nurse the wounds endured from the passing of Steven's mother, Rose Dobrowski, though children called her Granana. She was a regular fixture in the Dobrowski household the last few years.

In a phone conversation with the Dobrowski's, Mr. Favelle explained that the original owner of the house, Johnny Pistone, C.E.O. of Gypsum, Inc., demolished his old house and built the one they would be moving into, since Mr. Pistone decided to sell his company and move to Vienna with his family.

As a gift, Mr. Favelle considerably reduced the original selling price to an amount slightly under what the Dobrowski's could afford. To sweeten the pot, he said he would furnish the entire house with new furniture and appliances, except the finished attic, at no additional cost. How could the Dobrowski's say no to such a generous and sexy deal? Steven likened the declining of the lustrous offer to horse–kicking a man with metal cleats on the balls.

Steven and Keisha pulled into the driveway. Keisha nearly crashed into the moving truck because she was enamored with the house's beauty. Tiffany yelled for Keisha to stop, and she hit the brakes before the family's SUV made contact with the moving truck. The distance spared between the two vehicles was crepe-paper thin.

Mr. Favelle was parked in front of the house. When the Dobrowski's arrived, he didn't immediately leave his vehicle. He was preoccupied with talking to Dmitri, one of his associates.

Steven stepped out of the moving van and turned to Keisha and the children and said, "Well, what do you all think? You like it?"

"Yeah, Daddy," Brittany— the youngest child— said, holding Mr. Quacks, jumping up and down in place. "It's pretty. And Mr. Quacks likes it, too."

Ah, Mr. Quacks. The name Brittany gave to the stuffed animal— a duck— she and her dad won together at last year's fair playing the game where you are given three baseballs and must knock down all the bottles to win a prize. Brittany threw the first baseball and knocked down two of the six bottles that were arranged in a three-two-one configuration from bottom to top. The memory was poignant in Steven's mind, and often thought about in passing when his mind had time to wander aimlessly. When he did, the aroma of cheap corn dogs and stale beer crept into his nostrils.

"Dad, can we start bringing out things to bring inside now?" Tiffany asked, looking up at her dad, then pushed an entire Reese's peanut butter cup in her mouth. No nibbling or biting the cup and savoring the chocolate and peanut butter concoction one morsel at a time was in the cards when it came to her and her Reese's. Enter cup. Chew. Swallow. Rinse and repeat.

"My, my, my," Steven said, looking down at Tiffany. "Sweetheart, we need to wait for Mr. Favelle. He has the keys. Patience, please." He took off his glasses, wiped them with his shirt, then placed them back on his eagle beak.

"But, Dad," she said, "I want to set up my exercise room in the attic. I need to do some cycling, a little punching bag, and lift some weights. Seconds mean pounds, Dad. A few more minutes and with this summer heat, I'll be smelling like the bacon I ate for breakfast this morning." Another cup. Enter. Chew. Swallow.

"You're not fat, sweetheart. Please stop this self-flagellation."

Tiffany sighed. "Oh my, god, Dad, why do you always do this to me?"

"Do what?" he said, shrugging his shoulders.

"Use big words."

"I didn't use any big words."

"Really?" she said, placing a hand on her hip. "What about fag-ah-lay-shun? That sounds like a word suited for Jeffrey. Right, Jeffrey?"

Jeffrey didn't hear a word exchanged between her and her dad. He had his earbuds in his ears. He was listening to a new cello concerto he wanted to learn over the summer. He was an aspiring cellist who intended to earn a degree in music performance when he finished high school in three years.

"I'm sorry, sweetheart," Steven said. "All I'm saying is stop beating yourself up. You're rail thin. In all honestly, I'm concerned you're too thin. No matter what your size, I'll always think you're beautiful, okay?"

She looked up at her dad. "Thanks, Dad. I guess I'll do some laps in the backyard." She was a star athlete in high school. She would be a sophomore this year.

Mr. Favelle was still on his phone, but he did gesture the peace symbol and mouth the word *minutes* to Steven and Keisha. Two minutes maybe, based on the gesture. Hopefully.

"Babe?" Keisha said, looking up at Steven. "Come here, please." She placed her hands on his shoulders and lowered his head. She sighed. "Oh, babe, your bald spot is turning red. Why didn't you put sunblock on earlier today? I gave you the bottle, didn't I?"

"I'm sorry, honey," he said, then kissed her on her cheek. "You did. It's in the moving truck. I'll put some on once we're done with Mr. Favelle."

She folded her arms. "Listen now. I'm not playin' with you anymore, shiny top. I'm doing this because I love you. I care about you." She reached into her purse and pulled out a smaller bottle of sunblock. She squirted a generous amount of it on his bald spot and rubbed it in, but not well enough. White streaks were all over his head.

Mr. Favelle ended his call. He stepped out of his black Cadillac sedan and buttoned his jacket. A blast wave of hot air nearly knocked him to the ground. The suit he wore was Armani. A solid gold one. Silk. His dress shirt was solid black. The tie he wore matched the color of his suit. The knot of the tie was slightly below the neck of the collar. On his left hand he had two rings, one was a wedding band. The other ring was a pinky ring. Without question, it costed plenty of karats. It was a white–gold diamond ring with several stones. The largest stone was in the center and surrounding it were six smaller stones. His other hand had one ring on it—another ring on the pinky. Less flashy than the other pinky ring though. He certainly looked the part of some big-time mover and shaker, but was he?

With a thick, long cigar, partially smoked, sticking out of the side of his mouth, he approached Keisha and Steven with his arm extended. "Nice to finally meet you mugs in person."

"Likewise, Mr. Favelle." Steven said, shaking the man's hand. *Wow, that's a strong cologne.*

"How are you?" Keisha said overlapping Steven, also shaking his hand once Steven finished. *That cigar stinks to high Heaven.*

He shakes hands like a cake boy, Mr. Favelle thought. *Her grip, on the other hand, nearly broke my hand. Porca puttana!* He raised his hands up and said in a thick Italian tough-guy accent, "Uh-uh, not-uh. Didn't I tell youse two call me Tony? Now I'm not gonna tell youse again. When you buy from Tony, you become Tony's family. So, please, call me Tony, unless youse wanna be fitted with cement shoes and take a one-way skinny dip into Lake Michigan, okay?" He removed the cigar from his mouth and tapped it. The ashes fell onto Steven and Keisha's shoes. Keisha was wearing flip-flops.

Steven and Keisha looked at each other with their best what-the-fuck faces, then looked at Tony. Sure, Tony was talking tongue-in-cheek, but he had executed hits in the past. He was a made–guy in one of the local crime families. If he wanted to, he could make good on his in–jest threat.

Tony's grin retracted. He adjusted his tie and cleared his throat. "I'm sorry, folks," he said. "I'm kiddin' around with youse, that's all." Then laughed as he berated himself. *Idiot. Idiot. Idiot. You're not talking to your associates. These are decent people. Customers. You idiot!*

"It's alright," Steven said, then coughed up a pity chuckle. "We can take a joke." In Steven's gut, though, he believed Tony was implying he could be a dangerous man when and if he needed to be. *Let's get this over with quick,* Steven thought.

"May I please have the keys to the house now?" Keisha asked. "Please forgive me if I'm actin' a little brash. I don't mean to be rude, crude, and unrefined, but we have plenty to do before nightfall."

"No problem at all," Tony said, puffing out a large cloud of smoke. "Lady wants the keys to her palace, lady gets the keys to her palace." He reached into his silk jacket and pulled out a small-sized yellowish-brown envelope. Not an envelope you'd use to mail a letter though. This was considerably smaller. This was a coin envelope.

Steven flinched a little when Tony reached into his jacket. *Don't shoot! Get a grip. Do you think he'd shoot you in the light of day in a populated area?*

"Whoa, whoa," Tony said, looking up at Steven, "easy there, Sequoia. You don't mind if I call you that, do you?" He tapped his cigar again. This time Steven moved his shoes before the ashes could land on them.

"No, no. Call me whatever you like."

"I mean no disrespect," Tony said, "but you're a goliath if you're an inch. Tall. Very tall." He dropped the cigar onto the front lawn.

Tony handed Keisha the envelope containing the keys, which made a pleasant tone when they clanked together. "Thank you," she said, then smiled. Before leaving to unlock the front door of the house, she shook his hand once more. This time, when she gripped her hand, Tony faked she broke it. Dry humor. Still made Keisha chuckle though.

Steven wasn't much of a talker to people outside his little circle. He wanted to say something to break the silence. What though? He blurted the first thing that entered his mind. "That's a nice suit. I wish I could afford one like that. How much did you pay for it?"

"Nothin'. Nada. Not one dime. It was a gift. A gift from a man who now sleeps with the fishes." *Idiot. Tony, you've got to control the things you say.* He cleared his throat. "What I mean is he moved to Barbados and is alive and well… He and I spoke last week about some… business."

This was contradictory. Steven pointed this out. "You said *sleeps with.* I've seen enough movies to know what that means."

Tony cleared his throat and sashayed to the moving truck. He gave his face a once over in the large side mirror of the truck and straightened his tie again. He approached Steven and said, "I misspoke. He *swims with* the fishes— literally swims. When I say 'swims with the fishes', I mean the person is alive and well. When I say 'sleeps with the fishes', that means the person is one dead fuck, okay? My apologies for that… a… what do you call it… Hey, you kinda look like an educated guy. And if you're as smart as you are tall, I think you'll have the answer to my question. Tell me something. Who was the bald faggot shrink who smoked cigars and fucked his mother?"

Steven's eyes widened. He wasn't sure if Tony was trying to be funny or if he honestly didn't know the answer to his question. He didn't notice it before, but Tony used his hands a lot when he talked. A lot of pointing, and he would never point using both hands at the same time (except if he became angry). He liked to alternate both hands. His go-to point was a sideways 'I love you' sign. Thumb up, pointer and pinky extended outward. He sometimes did hand circles, most often at the start of his last sentence, especially if he had a lot to say. Listening and watching Tony for too long could make someone nauseous. Steven snickered. "Freud?"

"Yeah," Tony said with his eyes lit up. With his hand motion flair, he continued, "That's the sick fuck— oh, pardon my French— I'm thinking of. Freud. That fuckin' bald prick. He's a fuckin'—" He shook his head a few times. "I meant no offense to you. I'm sorry you suffer from alopecia. By the way, I can't help but ask you this question. Did a flock of birds shit on your head? What's all that up there on your melon scalp?" He waited a second or two for Steven to respond. "Ah, who gives a fuck. Anyway, I had a *Freudian* slip. Excuse me."

You can't remember who Freud was, but you can remember what alopecia is? Steven put up his hand. "No problem. You don't need to explain yourself to me."

A man dressed in a black suit approached Steven. He was a medium-built individual with a full head of carrot–colored hair parted to the side. He extended his hand and said, "Hi, there. By your color, I presume you're my new neighbor. My name is Terry Auckland. I live next door to you. Welcome."

"Nice to meet you. I'm Steven Dobrowski," shaking the man's hand. *My, my, my, what an oddball. By my color?*

Keisha walked up to Steven and said, "Babe, we decided we're going to wait for you to do the honors to open the front door of the house. We'll start unloading the truck and place things on the patio." She wanted to introduce herself to Terry. "I'm Keisha. Nice to meet you." She extended her hand out to Terry, but he didn't shake it.

He said, "I don't shake hands with Negros. Go back to the cotton field before I pull out my cat o' nine tails and whip you into tomorrow."

"Oh, yes, mastah," she said, bowing to him from the waist with her hands raised, then walked away. She took the verbal stomach punch like a pro. *How rude*, she thought. *I'll pray for you. I'm a woman of God. You're not going to get me to light up.*

"Who's the coon?" Terry asked Steven. "Your maid?"

"Excuse me? What?" Steven said, shocked. "That's my wife you're—" Steven clenched his fists. He took a step closer to Terry and said, "Let me tell you something, nobody talks—"

"Whoa, whoa, whoa," Tony said, placing his hands between Steven and Terry. "Steven, Amico mio, let me handle this, okay?"

Who was Steven to say no to Tony? He didn't. He wouldn't. He couldn't. Steven stepped aside.

Tony looked Terry in the eyes. He pointed BOTH hands at Terry. "Apologize."

Terry didn't say a word. He shook his head though. Bad idea.

Now Terry's once–straight tie was wrapped around in Tony's hand. The two were closer now than they were before. Their noses nearly touched. No Eskimo kisses for you, Terry. "Now, I'm gonna say it one more time, and that's it. Apologize to your neighbor for not playin' nice."

Terry shifted his eyes from Tony's to Steven's. "I'm sorry. I didn't know you were a coal burner."

Bad idea. Tony smiled widely, then delivered a swift punch to Terry's stomach. "Get the fuck outta here. Next time I'll put a bullet in your skull, you racist Irish spud suckin' mick fuck, you."

Terry fell to the ground and grabbed his stomach. Steven was unsure what to think. He wondered if this was reality or if he was asleep at the wheel on the expressway, on the verge of crashing and burning.

Tony turned to Steven. While gesturing towards Terry, he said, "You believe the nerve of this fuckin' carrot top fuck sayin' a thing like that? I for one am appalled."

Terry finally got the wind that was knocked out of him back in, and said, "You and your wife don't belong in this community." He stood and coughed. "Leave or be dragged out." Terry returned to his own house.

"That was crazy," Steven said. "I mean… I have no words. I'm gob smacked."

"Don't worry about that, Irish fire crotch prick, okay, Sequoia? He's nothing but a noisemaker— a fuss pot. Oh, by the way, he's not the only racist piece of shit in this neighborhood, let alone the city itself."

"What do you mean?"

Tony cleared his throat and once again wandered over to the mirror on the moving truck to do a hair check. He straightened his tie and tugged it downward a few times on the lower seam of his silk jacket. "Your other neighbor next door is one of the biggest fuckin' racists you'll meet. But he's worse than a racist. He's a covert racist. At least Terry is honest. This fat piece of German shit next door will mislead you. He's a slick talkin' kraut-eating prick, that's for damn sure."

"I'm not understanding," Steven said, shaking his head.

"He will likely try to tell you stories about your house that aren't true. You know, to shake you up. Make you wanna leave. Ignore him. You stand your ground. This is your house and you and your interracial family have a right to be in it."

Enough was enough. Steven had plenty of other things to do than to stand around and listen to Tony ramble and watch him gesture all the livelong day. He needed to help unload the moving truck, which Keisha and the children already started.

"Thanks. Listen, I enjoyed meeting you. Maybe we could have you over for dinner or coffee one night. I need to tend to some priorities here. I'm sure a respectable guy like yourself can appreciate the importance of taking care of business when it needs to be taken care of. Am I right?" Steven extended his hand.

Tony refused the offer of a handshake though. He didn't want to shake hands with someone whose grip was limper than the dick of a Viagra-withdrawn geriatric. He believed Steven was a closeted homosexual and used Keisha as a cloak. "Listen, you," he said, pointing. "We're family now, so we hug. Get the fuck outta here with your handshake, okay?" Tony extended his arms out for a hug.

While awkward, Steven complied. He didn't want to piss Tony off by turning down Tony's good-natured gesture of affection.

"Before I go," Tony said, "I wanna give you a little somethin'." He reached into his inside jacket pocket again and pulled out another envelope. Steven flinched again, but to a lesser extent that the first time. He handed Steven a letter-sized envelope. "This is my gift to you and your family. Buy something nice for that fucked-up— I mean fuckin' fun— house. Okay?"

Steven opened the envelope, albeit cautiously. His paranoia was getting the better of him, momentarily thinking Tony laced the contents of the envelope with Anthrax. Advanced Mafia-whacking tactics. Inside the envelope were several crisp one-hundred-dollar bills. A crimson money band wrapped around the brick of bills kept the greenbacks together. Steven's eyes widened. Sure, he'd seen a one-hundred-dollar bill before, though it was more like here today, gone tomorrow. Bills. Kids. Wife. Money waved goodbye soon after saying hello. He'd never seen one hundred one-hundred-dollar bills before though. Steven stammered, "I… look… I… we… this is…"

"Listen, I know you're a man of many words," Tony said, "but that's a gift from me to you. A GIFT! You refuse it, you hurt Tony's heart. You hurt Tony's heart, Tony might hurt you. Is that what you want?"

After a hard swallow, Steven said, "Of course I don't want that, Tony. You've been nothing but generous to us. How can we possibly accept this though?"

Tony snapped back, "Are you fuckin' deaf? …Didn't I say it was a *gift*? This is a *gift* from me to you and your family for taking this fuckin' house off my hands. This house was like a little dog that follows you around from room to room and bites your ankle when you don't give it enough attention. I bought this property as a favor to a friend of mine, the former C.E.O. of Gypsum. I didn't want it. I didn't need it. But this friend was – is – like family to me. You and your family popped and drained this festering carbuncle on my rosy-cheeked ass by purchasing this house. The contents of that envelope are my way of saying 'thank you,' okay?"

Steven stifled his laughter at Tony's ranting and gesturing. *Used two hands to talk to me now, eh, Tony? You brought out the big guns on me! Don't shoot!* "Okay, Tony. I understand your perspective. Thank you for the gift."

"Forget about it," Tony said. "I'll see you around, Sequoia."

"Alright. See you. Thanks again."

Tony didn't walk to his car, though. He walked towards Steven's other next-door neighbor's house. He turned his head towards Steven and said, "I'm gonna pay this kraut n' kielbasa eatin' dumpkopf a quick visit and kindly warn him not to fuck around with you and your mong— … family, like Terry did."

He almost said *mongrel* family, and wanted to, but stopped. Steven connected the dots, but it didn't matter. Tony could put two bullets in his chest and one in the head and still sleep peacefully.

Tony stopped and double backed to Steven's direction. "Hey, let me tell you one more thing. If this fuckin' guy next door fucks with you, I wanna hear about it. He fucks with you, he fucks with me. He fucks with me, I fuck him up with an ice pick. He'll swim with the fishes. Got it?"

"I think you mean he'll *sleep* with the fishes this time," Steven said. "You said *swims* with the fishes." He remembered with Tony *swims* means alive; *sleeps* means dead.

"Ah, see, you are too good," Tony said, smiling. "You are too fuckin' good for your own fuckin' good. And I love that about you." He turned back and walked towards the neighbor's house. "Take good fuckin' care, Sequoia."

Now Tony turned around and took no less than ten paces, then did an about face. "Hey, Sequoia. I've got one more thing to say to you." Using both hands, he said, "If you think I'm gonna buy this fuckin' house back from you because you and yours get the fuckin' heebie-jeebies, you can fuckin' forget about it. It's yours now. You fuckin' love that house like it's your woman. As for me, I'm fuckin' done with it. Don't fuckin' spit in my face by coming to me to buy that fuckin' house back. You got it? Fuck you. Take care, Sequoia." And off Tony went to make good on visiting the neighbor next door.

Before entering the house, Steven used his shirt to polish the gold-colored metal numbers that spelled out the address to the house: 6729. Their street name was Jefferson Ave.

For grins and giggles, he pushed the doorbell button once. *Ding dong.*

Steven unlocked the front door and pushed it open. The door continued to open until it tapped the wall and came to rest.

Standing on the porch, he turned to his family and said, "Here's to a new beginning and a bright future."

The front door slammed shut.

CHAPTER TWO

The Living Room Setup

The living room was furnished with beautiful furniture, courtesy of Tony. There were two couches. One couch was a plush white four-seater couch. At a ninety-degree angle was a smaller matching two-seater couch. In front of the larger couch was an oval-shaped three-tiered glass coffee table. On both ends of each couch were two glass end tables. They weren't oval-shaped though; they were rectangular.

Also, in the living room was an eighty-five-inch screen T.V. and a Blu-ray player. Speakers were distributed throughout the living room.

A fireplace— an amenity the Dobrowski's didn't have in the previous house— was across from the four-seater couch. It was made of granite and had a raised hearth.

The cherry on top of this delicious decorum sundae was a crystal chandelier that was suspended from the center of the textured ceiling.

Keisha and Steven entered the living room, both of whom were carrying a box of pictures, though Steven was also carrying his "World's Greatest Dad" coffee mug. It was a black coffee mug with white lettering in block capital letters. On the outside bottom of the mug, the children had the year the mug was given. Along the coffee cup handle were the names of the children. Whenever he held that mug, he had his children in the palm of his hand.

Today they were going to add their personal touch to the living room.

"Babe," Keisha said. "Why is the chandelier swaying?"

"To be honest, I don't know," he said. "Could be a ghost." He stopped the chandelier from swaying with his hand.

Keisha gasped. "Wow, that would be interesting, as long as it's a nice ghost. I've always wanted to have personal experiences with a ghost." She took a seat on the four-seater couch.

"We may have one here. This room is amazing. Tony spared no expense furnishing this house for us."

Keisha let out a light sigh, then said, "Yeah, I guess he has his good points."

Steven placed the box on the hearth and pulled out a picture. "Here's the first picture being placed on the fireplace mantel. Our family picture."

The family picture was taken last November, and was used for the front of the holiday cards the Dobrowski's sent out to family and friends. Steven cherished the picture, and sometimes would pick it up off the living room table in their old house and gaze at it, reminiscing about experiences with his children.

He stood in front of the fireplace. He placed the family picture on the far right-side of the mantel and took two paces back, stopped momentarily, then walked back to the picture and adjusted it. Once again, he stepped back to see if the picture was positioned to his liking.

"Looks good, babe," Keisha said.

"It does, doesn't it? Now I can add the rest of the pictures to the mantel."

As he approached the box to choose more pictures to place on the mantel, the family picture on the mantel slid and fell onto the hearth, causing Keisha to gasp.

"That's weird," he said. "I did place the picture far enough on the mantel, right?"

"Yes, you did," she said. "Maybe there is a ghost in this house. And, to be honest, I'm getting a little freaked out. It's one thing for a ghost to knock a picture off a table or a fireplace mantel when you're out of the room. It's quite another when it is performing live and does a number right in front of you."

"Honey, I assure you. There's nothing to worry about. All houses have spirits, some more obvious than others. Besides, you always said you wanted to experience paranormal events for yourself. You just said so. Here's your opportunity."

He placed the family picture back on the mantel, turning it a few degrees one way, then back a smidgen the other way. Before walking back to the box of pictures, he pulled upward on the mantel to ensure it was secure. It was, at least by his standards.

As he walked back to the box of pictures, the family picture slid and fell onto the hearth again.

Steven said, "My, my, my. Well, I think it's safe to say we definitely have a playful little spirit living in our house." He picked the picture up and held it in his hands, gazing at it.

"You mean poltergeist. And I'm slightly unnerved by it."

"Come on. It's not harming anyone. You and I have always been intrigued by ghosts. That's why we watch all those paranormal shows together."

"Babe, it's not the same. It's one thing to see it on T.V. or a movie. You can turn it off if it bothers you or you get too scared. But when it's occurring in your home in front of you, it's frightening, terrifyingly frightening."

"Wow. You flipped quick. I'm assuring you there's nothing to worry about. And, who knows. If the activity here continues, maybe we could have one of those ghost show crews come to our house and do an episode. Our episode could end up going viral on YouTube."

"You'd like that, wouldn't you," she said, then smiled. "I guess if the ghost isn't harmful to anyone, I can live with it. Maybe it has a story to tell us. Maybe that's why it is knocking the picture off the mantel."

"See! You're getting excited. I can tell! I love it!" He kissed her on the lips.

For a third time, he placed the picture on the mantel. Fortunately, it stayed put. He placed other pictures on the mantel, hoping they'd stay on it, but his gut told him they may not.

From the left to right, in birth order, he placed an individual picture of Jeffrey, Tiffany, Brittany, and even Mr. Quacks on the mantel. Some people gave Steven hell for displaying a picture of Brittany's favorite stuffed animal, as if Mr. Quacks was one of his children, including Steven's mother-in-law, Denise.

He didn't care though. As far as he was concerned, Mr. Quacks was a family member. In fact, when Steven introduced his children to new friends or long-distant relatives, he included Mr. Quacks as one of his children.

"What a relief," Steven said, pretending to wipe sweat from his brow. "Shall we bang some nails and hang some pictures now?"

Keisha sighed, then stood. "Yeah, I can't wait to see what happens next. Oh, I know! Maybe blood will fall from the walls like a waterfall."

"Now, that would be awesome!"

"You're straight-up crazy," she jested. "I can see all the pictures on the wall in my mind. We'll need nine nails."

He handed Keisha a hammer and a ring shank nail. "You should do the honors, my lady."

"Why thank you, kind sir," she said using a Southern belle voice. They kissed. Then she walked over to the left of the four-seater couch and placed the nail against the wall. "Alright, here goes." Before she could deliver the first blow to the nail, Steven distracted her.

"Maybe this winter we can paint the rooms. All of this plain, white drywall isn't too appealing to me."

"I kind of the like the white drywall. It makes the rooms look bigger." She tapped the nail a few times. "Ewww, yuck. What is that, Steven? Is that blood?"

A sanguine-hued liquid oozed from the orifice formed around the shaft of the nail and the puncture site.

"I don't know what that is, honey," Steven said. He rubbed his finger around the orifice. "Smells like rust and potpourri." He rubbed the substance between his thumb and pointer finger. "It's kind of warm. I don't know much about drywall, but maybe this chemical is a component of it."

Keisha sat on the couch. "This house is Twilight Zone territory. That's a bad omen, isn't it? I've read about cases like this Steven. Walls weeping blood. I just had to open my mouth about blood and walls. Now our wall is bloody."

"Blood? That's not blood, babe. How could it be blood? This is a new house."

"Yeah, but the land is the same, and there was a house on the land before this one was built. And, considering the fact Tony is likely in the Mafia, that leads me to believe the fool who owned the house before this one was in the Mafia, too."

Steven hesitated to respond immediately. After some thought, he said, "So what if he was in the Mafia? That's no concern of ours."

"People may have been whacked here. Can you imagine how angry a spirit would be if he or she was killed traumatically?" She sighed, then said, "I want you call Tony and tell him he can take his house back."

"What? Why?"

She pointed to the bleeding wall. "Need I say more? This house could end up being our grave."

"Alright, let's take a few breaths." He sat next to her on the couch and rubbed her back. "Let's pound in another nail. If the same substance pools out of that, it must be a component of the drywall."

Keisha placed another nail on the white drywall and lightly hammered it until the head of the nail was about one-sixteenth of an inch from the wall.

The same substance that exuded from the puncture site of the first nail started to ooze out of this one also, then slowly started to drip down the wall.

She dropped the hammer to the floor. "Call your new friend, Tony. Tell him to get over here and take his house back."

Steven chuckled slightly. "Honey, this house is fine. Everything is going to be fine. I'll text my friend Randy and see if he knows what this chemical might be." He removed his T-shirt and wiped the wall down. "We can't give this house back anyway."

"I know we can't, but I want to believe we can. This house is a lemon. The blood oozing out of the wall is a bad omen. I'm not going to become one of its victims."

“Honey, you're overreacting," he said, picking the hammer up to pound seven more nails into the wall. He hammered in two more nails. "Look around, babe. This house is a dream come true. Let's not run away so fast. I texted Randy and asked if the substance is a drywall component. And, I have something to show you. A surprise."

He summoned her over to the wall using the crook of his finger. She walked over to him. He pulled out the envelope Tony gave him yesterday. He didn't tell her about it yesterday because once the boxes were unloaded from the truck, the family ate dinner, relaxed, then went to sleep.

"Check this out," he said, opening the envelope.

"Oh my, God, Steven, where did you get all of that lettuce?" A smile replaced her pouty expression.

Steven did a chuckle-burp. "Excuse me. Tony. He gave us this money as a gift."

"There's enough there to buy a small island."

"Not quite that much. That brick has one hundred one-hundred dollar bills. Ten-thousand dollars."

Keisha put the brick of money back into the envelope. "Babe, I love you, but sometimes you can be a fool."

"What do you mean? I don't understand. I thought this little nest-egg would make you happy. Am I wrong?"

She handed him the envelope of money and sat back on the couch. "No, I'm sorry, I'm not. Not at all."

He scoffed and walked over to her. "Why not? We've got this magnificent house, fully furnished. We've got ten-thousand dollars cash. We've got three great kids who love us. We've got each other. Yeah, you're right. Things are terrible. Let's start drafting our suicide notes."

She exhaled, fighting to keep herself calm. She turned to him and said, "First, don't be joking about suicide. It's not funny. It's disrespectful. Secondly, you basically sold your soul to the Devil. That money paid you off to deal with this defective house. And, look, the chandelier is swaying again, and the blood dripping down the wall is about to land on the white Berber carpet. Wonderful."

"I'll take care of it," he said, leaping off the couch. He wiped the streak off the wall before it hit the carpet. "And it's not blood. It's… drywall stuff. Then he stopped the motion of the chandelier.

"I'm worried. This house doesn't sit right with me. And look at the wall."

"Honey, I get that, and that's to be expected. It's a new house, a new environment. But, please, let's give the house a chance. We haven't even been here a day and you're already wanting to pull the plug."

She didn't answer him. He stood and walked to the box of pictures near the wall. He had something else to say to her, but he kept it in a lock–box for now. He wanted to wait and hear what she had to say, if anything at all.

The wall had nine nails arranged in an upside-down V configuration. Steven placed pictures on the left side first. Two of pictures were from Steven and Keisha's wedding, one picture was from the Dobrowski's last Christmas, and the last picture was of Brittany— her First Day of Kindergarten photo.

"It looks nice," she said. She stood and walked over to Steven. "I'll do the other side."

And she did. From the bottom right, she placed a picture of Brittany, Tiffany, and Jeffrey. Their picture wall was nearly completed. Two nails remained.

The pinnacle of the upside-down V was for something special. Keisha reached into the picture box and pulled out a gift from her recently-departed mother-in-law, Granana. It was a crucifix. She held it in her hand and said a quick prayer. Then she stood on her tippy-toes and placed it on the top nail.

"It's beautiful, honey," Steven said. "I want to say something to you, and it may not bring a lot of comfort now, but I hope it does."

"I'm listening."

"Let's give the house a chance. If things go from bad to worse, we'll deal with it."

"Babe, you sound like a politician, and I think you know I'm a lot smarter than to fall for that. What do you mean by what you just said? I want specifics."

Steven put his hand up to the chandelier to stop it from swaying. "We'll take action. We'll do what needs to be done--whatever that may be."

"Would that include moving out of this house? Would you be willing to do that?"

The aroma of cigar smoke danced into Steven's nostrils. "What's that smell? It smells like Tony's cigar smoke."

"It does. Where's that coming from? I don't see any smoke."

Steven walked over to the sunroom door and opened it. The smell was intensifying. He started coughing, and couldn't stop.

"I'll get you some water, babe."

"Thanks," he said, strained. He followed her into the kitchen and took a big drink of water from the glass Keisha handed him. "I don't smell that cigar scent anymore. Do you?"

She took a big whiff. "No, I don't."

He sat on a stool in front of the bar counter and remained silent. A few moments later, he said, "Our son is gifted. Listen to how beautiful he executed that passage from Rachmaninoff's Second Symphony."

Jeffrey was in his bedroom practicing his cello. He started playing when he was four. Steven was his first teacher, but Jeffrey advanced rapidly; eventually, Steven had to find Jeffrey a new teacher. His new teacher— a professor of cello at Indiana Institute of Music— mentored Jeffrey for eleven years. Because of the move, Jeffrey needed to find a new teacher.

"It is lovely. I wish I would have learned how to play the piano when I was a kid."

"It's never too late, babe. If you want, we can get you a piano. We could put it in the sitting room. I could even give you lessons."

Steven took several years of piano lessons as a child, though it wasn't his primary instrument. He learned piano to supplement his overall music education. His primary instruments were violin and cello. Sometimes, he and Jeffrey would perform pieces together for fun. Never publicly though.

Jeffrey had aspirations to attend Julliard for his undergraduate and graduate degrees in cello performance once he graduated from high school two years from now.

"Maybe. One thing at a time. I'm still trying to adapt to the house. I do enjoy the paranormal. Maybe I'm being hypocritical. Maybe I need to accept this house and deal with it. Maybe I need to experience what all those people who have had to deal with ghosts went through, and from it I'd develop a greater appreciation for the spirit world and for those who are affected by it… And, who knows. Maybe the spirit or spirits here will become bored with our house and move to another. I think I'll get used to this house. Do you think I will, babe?"

"I know you will. Picture what's ahead. Jeffrey's graduation from high school, Tiffany's wedding, Brittany entering high school. Birthday parties for the grandchildren. I can smell the cotton candy and hot dogs just thinking about it. Also, you and I can conduct an investigation here to find out the spirit's story. It's haunting the house for a reason. We could make our new house our first case. Remember when we dreamed of becoming paranormal investigators? Want to do an E.V.P. session?"

Without hesitation, Keisha responded, "No, I don't. I have to live in his house, fool. I have no interest in communicating with any spirits in it. You want to communicate with the spirit, go ahead. Keep me out of it, though, and the children, too. We don't need to scare them."

Steven agreed. They chatted intermittently for about twenty minutes. Then Keisha stepped into the laundry room, which was adjacent to the kitchen. Meanwhile, Steven walked into the living room, which was adjacent to the kitchen.

When he entered the living room he was amazed. The family picture was on the hearth. Two of the four pictures on the mantel were toppled over— still on the mantel, but face-down. The crucifix that Keisha hung up before Steven choked was on the floor. And, finally, among the seven pictures on the wall, three were on the floor. The chandelier was swaying with more energy than it was before. He started an E.V.P. session using a voice recorder on his cellphone.

He was forthright with Keisha about the strange happenings in the living room. She said, "Maybe this spirit doesn't realize he or she is dead. Maybe they need help crossing over."

"That's a good point, honey. Are you sure you don't want to participate in this E.V.P. session with me?"

"I'm sure. Let me know when you're done."

Everyone in the Dobrowski family was intrigued with the paranormal. The family were huge fans of reality ghost shows, including *A Haunting*, *Ghost*

Adventures, *Paranormal Investigators*, and *My Ghost Story*.

Steven not only watched ghost shows on T.V., but he also frequently watched YouTube videos featuring paranormal activity, including demonic activity. Some videos he watched made his skin crawl. Demonic possession was one of his greatest fears.

Someone slammed a door, then someone screamed.

"Steven!" Keisha yelled. "The laundry room door slammed by itself. Nearly gave me a heart attack! But it was a wonderful thrill."

They both laughed.

The T.V. turned on un-commanded. A white screen with no sound. Steven reached for the remote to turn the T.V. off. He pushed the power button, but the T.V. remained on. Then a man in a black suit appeared for a second, then disappeared the next. A second later, the T.V. turned off by itself. He muttered, "Wow. That man had an unsightly scar on his forehead."

Ding-dong ding-dong ding-dong.

Three chimes of the doorbell sounded in quick succession a second or two after the T.V. turned off.

"I'll get it," Steven said. He walked to the door still clutching the remote in his hand. When he opened the door, nobody was there. He stepped outside to see if anyone was walking away. There wasn't.

Steven stepped back into the house and closed the door. He said, "It was nobody."

"Probably the ghost, right?" she said, chuckling afterwards.

"That's the spirit!"

He sat on the couch and placed his cellphone face-down on the three-tiered glass table in front of him. That was another quirk Steven possessed— he always placed his cellphone face-down. He leaned back and rested his head on top of the couch. He closed his eyes and listened to Jeffrey's cello playing.

Someone crawled into his lap. It was Brittany.

"Daddy? Me and Mr. Quacks are hungry?" she whispered.

He opened his eyes and smiled. "Guess what? Me, too."

Her hair was in pigtails. She was wearing an outfit Granana bought for her last year, for her birthday.

He patted Mr. Quacks on the head and said, "Hello, Mr. Quacks. I'm glad you're hungry, too."

"Can we have peanut butter and jelly?"

"You bet. Hey, did you sleep okay last night? I didn't get a chance to ask you this morning."

She placed a finger to her chin, then said, "Well, a few times I woke up. Someone was scratching my wall. And knocking on it. I wasn't scared though, Daddy. I just closed my eyes really tight and asked Granana to make it go away."

"Granana to the rescue, huh?"

"Yeah. She made it stop."

"I'm glad to hear that. You ready for some lunch?"

"Yes! And so is Mr. Quacks!"

He kissed her cheek. "Why don't you go to the kitchen. I'll be there in a minute."

She kissed him back on his cheek. Then she lightly placed Mr. Quacks' bill against his cheek. She walked to the kitchen and waited for Steven.

He laid his back on the couch for a bit longer, but an object landed on his stomach. When it struck him, it stung a little.

"Ouch," he said. Without lifting his head, he grasped the object. "A ring?" Then he opened his eyes. It was a ring.

Where did this ring come from? Why was it thrown at Steven? Whose ring was it?

Ding dong.

Steven peeked through the front door window. He mumbled, "U.P.S. Wonder what care package this is."

He opened the door.

"Greetings, sir," the U.P.S. worker said. "Here's your package."

Steven took it and placed to the right of him. It was heavy. Steven nearly dropped it.

"I'll just get a signature and then I'll be on my way."

"No problem," Steven said, picking up the stylus attached to the delivery driver's clipboard.

When the delivery driver left, Steven brought the package into the kitchen and set it on the couch.

Steven opened the kitchen window and said, "Hey, honey. You received a package from your mother."

"Oh, that's nice. I wasn't expecting anything."

Keisha stepped inside. She said, "Now that's a big package. I wonder what on earth she could have sent."

"Only one way to find out, right?" Steven said. "Maybe it's a pet snake." He chuckled.

"Not funny! You know that's one of my biggest fears." She was eagerly trying to guess what her mother sent her. Blown-up pictures when she was a kid? Her old toys from when she was a little girl? A dog, maybe?

Opening the scissors, she used one of the two blades as a straight razor and cut down the packaging tape that secured the flaps.

She opened the box and looked inside. Then she said, "Babe, this is wonderful."

Steven looked inside the box. "That's a nice-looking vase. Does it have any significance?"

Something crashed to the floor in the living room.

"I'll be right back," Steven said, standing up from the stool. "Probably the ghost playing games again."

"He sure is playful," Keisha said. "that's for sure. Never ends, but it never gets old." Then she chuckled.

Steven reentered the kitchen and said, "We were right. The ghost knocked over the family picture and crucifix. I put the items back where they belong. The chandelier has more moves than the entire cast of Saturday Night Fever combined. It's always gyrating and swaying. Why do you think the ghost likes that chandelier so much?"

"Who knows, babe. Maybe the spirit is of a child. Anyway, did you want to hear about the vase?"

"Sure," Steven said. He took a tall glass out of the cabinet and poured some iced tea into it.

Keisha explained, "This vase has been in my family for four generations now. My great-great grandmother made it, then passed it on to her daughter, and then to hers, and now to me."

"That's amazing. Not be rude, but I'm surprised your mother did something nice for you. It's taken me by surprise."

"I'm not going to lie. Me, too." Then Keisha screamed.

The sound of a door slamming startled her.

"Listen, ghost. Please stop slamming doors when my back is turned. I'm too young to join you in the hereafter. Got it? Good."

Steven laughed. Then he said, "You're funny, honey. That was good."

"Thanks. I pop off a good one every now and again. How are your E.V.P. sessions going?"

"Fine. Only a few Class B and C E.V.Ps., and I can't make out what's being said. You want to listen to them? Maybe you can ascertain what's being said."

"Listen, sucker!" she said lightheartedly. "I want nothing to do with trying to establish a kinship with your new friend, Casper."

"Fine. I understand. Where did you want to put those mirrors your mom sent you?"

Keisha's mom had included three mirrors. Two were of the same size and the third was larger than the two.

"I'm not—"

Ding-dong ding-dong ding-dong.

Steven stood and said, "I'll get it."

He opened the door, but nobody was there. He looked left and he looked right, but not a soul was in sight.

When he entered the kitchen, he said, "There's that cigar smell again. It's awful."

"It is. I'll pick up some candle warmers from that store on U.S. 12. What's it called again?"

"Rosco's, I think." Steven poured himself some more iced tea. "Would you like some?"

"No, thanks," she said. "Now, I want these two smaller mirrors to go upstairs. We'll put one in between our bedroom and the hallway bathroom and the other near the stairwell on the other side of the hallway bathroom."

Steven burped a little. "Excuse me. What about the other mirror?"

Keisha didn't reply right away. She was thinking of a prime spot for the bigger of the two-sized mirrors. The mirror was rectangular and had gold trim as its frame.

"Let's place it above the fireplace," she said.

Without hesitation, Steven got to work placing the mirrors where Keisha wanted them, starting with the upstairs first. Carrying both mirrors, he went to the second floor.

The second floor had a fairly straightforward layout. Once the top of the stairs was reached, there were two options: turn left or turn right. To the right were two bedrooms, a small storage area, and the stairwell to the attic. To the left were four bedrooms and one bathroom. Among the four bedrooms, three were on the right if one turned left. The master bedroom and hallway bathroom were on the left.

As he installed the first mirror in between the bathroom and master bedroom, more of the viscous liquid oozed out, further confirming in his mind it was a component of the drywall.

He also thought about his mother-in-law, Denise. They didn't get along at all.

As he installed the second mirror, something passed by him.

He said, "That looked like a mist of something. That must be the house ghost. Oh my. That would be a lame joke to tell people. We don't have a house guest, we have house ghost."

As he installed the second mirror, he couldn't help but look at himself. He touched and rubbed his mole and said, "I hate it. I hate this mole. I need to get it removed."

Then a door slammed near Steven. It was his office door. Steven gasped and lightly screamed.

The installation on the mirror was nearly finished. A few more turns of a screwdriver and it would be done. As he was completing the job, Keisha was irritated about something.

"Steven!" Keisha said, calling from the kitchen. "Are you upstairs?"

"Yes."

"Never mind. The ghost must be switching the chandelier light on and off."

After he had the second mirror installed, he walked down the hallway rubbing his hands together. He then blew into them.

"Awfully cold," he said, before turning onto the stairwell to go downstairs. After two steps, he stopped. Someone was groaning. The sounds were coming from the attic. He double-backed and stood at the foot of the attic stairs. The groans happened intermittently for thirty seconds before he said, "Tiffany?"

"Yeah, Dad," she said from the attic.

"Is that you groaning up there?"

"No, Dad. It's not me."

He was perplexed. If it wasn't her, who was it? The ghost?

"Did you hear them, also?" He rubbed his hands together and blew into them again.

After a moment of silence, she said, "Yes."

"Does it bother you?"

"No. It's kind of cool. We have a ghost in our house."

Steven was amazed at Tiffany's courage. Most people would be unnerved at a ghost groaning, especially if it was in the same room as them.

"Alright. Cool," Steven said, placing his hands in his shorts pockets. "Lunch will be ready soon."

Since Steven was upstairs, he figured he'd check on the other two children. He went to Jeffrey's room first. He knocked on the door and Jeffrey stopped his cello practice and opened the door.

Steven said, "I wanted to let you know lunch will be ready soon. I didn't get a chance ask any of you this morning because I was working in the living room. How'd you sleep?"

"Like a rock," Jeffrey said, "but I was woken up a few times from the sound of knocking and a few doors slamming."

"Does that bother you?"

"Nah. How could it? After all the ghost shows we've watched together and after all the horror movies I've seen, it's going to take a lot more than some knocks and slams to rattle my cage."

Steven laughed. "That makes me happy."

Finally, he knocked on Brittany's door. When she answered it, she was clutching Mr. Quacks in her hand.

"Hi, Daddy," she said.

"Hey, sweet pea. How did you sleep last night?" He rubbed Brittany's head, then Mr. Quacks'.

She sighed. "Well, the ghosty kept knocking on the walls. He woke me and Mr. Quacks up a few times. Give ghost a bedtime, Daddy. We need sleep!"

Steven laughed. "I'm sorry, sweet pea. Were you scared?"

"No. I wanted sleep though, and so did Mr. Quacks."

"Maybe tonight will be easier," he said, thinking over time everyone would adapt to the ghost in the house. "Lunch is going to be ready soon. Let's go downstairs."

"Okay, Daddy. Ready, Mr. Quacks? Let's go."

Steven picked her up and hoisted her on his shoulders.

Brittany was precocious for her age. She could read and write at two grade levels ahead of most children her age. She also had the ability to interact with spirits.

He went downstairs to the kitchen. Keisha was preparing some lunch for everyone. Turkey sandwiches and carrot sticks. Extra mayonnaise for Tiffany. No turkey for Jeffrey. Cut into four squares for Brittany.

He said, "I'll install the final mirror later. Jeffrey can help me."

Ding-dong.

"I'll get it," Steven said as he wiped the corners of his mouth with a napkin.

When he opened the door, a man wearing a cassock extended his hand and said, "Good afternoon, sir. My name is Father Thompson. I'm the priest at St. Matthews. I wanted to drop by and welcome you to the community and invite you to join our congregation."

"Nice to meet you, Father Thompson. Would you like to come in for a few minutes?"

"I'd like that. I can spare a few minutes before my church staff meeting."

Father Thompson was introduced to Keisha, the children, and Mr. Quacks. He spoke to Keisha about his church and its mission and vision while Steven did some more work around the house. Father Thompson also offered to do a house blessing. Keisha said she would call the church and set an appointment with the church secretary. Before Father Thompson left, he and Keisha prayed together, and, after the prayer, Keisha noticed a slight difference in the atmosphere of the house.

CHAPTER THREE

John Haber, Neighbor

Ding-dong, ding-dong, ding-dong.

Three rings in quick succession interrupted Steven from mixing his batter for pancakes. He answered the door, but nobody was there. He stepped onto the front porch to see if he could see someone walking away, but there wasn't a soul in sight. While looking, the front door slammed closed.

"This gag never gets old with you, does it?" Steven muttered. He opened the front door and returned to the kitchen to continue preparing his gourmet breakfast. The five bar stools positioned at the bar counter were tipped over. Some on their side, others upside down.

Talking out loud to the spirit, he said, "Upping your game, are you?" Steven said. "Oh, I'm petrified with fear and angst. Please don't hurt me, ghosty." Then he chuckled.

After adding some chocolate chips to the batter, he resumed mixing. The batter was thick and somewhat difficult to stir. It had a plaster of Paris consistency to it.

The laundry room was adjacent to the kitchen, and its door slammed. Steven jumped. "My, my, my. Enough already. I'm trying to make breakfast."

He sniffed the pancake batter, but the scent his olfactory sensors received sent back a response contradicting his expectations. He muttered, "Goodness, I'm never going to get rid of that Tony-cigar-and-cologne smell in this house. My, my, my."

Soon, the pungent aroma of bacon filled the entire house, replacing the Tony smell Steven was growing to detest. Who could blame him? It was a powerful smell, a knock-you-on-your-ass smell, like rotten eggs or a heaping pile of cow manure.

The sizzling of the bacon Steven was cooking in a pan was somewhat musical to his ears. Throughout the sizzling, random pops would occur from the grease exploding, sometimes burning Steven. A few times the grease splatter landed on the dime-sized black mole on the right side of his face, and this was akin to adding insult to injury. He hated that mole— a source of constant teasing since birth.

This morning, Steven was making his family his signature breakfast. This was the same breakfast he prepared every Wednesday and Sunday for the last two years. Prior to that, he made this special breakfast occasionally.

What was on the menu? Chocolate chip pancakes with a special syrup. The special syrup was a specific blend of chocolate syrup, pancake syrup, and hot fudge. The bacon was crispy for Brittany and not crispy for Tiffany. Jeffrey didn't eat bacon; he was a vegan. To accommodate Jeffrey's eating lifestyle, Steven made him Vegan French Toast.

Brittany was the first of the three children up. She walked down the stairs from the second floor to the first while rubbing her eyes with one hand and holding Mr. Quacks in the other.

She took a seat on one of the five bar stools along the counter in the kitchen and placed Mr. Quacks next to her on another stool.

Two of the five stools were tipped over when Steven entered the kitchen to make breakfast earlier that morning.

"Mornin', Daddy," she said, rubbing her eyes with a closed fist.

"Mornin', sweet pea," he said, flipping over the pancakes in the skillet with a spatula. "I hope you're hungry."

"Yes, very, and so is Mr. Quacks," she held Mr. Quacks up like a trophy.

Steven flashed a Duchenne smile, then waved and said, "Mornin', Mr. Quacks. Glad you're hungry, my feathered friend. Order will be up quicker than two shakes of a duck's tail."

She giggled at the joke her dad made and extended her arms upward. When she extended her arms, she knocked Mr. Quacks off the bar stool. "Oh, no," she said. "Mr. Quacks has ouchie now."

"He does? Well, let the doctor have a look at him." He walked around the counter to Brittany's side and picked up Mr. Quacks. He was laying on top of his head. His feet were slumped outward to the sides. Flashbacks of Daffy Duck diving into a swimming pool that was completely drained while he was in midair entered Steven's mind. He chuckled a little, thinking about Daffy Duck crashing head first in the empty pool, cracks forming throughout his body, then shattering into a pile of fragments.

He placed one hand against Mr. Quacks' back and gently turned him over with the hand. "It's okay, Mr. Quacks. Dr. Dad is here. I'll be right back."

"Okay, Daddy. You take care of Mr. Quacks."

He returned to the kitchen moments later with Mr. Quacks in one hand and gauze and tape in the other. He tore with his teeth a long piece of gauze and looped it around Mr. Quacks' head and chin. Holding the end of the gauze in place with the tape roll, he pulled a small piece of tape off and placed it over the exposed end of the gauze strip. He kissed Mr. Quacks on top of head, then said, "All better." Pointing at Mr. Quacks' bill, he said, "The 'bill' will be in the mail."

A raucous laugh erupted from Brittany. "Thanks for making Mr. Quacks all better, Daddy."

"You're welcome, sweet pea," he said, and handed her Mr. Quacks.

The odor of burnt flesh replaced the pleasant aroma of bacon cooking. The kitchen became veiled in a haze of wispy smoke. "Oh, my, my, my," he said, rushing to the stove. "Baking soda. I need baking soda."

Once the fire was extinguished, he removed the blackened strips of bacon from the skillet with his hands and placed them in the crispy stack of bacon. A disaster averted. No smoke detector activated.

He plated three chocolate chip pancakes, one stacked on the other, for Brittany. He cut the pancakes for her into smaller pieces and drizzled his special syrup over them. "Enjoy," he said, placing the plate of pancakes in front of her. "And here's some bacon."

While Brittany ate breakfast, Steven stepped outside to water the front lawn. To relieve boredom, he tried guessing what the clouds looked like. A boat. A heart. An angel. A face. Two dogs making whoopie.

"Hey, babe," Keisha said, calling Steven from the front door. "Did you want hamburgers or salad for lunch later today?"

"Hamburgers, honey. Thanks," he said.

"Great choice." She slammed the front door—accidentally.

"Good grief," a man's voice said, "I guess her crimson river is flowing, wouldn't you say?"

Steven snickered at the man's veiled reference to menstruation. He turned around and said, "I'm Steven. May I help you?"

The man was a short, portly gentleman. He was wearing a white dress shirt, with the top two buttons unbuttoned, and black slacks. His shoes clearly showed the clouds in the sky.

"My name is Haber. John Haber," he said, shaking Steven's hand. Limp-wristed Nancy boy, he thought. Would you like me to kiss your hand, madam? "I'm your next-door neighbor. It's nice to see someone took the plunge and bought the house. I thought it was going to be on the market for ages. Good for you. Congratulations."

"Thanks. We're all happy here."

John rubbed his thick salt-and-pepper beard. Then he said, "Really? No problems?

"Well, strange happenings pop up every now and again, but it's not like we've had blood coming out of the walls."

"I'm glad to hear that, my friend. That's a relief."

There was a company name tag clipped to John's dress shirt pocket. It's background color was maroon. In white lettering was the company name: GYPSUM, INC. Underneath the company name was John's photograph, and underneath his picture was his name. The last name was stacked on top of the first name. HABER, JOHN. In the upper right-hand corner were the letters P.T.E., which stood for part-time employee.

"I've heard that name before— Gypsum," Steven said. A second or two later, he snapped his fingers. "I remember. Tony told me the former C.E.O. of Gypsum used to live in this house."

"Well, not that house."

"Babe," Keisha said from the front door. "You better put some sunblock on your scalp. I don't want your head peeling like a flash-steamed tomato. And, not trying to be rude, but your new friend mini-Mister-Clean might want to do the same, too." She slammed the door again— accidentally.

John sighed and shook his head, then rubbed his bushy gray beard. "Aunt Flo is back in town."

Again, Steven snickered. Then he said, "I'm sorry. You were saying something about the house."

Before John could get a sentence out, Keisha opened the front door again and said, "Hi, mister. I'm sorry for not introducing myself. I'm Keisha, Steven's wife."

John introduced himself. Keisha reminded Steven she was going to the store in a few minutes and asked if he needed anything special while she was there. He didn't.

Steven said, "Please. What about the house?"

Because of the interruptions, John had to think a few moments. After he remembered, he said, "Your house was recently built. The C.E.O.— excuse me, former C.E.O.— had his old house raised and that one built. Not long after the construction of the house started, he decided to sell the house once it was finished. He also sold his company. Then he and his family moved to Vienna."

"That's odd," Steven said, fixing his comb–over. Damn wind is a double-edged sword, he thought. Cools me down yet messes my hair up. "Why Vienna?"

"I don't know why he specifically chose Vienna. I do know he was tired of the lifestyle he was living. He wanted to move somewhere else and run away from the history he had here."

"I can relate to that. To be honest, that's one of the biggest reasons my family and I moved here."

John sighed and shook his head. "You can't run from your past, my friend. Whatever you're running or hiding from will eventually catch up to you. You're fooling yourself to think otherwise."

"Duly noted. Thank you." He wiped his forehead with his hand, then said, "Would you like to come inside for coffee and a little breakfast? I have plenty inside and we could continue our conversation."

From his pants pocket, John removed his cellphone like it was a six–shooter. "Thanks for the offer. I have some time. I'll need to call the diner where I normally eat breakfast and tell them I won't be in today. They'll worry about me otherwise. I eat there daily before I go to work."

When they entered the house, Steven said, "That cool air feels nice, doesn't it? It's been hot as hell lately. The humidity up here is fierce."

"Up here? Where did you move from?" John asked as Steven lead the way to the living room.

"North Haven. It's south—"

"Pardon me for cutting you off. I know where it is. I pass through it when I drive to Muncie to visit my mother. Anyway, what's that music playing?"

"That's my oldest, Jeffrey. He's a cellist. He practices tirelessly every day."

"Fascinating. He's going places. So you said oldest. You have other children then?"

They entered the living room and remained standing. Steven said, "Yes. Tiffany is the middle child. She spends most of her time in the attic exercising. She's a star athlete. Track. Basketball. Swimming. Tennis. I don't think she'll ever meet a boy at this rate, but that's fine. Then there's Brittany, my youngest. She spends a lot of her time solving jigsaw puzzles and assembling model sets. She wants to work with real tools and build, but she's too young at this point. I picture her becoming an engineer one day."

John sat on the two–seater couch in the living room while Steven went to the kitchen to fix John a cup of coffee and some breakfast, but not the pancakes, since John told Steven he can't have chocolate. Steven graciously offered John some scrambled eggs with spinach and Parmesan cheese. To John, Parmesan cheese in eggs seemed odd, but he was a man who liked to experience new things.

Steven walked into the living room carrying a silver serving tray. On top if it were two plates of food, one for John and one for Steven. Even though he already ate, Steven wanted to make John more comfortable by eating with him.

"I'm sorry," Steven said, placing the serving tray on the glass coffee table. "Let me pick those up." He walked over to the hearth and placed the family picture on the mantel. Then he walked over to the crucifix on the floor near the picture wall. "Did they—"

"Yeah, the picture and the crucifix fell while I sat here. And now your chandelier is swinging like a pendulum. You have a ghost in your house?"

Steven chuckled lightly. "Yeah, I think so, but it doesn't bother us. To be honest, we all like it. We've always had an interest in the paranormal. Lately, I've been doing several E.V.P. sessions for fun. I'd like to ascertain what this ghost's story is. I always wanted to be a paranormal investigator."

John nodded while rubbing his beard.

Using a spoon, Steven sprinkled some shredded Parmesan cheese on John's eggs and handed the plate to John. "Here you are."

"Smells good," John said. He shoved his fork into the steamy, creamy eggs. "Alright, this should be adventurous." He took a little bite of the eggs and after swallowing said, "I have to admit I never would have thought to add Parmesan cheese to eggs. Delicious."

"Thanks. I never liked cooking until a few years ago."

John was nearly done with his eggs by the time Steven went to take his first bite. They eggs were that tasty to John, though he was hungry, also.

As they conversed, John asked, "Regarding the ghost in your lovely abode here, are you sure you know what you're dealing with?"

"What do you mean?"

"How do you know it's a friendly ghost? How do you know it isn't something evil or demonic?"

"Well, I figured if it were something demonic, plates and cups would be flying at our heads. We'd have scratches on our bodies. Nothing like that has happened. Sometimes it will push objects off counters or dressers, but it's never thrown objects directly at us. The activity has been innocuous."

John abruptly stopped chewing the eggs in his mouth, then forcefully swallowed so he could get his words out quickly. "For now," he said, straining. He coughed a few times, then had a few drinks of coffee. "Demons can masquerade as something friendly or playful to deceive you. Now, my friend, I know we just met and I'm not trying to be bossy, but I hope you know what you're dealing with here. A crucifix falling off a wall could be a sign of a demonic presence."

Steven didn't want to hear such things about the family ghost. He also didn't want to offend John, either; after all, John was trying to be a caring friend. Steven said, "I'll certainly keep that in mind. Perhaps my deep interest in the paranormal blinded my better judgment. Would you like some more eggs? I can whip up some seconds for us."

"Yeah, I'll have some more eggs, if you don't mind. Thank you."

Grabbing John's plate, Steven entered the kitchen to make some more eggs.

Meanwhile, John leaned back on the couch and whipped out his cellphone. He had about forty minutes left before he had to leave for work. Today was supposed to be an off day but somebody called off due to illness.

He stood and walked over to the picture that slid off the mantel for a second time. He picked it up and looked at it for several seconds, during which time he had flashbacks of his own family.

"Hi, mister," Brittany said, climbing on the larger couch.

John turned his head. "Well, hello, there, little one." He placed the picture back on the mantel and walked towards the couch. "That's a nice summer outfit you're wearing."

"Thanks. My Granana gave it to me for my birthday."

"Do you know what kind of flowers those are on your blouse?"

Brittany nodded her head. "Pretty ones."

After a light laugh, John said, "Yes, pretty ones. You're right. Lavender roses are pretty flowers." *I was once married to a woman like a lavender rose; she had all the beauty and elegance of a red rose without the thorns.*

"My name's Brittany. What's your name, mister?"

He introduced himself and shook her hand. As he talked to Brittany he had flashbacks of his own daughter.

"Uh oh," Brittany said. She exhaled a heavy sigh. "The picture fell again. I'll go pick it up for Daddy."

"Does it scare you when the picture falls off the mantel?" John asked, following her to fireplace.

"No, it's not scary. It's just the ghost saying hi to me."

Steven announced from the kitchen. "John, I'm sorry, I got distracted and burned the eggs. It'll be another five to ten minutes. Sorry."

"No problem. No rush at all, my friend. Take your time."

Brittany picked the picture up and presented it to John. She said, "I'm in the picture, and so is Mr. Quacks." Then she handed the picture to John, who placed it back on the mantel after looking at it.

Standing by the fireplace, John asked, "What else has the ghost done here? Are you willing to share that with me? If you're afraid, you don't have to."

Brittany walked over to the couch holding Mr. Quacks and climbed back on the larger couch. John followed her and sat on the smaller couch.

"I'm not afraid. The ghost sometimes slams doors in the kitchen. Sometimes the ghost throws things."

"Wow. That sounds scary to me. Does the ghost scare you?"

"No. My Granana protects me, and so does Mr. Quacks. The ghost doesn't bother me."

John was stunned with Brittany's bravery. He thought back to when he was around her age and had a ghost taunt him in the middle of the night. It was later discovered the little boy who visited John was a demon in disguise. John's older brother was practicing Satanism, which allowed the demon to infiltrate the home.

"Who's Granana?" John asked.

"She was my grandma. I miss her every day. She's in heaven now, but she still protects me from bad things."

"That's good to hear. Have you seen the ghost?"

Brittany coughed a few times. Then she said, "Yeah. The ghost wears a black suit. I see him sometimes walking up the attic stairs."

"Wow. And that didn't scare you?"

"Well, the first time it did, but I just closed my eyes real tight and thought of my Granana. Then the man went away."

"What's the ghost's face look like?"

"I haven't seen his face. Maybe soon I will."

Steven returned to the living room and handed John a plate of freshly-cooked eggs. Brittany excused herself. She wanted to go outside and play with Mr. Quacks. John shook her hand again and told her it was nice to meet her. He was mesmerized with how closely she resembled his own daughter at her age.

John said, "Cherish your family, my friend. That's one lovely little girl you have there."

"She's amazing. Smart. Perceptive for her age."

John finished his second helping of eggs. He said, "With your culinary skills, I'm surprised you're not a chef in a five-star restaurant.

Interestingly, John was more interested in learning about Steven's background than presenting his own. He asked a lot of follow-up questions when Steven revealed a little tidbit about himself.

Eventually, Steven asked, "John, do you know anything about drywall? I ask because when my wife and I put nails in the wall, this thick liquid oozed from it."

"Drywall wouldn't normally ooze liquid from a nail puncture." John said. "But, in the case of this house, I'm not surprised. You see, Mr. Pistone, the former C.E.O., of Gypsum, personally designed the drywall for this house— his new house. It was supposed to be a revolutionary drywall. He wanted to test it in his new house before offering it as a product through Gypsum though. Here's a fun fact: I was the forklift operator who loaded the palettes of the 'new and improved' drywall on the flatbed truck that transported them here for installation. Anyway, I guess the drywall wasn't as great as Pistone touted. I'd replace it. If you ask me, it sounds defective." He gave a thumbs-down.

Steven thanked John for the insight and indicated he would consider replacing the drywall, if needed. For now, the drywall wasn't creating a problem.

While finishing their breakfast, a mist formed around the coffee table. The odor of Tony's cigar and cologne were pungent. The mist didn't stick around for long, and when it disappeared, so did the odors.

When John left, Steven felt he met a lifelong friend. He was enamored with John's eloquence and wisdom, and he told his personal experiences with wit and humor. Each story had a lesson to be garnered from it.

Unbeknown to Steven, John said a silent prayer for the Dobrowski family before leaving for work.

CHAPTER FOUR

Brittany's Encounter

"Steven," Keisha said. "Steven!" nudging him lightly in his chest.

"Hmmm? What?" He said.

"I'm hearing creaks in the attic. Will you please check it out?" Her face was covered in some green goop to help prevent wrinkles. Her hair had several curlers in it.

"Of course, I will," he said, then yawned. The alarm clock indicated it was one-seventeen in the morning. He turned the light on next to his nightstand. Fortunately, it was bright enough for him to see around his side of the room, but not so bright as to disturb Keisha, who was nearly asleep already.

He slipped on his blue housecoat— a Father's Day gift from last year— and walked towards the attic steps after grabbing his cellphone off the nightstand. Someone was making the attic floor creak. Who was it? Tiffany? Maybe. Maybe not.

He stood at the foot of the stairs with one hand on the banister. "Tiffany?" he whispered up the attic stairs. "Is that you up there?"

There was no answer, but the creaks continued. Maybe she didn't hear him. He wouldn't knock on

Tiffany's bedroom door because if she was in her room, he would need to explain why he was disturbing her so early in the morning. He also wouldn't enter her room without knocking. His only alternative was to venture up to the attic and check it out for himself.

As he walked up the cold attic stairs, an arctic blast of air traveled past him. The creaks in the attic continued, but now Steven was making some creaks of his own as he traveled up the attic steps.

This attic was unlike most attics people envision when the word attic is mentioned. Often attics are pictured as drab, dark, and dingy. Not this attic. Far from it. This attic was finished from top to bottom. The walls were composed of drywall— the same drywall used throughout the other floors of the house. A gunstock oak hardwood floor adequately reflected the light from the two hexagonal-shaped windows, each on their own wall, during daylight hours.

The attic had plenty of space for Tiffany's exercise equipment she accumulated over the years as gifts from her parents and other relatives. Several pieces of exercise equipment were strewn across the attic floor: an elliptical, a stationary bike, and a weight bench. A royal blue Everlast punching bag hung and swung from the attic ceiling. Underneath it was a gym mat, but not the same color. The mat was gray. Its corners were tattered. A gym rope hung from the attic ceiling.

"Is someone up there?" He asked. His cellphone was out, and the flashlight was on. "Hello?" He said as he continued up the remaining few stairs. The creaking of the attic floor stopped.

Using the flashlight from his phone, he panned around the attic. The pedals on Tiffany's exercise bike were in motion. "That's interesting. A health-conscious ghost,"

He walked over to the exercise bike and stopped the pedals from rotating. The odor of cigar smoke and lasagna crept into Steven's nose. An orb of light swept across the attic and disappeared into one of the walls.

He pushed the record button on the voice recorder on his cellphone. "If someone is up here and wants to communicate, can you speak into this device or give me a sign, please? I'd like to hear from you." *Maybe this ghost is ready to tell his or her story and that's why it's making all these bumps in the night—and day.*

He reviewed the recording. No audio response—disembodied or on the voice recorder— but he did feel something poke him in the back. He said, "Maybe there are some Class B or C E.V.P.s on this." He was already backed up with reviewing, transcribing, and editing the inordinate number of E.V.P. sessions he'd been doing since his second day in the house.

He walked around the attic, feeling for any cold spots and searching for other signs of paranormal activity, but he found none.

As he was walking towards the attic stairs from the opposite side of the attic, someone spoke. It was faint chatter. He couldn't make out what was being said, but it was audible enough to hear. The talking sounded like it was coming from a radio.

Steven was persistent when it came to completing a task. If it took until sunrise to find the source of the faint chatter, so be it. He wouldn't be able to sleep if he went the bed without finding the source.

Eventually, the sound led him to the attic closet. He opened the door, slowly. The door didn't squeak; it opened seamlessly. As the door opened, the chatter became slightly louder since the door wasn't absorbing the sound. Even still, however, the chatter was unintelligible.

He shined his flashlight inside the closet. Resting atop a two-drawer metal file cabinet was a speaker— with the speaker part pointed towards the ceiling. He panned his flashlight around the closet looking for the radio, but he couldn't find one. Next, he traced the wires extending from the back of the speaker. He still couldn't find the radio. The back-and-forth chatter increased in speed. He picked the speaker up and reeled its wires in, hoping that would pinpoint where the radio was. He pulled and pulled, and eventually the leads of the wires were in his hand. The speaker was never connected to a radio, yet sound was emanating from it.

He placed the speaker on the file cabinet as he tried to process the reality he was experiencing. The chatter from the speaker continued. Part of him was scared out of his mind, but another part of him was intrigued at this paranormal phenomena. He asked the speaker a few questions but he never received a response. The chatter was still audible, but unclear. He couldn't make out many words. Wanting to get a better listen to the content of the conversation coming out of the speaker, he slowly lowered his ear to the speaker. Once his ear touched the speaker, a wave of static washed into his ears. He fell backwards, tripped over Tiffany's elliptical machine, and banged his head on the attic floor. The speaker went dead.

Moments later, Keisha called up from the attic stairs. "Babe, are you okay?"

Steven, slightly disoriented, stood and said, "Yes, I'm fine. Everything is fine."

As he walked towards the attic stairs, the bicycle pedals started rotating again, but Steven chose not to stop them this time.

Steven stood at the head of the stairs. "Good night, whoever you are," he said. "May you rest in peace, always. Please don't hurt my family. You're welcome to stay, but only if you don't harm my family. You want to hurt someone, come after me. But leave my family in peace… Please."

When he returned to the bedroom, Keisha was sound asleep in her purple nightgown.

Steven took off his housecoat and slipped back into bed under the covers. Soon after, he was asleep, but it was interrupted when a loud, piercing scream reverberated through the Dobrowksi house. It was Brittany.

Steven leapt out of bed and rushed to Brittany's aid. She was huddled in a fetal position on her bed. She was crying uncontrollably. Her hands covered her eyes. Her blanket was on the floor near the foot of the bed.

"Sweet pea," Steven said, sitting next to her on the bed rubbing her back, "what's wrong?"

"Is the scary man gone?" Brittany asked.

"What scary man?" he replied.

Keisha lingered into the room. "Are you okay, baby doll?"

"No, Mommy," Brittany said, trying to catch her breath. "The mean man tried to hurt me."

"Tell me, sweet pea," he said. "What man was in your nightmare?"

"No, Daddy. This was real. He was standing right there," Brittany said, pointing to the foot of her bed.

"What? A man is in the house? Where's my nine?" Steven said as he jumped off the bed and exited the bedroom.

"You don't have a nine, silly man," Keisha said.

Steven entered the bedroom armed with a five iron. "If there's a man in here, he's about to get some rough justice Jack Nicholson style." He searched around her bedroom. The closet. Under her bed. Inside the clothes hamper.

"Oh, babe, relax. There's no man in the house. She had a nightmare. Think about it. The house alarm didn't sound."

"No, Mommy," Brittany said. "It was the ghost. He looked mad. I don't wanna sleep in here. It's too scary."

"It's okay, baby doll. Mommy and Daddy are here for you and we won't ever let anything bad happen to you."

Keisha was a phenomenal mother for someone who had a poor home life growing up in East Chicago. She had been raised in a broken family and was sexually abused by her father. Her father impregnated her when she was fourteen, but the baby was born a stillbirth.

Steven said, "Tell you what, honey. I'll deal with this. You can go back to sleep."

Keisha accepted Steven's offer, but comforted Brittany a little while longer. Then she said, "I love you, baby doll." She lightly kissed Brittany on her cheek, then left the room and returned to the comfort of her bed.

Steven sat on her bed. "It's okay, sweet pea," Steven said, embracing her in his arms and rubbing her head. He rocked slightly back and forth. "Daddy's here… Daddy's here."

He asked her some questions about her nightmare, but she insisted it wasn't a nightmare. Steven stopped calling it a nightmare, though sometimes he would nearly slip up.

After drying her eyes and wiping her nose with some Kleenex, he said, "Now, please tell Daddy all about your night— I mean, the man you saw by your bed. Do you think you can do that for Daddy?"

She nodded. She wrapped her arms around Steven's neck, then became a fountain of information, spewing all the details of her encounter with this man. She said, "Well, first I heard scratching sounds on my wall. That's what woke me up. I was scared, Daddy. I couldn't yell for help but I wanted to. I put the blanket over my head. I wanted the scratching sounds to stop."

"Maybe it was a mouse trying to make a mouse hole. Or there's a tree outside your window. Maybe some branches were scratching against the house."

"No, Daddy. I don't think so."

"Keep going. You're doing great so far."

"Well, so then… I stayed under my covers. The scratching noises stopped, but I stayed under the covers. I was too scared to look around my room."

"Uh-huh," he said, rubbing the back of her head as it rested on his shoulder.

She took a deep breath. The heat from it ran across Steven's neck. She continued, "The covers were slowly pulled down, then stopped for a second. And then the blanket flew off me. I sat up and that's… that's…

that's when I saw the scary man by my bed." She cried, this time louder and harder than before.

Why did I make her relive this experience by telling it to me? Bad move. World's Greatest Dad? I think not. Moron. After his self-deprecation ended, he said, "I'm sorry this happened, sweet pea."

"Daddy, it was scary. His face was mean. He was gonna hurt me."

"No, no," he said. "That's not going to happen. Not while I'm around, it's not."

"When I screamed, he went away. His body blinked three times. It was like blink-blink… blink. I don't wanna see him anymore. Please keep him away."

"See? He got scared, too. Let me go downstairs and get you some milk. You'll feel better."

"No, Daddy," she said, tightening her arms around him. "I'll come with you. I can't be in here alone. That's when he'll come back and hurt me."

Steven choked from her stronghold. "A little less tight… Okay, thank you, sweet pea. Anything else you want to tell me?"

Brittany didn't respond immediately. "Well, he was wearing a suit… A black one."

"A suit?" *Terry better not be breaking into my house and scaring the hell out of my daughter.*

But what if the man in the black suit wasn't Terry, the Dobrowski's next-door neighbor? What if the man in the black suit wasn't human at all? What if he was the *GHOST*? Who was this man in the black suit? And what did he want? Or was Brittany so terrified out of her skull she believed it was real when it was actually a nightmare?

Steven and Brittany went downstairs to the kitchen. Mr. Quacks came along for the journey. They passed by the living room on their way to the kitchen. The crucifix and family picture were not in their places again. Steven didn't bother with those items though; he went straight to the kitchen where he poured her a glass of milk, which she drank in a few gulps. Then they went upstairs into Steven's bedroom. Keisha was fast asleep in bed. A night mask covered her eyes.

Brittany (and Mr. Quacks) slept in between Steven and Keisha that night. Fortunately, she slept well.

For two more nights, Brittany slept in her parents' bed. She didn't return to her room since her and Steven walked out of it the night she had her nightmare— assuming it was a nightmare.

On the third night around eight thirty, Brittany was playing in her parents' bedroom, laying on the floor in front of the bed with Mr. Quacks and some of her dolls Steven retrieved from her bedroom the previous day. She brushed the long blond hair on one of the dolls. Over and over and over… She didn't care much for dolls, but there wasn't much else for her to do since she refused to go into her room, even in daylight. Her jigsaw puzzles and K'Nex projects would have to wait until she developed the courage to return to her room.

Keisha walked into the bedroom and sat on the foot of the bed. She said nothing initially. She stared idly at Brittany on the floor and had a few flashbacks of her childhood, and they weren't pleasant. It's a wonder Keisha didn't become a homicidal maniac given her epic history of sexual, physical, and emotional abuse, courtesy of her father and some of his brothers. One memory that was seared into her brain and crashed into her forebrain while gazing at Tiffany playing with her dolls involved her dad, her Uncle Anfernee, and a friend of Uncle Anfernee's. A tag-team raping, it was. As one of the three raped her, the other two watched and cheered, like spectators at a baseball game. *Hit her again! Use your fist! Burn her nipple with your cigarette! Pound that shit harder! Slap that worthless bitch! Grip her throat tighter!*

Keisha wretched a little, but she didn't vomit. She laid this living memory to rest for now by hermetically sealing it in a coffin and burying it in a grave in her brain. Now her mind was like a blank slate. She could converse with Brittany about sleeping in her own bedroom.

"Hey, baby doll," Keisha said, wiping the tears from her face. "Ready for bath and bed?"

"Yeah, Mr. Quacks and I are tired," Brittany said. "Can I sleep in your bed again, Mommy? Please? Just one more night."

"Yes. That would be okay. If your room is still too scary to sleep in, you can. But, you know sooner or later you will have to sleep in your own bedroom, right?"

Brittany sighed and put the doll down. Its hair was falling out from excessive hair brushing. "Yeah, Mommy. I know."

"I have an idea. I think I have something I can give you that will make you feel safer in your room."

"Really? What?"

Keisha stood and walked to the egress of the door. "Follow me and you shall see."

And she did. They went downstairs into the laundry room. Keisha stepped into the walk-in storage closet while Brittany sat on the drying machine. The hum from the dryer made Brittany's eyes heavy. The warmth from the top panel comforted her. She lightly tapped rhythmically on the dryer door with her bare feet.

Keisha popped her head out of the storage closet with a smile as wide as the wingspan of an A380. "Ready for the surprise?"

Brittany finished a yawn she started before her mom startled her. "Yeah, Mommy," she said, then yawned again and stretched her arms sky high. "I'm ready."

"I hope you like it," Keisha said, walking out from the closet with her hands behind her back. "This is something I think you'll remember." She cautiously and slowly brought the arm containing the surprise from around her back. A red pillowcase covered the object. With her free hand, she pinched the top of the cover and like a magician yanked the cover off with flamboyancy and grandeur. "Surprise," she said.

Brittany's once-heavy eyes were now light as feather. "Wow, Mommy, you're really letting me have this?" Another yawn. No stretching though.

"Yes, I am." Keisha said, her tone joyful. "Do you remember this?"

"Definitely. That was Granana's. She had it next to her bed at her house before she went to her new home in Heaven."

What was this object being passed from mother to daughter that once belonged to the now-departed Granana? The object was a Michael the Archangel statue. It was snow white, made of porcelain. Michael was standing erect, with a sword in one hand and a shield tattooed with a cross in the other. The sword pointed downward and rested on the ground; Michael was leaning on it. His wings were fanned out.

After placing the porcelain statue next to her on the dryer, Brittany lunged off the dryer and wrapped her arms around her mother.

"Thank you, Mommy," Brittany said.

"You're welcome, baby doll," Keisha said, then kissed her daughter on the cheek.

Brittany was grateful for the statue. The possessions of Granana seemed to fill an emotional void in Brittany's tattered heart.

"Thank you again, but do you think I could have one more thing that was Granana's?"

Keisha placed Brittany back on the dryer and returned the storage closet. Brittany could see the shadow of her mother going from one box to the other trying to find something to supplement the Michael statue. The clinking and clanking of objects striking each other produced a symphony of sounds.

Eureka! Keisha found something. She stepped out from the storage closet and closed the door behind her. Her hair was slightly disheveled. She skidded her palm against the light switch. The sliver of light escaping through the thin space between the door and the floor disappeared. "Close your eyes," she said.

With Brittany's eyes blinded, Keisha removed the object, which rested on her hip. It was in between her waist and jeans.

When Brittany's eyes went from closed to open, an expression of amazement painted across her face. She said, "Wow, Mommy, really? I can have this, too?"

"You bet, baby doll. It's yours."

Brittany grasped the object from her mother's hand. The cold steel blanketed her body and soul with radiant warmth. The smell of vanilla tickled Brittany's nostrils.

It was a crucifix. A stainless-steel one. Granana kept this crucifix on her bed stand, near the candle warmer.

Brittany and Keisha walked to Brittany's room. When the door opened, a flood of winter-chill air hit them. They both shuddered, only momentarily though.

Brittany placed the Michael statue on her wooden two-drawer nightstand— the same one Granana had in her bedroom. Also, on the bed stand was a lamp.

The crucifix she placed in between the two pillows on her bed. Then she took a bath and changed into her pajamas. Soon after, she was asleep in her bed, grasping her Granana's crucifix in her hand.

CHAPTER FIVE

Scruffles

Ding-dong, ding-dong, ding-dong.

Three chimes in rapid succession startled Steven as he whisked some eggs, cinnamon, and vanilla for French toast. He hadn't even fired up the stove yet to warm his new non-stick skillet he purchased last night at Rosco's after work.

He opened the door, but nobody was there. He stepped onto the front porch to see if anyone was walking away in either direction, but there wasn't a soul in sight.

While outside, he did see John getting into his 1996 Buick LeSabre. John had that car since 1997. He purchased it after he signed a six-figure contract with a hospital, serving as a consultant. He was a hospital administrator whose main focuses were improving patient care and reducing costs. Now he was semi-retired working at Gypsum.

Standing outside of his faded green car, John waved to Steven as he placed his lunch box on the passenger seat. Steven waved back, and hoped John would spare him a few minutes before leaving for work.

And he did. He approached Steven with his hand extended. Steven shook his hand and they exchanged the standard nice–to–see–you–how–are–you pleasantries.

"How are things going with your spiritual tenant?" John asked, hoping Steven would say he removed it from the home.

"Alright. Nothing harmful has happened. Still lots of activity though. Doors fly open and slam shut. Objects get moved around; speaking of which, two days ago I was an hour late to work because the ghost hid my keys. I see orbs fly around in different rooms. And, for the life of me, every so often I smell Tony's cigar and cologne. The stuff I just mentioned doesn't bother me or anyone else in the house. Not even Keisha— she's gotten accustomed to it. But, last night, a message was written on the bathroom mirror while I was in the shower. It said OMICIDIO."

John shook his head. *Why hasn't he heeded my advice?* "So, other than all those things you just told me, things are fine?"

"Yes, things are fine. Brittany is sleeping in her own bed again. Tiffany resumed her daily exercise routine in the attic."

After John sighed, he said, "I don't like being the guy to say I told you so, but in this instance I need to be. I strongly feel that ghost you're hosting in your house is a wolf in sheep's clothing. Get it out of there before something happens that you'll regret."

Towards the tail end of John's last sentence, the front door slammed shut. The same thing happened two days ago, but this time the door was locked. Steven pulled the keys out of his shorts pocket— he always carried his keys with him after being late for work trying to find them— and unlocked and opened the door.

John said, "Well, that was fun and exciting." He reached down and picked up Steven's newspaper and handed it Steven. "Seriously, though, get rid of the spirit in your home. It's not a pet. It's not a toy."

"Maybe I should. I've conducted several E.V.P. sessions. I finally got some E.V.Ps. I thought this spirit would never talk to me. I'd turn on the voice recorder and not say anything for several minutes. Then I'd stop the recorder and play it back and get nothing. I'd spend hours listening to these recordings— much to Keisha's chagrin— and have nothing to show for it, not even any Class B or C E.V.Ps. That is until now. You should listen to some of them." Steven pulled out his cellphone and with a few taps he played one of them for John. Then he played the others, also.

The first E.V.P. he played said, "You… need to… leeeeave." The voice was raspy and drawled.

The next one said, "Strangled." The voice was quick and high-pitched.

The last one said with an angry tone, "Killer die."

Standing in amazement and horror, John said, "Take my advice and rid the house of the spirit. You need to smudge."

Steven didn't want to smudge his house. He wanted the spirit to stay. He felt a connection with it. Still, he didn't want to openly show his dissension, so he indulged John. He said, "I've heard of that before. Will you refresh my memory, please?"

"Smudging is a way to clear negative spirits from the home. Get some sage and burn it. Go through each room in your house and spread the smoke from corner to corner and all over using a feather or your hand. Chant an incantation. There are plenty incantations to choose from online. When I blessed my home, I chanted, 'All negative energy must leave at once. Only positive energy is welcome in this home.' I'm not all that creative. I just said the first incantation that shot in my ripened mind."

"I probably should smudge," Steven said. Then he countered. "However, part of me thinks it wants to say something. It has a story it wants to tell. Maybe I can help it."

"Get rid of it. It's not your job to help it, my friend. Your job is love and protect your family."

Steven agreed it was his job to love and protect his family, but why couldn't he do that and help a ghost? He didn't contend with John. He thanked him for his advice. They shook hands and parted ways.

After making breakfast and taking a shower, Steven decided to take Brittany to the park.

"Sweet pea," Steven said, calling from the main floor stairwell, his hand stroking the wood-stained banister. "After I read a little of the paper, we'll go to the park, okay. Are you ready?"

"Yeah, Daddy," Brittany said. A moment later she was at the top of the stairs holding Mr. Quacks. She scurried down the stairs and hugged her dad's leg. "I love you, Daddy."

"I love you, too, sweet pea."

They walked to the living room. Brittany climbed onto the couch and sat patiently as her dad picked up the pictures that fell off the fireplace mantel and picture wall, and replaced them. No broken glass, thankfully. The crucifix was further away from the wall this time. He placed it back on the nail after wiping off the corrosion-colored substance that trailed from the nail on the wall.

"Daddy, the light is moving again," Brittany said.

"Thanks, sweet pea," he replied.

It wasn't the light that was a concern right now. It was something else.

"What's that?" he asked.

He stood facing the picture wall, scratching the back of his head. A step or two forward. Now he was two inches away from the wall. A raised imperfection in the wall attracted his attention; it was red and inflamed, somewhat like a pimple. It was rough to the touch. He placed his nose closer to the imperfection. The odor of it was a cross between plaster of Paris and rotting carcass. He wanted the imperfection out of his wall, out of his beautiful picture wall, so he decided to iron it out. He pressed his crooked thumb against the lesion and applied pressure. First a little, then a bit more, then still a little more than that. It was starting to flatten. A little more pressure. BOOM. A viscous substance shot outward as well as radially from the imperfection onto Steven's face. Its color was that of a merlot that had dried on a napkin. The substance trailed from the lesion down the wall, slowly though. There were splatter patterns in all directions from the sheer velocity with which the viscous substance shot from the lesion.

Brittany pointed and cackled. She thought her dad staged the entire thing simply to get a laugh out of her. Steven ran to the bathroom and washed his face. It was a grisly site. The sink turned into a blood bath. The substance stained the porcelain sink bowl.

He pat dried his face with a white towel; it was now stained, also. The substance in the wall lesion was a nightmare.

His face now clean and pristine he entered the living room. Brittany was finger painting on the picture wall with the viscous substance.

"Sweet pea, my, my, my, what are you doing?" Steven asked her.

"I make pretty on the wall, Daddy," she said, her fingers still dancing in the viscous substance on the wall like it was a finger-painting project in art class. "But this paint is stinky. Gross!"

Steven cleaned her hands with the wet rag he intended to use to clean the wall. An aroma crept into their nostrils. The smell of rust and death nearly knocked Steven and Brittany on their asses. They went to the bathroom to finish the clean-up from Brittany's art project.

Now Steven returned to the living room to clean the wall. In his hand he held a damp rag he had dipped into a bucket of bleach water, then rung out. He pinched his nose with one hand and wiped the wall down with the other.

The lesion was now replaced with a pockmark. He didn't worry about this too much. He'd repair the wall later that night with some spackle and some touch-up paint.

After dropping the brown-stained rags and towel in the washing machine with an oil drum of bleach, he started the cycle. Heavy duty.

He sat on the longer four-seater couch. He removed the rubber band from the newspaper and opened it. The front-page headline was Gypsum Chief Accountant Still Missing. He read the article. Afterwards, he muttered, "Probably stole from the company and flew to a non–extraditing country. Corrupt piece of executive garbage." A split second after finishing his sentence, the newspaper flew out of his hand's into the fireplace. "Sweet pea, I think that's our cue to go to the park."

To the park they went. Mr. Quacks tagged along. Two's company, three's a crowd? Not to Steven. The more the merrier, even if Mr. Quacks was a stuffed animal. On the walk there, Brittany talked to her dad about the new K'Nex set he surprised her with the previous night. She and her dad were going to work on it after dinner. It was a construction set.

After spending some time on the slides, monkey bars, and various-shaped jungle gyms, Brittany was tired and hungry.

They closed their time at the park sitting in a double-glider swing. After a few oscillations on the swing, Brittany asked, "Daddy? Aren't ghosts awesome?"

"I think most are," he said. "How about you?"

"I do, too. Granana used to visit me at our old house after she died… I miss her."

Steven put his foot out of the swing. The back-and-forth motion was replaced with stationary silence. His Adam's apple moved up and down slightly from him swallowing. "She did?"

"Yeah, Daddy. She talked to me at night, after you and Mommy would tuck me in for bed." Several seconds passed by. "Dad?"

Steven rubbed his five o'clock shadow. With a single finger he rubbed his mole a few times. Lots of introspection. He released a heavy sigh. "What did you and Granana talk about?"

"Lots of stuff. School. Mr. Quacks. Her new home in heaven." Brittany yawned, then rubbed her nose.

He leaned forward and placed his hands on her shoulders. "Anything else?"

Brittany put a finger to her chin and twisted her lips. "I don't think so, Daddy."

"Did she say anything about me?"

"I don't remember, Daddy. Sorry."

"It's okay, sweet pea," he said, his tone flat.

"I miss her, Daddy. I miss her so much." She placed her face in her hands and cried.

He embraced her. While rubbing the back of her head, he said, "I know. You two were close."

Close? That's an understatement. Granana and Brittany had the strongest bond among the three children. They were essentially inseparable.

This seemingly indestructible bond wasn't formed as the result of a cataclysmic explosion, such as the Big Bang. It formed from the innumerable hours and days she and Granana spent together. Because Keisha had to leave before Brittany had to be at school, Granana would drive over every morning and help Brittany get ready for school. After eating breakfast, Granana drove Brittany to and from school during the school year and would stay at the Dobrowski house until Keisha arrived home from work.

On Wednesdays and Sundays, Granana, Keisha, and the children would attend church together. Steven used to be a follower and would attend church with the family, but eventually he recanted his beliefs and stopped attending church altogether. Keisha was a devout Catholic and she refused to allow Steven's views on religion stupefy the minds of her children.

As penance for not attending church with the family, he would prepare breakfast and dinner every Sunday and dinner every Wednesday for the family, including Granana.

Granana would drive over every Sunday morning and eat breakfast with the family, then drive Keisha and the children to church. She would return with them after church and stay for dinner and dessert. On Wednesdays, once church was over, she drove Keisha and the children back home and stayed for dinner and dessert.

"Daddy? Can we make a trip to visit Granana's grave?" Brittany asked.

"Of course, we can. Maybe in a few weeks we can all take a drive up there and visit. Lay some flowers down. Say a few words. Are you ready to go home and get some lunch?"

"Yeah, Mr. Quacks is hungry, too. And tired. He needs a nap."

Steven laughed. Patting Mr. Quacks on the head, he said, "Poor Mr. Quacks. We'll be home soon. It's nothing but a stone's throw away."

Brittany used Mr. Quacks as a way to express how she was feeling, and Steven was fine with that. He knew she was speaking about herself.

As the swing slowed to a stop, a dog approached the swing and sat near it. Brittany tried to step off the swing, but Steven put out his arm to prevent her from stepping off the swing. "Wait, sweet pea. That dog might be dangerous."

Steven stepped out first and rested on one knee. He slowly crept his hand toward the dog's head, preparing to retract it if the dog made any sudden moves. The dog was docile. Its pink tongue was hanging out and it was panting. He petted the dog a few times while keeping an eye out for its owner.

Brittany stepped off the swing and petted the dog. The dog gave her kisses on her face and cheek, which made her giggle.

"Daddy… can we please keep the doggy?" She asked.

"Sweet pea, that's a big doggy. And look at all that hair streaming off him. There'll be dog hair all over the house, in our food, in our drinks. Can you imagine biting into a hamburger or hot dog only to then pull a large ball of hair out of your mouth. Yuck. Besides, this dog might belong to somebody here."

"Please, Daddy. He's a nice doggy. Here, Daddy, pet him again," Brittany said, pulling his hand closer to the dog.

Steven pet the dog a few more times on the head. "Nice doggy. Good doggy." The dog tried licking Steven's arm, but its tongue missed each time.

Brittany laughed. "See, Daddy, he likes you. Do you like him?"

Steven let out a long sigh. "Yeah, I like him. I like him a lot. He's a cute dog."

"Yay! So we can keep him?" Brittany asked.

He scratched his head, then said, "We need to look around the park to see if maybe his collar fell off. We need to ask around and find out who this dog belongs to. It wouldn't be right to up and leave with him. We need to try to find its owner first."

And they tried, but no success. Furthermore, nobody at the park knew who it belonged to. They waited around a while longer at the park. Brittany was smitten with this dog. She and the dog ran and frolicked together while Steven continued to ask around about the dog with Mr. Quacks in his hand.

Steven approached Brittany, preparing to break the news to her they needed to leave the dog at the park so its rightful owner could find it.

He approached the dog and petted it a few more times. The dog's coat was filthy. Before he could burst Brittany's bubble, she popped the question again about keeping the dog.

"Please, Daddy? Please. Please can we keep him?" Brittany asked, petting the dog.

"My, my, my, that is one scruffy dog. He's filthy," Steven said.

Now Steven didn't want to break her daughter's heart. He figured it would be better to be a little diabolical about the situation and lead Brittany to decide to leave the dog at the park. He thought for a minute, gently squeezing Mr. Quacks in his hand, and then he had the answer he needed.

Mr. Quacks to the rescue! He said, "What about Mr. Quacks, sweet pea? Dogs love to chew things up, and Mr. Quacks is an ideal target. This dog could rip Mr. Quacks apart. I don't want to see anything bad happen to Mr. Quacks."

Brittany shook her head. "No, Daddy. He loves Mr. Quacks and Mr. Quacks loves him. Watch." She pulled Mr. Quacks from Steven's hand and gently pecked Mr. Quacks' bill on top of the dog's head while making smooch sounds. Then she placed the Mr. Quacks in front of the dog. After the dog briefly sniffed it, he began to lick it. "See, Daddy. They're buddies."

Steven chuckled. He knelt down and placed both hands on the sides of its head and began to massage it. The dog moved closer to Steven and licked his face. Steven laughed with a feminine tone. Now he was sold. Hook. Line. Sinker. Well played, doggy.

Steven said, "Okay, okay. We can keep him. Just until we find its family. For now, why don't you pick a name for it?"

Brittany thought for a few moments, and then exclaimed, "Scruffles!"

"Scruffles?" He questioned, combing the dog's coat with his fingers. Tufts of hair floated into the air like a gutted pillow in a gusty wind. "Why Scruffles?"

"Well, Daddy, you said the dog looked scruffy," Brittany said, then giggled as the dog licked Brittany's cheek some more. "So, I pick Scruffles."

"Scruffles it is," Steven said.

With their new Golden Retriever, they walked home from the park. Scruffles was part of the family—for now.

Walking up the driveway, Terry, the next-door neighbor was in his driveway washing and waxing his car. With a smug look, he said, "Nice dog, coal burner.

That bitch there is an upgrade from that nigger bitch wife of yours. I've got a sure-fire cure for your jungle fever." He lifted his polo shirt. A holstered gun on his hip. "You're circling the drain at this point. Tick tock."

After the word 'burn' in 'burner' left Terry's mouth, Steven covered Brittany's ears. Steven's blood went from a simmer to a rapid boil. A mile-high wave of rage washed over him. He didn't respond to Terry's off-color remark or his idle threat.

Through the front door the party of four went. When Scruffles entered the house, he walked over to the stairwell. He went up a few steps, then began barking and growling, his head titled upward toward the second floor. First a little, then a lot more.

Throughout the twenty seconds, Steven asked, "What's wrong, Scruffles?" then "What is it, boy?" Then he said, "It's okay, Scruffy-boy. It's okay."

Scruffles propelled himself up four more stairs in rapid succession, almost as if he were chasing after a toy bone somebody had thrown, then he abruptly stopped and looked up at the second floor and whimpered. Ten seconds later, he turned around and walked down the stairs and brushed up against Brittany's leg, still whimpering a little. She petted him a few times. "Let's go say hi to everyone, Scruffles," she said, holding Mr. Quacks.

It was Scruffles' first night in the house. Steven insisted Scruffles sleep downstairs in the living room, even though Brittany pleaded with him to let Scruffles sleep with her.

Brittany peeked her head out her door. The coast was clear. She tiptoed down the stairs and walked into the living room. Her sidekick Mr. Quacks tagged along for the adventure.

She knelt in front of Scruffles and petted him. Then she whispered, "Shhhhh, you got to be quiet if you come in my room. We don't want to wake up Mommy or Daddy. Especially, Daddy. Okay?"

Scruffles licked her cheek. The warmth from the kisses traveled to her heart.

"Good boy," she said, using her library voice. "Come on, Scuffs. Let's go to bed."

Brittany led the way and Scruffles followed. Up the stairs, she tiptoed again. In her room, she walked to her bed. Mr. Quacks was now resting with his head on her pillow. She climbed onto the bed and sat in the center with her legs crossed. Scruffles was near her bedside evaluating his environment, sniffing around. He approached the nightstand and sniffed the objects on it.

"You like that, Scruffles?" she asked. She picked up the Michael statue. "This is Michael. He and Granana protect us from the bad man living in this house."

Scruffles leaped onto the bed and rotated his body around so one side of his body was pressed against Brittany's leg.

Brittany examined the Michael statue closely. "See, Scruffs, Michael has this sword he'll use to slice the bad man to pieces. See the sword touching the ground?"

Scruffles sniffed the statue, then gave it a few licks. Then he laid his head down on the bed and closed his eyes. He let out a slight sigh.

"And this, Scruffles, is what Granana uses to protect us from the bad man."

Scruffles opened his eyes and turned his head towards the crucifix Brittany was holding in one hand and caressing it with the other. Sniff, sniff. Lick, lick. Back to sleep.

"You won't let anything bad happen to me either, will you, Scruffs?" She grabbed Mr. Quacks, who was laying on her pillow, and then said, "And neither will you Mr. Quacks."

Someone opened her door. It was her dad. Standing in a pair of boxers and a T-shirt while squinting his eyes, he said, "Who are you talking to, sweet pea? Why is Scruffles in your room?"

"I brought him up here. I think he was scared and needed to be with someone."

It was the other way around, and Steven was wise to it. He walked over to her bed and sat next to her. He rubbed her head for a few moments. The feeling of cold metal branded his ass. He pulled the object out from underneath him. "I didn't know you had this, sweet pea. Where did you get this?"

"Mommy let me have it. She said I could have it. It keeps the bad man away from me."

"Bad man?"

"Yeah, the man in the black suit. The man who scared me that one night, remember? I heard Scruffles growling downstairs. Maybe it was the man in the black suit."

"Do you like the crucifix?"

Brittany let out a lion's roar of a yawn and stretched. "Yeah, Daddy. Granana's crucifix is magic. It makes the bad man disappear. I miss her so much, Daddy."

"I know you do, sweet pea. In a few weeks we'll make a trip back to North Haven and visit Granana's resting place. Do you remember how Granana died, sweet pea?"

Brittany was tired of hearing her dad say they'd visit Granana's resting place in a few weeks, but she didn't bring it up. It could wait. She said, "Yeah, she got sick and went to the hospital. She died a few days later in her hospital bed."

Steven turned his head towards the wall behind him. He picked up the Michael statue that was still sitting on her bed. "I remember this. This was Granana's, too, right?"

"Yeah, Daddy. Michael and Granana are a team. Isn't the statue pretty?"

"Very pretty. I had one like this when I was your age. Mine had Michael extending the sword outward, you know, like he was about to slay some demons. This statue has Michael using the sword like a cane… Still, it's nice."

"Yeah, I love it."

Steven stood and placed the statue on Brittany's bed stand. Brittany wriggled under her covers, clutching the crucifix. She slept on her stomach and held the crucifix under her pillow.

He kissed her on her cheek, then Mr. Quacks, who was lying on the pillow next to Brittany. Then he petted Scruffles a few times.

"Good night, everyone," he said, before turning the light off and shutting the door.

CHAPTER SIX
Brickmail

The sound of broken glass and the blare of the burglar alarm sent shock waves through the hearts and minds of everyone in the Dobrowski household at three–seventeen in the morning, according to the Casio alarm clock that rested on Steven's nightstand next to his bed. Something struck a window on the first floor.

The barks and growls from Scruffles hopefully scared the burglar away. Too bad Scruffles wasn't downstairs to slice his canines through the meaty flesh of their ass. He was in Brittany's bedroom.

"Where's my nine?! Where's my nine?!" Steven shouted, running out of the bedroom. "An intruder!"

"You don't have a nine!" Keisha shouted back. "Stop saying that!"

"Everyone stay put! Lock your doors!" he said.

The second floor was dark as a cavern at night unless the hallway light was on, and right now the light was off.

Out of the small storage area nook on the second floor, Steven pulled out a five–iron from his oversized gray and maroon Titleist golf bag and slowly crept down the stairs. The shriek of the house alarm skewered Steven's eardrums like a hot-tipped arrow.

As Steven reached the bottom of the stairs, an orb shot past him and disappeared into the dining room.

Stepping into the front room— or, as Steven called it, a sitting room— barefoot, a hissing wind blew into the house. The rectangular sheet of glass in the picture window was reduced to infinite fragments. Only a few pieces of jagged glass hung from the top rails.

The flashing of red and blue lights illuminated the living room sufficiently for Steven to see the glass shattering culprit: a brick with a note secured using a tightly-wound red rubber band.

He shouted to the ceiling, "Honey, I know what happened. Someone sent us a message using Brickmail Express!"

Carefully stepping in between shards of glass, he walked over to the brick, he picked it up, removed the letter, and read it as police knocked on the front door. Steven opened the door and invited in the police.

Cut–out letters of various sizes, shapes, styles, and colors from newspapers and magazines were glued on the piece of canary–colored, legal–pad–sized paper. The message read as follows:

DEAR NIGGER BITCH AND NIGGER BITCH'S FAMILY:

THIS IS YOUR FIRST NOTICE AND IT MAY BE YOUR LAST… LEAVE WHITMOND LEAVE WHITMOND LEAVE WHITMOND… OR DIE.

Two uniformed officers were on the scene: Ofc. McGill and Ofc. Davies. McGill was medium-height and obese. His face was rosy and it was peppered with freckles. Davies was short, but muscular and toned. He had a shaved head and bad teeth.

Ofcs. McGill and Davies often completed each other's sentences. They were like a strange married couple.

Once preliminary information was collected, Steven showed Ofcs. McGill and Davies to the living room. When he turned the chandelier light on, three of the twelve bulbs instantly exploded. Steven played it off by saying that's never happened before, even though he replaced more than two dozen light bulbs in the last three weeks.

While completing the report, Ofc. Davies was sitting on the smaller love seat while Ofc. McGill was filling out his portion of the paperwork. The sound of Steven fumbling to make coffee prompted Ofc. Davies to look though the kitchen entrance. Adjacent to the kitchen was the laundry room. The laundry room door was open and Ofc. Davies could see into the laundry room. He turned away to see how his partner was coming along with the paperwork, then looked towards the kitchen again. He sprang up out of his seat like a jack-in-the-box and drew his weapon, running through the kitchen towards the laundry room door, which slammed shut before Ofc. Davies made it to the kitchen.

Ofc. Davies opened the laundry room door, but nobody was inside. He went out the back door and did a quick search. He found nobody, and quickly discounted anyone exited out the back door because the security light came on after he stepped out, not before. The front door in the laundry room was locked, including the deadbolt. The final spot Ofc. Davies checked was the garage, but it turned up nothing.

Steven entered the garage as Ofc. Davies was searching. He said, "What happened? What's going on?"

"I saw a man in a black suit enter the laundry room and slam the door. I can't find him anywhere. He's a slippery son of a bitch."

Steven wanted to be honest and tell Ofc. Davies it was a ghost, but Steven didn't want to risk being committed. Who knows what Ofc. Davies or Ofc. McGill would think hearing such an outlandish, yet true, admission.

"Sorry you missed him. I guess he got away."

After the report and statement were completed, the two officers provided Steven with additional information.

Ofc. Davies said, "We'll file this report and forward it—" while McGill stood erect as a grizzly's dick, arms equally erect at his sides.

"—to our detective bureau. If you have any—" Ofc. McGill said, his arms now folded as his partner looked at him and nodded with a dumbass smile on his face.

"—questions, call or email, or visit the station," Ofc. Davis continued. His eyes now back on Steven.

Now, when Ofc. Davies spoke, Ofc. McGill didn't look at him and smile and nod as he talked. Far from it, in fact. Instead, he essentially became straight-faced, and forcibly pressed his lips firmly together.

When Ofc. McGill talked, his arms were folded across his chest; when his partner interrupted him and talked, he placed them at his sides like a good tin soldier should.

It was obvious Ofc. McGill had to force himself to keep quiet. This didn't last long though. After Ofc. Davies spit out six, maybe seven words tops, Ofc. McGill interrupted him and resumed talking until Ofc.

Davies interrupted him again. Evidently, one couldn't let the other talk for very long, because each loved to hear the sound of their own voice.

With his arms folded and Ofc. Davies looking at Ofc. McGill while sporting that same shit-for-brains smile, Ofc. McGill said, "Your case number is—"

"— on the backside of this—" Ofc. Davies said while Ofc. McGill pressed his lips together, arms now straight as a board at his sides.

"— card. Please retain it for—" Ofc. McGill said, arms now folded.

"— your records. And if you—"

"— think of anything else that will—"

"— help forward the investigation please—"

"— contact the station immediately and ask—"

"— for the Detective Bureau. Someone—"

"— will be able to connect you with—"

"— a detective assigned to the case. Can you—"

"— think of anything else at this juncture?"

A few moments later, the dizziness Steven experienced from adjusting his head back and forth to make eye contact with the person speaking subsided, and then a eureka moment crashed into the forefront of his brain. He remembered the post he read on the Whitmond community forum website when he went on the site to post about finding a lost dog.

The post was titled "NEGRO at 6729 Jefferson Ave" and the contents of the post were:

"Hello community members. I'm making a public service announcement informing you that a Negro woman has moved into the house at 6729 Jefferson Ave. Her ogre-looking husband is White. Their ugly kids are mutts. Avoid contact at all costs. Hopefully they'll be out of our community soon."

He excused himself to go upstairs to his office to print off a copy of the post for them. Ofcs. Goofy and Poker Face remained silent until Steven returned.

While Steven was in his office upstairs, the stairwell light turned on and off randomly. A wispy mist danced around the stairwell light as this happened.

Ofcs. McGill and Davies discussed the phenomena and concluded Steven was playing games with them.

When Steven exited his office, the door behind him slammed shut, then opened again, only to slam once more. He turned the hallway light on, then walked to the stairwell.

He handed the post to Ofc. McGill, who started to say 'thank you', but then Ofc. Davies interrupted him and said 'you' after Ofc. McGill said 'thanks.'

About five more minutes of Ofcs. McGill and Davies competing for the center–stage spotlight passed, at which point the officers' business at the house concluded, and now it was time for these two traveling clowns to get back in their car and take their freak show back on the road, then return to the circus.

While McGill stood at attention with his lips clenched together, Ofc. Davies said, "May I use—"

"— your bathroom quickly, please?" Ofc. McGill chimed and folded his arms while Ofc. Davies nodded and smiled at him like a love-lust teenage girl, impressed his partner essentially read his mind— once again.

"Sure," Steven said through a strained smile, strenuously fighting to stop himself from unholstering one of their guns and firing manically into both their skulls.

While Ofc. Davies pee-pee danced to the hallway bathroom, Steven cordially escorted Ofc. McGill out the door. A minute longer around either of these two nincompoops, Steven would've gone bat–shit crazy.

The night was dead, absent of any breath in its lungs to exhale. The moon was nearly full, and the stars shimmered across the crepuscular sky. The day was summer, but the night was like winter; the temperature difference was palpable.

Ofc. McGill walked towards his car; Steven stepped into the house and waited patiently in the doorway for Ofc. Davies to do his follow-up jiggle and wash his hands. Ofc. Davies did neither. His pants had trickles of piss along his right pant leg and no faucet water ever ran while he was in the bathroom. Ofc. Davies didn't flush the toilet either. The following morning when Steven saw the unflushed toilet, he thought, *What's that about Ofc. Dumbass Smile Davies? Afraid you'll injure your trigger finger?*

Now, while Steven stood near the open doorway waiting for Ofc. Davies to leave the bathroom, grass rustled, yet there was no wind. Steven was intrigued with what critter might be in his yard and turned around. Steven peeked his head out from the front doorway. Another snake, maybe? No. A stray cat? Nope. It was Ofc. McGill traipsing across Steven's lawn in a military–march fashion, traveling towards Terry's house.

Why is he going over there? Steven stepped onto his front porch to get a better view. He played his presence off as if he were out there to get some fresh air, looking here and looking there, stretching and yawning, pointing at the sky in search for asterisms of constellations, just in case Ofc. McGill or Terry glanced in his direction.

While Steven pretended to be uninterested in the impending exchange between Ofc. McGill and Terry, the upstairs bathroom light turned on, which Steven noticed, but immediately turned his attention toward Terry's house again. Meanwhile, the upstairs bathroom light flickered on and off, randomly, as if someone was sending a message via Morse code. The front door slammed shut, causing Steven to scream like a schoolgirl, attracting the attention of Ofc. McGill, but Steven flagged him away.

Now, lights from inside Terry's house illuminated the front lawn, and his front porch light was on. Perhaps Ofc. McGill was going over there to ask Terry questions regarding the act of vandalism that had taken place at Steven's house. Steven scoffed at the notion of Terry providing any information about anything he witnessed related to the crime, that is if he had any.

Ofc. McGill knocked *six* times on Terry's porch door, with the interval distance between knocks starting off wide, then drastically shrinking from one knock to the next, and each successive knock was exponentially louder than the other: knock *knock Knock! KNOCK! KNOCK!! KNOCK!!!!* Immediately after his knuckles struck the door on the *sixth* knock, he returned to his military stance, his knuckles now slightly chaffed from the extreme knocking.

A portion of Terry's sidewalk and the lawn adjacent to it gradually illuminated. Terry had opened his storm door. Next, he opened the porch door. Ofc. McGill extended his hand to Terry. While shaking hands, they smiled at each other as one greeted the other. Ofc. McGill stepped into Terry's house. The newly-illuminated parts of the sidewalk and grass were now dark from Terry closing the door.

Soon after Ofc. McGill stepped into Terry's house, Ofc. Davies walked out of Steven's house and passed him without saying a word. No good night, sir. No thank you. No bye. Nothing.

After Ofc. Davies stepped out of the house, Steven went back inside and walked to the kitchen for a little nightcap. All the drawers and cabinets were open. He was convinced the spirit wanted to communicate. Why else would a ghost go through all the trouble?

Steven's curiosity kicked into hyperdrive. He muttered, "What do you want? Stop playing games, and tell me."

But he didn't get any disembodied response.

Idiot! You should have been recording! He removed his cellphone and started a new E.V.P. session. "The time is four-fifty-eight on July 12th. The energy around me feels thick and heavy. Wow, this pocket of air is freezing cold. There is definitely something here."

Maybe this ghost had unfinished business and that is why it was haunting the house. Steven decided to see if he could garner some information from the ghost. He asked some questions, leaving space in between each question to allow time for the ghost to respond.

"Can you tell me your name?... What do you want?... Are you angry?... How did you die?... Is my family in danger?... Are you a good spirit or a bad one?... What was your occupation?... How can I help?"

As he asked questions and recorded, something ran across his arm. The next morning, a long scratch was on that same arm. Ironically, when he noticed the scratch is when the pain started.

Because of upcoming business dinners and summits, he did not review the recording until the two days later, after work, and in his office at home.

Keisha and him had a huge argument about Steven's unhealthy obsession with the ghost living in their house. She demanded the house be blessed to clear the house of the spirit, but he refused. The agreement reached between the two was the ghost could stay as long as it didn't hurt anyone in the house.

The audio recorded from July 12th was uploaded to his iMac computer, cleaned, and then reviewed for answers to the questions Steven asked on July 12th, or any other information the entity wanted to share. Steven also had six more audio files to review. He ramped up the number of E.V.P. sessions and extended their duration.

As Steven listened to the recording, he transcribed it on a legal pad, just as he did for the innumerable other recordings. He made a two-column table: one column for the question (Q) and the other column for the answer (A).

July 12th at 4:58 a.m.

Q: Can you tell me your name?	A: No response.
Q: What do you want?	A: unintelligible
Q: Are you angry?	A: Yes.
Q: How did you die?	A: Painful.
Q: Is my family in danger?	A: unintelligible

Q: Are you a good spirit
or a bad one? A: No response.
Q: What was your occupation? A: Go away!
Now!
Q: How can I help? A: Get out of
here!

While reviewing the recording, Jeffrey entered Steven's office and sat on the love seat. He wanted to discuss his choice for a cello teacher.

Jeffrey said, "Dad, I found this cellist who used to tour internationally, performing solos and with orchestras. He recently retired from touring to focus on teaching."

"Sounds like an impressive performer if he's toured internationally as a soloist," Steven replied. He spun around in his swivel chair to face Jeffrey. "What else can you tell me?"

"He'd travel to the house for the lessons, so you and mom wouldn't have to worry about driving me there, waiting, and picking me up. And, he has connections with professors at Julliard, so if I meet or exceed his expectations, he can write me a recommendation letter."

Steven leaned back in his chair and sighed a little. "Why do I feel like this teacher is going to cost an arm and a leg?"

"Well, I think he's worth what he charges. He's a seasoned performer. He's been around the world playing with some of the greatest orchestras in the world."

"Do you have to audition or does he accept anyone?"

"For beginners, no audition," Jeffrey said. Then he silently yawned. "He prefers working with children to help provide them with the proper foundation for advanced playing. For intermediate to advanced, an audition is required, but I sent him some of my YouTube videos featuring my solos, and he said my playing was breathtaking. As a formality, I'll still need to audition, but basically I would be accepted."

"Mm-hmm." Steven twirled around and pressed a few keys on the keyboard. "How much does it cost per lesson?"

"Dad, before I tell you, please keep in mind the cello teacher I had when we were living in North Haven should have been charging twice what he did. He gave us a discount because he believed in my talent and because we were economically strapped."

"And, that was generous of him to do. I recognize us moving here meant we would need to find you a new cello teacher. I also understand the rate is probably going to be high. So, please tell me. I won't freak out."

"It's one–hundred–fifty per one-hour lesson."

Steven stood so quickly and forcefully, it pushed his executive-style swivel chair flying in back of him, striking the wall. He paced back and forth. "Are you serious? One–hundred–fifty dollars for one hour's work. That's insane. That's extortion. That's highway robbery! Christ! That rate must keep a lot of indigent kids with tremendous talent from learning how to play the cello. Good god! Talk about barriers to entry!"

Jeffrey was unsure what to say or do now. The news of the one–hundred–fifty-dollar rate wasn't the worst news he'd have to deliver to his dad about the cello teacher.

"Dad, please. I know it's expensive, but I've proven I'm committed to my musical pursuits. Please let me study with this teacher. He's the right person to take me to the next level."

Steven took a few deep breaths and walked near the wall where his chair came to rest. "I'll have to examine the budget and see if we can swing it, son. That's a lot of money. And, speaking of money, please stop leaving the hallway bathroom light on. I've turned it off several times this week for you. I'm sure you can—"

"Dad! Watch out!" Jeffrey shouted as he lunged up and swatted near his dad's neck.

"Ouch!" Steven shouted. "What the hell is all that about?"

"That was insane," Jeffrey confessed, shaking his head in disbelief. "I've never seen something like that."

"What happened?" Steven demanded.

"An arm came out of the wall and reached for your neck, Dad," Jeffrey said. He stood in shock, not saying a word for few seconds. Then he said, "That is unreal. I'm unsure what it was going to do, but I think whatever it was, it wouldn't be good. On one hand it's terrifying, and I think I need to change my boxers. On the other hand, it's pretty cool. I wish I had recorded it. Then I could put it YouTube and have a video go viral. YouTube pays if the video gets a lot of views."

Even though Steven was a big fan of the paranormal, he found Jeffrey's claim a little far-fetched. Sure, lights in the house flickered, they turned on and off, objects would get moved around, mists and orbs would appear out of nowhere and then disappear unexpectedly, and sometimes, the children would see the apparition of a man in a black suit. What the Dobrowski's experienced so far were typical of a haunted house. But an arm slithering out of the computer monitor— impossible, according to Steven.

"Get out of here with that," Steven said, feeling the back of his neck. "My neck burns like hell. I think you accidentally scratched me. I feel a long scratch. Will you take a look?"

Sure enough, Steven did have a two-inch horizontal scratch on the back of his neck. The wound was inflamed. It emitted heat and gave off an odor similar to rotten Durian fruit.

Keisha was in Brittany's room helping her with another jigsaw puzzle, even though Brittany didn't need any help. She stepped into the office. "What's going on?" She asked.

"Mom, this is insane. An arm snaked out of the wall by the door and scratched the back of his neck. The arm wasn't bare. It was in a white sleeve and a black suit jacket sleeve covered it."

"Say what? Excuse me? Let me see." She walked in back of Steven. Then said, "Oh, Lord Jesus, please bless this home and all those in it. That stinks. My goodness. Okay, now. That ghost has to go. That's it. We'll get Father Thompson over here this week and he'll push that angry spirit the hell out of here."

"Honey, please don't be so dramatic," Steven said. "It's not that bad. And I don't think some arm sneaking behind me scratched my neck. Jeffrey may have inadvertently scratched me when he swatted at the arm to get it away from my neck."

She hesitated to speak. This was a terrifying prospect to have some manifestation come out of a wall and attack someone, if it were true. She also was more inclined to believe Jeffrey scratched Steven, not some ghost arm doing it. She did believe Jeffrey saw something, but not an arm— that didn't make sense. The only thing that made Keisha consider an entity did it is the smell emanating from the scratch. Never had she smelled something so putrid. Still, she concluded based upon the evidence Jeffrey accidentally caused the scratch, not an entity. However, she still wanted the spirit gone, and a small part of her believed the spirit inflicted the scratch.

She stepped into the hallway bathroom and out of the cabinet pulled out some analgesic ointment. Then she returned to Steven's office and treated Steven's wound.

Before returning to Steven, she checked on Brittany and told her everything was fine with her daddy. She told Brittany she would be back in a few minutes.

She returned to Steven's office. Jeffrey returned to his room to practice. As she gently rubbed the analgesic ointment on Steven's arm, she said, "Babe, this might be a tipping point, don't you think?"

"What do you mean?"

"About this house and that ghost of yours, that's what I mean," she snapped.

Steven pouted as he walked to the sofa and sat. Keisha sat next to him, then continued her argument.

"Now, listen, babe. I'll admit I've enjoyed the knocks in the middle of the night and the pictures being pushed off the mantel and the light bulbs exploding and the doors slamming closed and the chandelier swaying every which way along with a laundry list of other things, but when we start getting hurt, I think that's when we need to give serious thought and consideration to what's truly important. So, tell me, babe. What's more important? The show the entity puts on for our amusement or the safety of you and our family?"

"That's a no–brainer. The latter, of course."

Keisha decided to use the door–in–the–face approach. "Good. Let's put the house up for sale then. We can find a house just as good and—"

"No, we can't," Steven snarled. He took a deep breath. "This is a house we shouldn't even have, but we do, and we should be grateful. As the sole owner of property, Tony lowered the price of the house well under what we could afford as a favor to us, so we could purchase the house. We'd have to work the rest of our lives to afford a house like this."

Keisha wasn't a fool.

She said, "That's not true. We'd be able to get a house like this. Maybe not tomorrow or next week, but eventually. It wouldn't take the rest of our lives, either. And, just for the record, I don't need a big house to make me feel good. All I need is you and the kids."

His heart melted like a stick of softened butter on a hot griddle. He was putty in her hands. They embraced, and he kissed her on the cheek. Then on the lips.

"There is another reservation I have with leaving this house, though," Steven said. "I don't want to stay here only because I get a thrill out of seeing paranormal things happen around here or because I want to find out this ghost's story. It's a matter of principle. If we leave, we lose. This our house now. Not the entity's. Not any other ghost. Ours. And I'll fight for what's rightfully ours."

She was mildly turned on by him shedding his skin and showing his reptilian armor— acting rough and tough.

"I want to stay here, too. With that said, instead of picking up moving somewhere else, how about we get Father Thompson over here and piss holy water all over this mother?"

"Excuse me? Honey, what's gotten into you? You don't often talk like that."

"Like what? I didn't say anything."

"I don't want the house blessed. I don't want the spirit pushed out, at least not yet. I'm trying to make a connection with this spirit. My instinct tells me it wants to tell a story to me, but it isn't ready yet. It wants to ensure I can be trusted. Also, we agreed the spirit could stick around as long as it didn't hurt anyone."

She threw her hands up. "Fine, but what if what Jeffrey saw is true? What if the entity becomes more and more aggressive, and not with just you, but with the kids or me? What if we need to push the entity out? What if it doesn't leave? Then what?"

"If we need to push the spirit out, we will. If that doesn't work, then we'd leave. Family first. But I'd put up a fierce battle before I raise the white flag and leave our house."

And on that note, Keisha kissed Steven, then returned to Brittany's room.

CHAPTER SEVEN

Die Another Day

Around two in the morning, Tiffany stormed into her parents' bedroom. "Mom! Dad!" She said, her tone frantic. "Please wake up!"

"What is it, sweetheart," Steven said. What's wrong?"

"Dad, listen. I woke up because I heard creaking and stomping in the attic. So, I stepped out of my room and stood by the attic stairs to get a better listen. Then I heard a struggle. Like two people were fighting. Then I heard someone choking. It sounded like someone was dying. I get chills just thinking about it, let alone talking about it."

"Jesus, Lord," Keisha said. "Steven, what are you going to do about this? That is scary."

"I'll go check it out," he mumbled.

He stood and put on his housecoat. Then walked zombie-like towards the attic stairs. He stood at the foot of the stairs, but he heard nothing. He turned the stairwell light and started to climb the stairs. One step at a time. No matter how lightly he stepped on a stair, it produced a creak, unlike the stairs in the main stairwell leading to the first floor. Those stairs never creaked, or if they did, the sounds were imperceptible.

When Steven was about to approach the halfway point, he heard a door on the second floor open. Then the attic light turned off.

"Jeffrey? Is this another one of your pranks?" Steven called out from the attic stairs.

"No, Dad," Jeffrey said. He turned the stairwell light back on. "I thought Tiffany left the attic light on, so I turned it off."

"Thank you, son. Good night."

When Steven reached the attic, a few orbs were floating around the attic space. The hairs on his arms were slightly raised and his senses were heightened. He turned the attic light on and took a seat on Tiffany's weight bench. The attic was fully illuminated.

Interested in catching some audio evidence, he started his voice recorder app on his cellphone and held it up. Then he said, "If anyone is here and wishes to communicate with me, please speak into this device I'm holding in my hand."

After ten minutes of recording, Steven stopped the recording and played it back, holding the speaker of the phone to his ear. No voices were captured.

He muttered, "I'll have to upload the audio and see if there is any Class B or C E.V.P.s on here. Keisha is going to kill me with all this time I'll need to spend catching up with these E.V.P. sessions."

She was irritated with Steven lately. He'd come home from work, make a plate of dinner for himself, and go to his office to edit and transcribe E.V.P. sessions. She tried to be understanding though. She hoped Steven would come to his senses and stop playing paranormal investigator in their house.

When he turned his cellphone off, in the reflection he saw someone. It was the man in the black suit the children had seen several times already. Steven gasped and turned around, but there was no one there.

He had enough excitement. It was time to go back to bed. He turned off the attic light and started to walk down the stairs, but something fell and crashed to the floor. He double-backed and turned the attic light on, but it wouldn't turn on.

He frantically flipped the switch, but it was no use. He pulled out his cellphone and tried to turn it on, but it wasn't responding either.

Out of desperation, he tried the turning the attic light on again, but it remained off. He figured it was a burnt bulb. What perplexed him was why wasn't his cellphone working? He tried turning it on using the home button and the on–off switch on the side. Nothing seemed to be working to power on the device.

He gave up trying to turn his cellphone on and decided to investigate what crashed to the floor without any light source. With caution, he slowly entered the attic. The atmosphere of the attic was different though. The air was electrically charged and dense. It was menacing.

The attic light was flickering a little. Steven left the switch up before investigating the attic. The light would flicker a little, then die out. The intensity of the light was minimal. It had little life in it when it turned on.

Near the weight bench was a two–tiered shelf. On the shelves were stacks of weights:
One–and–a–quarter pounds, two–and–a–half pounds,

five pounds, ten pounds, twenty–five pounds, and fifty pounds.

Two ten-pound weights were knocked off the shelf. He picked them and placed them in the stack on the shelf.

An orb of light flew towards Steven, then turned sharply to his right. It disappeared into the attic wall.

Steven addressed the spirit. He spoke faintly. "I'll say it again. Please don't harm my family. Leave my wife and children alone. I don't know if you're angry or playful, but I don't like the idea you can knock over weights. If you're going to stay here, you need to have a little more respect. Otherwise, I'm going to eradicate you from the house. I'll smudge the house and push you out of it. I hope we understand each other. Rest in peace. Good night."

He said his piece and now he was ready to go back to bed. He walked to the attic stairwell and pushed the attic light switch down so it was in the off position, but the attic light turned on. The attic was as bright as it was when he first turned the light on before the weights fell to the floor. He toggled the switch several times to turn the light off, but the light stayed illuminated.

The attic light started to pulsate, almost like a heartbeat, first slowly, and then slightly faster. The light seemed to be mimicking Steven's heart rate, and a feedback loop started between the two. The light would pulsate and increase in intensity which would increase Steven's heart rate, which, in turn, would cause the light to pulsate more and increase in intensity.

Steven swallowed hard and approached the attic light. He was going to remove the light fixture covering and remove the light bulb.

As he approached the light, it pulsated faster and faster. The brightness of the light intensified, also.

He stood under the attic light and reached for the fixture. When his fingers contacted it, the bulb exploded, as did the attic stairwell light, causing Steven to scream and leaving him in a cavern of darkness.

He stood still, terrified to move. He reached for his cellphone and tried to turn it on again, but it was dead.

After taking a breath, he walked towards the attic stairs, praying tonight's ghost show was over. He stepped onto the attic stairs and made his way down them.

Someone speaking unintelligible words and the sound of static stopped Steven from walking any further down the stairwell. The chatter seemed as if it was behind him. But it wasn't.

He pulled out his lifeless cellphone, the source of the unintelligible words. The thick cloth of his housecoat distorted the sound, but now that it was out, the words were understandable. He remained stationary on the stairs as the words flowed randomly out of his phone:

** = static

[**** omiicdio ** quell bastardo ******** strangolato ************* vaffunculo! **** ucciderti *********** lasciare ora *********** rimanere e morire **** uscire di casa o morire! *********** Uccidi la tua famiglia! *****]

The static and voice ceased. Then his phone jingled a jangle, which induced Steven to gasp and shudder. The display on the phone indicated the caller was NO DATA. The number of the caller was (xxx) xxx xxxx.

There were two icons on the display, one to accept the call; the other to decline it. His spirit of inquiry was alive and well. He accepted the call and placed the phone to his ear, but he didn't say hello immediately.

Nothing but silence. Finally, he said, "Hello?"

[**!**!**!**!**!**!**!]

Loud static blasted into Steven's ear like a bullet out of a gun, causing him to lose his balance and fall down the stairs as if he'd just been shot in the heart.

Everyone in the house awoke to the crashing sounds. They rushed out of their rooms to the attic stairs, where they found Steven lying on his back on the stairs upside down.

"Daddy!" Brittany shrieked. "Daddy! Wake up, Daddy! Wake up!"

"Lord, Jesus, have mercy!" Keisha said. "Babe, wake up."

"Shouldn't we call 911?" Jeffrey asked.

"No," Steven said, his tone subdued and quiet. "I'll be alright." He felt the back of his head. "I'm bleeding a little. Let me get up and go to the bathroom, please."

"Excuse me?" Keisha snapped out of concern for her husband. "You're not moving about right now. You sit up and stay put. I'll get some things to tend to your injuries."

As Keisha sprinted to the hallway bathroom, while fighting back tears, Brittany asked, "Daddy, are you gonna die? Please don't."

He hugged her breathlessly, battling to fight back his own tears, and said, "Not today, sweet pea."

Steven called off from work. While he was not seriously injured from his tumble down the stairs, he believed it best to spend the day resting. The only injuries he sustained were a sore back and a small cut to the back of his head.

Against Keisha's protests, he refused to go to the emergency room. She feared he may have a concussion, but he said he was fine and didn't need any further medical attention other than what she provided.

All six stove burners were on when he entered the kitchen to prepare breakfast for his family. He turned them off, except for two and then placed a skillet on each one. Then he adjusted the flame for each lit burner, increasing one and decreasing the other.

French toast and scrambled eggs were on this morning's menu. Of course, for Jeffrey, he'd prepare Vegan French Toast. Beverages included freshly–squeezed orange juice and milk for Brittany and Tiffany, almond milk for Jeffrey, and dark roast coffee for Keisha.

Ironically, Steven disliked cooking for the longest time, and Keisha used to prepare most of the dinners while the now-older children were growing up. This changed, however, when Steven resigned from his position as a package handler at a parcel company and started his internship at a marketing firm, and simultaneously Keisha started her teaching career.

Because of her demanding job, Keisha had little time to prepare dinner each week. She was a first–year teacher in an urban school. Not only did she have all the duties of any other teacher, she had to attend weekly bullshit, waste–of–time, first–year teacher meetings and complete a year–long mentoring program mandated by the Indiana Department of Education, which required weekly activities that needed to be completed. Activities included writing informal self–reflections of her teaching, recording her teaching several times throughout the year and analyzing it in a separate video, which then had to be sent to the I.D.O.E., and meeting with her assigned mentor once a week. Long story short, most of her time was devoured by the Monster of Teaching.

To his credit, Steven stepped up to the plate and cooked dinner several times throughout the week. Consequently, he became an avid chef, often constructing new recipes that were outside of the box, yet were also creative and flavorful.

Tiffany entered the kitchen and said, "How are you feeling, Dad?"

"Better, sweetheart," Steven said. He flipped the French toast slices over in the skillet. The sizzle sounds were symphonic. "How'd you sleep?"

She opened the refrigerator and pulled out the freshly–squeezed orange juice contained in a glass pitcher— another possession of the late Granana. Then she said, "Alright. My closet door rattled a few times last night. Like there was someone in there who wanted to escape, but couldn't."

"Oh, my, my, my. That's something different. Were you scared?"

"Not really. I don't let the things this ghost does around the house irritate me. On one of the episodes of

Spirit Survivor someone said fear feeds the spirits, especially if they're angry or evil."

"It's true. Fear and anger are both powerful forces that entities with malicious intentions feed off of. Do you think the spirit we have here is angry?"

Tiffany gulped her orange juice down. As she poured herself another glass, she said, "No, I don't think so. I think it's playful."

Steven nodded. "I think you're right. It's playful— sometimes a little too playful." Sounds from the living room prompted Steven to say, "I guess that's the entity knocking the family picture off the mantle and the crucifix off the wall. I don't understand what its fascination with those items is. Any idea?"

"Maybe he never had a family. Maybe someone in his family killed him. Maybe he was an agnostic or an atheist in his physical life. Could be any of several reasons."

Steven appreciated the cognizance Tiffany offered. While he had different postulates about the entities reasons for knocking the family picture off the mantle and the crucifix off the wall several times a day, she prompted him to think in a different direction.

"Those are all reasonable possibilities. You're perspicacious, and that is a wonderful attribute to possess."

Tiffany lowered head and shook it. "Dad. Why. Why?! Why do you have to use big words? I mean do you have to be Mr. Merriam Wordsmith all the time? And, I'll tell you something else. When you use words that are big or not commonly used, it makes you sound… I think the word is pretentious."

He let out a hearty chuckle. "Pretentious. Great word. And, I'm sorry for shooting my mouth off like I'm some ivory–tower professor. Perspicacious means having great insight, which you do. Anyway, while we're chatting, I wanted to ask you something else. Are you happy here?"

After Tiffany poured herself a glass of milk and grabbed an egg from the fridge, she said, "Yes, I do, Dad. I have my own exercise room and now I have my own bedroom. I didn't have that before at our old house. This house has been a blessing." She cracked the egg against the rim of her glass and opened the shell, dropping the egg into her milk.

"Knowing you're happy makes me happy. What about the entity though? Don't the strange happenings around here bother you?"

"Not really. The occurrences are relatively infrequent. The entity hasn't done anything to make me feel threatened." She chugged her milk–and–egg drink down.

"I'm glad to hear that, and if it ever does, you tell me immediately."

"Of course, Dad," she said, pouring herself another glass of milk, sans egg this time.

"How do you feel about moving, sweetheart?"

"I wouldn't want to move. I love this house."

He smiled a little, then said, "That's good to hear." He turned his back to Tiffany to flip the French toast. Afterwards, he said, "Your mother is something else though. At first, she wanted to move. Did you know that?"

"No, I didn't? Why?"

"Just new–house–with–a–ghost–in–it jitters. But she stayed. She has garnered so much from experiencing a ghost in her own house rather than vicariously experiencing it on T.V. or on YouTube. Still, she is riding my ass like a Clydesdale about the spirit. She wants it out of here. And if that doesn't work, she wants us to move to a new house. Pisses me off," clenching his fists.

"I think she wishes you'd spend less time with the ghost and more time with her and us. I will say it is interesting when you can see the objects move without a source right in front of your eyes. I mean who knows if the stuff on T.V. is faked for ratings. Having a ghost in our house has solidified my belief there is life after death, and that is a liberating feeling. Excuse me, Dad. Unlike ghosts, we still have to empty our bladders and bowels." She stood and entered the downstairs hallway bathroom, which was adjacent to the kitchen.

As Tiffany finished her last sentence and entered the bathroom, Jeffrey entered the kitchen and sauntered to the fridge. He poured himself a tall glass of almond milk, then sat at the kitchen bar counter.

"I know you didn't ask me, Dad," Jeffrey said, "but if I had a say in the matter, I wouldn't want to move either. I love this house. My room is so much larger than my old one, and acoustically it makes a huge difference with my cello practice."

"It's good to hear you love the house, son. What about the entity in the house? Does it bother you?"

"No, it doesn't. Sometimes I've seen him go up the attic stairs when I use the bathroom around two or three in the morning. Sometimes he'll knock my cello and cello bow over in my room. He's never done anything malicious to me, thankfully. If he did, though, I might have a different opinion about staying in the house."

"That's good to hear. He better not touch you either. He does, you let me know right away. Will you set the table, son? Breakfast is almost done."

"Sure, Dad," he said. After grabbing plates, forks, spoons, knives, and napkins, he entered the dining room.

Steven continued to prepare breakfast. The aroma of cinnamon and vanilla inebriated the senses. The crackle of grease from the sausage links cooking were pleasant–sounding.

"Daddy?" Brittany said. "Will you fix Mr. Quacks, please? He has ouchie on his leg." Tears were streaming down her face.

"You bet, sweet pea. Dr. Dad to the rescue."

Steven dried the tears of Brittany's eyes and assumed the role of Dr. Dad again, tending to a wound on one of Mr. Quacks' feet. From wear and tear, the threading started to go, and Mr. Quacks' wounded limb started to bleed stuffing. Steven quickly sewed the dangling limb from Mr. Quacks' body, then wrapped the small Band-Aid around his orange limb. In the kitchen, near the bar counter was a desk that matched the cabinets and drawers. He opened the middle drawer and pulled out a small plastic box.

"Tiffany, please flip the French toast over while I fix my buddy, Mr. Quacks," he said.

Steven threaded a needle and within minutes Mr. Quacks was as good as new. Before handing Brittany Mr. Quacks, he kissed Mr. Quacks' ouchie— to use Brittany's term.

"Yay! Daddy fixed Mr. Quacks!" Brittany said to Keisha, who walked into the kitchen moments before Steven finished up the operation on Mr. Quacks.

"I'm so happy!" Keisha said. "Go wash up for breakfast."

Steven kissed Keisha on her lips. Not a peck either. A long kiss. When he tried to break away, she pulled him back.

She whispered, "You were like an animal last night, Tiger."

"Oh my, God. How's about a little spoiler alert courtesy?" Jeffrey quipped.

Steven returned Jeffrey's serve by saying, "What? Your mother and I had passionate, untamed sex last night, and more than once, I might add."

"Okay, lover boy," Keisha said to Steven "I think that's enough chest–bumping for one day. That's your son, not your executive buddies at the marketing firm."

Steven stepped into the dining room with a platter covered with French toast and sausage. He said, "Jeffrey, I told you to set the table. Why didn't you do it?"

"I did, Dad," he called out from the kitchen. "I swear I did."

"I see. I got it," he said with a harshness in his tone. "Okay, you set the table, yet the plates are stacked and the silverware is in a big pile. I guess the ghost in the house undid all of your work setting the table. Is that it? The ghost is trying to get you in trouble?"

Jeffrey was stymied. The way Steven was talking was uncharacteristic of him. He looked at his mom.

"Babe, do you think we can get a birdbath for the backyard? I think it would be a nice addition to our house."

That seemed to break the spell. Steven was receptive to the idea of a birdbath in the backyard, and it helped him solidify the idea Keisha was committed to staying in the house, though Steven was on guard. Keisha could flip on him without warning. In between their love-making sessions, she brought up the idea of blessing the house and pushing the spirit out again last night and went further to say if it didn't work, she'd take the children and move. She was shaken up by Steven's tumble down the stairs and she believed the ghost did it, even though she didn't openly admit that to Steven, primarily because he would deny it outright.

Steven returned to the kitchen and instructed everyone to please sit at the dining room table. He removed the last links of sausage from the pan. He turned off the burner and joined his family at the table.

Before Steven could plate Brittany's food, Brittany asked, "Daddy, may I eat off Granana's special plate? Please?"

"Why do you want to use that plate, sweet pea?"

"It'll make me feel like Granana is with me. Please, Daddy. I won't break it. I'll take good care of it."

Steven sighed. "Well, sweet pea, I honestly don't know where it is."

"I do, Daddy. I'll go get it."

She jumped out of her seat. Before she could get to the kitchen, Steven said, "Stop. Come back here, sweet pea. I'll get it for you. Please don't meddle in my things unless I say it's okay. Understand?"

"Yes, Daddy."

"Good. I'll get the plate."

And he did. In the garage, he had a box that was labeled ‘Granana (Mom)’. He opened the box and pulled out a black tote bag. From the tote bag, he removed the plate. He held it in his hands, thinking about Granana, his deceased mother.

He sat in a recliner that was originally going to be placed in the living room. The recliner was drabby. It had tears and rips. The stuffing was coming out of it. Something that decrepit didn't belong in the living room, so it was placed in the garage. Steven would sometimes sit in it after cutting the lawn or watering the flowerbeds.

He nearly fell asleep, but stopped himself.

Before giving the plate to Brittany he washed the plate with dish soap and a scour pad. But apparently that wasn't good enough. Next, he sprayed the plate with all–purpose cleaner containing bleach, scrubbed it with the scour pad, then rinsed it thoroughly with the sprayer followed by drowning it in a sink of fresh–faucet water.

He placed the plate in front of Brittany. She said, "What a beautiful plate."

And it was. The plate was snow white with gold trim. Engraved in the center of the plate in elegant-looking cursive writing was 'Granana.' Underneath that were the names of the people in the Dobrowski household, starting with Steven and ending with Brittany. Mr. Quacks' name was included, also. Along the entire circumference of the plate were the words 'We love you' written six times. In between each 'We love you' was a picture of one of the Dobrowski household members.

Indisputably, this plate stood out compared to the dining set the Dobrowski's owned (and still used):

solid red and orange plates. Steven bought this plate set and presented it to the family the same night Granana was presented with her personalized plate.

Over breakfast, the dining room light flickered several times, but after a while everyone ignored it.

Brittany said, "Daddy, I was so scared last night when you fell down the stairs. I thought you were going to die."

Steven rubbed her head. "Another day, sweet pea, and not for a long, long time."

While eating breakfast, Tiffany talked about the sports she was going to try out for this year, Jeffrey discussed his progress on the cello pieces he was studying, and Brittany asked if she could get some tools and wood to start building real things.

As they ate and conversed, some of the kitchen cabinets and drawers opened and slammed shut. Not all at once. A cabinet would open, then close. Then another. Then a drawer would open and slam shut.

Keisha dropped her fork onto her plate and said, "Steven? I hope you won't get mad, but don't you think it's time to help this ghost move on from the world of the living?"

"Why?" He queried.

"Because I think it's improper for this ghost to stay in our house. It should be in Heaven, singing with angels."

Steven whined like a toddler wanting a toy off a shelf in a store. "I want the ghost to stay. It's not hurting anybody here. And, to be honest, the children aren't bothered by it either. You seem to be the only one banging the I–want–the–ghost–gone drum. Can't you thump out a new beat?"

She dropped her fork on her plate. "Now, listen, sucker. I have kept up my end of the bargain and let the ghost stay, but I am tired of living like this. I'm tired of you coming home and spending all your time in your office trying to court that spirit. What you're doing is wrong and I think I'm going to get Father Thompson in here and have the house blessed."

"Don't you dare!" He shouted. "I'm so close to reaching the spirit. It has something to say but its ensuring it can trust me. Please, don't push the spirit out. Doing that would be like taking the family pet miles away and leaving it somewhere. Don't do it."

Keisha picked up her fork and continued eating without responding to Steven's plea. He didn't push her for a response either. He'd smooth things over with her later in the day when the children weren't in earshot of their conversation.

CHAPTER EIGHT

Tiffany's New Friend

Scruffles stood at the foot of the first floor stairs, snarling and barking at something— or someone.

"What is it, Scruffs?" Brittany said. "There's nobody there."

He ran up a few stairs, then stopped, continuing to snarl and bark.

"Come on, Scruffles," Steven said. "Let's go for a walk."

But Scruffles ignored Steven. He kept right on snarling and barking. Then he lunged up several more steps while barking, but stopped abruptly and whimpered. Shortly after, he walked down the stairs.

Steven said, "Why do you do that, Scruffs? That's the fourth time this week."

Steven placed a harness around Scruffles and, not soon after, they were out the door for their walk.

His next–door neighbor, Terry, was outside washing and waxing his car, as he always did on Saturday afternoons, provided the weather was favorable.

As Steven and Scruffles passed Terry's property, Terry quipped, "Afternoon, coal burner," to which Scruffles growled a little.

Steven didn't respond. It wasn't in his nature to engage in conflict, sometimes to a fault. When people picked up that Steven was passive, many took advantage of it.

Perhaps his passivity stemmed from his upbringing. He was the first and only child, and the direct result of unprotected sex. His parents were young and clueless when it came to the upbringing of a child. He and his father had a rocky relationship. His dad was a drunken, emotionally and physically abusive son–of–a–bitch, which turned Steven into a whipped puppy. Eventually, when Steven was eight, his dad left the family and never returned, and Steven's mom filed for divorce six months later.

After Steven's dad left, Steven had to grow up fast. When he was old enough to start working, he delivered newspapers to bring in income to help his mother pay the bills. He supplemented his paper-route income with washing cars at a car wash on Saturdays in the summer with his best and only friend, Josh.

As Steven passed the houses in the neighborhood, a gentleman who Steven hadn't seen before was outside watering his lawn, and near the sidewalk, too.

"Good morning, fella. And good mornin', pooch," said the gentleman. He was in his eighties. He looked like post-nineteen-eighties Johnny Carson. A dead ringer.

"How do you do, sir. I'm Steven. I live down the block from you."

The older gentleman stood with a pensive expression, then said, "Oh, right. I remember now.

You're the fella with the Negro wife and chocolate milk children, right? I'm George Zeiter, by the way."

"Oh, you're a racist, too, huh?" Steven asked, as he walked away from the man.

"Now just hold it there, fella. You need to understand I grew up during a time when Blacks and Whites didn't mix. And my father was one of the biggest racists you'd ever lay eyes on. Once, my daddy saw a black teenage boy approach an elderly White lady. He kicked that guy's ass. My dad embodied racism. But me? No. I'm not a racist. I just sound like one. Sometimes I don't think before I speak as I should. I'm sorry." He took out a Kleenex from his back pocket and wiped the sweat from his forehead.

"Times have changed. You should get with it. And I don't appreciate your off–color remarks about my children."

"What did I say? I honestly don't even remember."

"I don't want a confrontation or a discussion. I need to be going now. Have a nice day."

Scruffles and Steven continued around block. Steven didn't want to walk Scruffles too far since it was extremely hot. A heat advisory was predicted, but was canceled. Even still, it was blazing hot, and the humidity didn't help.

When Steven and Scruffles returned home, Steven checked the mailbox and thumbed through the stack. The cool breeze was a warm welcome compared to the blistering heat and humidity experienced during the walk. One of the letters in the stack was addressed to Jameson T. Auckland, 6725 Jefferson Ave., Whitmond, IN, 46324. The return address was from Plano, Texas.

The letter was a personal letter. The sender's name was Emily Auckland-Goetz.

"So, your first name is Jameson, not Terry, eh," he muttered. "He's not getting this letter. I don't care if it's from his daughter or not. Racist, fascist maggot."

A victorious smile painted across Steven's face as he walked up the driveway and sidewalk with Scruffles, all the while looking in the direction of Terry's house.

Once inside his house, he bolted up the stairs like a child on Christmas Day, eager to use his iMac desktop to do some sleuth work on his non–White–race–hating neighbor. Maybe other people in the Whitmond community have had problems with him. Perhaps he coerced other families out of the neighborhood.

Steven strongly disliked Terry, and wanted to shake him up. Make him sweat a little. Maybe his phone number— cell or landline— was listed.

A little prank call might send a message, Steven thought. *Maybe a few texts will let him see how it feels to be persecuted.*

On the Whitmond Residential Phone Directory website, with chicken-peck strokes— one finger on each hand did the typing— on the keyboard, Steven typed in AUCKLAND, JAMESON. What did the search return? No matches. Next, he tried AUCKLAND, TERRY. Zero for two. Too bad. Out of curiosity, Steven wondered if any Auckland's were listed in the directory. His fingers now beaks, he typed in AUCKLAND. The results? One-hundred-and-forty-two. He muttered, "My, my, my. There's an entire army of these jerks." A numbers guy, he looked up the population of Whitmond; the answer:

3,682. After some additional virtuoso chicken–pecking on a new instrument, his financial calculator, he said aloud, "So, four percent of Whitmond's population has the last name Auckland. My, my, my."

Someone knocked on Steven's door. He stuffed the letter at the bottom of his top–right desk drawer.

"Dad, I'd like you to meet a new friend of mine," Tiffany said. "Sebastian, this is my dad, Steven. Dad, this is Sebastian."

"Nice to meet you, Mr. D," Sebastian said. He approached Steven and shook his hand.

What a wimpy handshake, Sebastian, Steven thought. *Perhaps you should call yourself "Sebastina."*

They talked briefly about Sebastian's background and aspirations. Steven was sizing him up to see if he was a good catch or not, even though Tiffany and Sebastian weren't dating.

He was an intelligent young man who aspired to be a scientist, perhaps even attend medical school. His marks in school certainly demonstrated he had aptitude to write his own ticket anywhere. He and Tiffany would be attending the same high school this upcoming school year. They likely wouldn't have any classes together, however; not unless it was an elective. Steven was in AP–everything; Tiffany was in regular everything, and remedial math.

While Tiffany was toned and muscular, Sebastian was sickly thin and weak. His grandfather, on numerous occasions, said he looked like an Ethiopian boy. Tiffany started him on an exercise regimen, which he was fine with, but only did it so he could spend time with her.

"So, Tiffany's going to beef you up a little, huh?" Steven asked.

"She's going to try," Sebastian replied. "I think— Oh my, goulash! What was that?"

Someone forcefully pounded on the closet door in Steven's office, but nobody was near it.

"Don't worry about that, Sebastian," Tiffany said, punching him playfully in his shoulder. "That's the spirit I was telling you about. He's just saying hi to you. Letting you know he's here."

"H-hi, ghosty," Sebastian said while nervously waving towards the closet. "Nice to meet you."

Tiffany opened the closet door to show nobody was in it. She knew Sebastian would try to find a way to rationally explain the pounding sound.

A few days when Tiffany told Sebastian in a text her house was haunted, he didn't believe it. It's not that he believed Tiffany was a liar. He simply didn't believe in the paranormal altogether, though this even put him into a temporary state of cognitive dissonance. An isolated occurrence of something unexplainable within a rational framework wasn't going to swing his pendulum to the opposite side, but this event did nudge it.

Tiffany and Sebastian spent two hours in the attic exercising and talking after he was introduced to Steven. Before Sebastian and Tiffany went upstairs, Steven asked Tiffany to stay a minute and told Sebastian he may go up to the attic and wait for Tiffany. He had a few follow–up questions for her regarding Sebastian.

When she returned to attic, Sebastian told her someone was knocking on the wall and someone passed him in the corner of his eye, yet nobody was around.

To that, she said, "I told you there was a spirit in our house."

"Yeah," he said, "I'm starting to believe in the spiritual realm more and more."

"I promise you this house will turn the most skeptic peeps into believers. What did you think of the stool in the sink?"

Sebastian stood on the puzzle mat he was doing push–ups on and asked with veiled sarcasm, "Somebody pooped in the sink?"

"Really? Pooped in the sink? You know what I'm talking about, don't even play with me, boy."

Sebastian laughed. "My bad. Well, we didn't witness the stool be placed in the sink, so I can't comment."

She sighed, then swung her gorilla–sized leg over the exercise bike seat. "Just play along for the moment. Pretend we witnessed the bar stool fly across the room and land in the kitchen sink. What would you think then?"

"I'd think I need to run like a fierce hurricane wind and get the fluff out of that room. That would be terrifying. Have you seen that happen?"

Tiffany used the towel that she had draped over her shoulder to wipe her face and neck. "No, I haven't, but that would be pretty cool to see."

"I don't think so. That sounds like the work of an angry spirit or a demon."

"Oooh, listen to you using words outside of the rational world," she said, then chuckled.

Sebastian said, "Sheesh, you're a haughty one, aren't you?"

"Haughty?" Tiffany said. "Really? I'm haughty now, am I?" She pedaled a little faster.

"I'm being playful with you." He laid down on the weight bench and struggled to lift the barbell out of the catch.

"I've told you, I don't understand big words. Talk normal." She was fighting not to laugh at Sebastian straining to lift the barbell. The grunting noises he produced made Tiffany think he was constipated.

Sebastian continued to grunt as he strained to lift the barbell, then stood, flexed his arm and squeezed his muscle, and said, "That was a good workout."

Tiffany burst into a fit of laughter. "I'll adjust the weights for you in a second." She pedaled at a rate of speed that made it difficult for a bystander to see her feet and the pedals. It was a blur.

"Thanks. And haughty means arrogant, conceited, or egotistical."

"Oh." She slowed to a stop, wiped her face, and stepped off the bike.

She walked to the far–right side of the attic where a bathroom scale and a table sat against a wall.

On the same wall was a large dry–erase board she used to track her weight, height, and BMI score. The dry–erase board had thirty–one rows and four columns. Each row was labeled with a date for the current month; each column had its own label, which were, from left to right: DATE, WEIGHT, HEIGHT, BMI. Next to the dry–erase board was an oval–shaped full body mirror, but it didn't hang on the wall. The mirror rested within a frame. The mirror could pivot forward or backward. It was a cheval mirror.

She stepped on the scale and recorded her weight on the dry–erase board. Then she measured her height using an old tape measure her Uncle Jamal— one of Keisha's several siblings— had given her a few years ago while she was helping him change the transmission in his 1953 Studebaker. She recorded the height on her dry–erase board. Using the two measurements, she calculated her BMI and wrote the score on the dry-erase board. A slight decrease, finally. She exhaled a sigh of relief.

Sebastian stood in amazement, concern, and disbelief— all at once. "I'm confused."

"About what?" She asked, removing some of the weights off the barbell.

"About two hours ago, before you did any strenuous exercise, you weighed yourself. You measured your height. You calculated your B.M.I. You recorded the data on your marker board. Then about thirty minutes later, you did it all over again. Then some time later again. And now once more. What's that all about?"

"What? I worry about my physique. I need to stay in shape. I don't want to end up obese like my Grandma Denise is. Weights are set for you." She unwrapped a Reese's peanut butter cup. Enter. Chew. Swallow. And then once more. "You sound concerned. Why?"

"I don't know. I mean it's not wrong to worry about your health, but I'm inclined to conjecture you're obsessed."

"We're on that merry–go–round again, huh?" she jested.

"I'm confused." He lifted the barbell out of its catch and started his reps.

Using air quotes, she said, "Conjecture. I can tell you, my brother, and my dad are going to become the best of buds. They seem to get a stiffy when they try to prove how smart they are by using arcane words."

"Arcane? What's that mean?" Sebastian queried.

Tiffany started to heckle Sebastian as she climbed up the rope dangling from the ceiling. "Wow, Sebastian. You mean there's a word you don't know what it means? I thought you knew the dictionary frontwards and backwards. What is up?" She climbed down the rope, then back up.

"Oh, that is funny. You are so funny," he said. "I'm sorry if I've presented myself as some pompous asparagus."

"No problem. You're fine. Arcane means understood by few. I've started reading the dictionary at night to try and impress my brother and dad in the future. Now I have another contender: you."

"The attic light is flickering again," Sebastian informed Tiffany. "Cool. And, no, let's not compete in that way. I'll try to speak like a regular person. And, you know what? I think you are right. I don't want to use big words as a means to prove my intelligence. When you put it that way it made me feel dirty— like I need a shower."

Tiffany chuckled. "Well, you are sweating pretty bad," then wafted her hand in front of her nose.

"Ha–ha."

A loud crash snuffed out the back–and–forth banter between Tiffany and Sebastian like a fire blanket to a candle flame.

"What the fluff!" Sebastian exclaimed. "Hey, two weights on your shelf just fell to the floor."

Ah, yes, that was Sebastian. Never uttered a bad word, but implied it. Fuck was fluff; ass was asparagus— or 'asparagi,' a word he heard Joe Gatto use on an episode of Impractical Jokers, one of his favorite T.V. shows.

Tiffany walked over to the weights. There were two ten–pound weights and one twenty–pound weight on the floor. She placed them back on the shelf.

"Are you a believer now?" she asked Sebastian.

"I'm getting there, but not entirely just yet."

Sebastian was startled by the weights hitting the floor, but he didn't immediately attach that to an entity. The weights could have been off–center or maybe vibrations over time gradually moved the weight, ultimately leading to its fall to the floor.

They exercised for another hour, then went downstairs to get something to eat.

Tiffany said, "Have a seat in the living room. I'll make us some sandwiches."

And he did.

"Hey, Tiff. The chandelier is swinging wildly in here. And there's a picture face–down on the hearth. Oh, and a crucifix. And there's some nasty crimson-colored goop streaming down the wall."

Sebastian believed she was staging the living room to convince him spirits exist.

"That's okay. I'll put the things back when I bring us the food."

He put the family picture back on the mantle. He stopped the chandelier from swaying. The goop on the wall wasn't streaming down the wall; it was dry. He replaced the crucifix on the nail.

He turned the T.V. on and flipped through the channels. Nothing but wall–to–wall shit. He settled for a CNN.

A few minutes later, Tiffany called from the kitchen. "I'll be out there soon."

"Okay. No problem."

The sliding glass door to the sunroom opened and the blinds shook a little, but no one was around. Sebastian stood and walked over to the sliding glass door. He pulled the blinds back a little and looked out the sunroom windows. Brittany was in the backyard playing with Scruffles.

He let out a sigh of relief. "That's who opened the sliding door. What's that smell? Nasty." He called to Tiffany. "Hey, Tiff? Are you cooking something for lunch?" He coughed and choked from the smell.

"No. I'm making us roast beef sandwiches."

"Great. My favorite. You are too nice," he stammered out in between coughs and chokes.

When he turned around to walk back to the couch, he immediately stopped. The chandelier was moving again, but not as erratic as it was before. The family picture was on the hearth again. The crucifix was on the floor again.

"What the fluff is going on here," he muttered. "She has to be staging this for her own amusement. Just to prove me wrong. Just to win the bet."

Then the sliding door slammed shut behind him.

"God damnson it!" he shrieked, turning around and clutching his chest.

The instant the sliding door slammed shut, the chandelier light turned on and flickered and swayed erratically.

She peeked her head out from the kitchen and said, "Do you believe me now?"

He sat on the couch and calmed himself. She entered the living room and handed him a plate. A roast beef sandwich cut into four triangles, just the way Sebastian liked his sandwiches.

"Eat. You'll feel better, dimple butt," she said.

"Thanks… melon chest." He took the plate from her.

She gasped. "Sebastian! Melon chest?"

"Sure. If you're going to call me dimple butt, I think it's only fitting to give you a nickname, too."

"Okay, I won't call you dimple butt anymore. I can't help it, though. It's a cute name. I can't believe that was your nickname as a baby."

"It's cool. You can call me dimple butt and I'll call you melon chest, but let's only say those names when we're alone together."

"Cool. So, what do you think of my haunted house? Pretty cool, huh?"

No, it's not cool. I'm in a state of shock." He bit into one of the triangle pieces and grimaced. A fountain of mayonnaise squirted into his mouth. He hadn't even bit completely through the sandwich yet. He removed the sandwich from his mouth and said, "Wow. You must like mayonnaise."

"I do. Don't you?"

"Yeah, but in moderation," he said, removing the top piece of each triangle piece to scrap off the excess mayonnaise.

"Wait, wait," Tiffany said. "Here, put it on my sandwich."

And he did. He scraped the excess mayonnaise from all four triangle pieces onto her sandwich. Tiffany liked to eat her sandwich uncut.

Sebastian was perplexed at the unexplainable events that had unfolded while he was over at Tiffany's house.

He asked her, "Tiffany, how can you live in a house like this and not be afraid?"

"Simple. Because the ghost hasn't hurt me or anyone else in the house. If it tried to attack me, then I'd be terrified, and my position on this entity would change. Until then, it's all good."

"Wow. You're braver than me."

When he left, she asked him, "Will you come back over sometime even though my house is haunted?"

And he said, "To spend time with you, most definitely."

CHAPTER NINE

Granana's Grave

The Dobrowski's walked several feet up a concrete path, then turned and walked through a maze of headstones before reaching Granana's gravesite.

"Hi, Mom," Steven said, looking down at his mother's grave with his hands overlapped in front of him. "I hope you're enjoying Heaven. I miss you. I'm sorry I didn't get a chance to say how much I love you before your departure. One day, we will be reunited. Rest in peace, Mom."

"That was beautiful, Steven," Keisha said. She wouldn't call him his pet name in front of anyone's grave, especially a close member of the family.

"Thank you," he said. He hugged her. "I guess you're up to bat."

She nodded. After placing a bouquet of flowers against the headstone, she said, "Hi, Granana. This is Keisha, your daughter-in-law." Then she chuckled lightly. "Listen to me. Of course you know who I am. Anyway, we're all doing fine. Our house is a little haunted, but I'm sure you're there sometimes keeping the spirits in line, just like you gracefully did with your grandkids. They're here, too. Like Steven said, one day we'll be reunited, and I look forward to that day. You were a wonderful woman. You helped me be a better mother. You taught me so much, and for that I will be eternally grateful. May you rest in peace."

"Well put," Steven whispered.

"Dad? May I say my words now?" Brittany asked.

"Let's let Jeffrey and Tiffany go liked we rehearsed, okay?" He said. Then he whispered in her ear, "I wanted you to go last because I know Granana wants to save the best for last. Okay?"

"Okay!" She said with exuberance.

Jeffrey placed a bouquet of flowers next to Keisha's, and, afterwards he stood at the foot of Granana's grave and didn't say anything immediately. After some thought, he said, "Granana… I hope Heaven is nice and they're treating you like the queen you are. You were a true inspiration to me. You knew so much about music. We had some good times preparing for and performing at competitions. Your piano playing was heavenly. Remember when we performed Rachmaninoff's Sonata for Cello and Piano? That was our last competition as an ensemble. I— we, I mean— won first place. I think of you every day. I love you, and enjoy Heaven."

"Jeffrey, that was lovely," Keisha said. "Tiffany? Are you ready to say what you'd like to say?"

"Sure," she said. Before speaking she laid a bouquet of flowers against Granana's headstone. She wiped tears from her eyes and forced herself into soliloquy mode. "Hey, Granana. I'm not really good at this, but I'll give it my best shot, just like you used to say to me. 'Give your best shot, kiddo.' We had some amazing times together. After school, you and I would do Pilates together. We had so many laughs. I still can't believe you're no longer here physically, but I feel you in spirit… I met a boy. His name is Sebastian. He's cute and smart and kind of funny. You'd like him. He has that dry, witty British sense of humor. I wear your pearls of wisdom like a bracelet. They are always with me. Rest peacefully." She wept.

Keisha embraced her and said, "That was so wonderful. Granana's heart is definitely touched by that."

Now it was Brittany's turn to speak. She, too, placed a bouquet of flowers, specifically lavender roses, Granana's favorite. "Hi, Granana. Brittany and Mr. Quacks here. I hope you'll visit me like you used to do at our old house. I miss our talks. I gave you some flowers, Granana. A card is inside it with the new address in case you don't know it. Please come and visit me, Granana. If you are in our new house, I want to thank you for protecting me from the bad man living in our house. I know if he does something mean to me, you'll bend him over your knee and blister his butt raw." She took a deep breath and exhaled. She wiped her eyes. "That's all Mr. Quacks and I have to say. Enjoy Heaven. You deserve it. Be in peace." And then Brittany turned to Steven, clutched his leg, and started bawling.

Steven comforted her by rubbing her back. Then he picked her up and embraced her.

After Brittany calmed down, Steven said, "Would you all let me be here alone for a few minutes, please? I would appreciate it."

"Sure," Keisha said. "We'll meet you back at the S.U.V."

"See you in a bit," Steven said.

"Take all the time you need," Keisha said. Then she caught up with the children.

Steven stood looking at his mother's grave. The headstone was granite, consisting of a rectangular-prism base with a candle flame on top of it. Engraved on the flame was her name, under that was her birth and death dates, and under that was an inscription, in italics: ROSE DOBROWSKI, 4/12/1946-4/17/2018, *Your flame flickered out, but your spirit shines radiantly.*

A few minutes passed. He was still silent.

"Steven... Steven..." an angelic voice said.

"Mom?" he replied, looking down. *This can't be. I'm hallucinating again.*

"Steven, please come closer. Please."

And he did, stepping forward a pace or two.

"No, Steven, not in that sense. Come closer to me. I have something for you that will blow you away."

He knelt down.

"That's it. Come even closer now. Put your ear closer to me. Please."

And he did. His head was turned so his left ear was pointing towards the grass. It was about two inches above her grave.

"That's it," she said, still with an angelic voice. "Be patient. Wait there."

From the inside of Granana's grave, the barrel of a shotgun seamlessly and inaudibly pierced through the ground centimeters below Steven's left temple, followed by a deafening blast.

Steven released a blood–curdling screamed, then coughed and choked. Afterwards, he stammered, "What happened?" He breathed heavily.

He was in motion. Keisha in the driver's seat in their S.U.V. The Dobrowski's were driving from Whitmond to North Haven before the school year started to pay their respects to Granana. Steven drove the first half of the three–and–a–half hour journey, then Keisha took the helm.

"You fell asleep, babe. I guess you had a nightmare, huh?" She asked. She smiled at him and then put her eyes where they belonged— on the road.

As Steven did some breathing exercises to calm himself, he pulled the lever to recline the seat back and thrust his body against the seat.

"Ouch!" Jeffrey said. "Dad, please."

Steven pulled the lever again and raised the back rest. Then he said, "Sorry, son."

"Daddy? Are you okay now?" Brittany asked. She was petting Mr. Quacks' head.

"Yeah, sweet pea. I'm okay."

Keisha handed him a tissue to wipe his sweat–laden face. Then she said, "Do you want to share your nightmare? I minored in psychology. Let's put my dream analysis course to good use."

As he wiped his face, he said, "It was awful. I don't know if I can even muster up the courage to discuss it. Besides, I only remember bits and pieces."

That was a little fib. He remembered it, and he remembered it well. He certainly tried to forget it, but that proved to be an impossibility. That dream was permanently cauterized into his brain.

"If you need me, I'm here," Keisha said.

Tiffany removed the cap from a bottle and said, "Dad, here's a bottle of water. Have a few drinks. You'll feel better after you do."

"Thanks, sweetheart," Steven said. "I think you're right." He took the bottle from her and spilled a little on his dress slacks. He was still shaken up by the dream he just had. His hands still trembled.

After a few sips, he placed the bottle into the cup holder near the gear shift console. He laid back down, but forced himself to stay awake, even though he was devitalized and wanted to sleep.

He laid there relentlessly asking himself, *What the hell was that dream about? What did it mean?*

But no answers registered.

When they arrived at the cemetery, Keisha asked, "Okay, does everyone have their index cards to read from when you say your words of respect to Granana?"

Keisha had everyone, even Steven, write out what they wanted to say on index cards ahead of time for two reasons. First, she wanted to screen what they wanted to say to ensure there wasn't anything inappropriate. Second, if someone became emotional while reading, the cards would help him or her remember where to pick up once he or she composed him or herself and was ready to continue.

Keisha also conducted a Granana Visit Rehearsal. Steven read his cards first, then Keisha, followed by Jeffrey, Tiffany, and Brittany, respectively. The speeches in Steven's dream were those he had heard during the two rehearsals. One was last week and the other was yesterday night over dinner.

The dinner consisted of some foods, many of which Granana used to regularly prepare: oven–baked chicken, homemade garlic mashed potatoes, steamed baby carrots, butter rolls, and homemade lemon meringue pie for dessert. The dinner was dedicated to Granana.

The Dobrowski's walked several feet up a concrete path, then turned and walked through a maze of headstones before reaching Granana's gravesite.

The Dobrowski's replayed the motions of their Granana Visit Rehearsals. Four bouquet of flowers were laid against Granana's gravestone— the same gravestone in Steven's dream. In fact, his dream seemed to be more of a premonition than anything else, because the reality experienced mirrored his dream.

After everyone delivered their words, Steven asked Keisha if he could have some time alone at his mother's gravesite. She and the children walked to S.U.V. and waited for him.

For several minutes, Steven stood at the foot of her grave, but said nothing. He backtracked from whence he came and eventually reached the concrete path that would lead him to the S.U.V. Something— maybe an external force or perhaps his spider sense— compelled him to turn around and face the direction of Granana's grave.

And he did. Granana was standing on her grave, several feet away, looking at Steven. She had a menacing scowl on her face. She was wearing the same dress she wore at her funeral: A white lavender–patterned dress. Her arms were at her side. She slowly raised her right arm. Then she balled her hand into a fist except for her pointer finger, which she dragged across her neck. Then she vanished.

Steven stood in shock, blinking several times, trying to process and attach meaning to the ghostly encounter he had with his mother's spirit— if it was truly her, that is.

The Dobrowski's were nearly one hour outside of Whitmond, but traffic was backed up for miles on the expressway due to a pile–up. According to a news report, at least six people were killed and the number injured was unknown.

In the back seat, Brittany was asleep hugging Mr. Quacks. Tiffany watched kickboxing videos— a new area of interest for her— on her cellphone. Jeffrey was listening to Elgar's Cello Concerto in E minor— a piece he needed to learn for his next concert. He would be the soloist, performing with the local symphony orchestra.

Keisha was once again in the driver's seat. For the round trip, Steven drove the first half of the leg.

Since the dismal experience of paying respects was over, Keisha now could break the good news she had. "I have something to tell you," she said. "I think you'll be happy."

Steven said, "Lay it on me, my sexy honey."

"The principal from Whitmond Middle School called me yesterday afternoon and asked me to interview."

"That is good news." Steven turned the air–conditioning dial to a lower setting.

He didn't believe what he was saying though. Once they see what color she was, they'd find a way to disqualify her from consideration. He figured he'd let her interview and lose gracefully. Besides, putting the thought in her head that she likely wouldn't be hired would make her perform poorly in the interview. Better for her to present herself with confidence and lose than to go into the interview and trip over her own feet. He said, "I'm sure you'll do wonderfully in the interview, and they'd be crazy to not hire you."

"Thanks, babe. That means—"

Steven put his finger up. His cellphone was jingling.

"It's Abode Alarm," he said. Then he placed the call on speaker so Keisha could hear the conversation. "Hello. Steven Dobrowski speaking."

"Yes, sir. This is Greg Nystrom with Abode Alarms. We've received a signal your burglar alarm was tripped. Is everything okay?"

"Lord, Jesus," Keisha said. "Thank goodness John watched Scruffles for us."

"We're fine, but we're not even home at the moment," Steven said.

Greg said, "Police are en–route to your house to investigate. Is it okay if they enter the home to search for an intruder?"

"Hell, yes. Please do," Steven said.

"I'll place you on hold and keep you posted."

Fifteen minutes passed and still no update. In the interim, Keisha and Steven kicked around the possibility punk teenage kids peeked in the windows and saw the numerous electronics in the living room.

Steven instructed the children not to say a word while he and their mom were on the phone with the alarm company.

Another ten minutes passed and Greg had an update.

He said, "Officers arrived on the scene and found the front door open. No forced entry. Nothing appears to have been vandalized inside the home, but a picture was knocked off the wall, some kitchen stools were tipped over and one was in the kitchen sink, and all the drawers and cabinets were open with their contents spread all over the kitchen counter and floor. There were some broken plates near the door."

"My, my, my," Steven said. He turned the air conditioning back up. His blood was boiling about this situation.

Greg said, "Officers arrived on the scene and found a large swastika along with a message spray painted on your garage."

"What did the message say?" Keisha asked, fearing the answer and silently berating herself for asking.

"Sorry, ma'am, I didn't ask," Greg said.

Steven said, "We'll be there as fast as we can. We're up to our ass in backed–up traffic."

"That's—" Greg started to say, but Keisha interrupted him.

"Steven, your language, Please," she scolded.

"That's okay, Mr. Dobrowski," Greg said. He cleared his throat, probably from trying not to laugh at Keisha admonishing Steven. Then he said, "Get there when you can."

"Are you still in communication with the officers?" Steven asked Greg. He tapped his fingers nervously on the window and lock control panel on his side of the vehicle.

"No, sir, sorry. I'm not," Greg replied.

"For heaven's sakes," Steven said, "I hope it's not Tubby McDuff and Smiling Davies." He tapped nervously again on the passenger–side control panel.

Greg said, "I wrote down the officers names. Just a second, sir. The officers responding to the scene are Ofc. Brannigan and Ofc. Halsted."

Steven exhaled a sigh of relief. "Well, thank God for small favors."

Once the call ended, Keisha and Steven debated whether it would be better to stay on the expressway or get off on the next exit and navigate back home using city streets. Steven suggested city streets, but then Keisha tweaked his idea a little. She suggested they use city streets until they pass the accident, then get back on the expressway.

And they did. They arrived home forty–five minutes after the decision was made. Keisha broke many traffic laws along the way.

While they drove home, Keisha questioned why there were broken plates near the front door. Steven pointed out maybe the ghost was trying to protect the house.

When they pulled into the driveway, the graffiti was covered with some emergency blankets, courtesy of the officer responding. The message on the garage said: TAKE YOUR NIGGER WIFE AND MONGREL CHILDREN SOMEWHERE ELSE.

A report was filed. The officers told Steven and Keisha the detective assigned to the case would contact them. Steven told the officers they had a similar incident happen not too long ago and asked if the same detective handling that case could be assigned to this one. The officers said they would relay the information to the Chief of Detectives, since ultimately she decides which detective would be assigned the case.

After Steven covered the graffiti with a bed sheet, he gave the officers back their emergency blankets. Once the officers left, he drove to Rosco's in his recently–purchased Hyundai Elantra, a vehicle he purchased about a week ago.

Finding a parking space was about as easy as running with one leg. Eventually, he was able to get a space relatively close to the main entrance.

While at Rosco's, he purchased some lawn care products to nourish his lawn and some spray paint to cover up the graffiti.

While standing in line waiting to check out, a woman approached him from behind. She said, "Excuse me," her tone stern.

Steven turned around, and in front of him was an elderly tall lady, though slightly shorter than him, with brown hair, wearing a solid purple dress and a matching hat, standing with her head tilted slightly upright. "Yes, ma'am? Good after—"

"Where do you get off bringing that tree-swinging chimp jezebel wife of yours into our community? I don't care if she is your wife. We are a community cut from the same cloth— the same *white* cloth. We don't want any black sheep in our white flock. You, your nigger wife, and your cocoa puff children should leave the community before things spiral out of control, you coal burner."

Steven's face turned redder than the festering pimple on his ass. He swallowed hard, then said, "I beg your pardon?"

"That's right," the woman snapped back, stepping forward shaking one of her skeletal, wrinkly fingers at him. "You heard me. You need to take that

Michelle Obama look–alike along with your ugly mutt children and leave. There's no future for you and your family if you stay."

"Are you threat—"

She interrupted him. Locking her eyes with Steven's, she extended her right arm outward and said, "Sieg Hiel!" then briskly walked away. The sound of her heels striking the tile floor was thunderous. *Click-clack-click-clack.*

A few customers within earshot of this exchange were stunned; the majority nodded in agreement like congregation members in a T.V. preacher's audience as the lady spoke her piece, and many people flashed her the same salute as she walked passed them. *We're not going anywhere*, he thought. *You don't like it, you can move, you Crypt–keeper–looking, Hitler–dick–sucking bitch.*

As Steven pulled into his driveway, Terry was outside vacuuming his car. Steven parked in the garage and walked down his driveway to check the mail. Steven tried to avoid eye contact. He wasn't in the mood to hear Terry's shit, especially after his house was vandalized and he was implicitly threatened at Rosco's.

Steven removed the mail from the box and walked up his driveway, still avoiding eye contact.

I get the feeling he's staring at me, Steven thought. *Go in the house through the garage.* "Don't look his way. Just keep walking," he muttered faintly.

As Steven was about to escape Terry's eyesight, Terry shouted, "Yo! Hey!"

Steven backed up a few paces. "What?" He said, his tone sharp and bitter.

"Just sayin' hi, neighbor. How are you and your camel lips wife doing? I placed a peace offering on your front porch. I hope you like it." Then Terry walked to his front porch and went inside his house, laughing along the way.

"Man, as if I don't have enough to deal with," Steven muttered walking to his front porch with caution.

There was a package near the front door. A red wrap–around bow had an inviting appearance, but Steven wasn't going to let that deter him from proceeding with caution.

He set his Rosco's bag on the bench that sat in front of the dining room window. He knelt down and placed his ear to the package. No ticks. No sounds. Nothing.

He carefully untied the bow and opened the package. Inside was several pieces of fried chicken and watermelon. There was no note or card in the box, only the food items.

You fucker, he thought. *How'd you like to sleep with the fishes?*

When that idea entered Steven's head, he immediately thought of Tony. Steven considered hiring Tony to do a nice hospital job on Terry. A baseball to the kneecaps and a tire iron to the chest. That might send Terry a message not to fuck with Steven's family.

At this point, Steven wasn't surprised. After the brick through the window with the racially–charged message, the swastika, the elderly gentleman down the block, and the old lady at Rosco's, Terry's gift was likely the kindest racial statement among them, and it was a step up from Terry's hateful attitude towards Keisha when the Dobrowski's moved into their new house.

Steven picked up the box and his Rosco's bag and walked into the garage, where he pitched the box of food.

CHAPTER TEN

The Attic Speaks

The time was one–twenty–seven in the morning. Steven couldn't sleep all too well, and not only because of frequent knocks and pounds occurring in his house throughout the night. Work was becoming more hectic and his boss was sending him all the wrong signals, which included leaning on his desk to accentuate her abundance of cleavage, intentionally dropping things as she walked out of his office so she'd have to bend over and pick them up, and seductively and sensually licking her lips as she would listen to Steven answer her questions about his progress on certain accounts.

Work wasn't the only issue weighing heavily on him. Two days ago, he received another letter much like the one that was attached to the brick. This time, however, it wasn't sent via brickmail; it was neatly folded into thirds, and stuff in the mailbox without an envelope. The letter said: TIME IS RUNNING OUT. LEAVE THE COMMUNITY. TAKE YOUR BUNNY BACK TO THE JUNGLE. STAYING SIGNS AND SEALS YOU AND YOUR FAMILY'S DEATH WARRANT.

The detectives were actively investigating the incidents. The chief of police, Chief Jenkins, personally called Steven and said he placed one of his top detectives on the case. Although Steven wasn't directed to contact the detective investigating the incidents, he intended to do so in a few days, if he could remember.

What ate away Steven is how the intruders were able to enter the residence with no forced entry. Keisha and Steven always checked that the doors were locked independent of each other. Steven checked the front door after Keisha locked it and checked it herself. Steven knew with certainly the front door was locked, as were the other entry points to the house.

He swung his legs from under the covers onto the floor, stood, and put on his blue housecoat. He took in a deep breath, then exhaled. The smell of cigars and cologne were prevalent. Steven deduced the scent was attached to the spirit haunting their house. Since Keisha and Steven moved in, Tony hadn't been in the house, so the scent that continued to creep up now and then couldn't have been from Tony.

Steven stepped out of his bedroom and accidentally closed his door too hard, which caused Scruffles to bark. This was mildly irritating to Steven, only because all sorts of knocks, pounds, and scratches happened throughout the night, but Scruffles never barked at those anymore. Perhaps Scruffles adapted to the characteristic sounds of the ghost or ghosts.

"My, my, my," Steven muttered. "I've told Jeffrey countless times to stop leaving the hallway bathroom light on." Steven smacked the light switch, turning off the light and simultaneously causing Scruffles to bark again.

As he walked out of the hallway bathroom, Steven stood in front of one of the housewarming–gift mirrors from Denise that he had hung up several weeks ago; this mirror was on the wall near the stairwell in the upstairs hallway. Denise would be visiting the Dobrowski's soon. Steven wasn't looking forward to that at all.

Standing in front of the mirror, he adjusted his combover. He wanted to get a hair transplant when the money was available to have one. He started losing hair in his 20s, and it progressively declined from then.

Another source of angst was the mole on the right side of his face, about a half inch below his right eye and slightly right of his nose. Since childhood and onward, he was teased about his mole. In public, adults wouldn't say anything to his face, but they would stare, point, converse, and giggle. Children and teenagers were more cutthroat, however. A common taunt from teenagers was extracted from an Austin Powers movie. They'd point and say, "Moley, moley, moley, moley." It made Steven angry, and he wanted to see them suffer, but he never acted on these impulsive thoughts.

As Steven was about to step onto the stairs to go downstairs to get something to drink, talking from the attic attracted his attention.

He didn't jump to conclusions. The alarm didn't sound. Couldn't be an intruder.

He walked towards the attic stairs and listened. He heard two people conversing, but the timbre of their voices was distorted due to the acoustics of the attic and the spiral–shaped stairwell.

One man said, "You-a better give what's owed to me. You've been cheating me out of money for months now. Ladro!" This man had a thick Italian accent.

Another man said, "You're crazy. I haven't cheated you out of nothing."

"I'm-a gonna go to the proper authorities if you don't give me what's mine. You'll rot the rest of your life in prison. Now pay me my money!"

"Alright. I'll give you what's coming to you. Just relax. I don't want a war, my friend."

Moments later a struggle ensued. Then the sounds of someone choking and gagging caused Steven's stomach to churn. Someone's shoes pounded against the attic floor.

The man accused of being a thief said, "You miserable fuck, you. Threaten me."

Another man with a husky voice said, "Let me hit this fuckin' scumbag!"

"No, no. We don't want any blood evidence left behind," said the accused the thief. "Tighten that ligature... Motherfuckin' mutt, you. Die already."

The sounds of choking and gagging eventually became weaker, then eventually died out.

"Alright, boss. Now what? Does he sleep with the fishes?" said the man with the husky voice.

"No, we're gonna grind him up."

"Sausage?"

"Not exactly. We gotta get him in the trunk. Wrap him in that plastic from over there and let's get him out of here. And we gotta be careful of the neighbors, especially that no–off–switch talkin' nosy fuck, John, next door. That miserable fuck will want to talk until sunrise if he sees us. He's a fuckin' night owl."

"So if not sausage, then what?"

"Are you gonna be a fuckin' chatty Kathy doll all fuckin' night? We've got work to do, okay? Come on, turn him over... That's it. Let's wrap this yappin' fuckin' mutt up good. Piece of fu—"

Steven turned the stairwell light on and instantly all the noise stopped. No more talking. No more footsteps. No more sounds of plastic being wrapped.

For a moment, Steven wondered if turning the light off would induce the chatter to pick up where it left off, but he didn't try it.

He circumspectly walked up the attic stairs. When he reached the top of the stairwell, he turned the attic light on, which exploded.

"Ah, damn it. Not again," he whined in a soft, quiet tone. "Tired of replacing bulbs all the freakin' time."

Fortunately, his cellphone was in his housecoat pocket. He removed it and turned the flashlight on, and when he panned around the room, he found nobody, as he suspected he would.

He walked further into the attic, contemplating whether or not to do another audio session with the ghost. His last session turned up one Class C E.V.P., though it was still unintelligible.

He stood near the attic window and started to talk aloud, hoping the ghost would give him a sign. He turned on his voice recorder, then proceeded to ask questions.

"It's July 28th at one–fifty–six in the morning. I heard you and your friends talking up here. Can you talk to me about what happened?... You must have wanted me to hear that, am I right?... Is there something you want from me?... Why don't you—"

Someone wrapped something around Steven's neck. He choked and gagged, falling to the floor. The object wrapped around his neck tightened, cutting off his air supply.

When he woke up, he checked his phone. It was four twenty-seven in the morning. He had to retrace his steps in order to remember how he ended up in the attic.

After some thought, Steven was convinced someone was murdered in the house and the ghost or ghosts wanted Steven to expose the murderer. Or perhaps the ghost was the murderer and was guilt-ridden by it.

In Steven's mind, that's why the ghost was making its presence known. To get attention.

But was that what the ghost or ghosts really wanted?

Steven returned to his bedroom and decided to take a hot bath. He had several abrasions around his neck, as if someone garroted him.

Most people would be terrified of something like this happening. Not Steven though.

As he laid in the soapy tub water, he dipped a washcloth in under the faucet and rung it out. After he turned the water off, he folded the damp, steamy rag once, laid back, and placed it over his eyes.

He laid in the tub for ten minutes. The steamy rag was cool now. Still, it felt good. He hadn't been sleeping well, and his eyes were sore. The rag was comforting, even when cool.

The sound of someone writing on the bathroom mirror prompted him to say, "Honey? Is that you?"

Nobody answered, and he didn't look to see if it was her. He laid there, thinking about the times he would leave her notes on the bathroom mirror, and her him. When they were first married and lived together, they did this ad nauseam. It reminded Steven of being in study hall where you weren't allowed to talk, but you could write and pass notes. Over time, they wrote each other notes less often, but still did it, nonetheless. Keisha and Steven both were of the mind some is better than none.

Still laying in the tub, he removed the washcloth and opened his eyes. Standing next to the tub was the man in the black suit. He shifted his eyes to the bathroom mirror and written on it was the word OMICIDIO. Then the man in the black suit and the message on the mirror vanished.

Who was this man in the black suit? Was he the murder victim or the murderer, or neither? Did he intend for Steven to search for answers and tell his story or did this man in the black suit have malicious intentions of his own?

Two days had passed since Steven's encounter with the man in the black suit. The face of the man in the black suit looked familiar, but he couldn't place where he saw it.

Another hate letter was left in the Dobrowski's mailbox, and this prompted Steven to contact the detective assigned to the case.

He sat in the dining room when he made the call. He placed the phone on speakerphone. This way he could read market research reports for work and drink his coffee while speaking to the detective.

"Whitmond Police Department," someone with a perky feminine voice said. "Officer Leonard Santiago speaking."

"Leon—?" Steven said, confused about the discrepancy between the voice and the name, but then figured it was irrelevant. "Can you connect me to the Detective Bureau, please?"

The officer did, and someone in the Detective Bureau answered. Steven asked to be connected to the person handling the brickmail and graffiti case. As Steven waited, execrable elevator music played.

This music is making me suicidal, he thought. *Glad I don't own a nine. I'd blow my brains out.*

"Good afternoon, Detective Auckland speaking."

"Yes, detective. This is Steven Dobrowski. 6729 Jefferson Ave. I'm calling to touch base with you. Any progress on any of the cases?"

"One moment, please."

Cursed elevator music!

About two minutes later, Det. Auckland said, "Yes, Mr. Dobrowski. Let me bring you up to speed about the cases. First, regarding the brick case. The letter had prints, but they were yours, so it wasn't much use. We interviewed neighbors with the hopes someone witnessed the vehicle— if one was involved— or the assailants, but that produced no fruit either. We'll continue to pursue any leads we can. With me so far, Mr. Dobrowski?"

"Yes, sir," Steven said, mad as hell the brick case was essentially dead in the water.

"Regarding the graffiti, one of your neighbors saw two punk teenage kids leave the area right around the time your burglar alarm was activated. We have descriptions and we will continue to pursue any leads we can."

"Alright. What about the letters in my mailbox? Any leads?"

"None at this time."

Steven sighed, then remained silent.

"Mr. Dobrowski?"

"Yeah? Sorry, I'm still here." He was momentarily distracted because the dining room light was rapidly and randomly turning on and off.

"It's a damn shame the society we live in today. I'm sorry for your misfortune. If something noteworthy happens in our investigation of these incidents, I'll contact you. Is there anything else I can do for you today, sir?"

Steven let out a light sigh, slowly. Then he said, "No, not that I can think of."

"Alright, well take care then, and we'll be in touch."

"Oh, wait. I didn't catch your name. I'm sorry. Say it one more time, please?"

The man on the phone was briefly silent. Then he said, "Auckland. Detective Auckland, Badge Number 573."

"Auckland, huh? That name is ringing some bells, but I can't quite put my finger on it. Do you have any relatives working at Blue Chip Advertising?"

"I don't think so. Sorry. Have a good rest of the day."

The fact that police had no useful leads aside from descriptions of two teenage kids was a kick in the balls to Steven. Someone or a group of people is harassing him and his family and it seemed the police were completely inept. He considered installing security cameras around his house, but then he figured the money might be better spent on something else, such as Jeffrey's cello lessons.

Steven resumed reading his reports. He had to create a slogan for a new, kinky peanut butter called ButtNutt.

Ding-dong

Opening the door, John extended his hand with a warm smile and said, "How have you been, my friend?" In his other hand, John had a bottle of wine.

"Alright," Steven said, shaking John's hand. "Work is kicking my ass."

Steven showed John to the living room. John sat on the smaller couch with his Popeye–sized arm along the rest. As he sat, the crucifix and the family picture were knocked out of place. John shook his head and spoke. "I see you haven't gotten rid of the ghost yet. You're heading for trouble, my friend. Get it the hell out of here. Ouch!"

"What happened?" Steven asked, as he stopped the chandelier from swinging, placed the family picture back on the mantel, and hung the crucifix back on its nail.

"I got a shock. I'm okay. Is someone smoking a cigar?"

"I don't understand why that smell comes and goes. Nobody in the house smokes. Well, I mean they better not be smoking." Great. One more thing I have to look into now.

"Well, over by your sunroom doors, I see wispy smoke. Is the smoke coming from the vent on the floor?"

Steven walked over the sliding glass doors of the sunroom and took a few whiffs. Then he said, "No, this smoke smells like cologne." Damn that Tony–cologne smell!

"That's evidence of a spirit. I suppose the items you put back will be misplaced shortly. The chandelier will start to dance again, too. Please get rid of the spirit that's in this house. It doesn't belong here. Keisha vocalized her frustration to me about you and your obsession with this spirit. You're on the path to divorce."

"No, I don't think Keisha would ever leave me," Steven countered. "A few weeks ago, she threatened to leave and I put her in her place."

"Is that so? How'd you do that?"

"I told her she wasn't a true Catholic woman if she left me. She'd be breaking up the family. That's a sin!"

"My friend," John said, shaking his head. "You're royally screwing up. Now, listen. I'm not suggesting you give up your interest in the paranormal altogether. You and Keisha spoke last week about starting your own group. Do that. Investigate other people's homes and their ghosts, and help them. Explore abandoned houses that are haunted. But, please, understand it's not normal to live side–by–side with a spirit in the way you are doing so."

Steven thanked John for his concern, then excused himself to the kitchen to prepare some coffee. John perused his cellphone while trying to avoid snapping on Steven for not heeding his earlier advice to smudge the home.

Steven handed John a large cup of coffee. After taking a sip of coffee, John placed it on the glass coffee table in front of him. Billows of steam rose from the cup like ghosts out of their graves.

Sitting on the larger couch, Steven crossed his wooly mammoth legs and pointed them away from John. His cup of coffee was on the same table as John's.

John said, "Sorry I've been distant lately, my friend, but I've been working overtime at Gypsum."

"No need to apologize," Steven said, raising his cup to his lips. A long sip later, he said, "Need to make that paper."

John squinted an eye, then caught on to what Steven was implying. "Ah, yes, my friend. Social Security goes only so far. Our government is about as useful as a car with square tires."

Steven placed his cellphone face–down on the glass coffee table. "Tell me about it. I worry about money for the future constantly. Retirement. Investing. Paying for my children's college tuition. I feel as if I'm swimming with concrete water wings in an oceanic abyss of worry."

They talked for several minutes about John's family. Up to this point, Steven was in the dark about specifics of his children. John had two children, a boy and a girl, but only one of the two was alive. John's son, Jesse, tragically died, though John wouldn't share the specifics about his son's untimely death, and Steven didn't pick and prod, either.

Steven asked, "What do you know about my next–door neighbor?"

"Oh, Terry? Not much, and I don't like the guy anyway. He wandered over to my house six years ago when he moved into the neighborhood. I was outside mowing my lawn. His introduction flowed like a salesman's pitch. I think he rehearsed it."

Steven nodded with a pensive expression.

John sipped some coffee then offered more details about his perceptions of Terry. "Anyway, we would talk briefly in passing, but the guy rubbed me the wrong way not long after we met. He would spout and tout all sorts of racial biases, especially about Blacks and Jews. I didn't care for that sort of stuff. Once, he invited me to one of his KKK meetings. I politely declined with a terse explanation. Afterwards, I broke off contact with him altogether. And he left me alone. I don't know if he's still a KKK member."

"That makes a lot of sense," Steven said. "He's said awful things to me about my wife and children. He's said horrible things to my wife and children, too. And he's made some passive threats."

"I'm sorry to hear that, my friend. Perhaps I should have warned you about him. I didn't say anything because so much time elapsed from my last interaction with him I didn't want to slander his name. Hell, he could be a god damned born–again Christian volunteering at the local soup kitchen and reading books to the blind for all I know."

"Far from it. He's hellbound, that's for sure."

"Did you file police reports when he made the threats?"

Steven shook his head, then rubbed his mole. "I thought about calling Tony and letting him deal with it. A busted jaw and a broken leg. A few fractured ribs. That will send a message alright."

"No, my friend, I don't think that's a good idea. Tony is not someone you want to be involved with. He's a bad man. He's in the upper echelon of the Sorrentino family."

Steven's once pensive face was now one of surprise. "Really? Which of my two legs are you pulling here?"

John crossed his eyes at Steven for a moment or two, then admonished him. "Now, c'mon. You're a bright young man. So don't sit there and give me the babe in the woods routine. You know damn well he's connected to the Mafia."

Steven broke into a short fit of laughter. "I know, I know. I didn't want to believe it's true. Still, though, I want to see Terry suffer. A little hospital job. He might be the guy behind the brick throwing and hateful letters."

"Listen to me," John said, leaning forward and locking eyes with Steven's. "You're a family man, and a damn good one. You don't want to involve yourself with someone who is in the Mafia, and you don't want to put yourself in a position where you could go to jail for being an accessory. You need to be smart about this, my friend. Go to the police."

"What good will that do?" Steven said. He took another sip of his coffee. "A report is filed. Then what? Pigeonholed. I talked to the detective today about the other incidents and they have no leads. Regarding Terry and his threats, there isn't any evidence to prosecute him. Something needs to be done though. I thought I'd never need to deal with Tony again, but now..."

"Well, you're gonna do what you're gonna do. Based on what I've seen and heard regarding Tony, he's a force to be reckoned with. I could share some stories with you about Tony, my friend. He used to hang out with my former boss, Mr. Pistone, and the C.F.O and chief accountant many times here at this house — well, I mean the one before this house replaced it."

Now Steven loved listening to John tell stories and John was a captivating storyteller.

Steven said, "What do you know about Tony?"

John's face lit up like the night sky on the Fourth of July. He loved to tell stories. He took another sip of coffee, coughed, and cleared his throat. "This is only speculation, so please take it at face value, but it's more likely true than not."

John took a big sip of coffee this time. Then stood momentarily and sat back down. With his legs stretched and his whistle wet, he was ready to sing. "Tony and his associates were the muscle within the Sorrentino family. Tony was the intermediate between Mr. Pistone and the Sorrentino family. When they discovered a new establishment planned to be constructed in Paris City, Tony and his cronies would strong-arm the owner of the prospective building and force him or her to contract with Gypsum, Inc. to construct the building. Design. Materials. Construction. The whole nine yards."

"Wow, that's some juicy fruit," Steven said. Now his face was as bright as John's, beaming with a curious and intrigued look, wanting to hear more, but before John could continue, a thunderous bang rang out from the kitchen. It sounded like a someone had dropped a heavy textbook onto a tile floor.

John jumped, spilling some coffee on himself. "What was that, my friend?" John asked. "Your ghost again?"

"I'll check it out. Sometimes Jeffrey likes to play pranks."

Steven entered the kitchen. No one was in it though. Then the back door opened. Jeffrey walked through the kitchen and said hello to his dad. *My, my, my. Son, when will these pranks of yours stop?*

Steven returned and said, "Nothing to worry about."

"I don't know, my friend. That sounded angry."

"It's fine. What were you saying about Gypsum?"

"Right. Now, Gypsum, Inc. started out as a small drywall company, founded in 1927 by Mr. Pistone's grandfather, George. It was passed down from one generation to the next. Now when Mr. Pistone's father died— his death was ruled a homicide— his son, Mr. Pistone became C.E.O. and immediately expanded the operation from manufacturing drywall to doing a host of other things on top of that. Sure, manufacturing drywall is still a large part of our organization, but now Gypsum, Inc. does installation and construction. In fact, it was a Gypsum, Inc. construction team that built this house— your house."

Steven's mouth hung slightly open, wanting to be spoon-fed more of this story. "Mr. Pistone's father was murdered? Was he involved in organized crime?"

"No. Not at all. He was a straight shooter. Anyway, once Tony strong–armed the owner of the prospective building, Mr. Pistone would draft a contract charging the owner market price for materials, labor, blah, blah, blah plus a fee paid under the table." John sipped his coffee, then continued. "A cut of that fee went into Pistone's pocket and the remainder went to the Sorrentino crime family."

"This is like Goodfellas stuff," Steven said, his eyes wide open. "What if the owner refused to play ball?"

"I'm glad you're enjoying this," John said, chuckling. "Well, the owner would probably be tortured or killed or once their business was constructed, associates in the Sorrentino crime family would burn it to the ground. I don't have all the answers, my friend. I'm sorry. Withstanding that, the point I'm trying to get to is Tony is a bad man. He's a criminal. He's killed people."

"I think I'll heed your advice and let sleeping dogs lie."

"Smart man. They're all scumbags. Mr. Pistone finally had enough of the Sorrentino family. He regretted becoming involved with organized crime. He was concerned about the example he was setting for his children. He washed his hands clean and moved his family to Vienna. He sent me a postcard about a week ago." John consumed the remaining coffee in his cup, then said, "The chief accountant disappeared from the Mafia landscape, also. He apparently had enough. He was a piece of shit. He abandoned his wife and children. Now the for—" John rubbed the top of his head a few times while looking at the ceiling.

"What's wrong?" Steven asked.

"I thought a spider landed on my head. That was weird. Something ran across my scalp." John continued to rub his head. "It's tingly." John looked up and saw the living room chandelier swinging back and forth.

"That is weird. You okay?"

Before John could respond, the alarm system blared again.

While Steven excused himself to tend to the alarm, John sat on the couch and continued to rub his scalp. The tingling sensation evolved into searing pain. *There goes the crucifix and family picture. And the chandelier is dancing again.*

"My, my, my. Sorry about that," Steven said. "This alarm system is possessed or something." He picked up the fallen items and stopped the chandelier from its back–and–forth motion.

"My head hurts bad, my friend," John said. Now his catcher–mitt–sized hand closed except for his pointer finger, which he used to trace the line of pain, traveling from front to back.

"Wow," Steven said, "that's a long scratch."

"Scratch?" John said, standing to his feet and walking to the mirror that hung above the fireplace mantle. "What the hell?"

"Want me to get you something for it? Maybe some ice? Or some medicinal cream?"

"No, my friend, that won't be necessary," John said, walking towards the front door without stopping. "I think I'll be going now. Nice chatting with you. Thanks for the coffee." He closed the front door behind him and went home.

The pain from the scratch lasted for a week. John had to call in sick from Gypsum two consecutive days. His bed became his grave for the first day–and–a–half after the scratch appeared.

CHAPTER ELEVEN

The Patio Dinner

The patio table was set with plates, utensils, cups, and napkins, and the food was ready. Steven prepared a delicious spread of summer foods for dinner on the barbecue: his signature hamburgers, hot dogs, vegetable shish kabobs, and an organic–based salad, lightly drizzled with Steven's personally–created homemade salad dressing, a vinaigrette.

Steven was feeling a little better now that he made some headway on the accounts he was assigned to by his overbearing, lust–drunk nymphomaniac of a boss. Later that night, he would need to work more on the accounts, as well as complete detailed research on a new account his boss sent to him while he was driving home from Rosco's earlier in the day. Speaking of which, the older lady who confronted him about Keisha still weighed heavy on his mind.

The hamburgers were cooked with Ray's Honey Barbecue Sauce with some additional honey and molasses added to the meat. Seasoning included fresh garlic, a little butter, and some salt and pepper. Shredded Parmesan cheese, Steven's favorite cheese, was added to the mix. Yes, it was a hodgepodge of ingredients. Once all those ingredients were in the large glass mixing bowl,

Brittany let loose and mixed it all up. When she worked in the kitchen with her dad, she wore her Daddy's Little Helper chef hat, which Steven had specially made for her several months ago, before the family moved into their new house.

Over dinner, the family conversed about usual family things. How was your day? What did you do today? Those questions rarely generated meaningful answers. Common answers included Nothing, fine, alright. No substance or descriptive dialogue.

Eventually, all the pistons fired, and the conversation revved up with interesting topics.

"I received a call for another interview today," Keisha said.

"Wow!" Jeffrey said. "That's awesome. Where?"

"Portage Middle School," she said, then licked a splotch of ketchup from the corner of her lip.

"That's good news, Mrs. D," Sebastian, the new friend of Tiffany's, said. "I'm sure you'll be hired. It would be injudicious of them if they didn't."

"What?" Tiffany said, her tone confused and mildly agitated? "In Jewish what?"

Steven, Sebastian, and Jeffrey cackled, knowing Tiffany was about to tear into Sebastian for using a word whose meaning she was in the dark about.

"No, no, Tiffs," Sebastian said, then huffed and puffed on the lenses of his spectacles. "Injudicious. It means showing poor judgment." Then he ran his pencil–like fingers through his thick, sandy blonde hair as Tiffany chided him for showing off in front of the family and confusing the hell out of her. She was also irritated at him because he told her he wouldn't show off with big words, and he lived up to that up, until he rubbed shoulders with Jeffrey and Steven.

Jeffrey said, "So, Sebastian. Why don't tell my dad about the thing you told me?"

"Please do," Steven said.

"Well, I have some friends who do ghost hunts."

That's pretty cool," Keisha said. "See, babe, we should become ghost investigators on the side. Maybe we could start that after this entity leaves."

Steven swallowed his bite of hamburger. Then he said, "I don't think it's interested in leaving. Go ahead, Sebastian. I'm interested. Tell me more."

And he did. Sebastian said, "My friends will use different equipment to detect and document evidence of paranormal events. Equipment they use includes EMF detectors, infrared cameras, digital recorders, and still cameras. All evidence collected will be shared with the family, edited only for enhancement of paranormal phenomena. The entire investigation will be live–streamed and recorded."

"That sounds fascinating," Keisha said. "I'd love to see what their investigation uncovers. What do you think, Steven?"

"I don't know," Steven said. "I'm not too keen on opening the house up to strangers and showing off the ghost like some freak in a sideshow at the circus. The ghost and I have a personal connection."

"Please, Dad," Tiffany said, her face with a smorgasbord of condiments smeared around her lips. There wasn't enough mayonnaise on her bun. She placed her hamburger down, removed the top bun, squirted a foothill of mayonnaise on top of the partially–eaten burger.

"Tiffany, I'm having second thoughts now, because it might be dangerous," Keisha said. "What if they anger the spirit and somebody gets hurt, or worse, killed. As the homeowners, your father and I would be liable and money is already tight even with two incomes. We'd be financially ruined if something bad happened to Sebastian or one of his friends."

"Don't we have homeowner's insurance?" Tiffany asked.

"Sorry, I don't recall seeing an 'injury or death resulting from a ghost' clause in the contract," Steven said, his tone sardonic, chuckling towards the end of his lame joke. Everyone at the table chuckled.

"They'll sign a waiver. Look." Tiffany said.

Steven and Keisha believed a waiver wouldn't exclude them from liability, but they weren't attorneys either. Maybe a waiver would absolve them of any liability from injury or death.

"Also, Mom and Dad," Tiffany said, "if compelling evidence is collected, news stations might want to air it on their programs. We'd get paid for that, and here's what I propose we do with the money: I propose that money is put towards Jeffrey's cello lessons."

"Wow, sis, thanks," Jeffrey said. He clasped his hands together and said, "Dad, please. Mom, please."

The notion of being paid money for paranormal phenomena never entered Steven's mind. He wanted to provide his son with the best possible cello teacher, and he believed Jeffrey deserved it. The added income would certainly help. Steven's stance on the matter was that they may as well get some benefit from having an angry ghost in their house, and a monetary benefit sweetened the pot. Ah, yes, the seductive allure of money.

After pondering Tiffany's proposal, Steven said, "They can do it."

Keisha replied, "Thank God. Maybe the investigation will provide some closure to the entity and it can get the hell out of the house."

Steven slammed his burger onto his plate. "Excuse me?"

Everyone at the table gasped. They were startled at Steven's drastic shift in demeanor.

Keisha tried to backpedal. "Babe, I'm sorry," she said. "I didn't mean to upset you. Forget what I said, please."

With his fists clenched on the table, Steven said, "It's okay. I'm not mad. I'd like to know what you mean by that though."

Keisha sighed, regretting she opened her mouth. "I think we need to release the entity. I think it's wrong for us to continue to let it stay in the house. We should be trying to send it to Heaven. We've had our fun with it, now it's time for it to leave. It doesn't belong in our house."

"What if it likes being in our house? What if it doesn't want to go to Heaven?" Steven inquired.

"If it doesn't want to go to Heaven, that to me means it did something terrible on Earth, and it doesn't want to face God. And that would be another reason I don't want it in the house any longer," Keisha said.

"I'm confused," Steven said, picking his burger up off his plate. "I thought we both were enjoying this wave. I thought you liked the entity in the house. That's what you told me a few nights ago after our get–freaky sessions."

Jeffrey and Tiffany shook their heads with embarrassment. Brittany was too young to connect the dots about what Steven implied.

Keisha wiped the sweat from her forehead with a new napkin. Then she said, "I enjoyed its company at first. I admit it, I did. But it's not fun or funny anymore. It's not normal for us to be mingling with a ghost. I want it out of the house."

"I've spent several weeks trying to communicate with it. I'm making progress. Maybe instead of fighting with me you could join me. You could investigate with me. Once it tells me its story, we'll help it cross over. I don't think it would leave until I discover its story anyway."

"I worry it could be dangerous, Steven. Just last—"

"It's not dangerous, okay. You're jealous. Period."

"I've said my piece," Keisha replied. She was tired of Steven's incredulity and stubbornness.

In an attempt to steer the conversation another direction, Steven said, "How's the burger, Sebastian?"

"Delicious," Sebastian said.

"Well, that's good to hear. Go on, Sebastian, eat up. Have some more. There's plenty. Please eat up. All of you eat up."

"Thank you, Mr. D," Sebastian said. He used his plastic fork to stab another thick hamburger patty from the baking pan and place it on a Brioche bun. "Now for some barbecue sauce. May I?" he said, pointing to the near–empty bottle of Ray's Honey Barbecue Sauce that was out of his grasp.

"Here you go," Brittany said, passing the bottle to Tiffany who passed it to Sebastian.

The bottle had a tiny amount of sauce, in patches, glued to the walls inside the bottle. He turned the bottle upside down, then squeezed and shook the bottle several times with one hand, but no sauce shot out from the spot. He wasn't one to give up easily, so he tried again, though this time with considerably more force. Again, no sauce. Visibly agitated, he shook the bottle once downward towards his hamburger bun and squeezed the bottle with both hands with maximum force. A small splotch of that sweet, tangy sauce landed on his bun. For a few seconds he stared at the bun, then commented. "That ought to be enough." The crowd laughed wildly.

"My, my, my. I think that bottle is done," Steven said. "I've got two unopened bottles of Ray's sauce in the house. I'll get a new bottle for you." Steven excused himself.

"See, Tiffany, let this be inspirational," Keisha said. "Stick with something you'll achieve. I wish you would have stuck with piano."

"Mom, please, let it go," Tiffany said, squirting thick layers of ketchup, mustard, and barbecue sauce on her bun. "I know you took lessons for many years as a kid and wished you would have become a concert pianist, but I wasn't good at piano because playing piano didn't interest me. I'm sorry."

That was a lie. Keisha made all sorts of bogus stories up about her childhood. She refused to dampen her children's spirits by sharing all the horrific experiences she endured as a child. Providing her children with the best emotional, physical, and spiritual upbringing was her top priority.

"Here you go, bud," Steven said, handing the bottle to Sebastian.

"Thanks, Mr. D," Sebastian said.

As Steven sauntered to his seat, he said, "Alright, everyone. Eat up. Plenty there."

While Tiffany finished off her fourth hamburger, Steven poured himself a glass of wine— a merlot John had given him as a gift. John had a wine cellar in his house.

He swirled the purplish liquid in his glass and placed his eagle beak of a nose into the convex glass. After a lengthy inhale through his hairy nostrils, he exhaled through his mouth, twice as long though. He gripped the rim of the glass with his chapped and cracked lips, then tipped the glass. He swished and swirled the liquid from one side of his mouth to the other. As he agitated the liquid, his cheeks puffed out, not both at the same time though. Left cheek, right cheek, left cheek, right cheek. He swallowed the liquid and placed the wine glass on the table. Then exhaled with an O–face. Then he poured himself more of the dark–violet vino.

Tiffany grimaced while her dad performed his circus–act of wine drinking. "What are you doing?"

"John taught me how to properly drink wine last night while I was over at his place. We sat on the porch and drank wine and chatted for hours."

Keisha was furious. This patio dinner was the first time in a long time Steven joined the family for dinner. He spent the majority of his time outside of work conducting E.V.P. sessions and listening, editing, and transcribing them. He could make time for the ghost and John, but not his family. Had she not demanded Steven join the family for dinner, he would have been in his home office reviewing audio.

"Weird," Tiffany said referring to Steven's wine–tasting show, then ate the crumbs that remained in the pie tin, going so far as to lick the pie tin itself to ingest the fragments of the flaky crust too small to grip with her ruler–length fingers.

The evening continued with idle chatter and laughter. The six o'clock news would be on in twenty minutes. So, now it was time to reveal and serve the dessert: raspberry lemon cream pies.

Twelve individually–sized pies rested in muffin tin on a silver platter Steven held on his hand. He carried it out like a waiter at a five–star restaurant; he even had a cloth napkin over his arm and white gloves on his hands. This was for show though.

Steven served the first individually–sized pie to Sebastian, since he was the guest. He placed the pie in front of him, serving it to Sebastian on the right. Then he patted him lightly on the back after Sebastian thanked him.

The dessert was quickly devoured, and Tiffany was already on her third pie while Sebastian was finishing his first.

Tiffany said to Sebastian, "Please hand me a napkin."

"Sure," Sebastian said, picking up a napkin off of the stack.

"Thank you, dimple butt," Tiffany said.

The environment changed in an instant. Plates, pie tins, and cups on the table slightly popped up in the air then immediately landed when Steven hammered his fist onto the glass patio table and said, "What?" His tone was sharp and bitter. After his fist contacted the table, he lunged up out of his chair and threw it in back of him, striking the back of the house with a clatter, then speed–walked to Sebastian.

A thunderous silence followed for about ten seconds while Steven stood over Sebastian and mean–mugged him until Steven shouted, "You've exposed yourself to my daughter? You son of a bitch."

Everyone froze in fear, unsure about what Steven was going to do. Brittany was holding back tears.

Steven pounded his fist again on the table several times in succession while shouting, "Answer me, you motherfucker!"

"No! No sir! Absolutely not. Never," Sebastian said, cringing in his seat.

Now Tiffany stood and walked over to her dad as Sebastian was answering. When Sebastian finished talking, Tiffany said, "What's wrong with you, Dad? Are you out of your mind?"

He turned in her direction and stuck his furry finger in her face. "God damn it! Don't you ever use that tone of voice with me again. You hear me?!"

"Sorry, Dad," Tiffany pleaded. "Take it easy, please. What's wrong?"

Steven shouted louder now with both fists clenched. "Dimple butt! Dimple butt! Dimple butt! That's what's wrong, god fuckin' damn it to fuckin' god damn Hell! Did this sick twisted pimpled–faced four–eyed needle dick pervert expose himself to you? I'll kill him! It's my job to protect you from sick fucks like this!"

"Jesus Christ Almighty, Steven," Keisha said with an assertive tone, standing and staring at him. "You need to calm down right now." He walked towards his seat but didn't sit. She continued. "You use big words all the time, but you don't know what dimple butt means? Sebastian, I'm sorry for Steven's behavior."

It appeared the animal in Steven was now caged. He whispered, "I... I'm... I... I need to go inside."

Was it paternal instinct in overdrive? Or was something more sinister behind the scenes pulling the strings?

Steven woke up around seven thirty, and instantly recalled his tirade at dinner. His stomach turned. He wanted to apologize to Sebastian personally. In the meantime, he apologized to everyone individually in the house, the last person being Keisha, who was sitting on the couch, watching CNN. She accepted his apology, and now they were watching T.V. together, Keisha in his arms.

"I know you've accepted my apology," Steven said, "but I want to apologize again. I don't know what came over me. I was madder than a bear with a hornet sting on his rear."

"It's okay, babe," Keisha said. "It's history. And, speaking of bear, Sebastian wanted to tell this himself but I'm going to tell you anyway, because it's obvious you're saturated with remorse. He said he lauded you for going into papa bear mode."

That brought some comfort to Steven, but he still was wrestling with how out of character he was.

Sure, he'd been angry before, and occasionally raised his voice, once in a blue moon. Up to that point, never had he gone to the extent he did that night.

"I've had enough CNN," Steven said. "Let's watch something else."

"Alright," Keisha said, changing the channel. "I think Judge Hoss is on right now."

"That's fine. I love that show. He sure pounds that gavel awfully hard though. He pounds it like it were his lady."

A few minutes passed. The case was about a man being sued for borrowing $500 from his girlfriend— now ex–girlfriend— but never paid it back. He claimed it was a gift. Standard civil case. Same shit, different smell.

"Throw the book at him, Boss Man Hoss!" Steven shouted at the T.V.

Keisha laughed. "O.K., old man."

"Old man?"

"Yeah. Talking to the T.V."

"Hey," he said, "it's good to try new things, right?"

She nodded. "I guess," then snickered.

"Right. Now you do it. Go ahead. Give it a go. Let loose. Get wild. Get freaky."

Now she was hysterical with laughter. "No, babe. That's all you."

"What the—" Steven said. He picked up the remote in front of him and changed the channel back to Judge Hoss. "I guess the ghost has a new trick." Then he placed the remote on the glass table in front of him again. Now his dogs were on the table, also.

Keisha scoffed, then said in a matter–of–fact tone, "It's not the weirdest thing the ghost has done so far."

Steven laughed. "I know, I know. All houses— What the heck." Swiftly, he knocked his dogs back onto the floor, which produced a thunderclap of noise, and picked up the remote again. "I don't get it."

"I guess the ghosty doesn't like your taste in television programs," she said, then chuckled, as she rubbed in the lotion she squirted in her hands just seconds before.

"Very funny. Ha–ha," he said, placing his man's best friends back on the table. "If the ghost is doing this, it better stop it. I'm not fooling around here."

With a seductive tone, she said, "Oh, babe, you're making me hot and bothered. Talk rough and tough some more." She placed her hand down his shirt and rubbed his Sasquatch chest with her soft vanilla–scented palm.

The verdict of the civil case was about to be rendered. He missed the boat on the cues she was sending him.

"What the hell! Again, the channel changed back to C.N.N. Third time now. Maybe the T.V. is defective. This is irritating."

Keisha sighed. "It is. I'm starting to get annoyed now."

"Ridic—" he said, then stopped. He leaned back, and became pensive, briefly. Then he placed his finger to his lips and slightly shook his head. His spider sense was receiving more signals than a deaf person. He placed his right hand on the remote and loosened up his trigger finger, his eyes locked on the T.V. screen. Now the T.V.

was off and his enemy was right in front of him. He sprung off the couch as if he had fallen from the sky and his bare ass landed on a hot plate. He twirled around, pointing to the stairwell, and said with a victory–laced voice, "Got you!"

Raucous laughter erupted from the stairwell.

Steven said, "Come out and take a bow, you little wisenheimer, you."

"I'm sorry, Dad," Jeffrey said, walking down the stairs and clutching his stomach with his free hand, remote control in the other, still laughing about his dumbass prank. "And Mom."

Keisha put a hand up and shook her head, walking out of the living room to have a late–night snack.

"Man, why do you do that?" Steven asked, not really wanting an answer. "Always pranking, always playing. You should start your own show: Prank Yankers. How can someone so mature be so immature?"

"What do you mean?" Jeffrey asked.

"I mean you're a phenomenal cellist. You have a tremendous gift. You are dedicated to your music; you're serious about it. But when it comes to real life, you cut up too much. Enough already with the pranks. Please?"

"How'd you catch me, anyhow?" Jeffrey asked, truthfully clueless as to how his dad outsmarted him.

"It wasn't hard. I knew there had to be a logical explanation. I turned the T.V. off and instantly saw your pearly whites flashing like a neon sign in the reflection of the T.V."

"Wicked, dad. You've got wicked mad skills. Wicked mad skills. You're wicked," he said, walking towards the stairwell. "Good night. Love you."

"Love you, too, son. Good night."

Steven plopped himself on the couch and resumed watching T.V. Fair Justice with Judge Hoss was now over. The program airing now was a one-hour court reporting program called The Court Transcript. After watching a few minutes of the news program, he leaned his head back; the ceiling started down on him. His eyes were heavy, and a second or two before he was about to doze off, a voice interrupted.

"Dad?" Tiffany called, her voice distant.

"Yeah?" Steven said, lethargic and faint.

"Where are you?"

"I'm... I'm hanging in the living room."

The sound of rapid footsteps sent vibrations through Steven's feet. He placed them on the glass coffee table again.

"Dad?... Dad?"

"Huh? What? Everything okay, sweetheart?" Steven mumbled, rubbing his eyes.

"Dad, I just wanted to say I'm sorry about what happened today during dinner. I feel like I caused the whole thing. I should have censored myself." Tiffany placed her hand on her dad's arm, which was extending along the arm rest. "For what it's worth, I'm sorry."

Steven opened his eyes and placed his other hand on her hand, which was still on his arm, and said, "Oh, sweetheart, you needn't apologize. It's really my fault. I overreacted without thinking first. So, I'm sorry."

"It's okay, Dad," she said, then leaned and kissed his stubbly cheek. "Good night."

"Good night," he said, his head now resting on top of the couch.

The sound of footsteps racing up the stairs were like gentle strokes along Steven's head, and soon he was nearly asleep again.

Someone climbed on Steven's lap. He opened his eyes and lifted his head to see who it was. "Hey, sweet pea," he said, then flashed a closed smile.

She whispered, "Daddy, can I please have some Apple Squares?"

"Sure, sweet pea, but only a small bowl, okay?"

Brittany nodded with a smile.

Steven stood, and before he could walk around the couch to venture into the kitchen, Keisha said, "I'll do it, babe. You relax."

"Really?" He asked, unsure.

"Yes. Please sit and watch your court shows. I'll get her some cereal. Come with me, baby doll."

Again, he assumed the position of sitting on the couch with his head arched back. Minutes later, his stairway to slumber was spoiled when a voice called from a distance.

"Dad?" Brittany said.

This house is going to put me in an early grave. "Yes?" he replied, even though he wished he pretended to not hear her, so he could stay put and play a much–wanted game of forty–winks.

"Can you come up here please? I need to show you something."

He hesitated to respond, but moments later did. "Sure, sweetheart. I'm on the stairs as we speak."

When he reached the top, Brittany was sitting in the hallway crouched against the wall, her knees near her chest, and her head down. She was wearing blue pajamas. He approached her, bent down at both knees, and said, "Hey, baby doll, everything okay? I thought you were going to have some Apple Squares."

At first, she didn't offer a response, but then she shook her head, slowly. She was hugging a picture frame, but Steven wasn't concerned about that now; he was concerned about her.

"Something wrong, sweet pea?" He asked.

She nodded her head slowly, not making eye contact with him. She could still see him though.

He reached out his hand to touch her shoulder, but she pulled away from him, and he relented. A few seconds later, he asked, "Are you sick?"

After a brief hesitation, she nodded her head, this time a little faster than before. Still, the motion was slow.

"Is it your tummy?"

She shook her head, slowly.

"Does your throat hurt?"

Brittany sighed. "No," she said, mildly agitated. "It's not my tummy. It's not my throat. It's not that kind of sick."

Steven's face morphed to one with a ruminative expression for a few moments before responding. "Oh, I think I know what's wrong... Everything will be okay, sweet pea. It's going to take some time, but you'll be okay. I promise... Okay?"

She shook her head a few times, but the back–and–forth motion was subtle, almost indiscernible.

Steven adjusted his focus. "What's that you got there?"

Brittany sighed and closed her eyes. A few seconds later, she opened her eyes, and slowly turned the picture frame around, so Steven could see it. As she revealed the picture she was embracing she blinked abnormally. Not rapid successive blinks though.

"Sweet pea, why do you have that up here? That belongs downstairs with the other pictures."

She didn't respond. Her head was still down.

His heart sank for focusing on the picture being out of place rather than on her emotional state. After some reflection, he said, "You miss her, don't you? You miss Granana."

"Yes, I do," she said, embracing the picture again and fighting back tears and forcing herself not to cry. "I miss her so much."

Thinking as if he had just scored the tie–breaking touchdown to win the Super Bowl, he reached out to rub her head, thinking she'd welcome it, but she didn't. She pulled away, and this time more forcibly than before. The cold stare he received froze him in his place, though a few seconds later he did slowly retract his arm and rest it back on his bare knee. His stare was pensive once again. He scratched his Titleist T-shirt to relieve an itch.

She remained crouched against the wall embracing the picture with her head down. The only movements from her included random blinking more than the average person would and a subtle rocking motion.

Finally, he stood and spoke. "Come on, sweet pea. Let's get you to bed. Scruffles is probably wondering where you are." He stood and said, "Come on, kiddo."

"No," she said, her tone defiant, not looking at him.

"No?" he said, shocked. "Excuse me?"

She gave him a menacing look, albeit briefly. Then lowered her head again.

He swallowed hard. Then he said, "Scruffles misses you. Come on. Let's go, sweet pea."

"No," her tone sharper and bitter than the last refusal.

He stood silent for several moments, then responded. "Sweet pea, Scruffles is waiting for you. He's all alone in your room."

Brittany released a heavy sigh. Then she stood and said, "Follow me," taking his hand to lead the way.

Her touch instantly melted his frostbitten heart, and he followed her lead. Up the attic stairs they went in absolute silence. The silence was eating away at him though. No sound at all. Dead quiet.

Now in the attic, Brittany walked over to Tiffany who was standing near her new treadmill. Tiffany was wearing a white Nike shirt and a pair of black Adidas shorts.

Steven glanced around the attic, then said, "I like how you've rearranged your exercise equipment. Good work. It looks nice... I see you took my suggestion to put the bike near the window. Now you've got a nice view to look at as you cycle. This attic is getting awfully cluttered though. Not a lot of space left."

Tiffany failed to respond. He glanced up at the ceiling where the hook Tiffany's rope hung from. "The ceiling is leaking. Look at it." The hook was still there, but not the rope.

Tiffany offered no response. She only stared. Brittany remained next to her, staring also, with the picture frame now turned so the clasp it hung from was touching the little frills on Brittany's pajamas. She wasn't embracing the picture any longer; instead, she held the frame's sides.

He remained slightly ahead of the stairwell, looking at Brittany and Tiffany, waiting for a response, but he received none. They simply stared.

He clasped his hands together, fingers not interlocked, and blew into them, then rubbed them together. He asked, "What's going on?" while placing his hands in his pockets.

They didn't answer. *Why don't they blink? That's odd.*

Their stares made Steven wish he was blind.

"What?... What's going on?" he asked, his voice desperate. *They haven't blinked. What the hell is that about?*

They continued to stare; no words uttered.

"Whatever it is, you can tell me." *Why won't they blink?*

No answer. They simply stared.

"Tell me. What's going on? I can't help if you don't tell me." *What's that noise? Sounds like a knife against a grindstone.*

They stared on. Their cold stares burned through Steven like a white–hot arrow.

"Girls, whatever it is, we'll fix it. Now, please, tell me." *They haven't blinked a single time yet. How the hell are they doing that?* He continued, "Do you girls hear that noise? It sounds like a knife being sharpened." *Why don't they talk? Why don't they blink?*

Steven's blinking became abnormal and erratic, and stayed that way. *Blink blink... blink blink... blink blink blink... blink... blink blink...*

A minute or so later, Steven said, "What's wrong? What happened? And what is that noise? Where's it coming from?" *They don't blink. What the hell is going on with their eyes?*

Not moving from where he stopped when he entered the attic, he said, "Girls, whatever is I can help fix it. Please, tell me. Don't you know—"

"We know," Tiffany said, her tone dry but firm.

Steven once again went from to–the–rescue dad to pensive Steven. Finally, he said in a resigned tone, "Oh... I see," then looked down.

Seconds became minutes. Tiffany and Brittany were like statues. They just stared. No blinks.

He looked up at his two daughters, blinking several times, then said, "What now?"

Tiffany and Brittany, in sync with each other, pointed to their left, not taking their eyes off their dad. Steven's abnormal blinking continued, then he looked where the girls were pointing.

[blink]
NOW

The attic was as empty as it was full, except for a wooden table centered within the attic space, underneath the hook. Brittany and Tiffany stared. Steven was wearing a black seersucker suit with a white shirt and a matching black tie. His dress shoes were black. Steven looked toward the metal hook that hung from the ceiling. His eyes followed a sanguine-colored viscous substance free–falling from the orifice of the hook onto the table. When it hit the table, it exploded with a sonic boom.

He did a once–over on himself, then looked back at Tiffany and Brittany, who were still pointing at the table and staring at him. "I see," he said, resigned. He nodded his head. "Okay."

[blink]
NOW

Jeffrey and someone else approached the table from opposite sides and placed a set of stairs against it. Jeffrey and the other person were wearing a matching black suit, identical to Steven's. The other person, however, wore a black hood to mask his identity.

Steven looked back at his daughters. They were still pointing to the table. He nodded and whispered, "Okay, I'll do it," his voice trembling, slightly though. "I guess it has to be done."

They said nothing, but only stared without a single blink. He walked towards the wooden table. Once there, he climbed up the set of stairs Jeffrey positioned moments before, stepped on the table, and turned to face his daughters.

[blink]
NOW

Brittany and Tiffany were wearing matching black dresses. They weren't standing and pointing, however. They were seated in a wooden church pew. The church pew matched the wooden table upon which Steven stood.

The sound of a blade being sharpened resumed. Steven continued to excessively and erratically blink in a short period of time. Blink… blink… blink… blink blink... blink… blink blink…

[blink]
NOW

Seated in the pew on Brittany's right was Mr. Quacks. Tiffany and Brittany hadn't moved a single muscle. They were motionless— as if stone–dead.

Steven massaged the front of his neck with his thumb and two fingers while rapidly and randomly blinking.

[blink]
NOW

A thick rope with a tightly–coiled noose hung dead–still behind Steven. He couldn't see it... He didn't need to though... He knew what was coming.

Steven's mind raced in a machine–gun fire fashion.

(*I work tomorrow, need eggs for quiche, why won't they blink, racist neighbor, need to cut the grass, market projections, she vomited blood, car needs new plates, why don't they blink, pay NIPSCO, smoke a cigarette, water the lawn,......*)

[blink]
NOW

In a solid white dress behind the pew was Keisha. Brittany and Tiffany were static. They hadn't moved a micrometer since Steven first saw them sitting in the pew.

(......*murdered weeds, need a trim, walk Scruffles, focus groups, brickmail, hate my job, clean the gutters, not a single blink yet, light a smoke, make dentist appt, choking life out, water the flower beds, head struck floor, emotional scars, quarterly performance evaluation meeting, shattered mirrors,*......)

[blink]
NOW

Scruffles was next to the pew, closest to Brittany. With his head slightly tilted, he looked at Steven standing erect as a board on the wooden table in his black suit with an expression of bewilderment.

(......*my soul is eternally damned, no blinks yet, be a team player, school registration, junkets, drywall, convulsed repeatedly, wash car, Gypsum, Inc., cello lessons, passed out, sweet nicotine, slogans, still no blinks, crazy boss, pay mortgage, Nazi lady, dog hasn't blinked, mow back lawn,*......)

[blink]
NOW

A solid black dinner plate with a large cursive D on it was on Keisha's palms. Scruffles' head was on the floor. His eyes were on Steven.

(......*mom is dead, my job sucks, fertilize the yard, gay store owners, profit, feed Scruffles, they won't blink, market demand, dying wish, busted picture window, alopecia, rode to hospital, blood money hungry, no one has blinked yet, buy new hallway mirror, screams of pain, wise neighbor,......)*

[blink]
NOW

In the palm of Keisha's hand was the solid black plate. In her other hand was a solid crimson–red cereal box with black lettering.

(......*for the team, my face is ugly, blood spewed out, still no blinks, false alarms, make vet appt, market trends, nitrogen-rich soil, Vegan French toast, forklift operator, need gas for riding mower, scratch on neck, Waggin Trails, cancer stick please, five iron, entered a coma, lots of ricotta, want new job, crucifix won't stay up, man in black suit,......)*

[blink]
NOW

Keisha— who never moved her head once— poured the contents of the solid crimson–colored box onto the solid black plate. Her eyes stayed fixed on Steven as the pile became higher on the plate.

(......*profit, by the hearth, sprinkling the sidewalk, poison for rats, on my way out, her gray hair, food was source, need a shower, Sieg Heil lady, swim with fish, kids fell, dimple butt, weeds, new car, pushy boss, please give me a cigarette, no blinks, flash–steamed scalp, Mafia Tony, cost–benefit, bottle of*

Merlot, mole is ugly, she died, buy more shampoo, Apple squares cereal, pranks,......)

[blink]
NOW

As if Steven's brain was a book, Jeffrey read it, and, standing with one foot on the table and the other on the top stair, popped an unlit cigarette in between his dad's ashen lips, fully aware Steven couldn't have done it himself, since his hands were like maracas. Within the same second of the cigarette contacting Steven's dry, pale lips, the hooded gentleman in the black suit mirrored Jeffrey's position and extended his blemished hand holding a lighter towards the cigarette and thumbed the lighter switch wheel. A flame erupted from the lighter, igniting the end of the cigarette. Steven never touched the cigarette, keeping his hands at his sides at all times after massaging his neck, and instead took a drag, puffed out smoke, took a drag, puffed out smoke, another drag, another smoke puff... while his thoughts continued to race.

(......*never sleep, work kills me, make the bed, fair market price, never again, balding head, eating food, write another check, wash the clothes, schmooze the clients, find the ghost, by myself......*)

[blink]
NOW

A priest, Father Thompson from St. Matthew's, was next to the pew, the side opposite Scruffles. In one hand was a bible; in the other, a rosary. He stared at Steven, and never stopped.

(......unemployment, edge the yard, life out of eyes, take kids to store, pay cellphone bill, make time, clean that room, why don't they blink, prune the garden, no rest ever, black coffee, never enough time, fucked–up childhood, no rest ever, sprinkling chocolate shavings......)

[blink]
NOW

A black casket with no lining was about two feet to the left of Scruffles. Keisha continued to pour the substance out of the cereal box onto the plate. The pile on the plate was well over her head at this point. Jeffrey and the hooded individual unfurled a sheet and draped it inside the empty casket.

(......she vomited blood, choking life out, convulsed repeatedly, screams of pain, blood spewed out, kids fell, eating food, life out of eyes, scent of death, cellphone bill, poison for the mind......)

[blink]
NOW

A cremation oven was near the casket. The substance pouring out of the box was nearly ceiling high and growing. Jeffrey, Tiffany, Brittany, Scruffles, the priest, the hooded individual, and Mr. Quacks were staring and not moving.

(......mail the letter, pay for lessons, fix the motor, they still haven't blinked, dead man walking, no respect, rude man at store, chop firewood for winter, tired from work, in the grass......)

[blink]
NOW

The man in the black suit was standing next to the cremation oven. He had a thin, long scar on his forehead; its shape was a backwards C. The cremation door oven was open; flames were licking the top of the oven.

(......make doctor's appt., sales pitches, nobody likes me, every day pain, student loans, seductive boss, alimony, killed the weeds, child support, not a single blink, supply and demand forecasts, my days are numbered, her advances......)

[blink]
NOW

Tiffany, Brittany, and Mr. Quacks were in the pew. Keisha was peeking around the never–ending pile on the plate to see Steven. Father was holding his bible and rosary. The man in the black suit looked as though he had coal for eyes. Jeffrey and the hood–headed individual were almost finished. Except for Steven, everyone else was like Mr. Quacks— motionless and not blinking.

(......college fund, die another day, coon, they haven't blinked once, another cigarette, recipe for

scones, freak with glasses, profit drives all, on my way out, food with love,......)

[blink]
NOW

All eyes were on Steven. Jeffrey and the hooded individual walked in synchronization. They walked up the steps. Jeffrey and Sebastian each took one of Steven's arm and placed them behind his back. Jeffrey bound Steven's hands with a long and wide strip of black cloth. Then he bound Steven's legs together at the ankles with another black strip. Instantaneously, one after the other, Jeffrey wrapped a black blindfold around Steven's eyes, the masked individual removed his hood and placed it over Steven's head, then Jeffrey placed the noose around Steven's neck and tightened it. The once–hooded individual said, "Mr. D, it's a shame it's come to this... I hope this show you're about to put on lasts a long time." Jeffrey and Sebastian (the once–hooded individual) walked down the stairs. They each retrieved an axe that rested against the side of portable staircase— the side not seen by the witnesses. Standing to the side of the table, they chopped the front legs of the table in synchronization. Whack... whack... whack... whack... The table's legs gave, and Steven was in free–fall... then the rope became straight as a board in an instant. Every muscle in his body seemed to tense.

"Steven! Steven!" Keisha shouted as she shook his arm.

Choking, coughing, gagging ensued for roughly fifteen seconds while Steven grasped his throat. Keisha was on the couch next to Steven. Jeffrey stood in front of his dad with Brittany and Scruffles. Tiffany was to the right of Steven, standing near the couch.

Once the involuntary reflexes stopped, he said rather hoarse, "What's going on?"

"You were having a dream," Tiffany said. "We tried to wake you up several times."

"Are you okay?" Keisha asked. "Do you need some water?"

"Yes, please," he said.

As Keisha walked to the kitchen, Steven muttered, "What are these doing in my lap?" Then he said, "Jeffrey, please put these back where they belong."

Brittany said, "Jeffrey, I'll put Granana's picture back, and you can put the other picture and cross back."

By this time, Keisha provided Steven with a glass of water. He was taking slow slips. His throat was sore—*profusely* sore.

"You feeling a little better, Dad?" Tiffany asked, while Keisha rubbed Steven on his shoulder. Brittany was adjusting Granana's picture, so it was properly centered. Jeffrey placed the crucifix back on its nail, then walked over to the fireplace mantel to put the family picture back.

"A little," he said, his voice strained. "I'll be alright."

"Do you want to go to the hospital, babe?" Keisha asked. "It looks like you need to. It's pretty bad."

"No, I'll be fine," he replied, his voice sounding like it was a smoke–filled chimney.

"What were you dreaming, Dad?" Jeffrey asked.

"Yeah, good question. Tell us, Dad," Tiffany added.

Strained and sickly sounding, Steven said, "Plane crash. Lake Michigan. I was drowning."

The family asked him a few more questions about the dream. He entertained a few questions, then gestured time out. Enough was enough. He needed to rest.

Tiffany and Jeffrey told their dad good night, then returned to their rooms to go to bed. Brittany climbed up and sat on Steven's lap and whispered, "Are you okay, Daddy?"

Steven smiled, momentarily forgetting how painful his throat felt. "Yeah, sweet pea," he said, "I'll be okay."

She placed her head against his chest, then sniffed a little. "Daddy, you stink."

Keisha chuckled. "Brittany, that's not polite to say." Keisha moved closer to Steven and took a big whiff. "Wow, Steven, you do stink. Why were you smoking?"

"I don't smoke," he said. "I don't know where that odor came from."

Steven started coughing and choking again. He drank some more water, which helped. Brittany asked, "Daddy, are you sick?"

"A little, sweet pea. A little. I'll be okay though. A good night's sleep will help."

Brittany put her arms across his chest and said, "I love you, Daddy. Feel better."

"I love you, too, sweet pea," he said.

Keisha escorted Brittany upstairs to tuck her in while Steven rested on the couch, his throat inside and out. He needed to use the bathroom, and he did. Sitting on the commode, he massaged his neck with his thumb and two fingers, since it felt as though the pain was increasing. *It feels like someone placed a red-hot horseshoe around my neck.*

When he went to wash his hands, he looked at himself in the mirror and noticed several abrasions around his neck. He rubbed copious amounts of analgesic cream on it, then figured he'd had enough adventure for one day. As he walked up the stairs, he thought: *What was that elaborate, terrifying dream all about? What that hell did it mean?*

CHAPTER TWELVE
Tiffany's Encounter

"Mom, Dad, please listen to me," Tiffany said, standing in front of her mom and dad with a towel wrapped around her and another wrapped around her head. "This is weird, scary, and cool all at the same time."

"That's quite a trifecta," Steven quipped. "I can't wait to hear this. My rabbit ears are perked up and ready for business." He was sitting on the couch next to Keisha.

Tiffany said, "I was in the bathroom taking a shower. When I stepped out of the tub, I wiped the mirror down with the hand towel. I brushed my teeth. After I rinsed and spit, I looked up. In the mirror was the man in the black suit. He replaced my reflection. He was looking at me from within the mirror. The look on his face was not angry, but evil."

"Lord, help me," Keisha said, bringing her hands to the sides of her face. "Babe, what's that mean? That's freaking me out. I told you we should have gotten rid of that malevolent spirit!"

"It's not malevolent. I'm not sure what it means," he said. "Are you sure that's what you saw and are you sure the man in the black suit wasn't standing in back of you?"

"Yes, I'm one–hundred percent sure that's what I saw," Tiffany said, drying her hair with a towel.

"I've had it, Steven," Keisha said. "I'm going to call Father Thompson from St. Matthews and ask him to bring his holy heinie here to bless the house. I don't have a good vibe about what she told us. Your fun with this ghost is over. You want to play with ghosts? Go find some abandoned haunted houses to investigate. Go help those ghosts. This is our house and I'm not sharing it with this entity you've become obsessed with anymore."

Steven stood and shouted, "The hell you will. You better keep the priest away from this house! I'm on the brink of discovering what this entity's story is. I've spent weeks upon weeks doing audio sessions trying to capture any evidence to help this entity. Don't cut my balls off like this. I'm sure the entity meant no harm, and Tiffany said herself that the experience was cool and weird."

Keisha stood and countered back. She said, "Damn it, Steven. Oh, Lord, excuse my language. She also said it was scary, and rightfully so. She said it had an evil look on its face. Can you imagine looking into a mirror and instead of your reflection being projected back someone else's is?"

"You hypocrite!" Steven blustered. "You hypocritical bitch! Over the years, you've professed your interest in the paranormal. You've claimed for years and years it would be cool to live in a haunted house. You've said countless times when we've watched all those paranormal shows over the years you wished you could experience what they experienced. But then when it happens, all of a sudden you want to pull the plug and force the spirit out."

Keisha didn't say a word. She walked to the sunroom's sliding door, opened it, and went outside in the backyard through another door in the sunroom that led to the patio.

"That was terrible of you talk to Mom like that," Tiffany said. Then she walked out of the room.

"I'm sorry, sweetheart," he stammered. "I don't know where that came from." He sat on the couch and leaned his head over the head rest.

Indeed, Steven had never talked to his wife like that in all the years they'd been together. Never called her a mean name. Never raised his voice at her. It was as if Steven wasn't Steven.

He stood and walked over to the fireplace mantel. He looked in the mirror above the fireplace and wondered if Tiffany hallucinated. He touched the mirror and ran his fingers around it, all the while contemplating how it was possible for a reflection to be replaced.

He stepped into the upstairs hallway bathroom and inspected the mirror. It was filthy. Toothpaste, mouthwash rinse stains, and dried water drops littered it.

After exiting the bathroom, he stood in front of the mirror that hung on the wall in between his bedroom and the hallway bathroom. Standing in front of the mirror, he fixed his few strands of disheveled hair. He removed the piece of greasy sausage that seemed to be forever stuck in between his coffee–stained front teeth.

The brightly–lit hallway gradually turned to dusk as Steven walked down the hallway to get to the stairwell. A step or two before he reached the stairwell, he stopped abruptly, sensing someone (or something) was eying him up and down. An eel-length current of electricity slithered up his spine, then back down, causing Steven to shudder. The unheard wind was now howling. Steven's plum–sized testicles pruned to the size of a raisin as an icy–hot blast of air passed him. The hair on his arms was standing on end like soldiers in formation.

The man in the black suit was leaning out of the mirror Steven had just stood in front of, but Steven feared turning around to see what it was, and what would happen if he did. This was the first time he believed the spirit might be dangerous. The few seconds that passed by as he stood contemplating what to do seemed like days. Finally, he slowly turned his head to the right, and for every micrometer increase in the arc length of his head turning, the man in the black suit leaned back into the mirror, so once Steven had any semblance of a decent view, the man in the black suit was no longer there. Dusk became dawn again, and his physiological and psychological states returned to a state of homeostasis. He concluded his mind was playing tricks on him or his eyes needed to be examined; cataracts were a possibility.

His curiosity peaked, he approached the mirror with hyper–vigilance, and gazed in wonderment at the innumerable cracks radiating throughout the entire length of the mirror. Every which way had cracks. Steven's face was a jigsaw puzzle made up of several shapes and sizes.

"My, my, my. That is certainly different," he muttered while shaking his head in disbelief, at which point the puzzle pieces in the mirror fell to the floor.

He ambled down the hallway, bewildered by the mirror cracking without making a sound, and as he passed the matching mirror near the stairwell, his white short–sleeve cotton T-shirt was reflected as a long–sleeve black seersucker, unbeknown to Steven himself.

After he cleaned up the glass and threw the mirror's frame and its guts in the trash, he joined Keisha on the back porch.

He said, "I apologize for my behavior. I don't know where that came from, and that's no excuse, but I still wanted you to know that I felt like that wasn't me talking."

She wiped her eyes and blew her nose, which was raw–red. She said, "Steven, I accept your apology, but we still need to discuss this entity in the house."

"Alright."

She took a deep breath and exhaled. "I can appreciate your interest in the paranormal. But I was wrong to say I wanted to live in a haunted house. I was wrong to say I wish I could experience what it would be like to interact with a ghost on a daily basis."

He put his arm around her. "No, honey. It's good to want those things. We're lucky. We get to see things in our home that most people don't."

"That's what I want to get to discussing. Our home. This isn't normal, babe. It would be one thing if you and I went to haunted locations and investigated together, because we could leave if things became too intense or dangerous. It's quite another to willfully live in a haunted house, and I think the entity's power is increasing. Eventually, it's going to boil over."

"I understand how you feel. But I still don't think we need to push the entity out. It hasn't hurt anyone. It just does things to make its presence known.

It's playful. Alright, a time or two it's been a little too playful."

She sighed and wiped her eyes again. "I had an experience similar to Tiffany's a few days ago. I was in our bathroom taking a bubble bath. The lights started to flicker. The odor of rotten eggs replaced the smell of my raspberry candles that were burning. Then the lights turned off and my candles blew out due to a strong gust of frigid air. I stood and reached for the light switch. I toggled it back and forth, but the lights wouldn't turn on."

"Wow, that's quite an experience."

"I wrapped a towel around myself and opened the bathroom door, and when I did, standing a few feet in front of me, was the man in the black suit. I know the look Tiffany described because I think it was the same look the entity gave me. It was a menacing look, babe. I was scared out of my mind. I almost fainted."

"What?!" Steven snapped. He stood and said, "Why didn't tell me this before? Why didn't you tell me right after it happened?"

She again took a deep breath. "I couldn't. For the past few weeks, your interest in this entity inhabiting our house has taken control of you. You go to work, you come home. When you're home, you spend hours in the living room and attic, recording audio. Then you spend more hours reviewing and editing the audio. When you would talk to me about your ghost investigation you would light up. You know, the same way you would look when you first saw me after a long day at work or school. I miss that. Anyway, you see, I couldn't tell you because I want you to be happy, and it seems this ghost adventure of yours makes you happy. I didn't want to rain on your parade. Another reason— and the main reason— is because of fear. You're attitude towards me has deteriorated. I feel like you put this ghost above me. I try to talk to you about pushing it out and you go all crazy on me. It's not right."

Steven swallowed hard, then sat next to Keisha again. He rubbed her back as he took a deep breath. Then he said, "Perhaps I have allowed this quest to tell the entity's story overtake me as a person. I'm sorry."

She nodded and said nothing.

He kissed her on the cheek. Then they embraced.

Keisha asked, "So, I'm curious. What has the entity told you? You've never shared that sort of information with me. Tell me. I want to hear this entity's story."

"I can't lie to you. Not much."

Steven was reluctant to reveal to her the entity's E.V.P.s escalated in terms of the spirits tone as well as the content of the messages. The ghost recently threatened violence, but Steven turned a blind eye and a deaf ear.

She shook her head, then spoke. "Babe, think about this logically. You have it set in your mind this entity has a story it wants to tell you. So you spend hours trying to communicate with it but have nothing to show for it? Does it sound like this entity wants to share a story with you?"

"No. When you frame it like that, it doesn't seem like it does." She's trying to pull me away from what I enjoy. How selfish.

"I'm going to tell you what I think. I hope you will listen until I finish."

"I will."

"I think this entity is evil. I think it is lurking around the house, gaining power, and once it has enough power, it's going to release it with a fury. I don't want that to happen."

"Uh-huh," he said, not wanting to hear what she had to say. She wants me all to herself. She's jealous I'm devoting my time to seeking the entity's story.

"That's all you can say? I think this entity is going to hurt us and all you can say is 'uh-huh?'"

"Can you elaborate?" he asked.

"It's a vibe I have. The entity started off doing relatively innocuous things, but not lately."

"Okay, okay. I understand what you really want. I'll spend more time with you and less time trying to interact and communicate with the entity. How's that sound?" he said, insincere.

Keisha was frustrated. It was as if Steven didn't understand a word she said.

She said, "I want the entity out of the house. I want to go back to our old lives when we would watch paranormal events on T.V. or YouTube, not interact with a ghost in our own house."

Easy, Steven. Tame the rage, he thought. He forced a smile, then said, "There's the hypocritical part. You said you wanted to experience paranormal events for your—"

"And I have, and I'm ready to be done with it. I never said I wanted to spend the rest of my living days experiencing paranormal events in my own house."

He stood and slammed his chair into the patio table. "Unbelievable."

"What?"

"You are something else. I can't believe you."

Keisha was angered, but she pushed it down deep in the pit of her stomach. She approached him and spoke. "I'm unbelievable, huh? Take a look at this! Is that unbelievable?" She pulled up her sleeve and presented her arm. She had a five-inch scratch on the back of her arm.

Steven gasped. "How did that happen?"

"Your entity— the one you're always trying to have play dates with. The one who is playful and doesn't harm anyone. Because I sure as heck didn't scratch my own arm, sucker!"

Steven believed Keisha inflicted the injury on herself as a way to convince him to stop his pursuit of interacting with the ghost and push the entity out so he could devote more time to her. A volcanic eruption of rage nearly spewed out of him. He wanted to punch her in the face.

But he didn't. He calmed himself and considered the possibility the entity did it.

"When and where did this happen?"

"Remember the bathroom story I told you about?"

"Yes."

"That's when and where. When the entity and I were face to face. When I opened the bathroom door I immediately felt a singe–like sensation on my arm. When I looked at it, the scratch started to form. A few minutes later, it was bleeding and felt as though a million fire ants were crawling on my arm. It's healing nicely though."

They talked for several minutes about her experience. Steven was furious at the entity for hurting his wife. He knew he would need to take action, and he planned to do so.

Keisha sharing her experience prompted him to share one of his own.

He said, "You remember when I wore the neck brace for a week because I said I had a sore neck from sleeping on it improperly?"

"Yes."

"Well, I lied. Truth is the entity... Well, maybe the pictures I took will tell it better than I can."

Steven was referring to the instance in which the entity garroted him in the attic the night he heard the altercation.

"Sweet Jesus, Mary, and Joseph, Steven!" she shrieked. "You could have been killed. That looks like someone wanted to strangle you to death. You're lucky to be alive. And after this happened, you still tried to play with the ghost? Are you crazy?"

He lowered his head. "I'm sorry. One night I heard what I think is a residual haunting," referring to the altercation between the two men— one accusing the other of cheating him out of money— followed by the third man killing the accuser.

He explained it to her, and she was mortified at the story and angry at him for not sharing this information earlier.

Then he said, "I think the entity wanted me to experience his death. I don't think it wanted to hurt me or kill me."

The back door swung open. "Mom! Dad! You won't believe this!" Tiffany shrieked.

"That was terrible of you talk to Mom like that," Tiffany said. Then she walked out of the room.

Tiffany was furious and appalled at her dad's conduct towards her mom. All her mom was trying to do was protect the home from a potential evil entity living in the house, but her dad was blinded by his love for the paranormal and his obsession with discovering the entity's story.

Tiffany finished telling her parents about the encounter with the man in the black suit while she in the bathroom. Tiffany explained when she looked in the mirror after rinsing and spitting from brushing her teeth, she looked in the mirror but didn't see her reflection; instead, her reflection was replaced with the man in the black suit. She also mentioned his stare was evil.

Keisha insisted a priest come to the home to bless it, but Steven declined. He said, "The hell you will. You better keep the priest away from this house!"

She went upstairs to her bedroom with the towel around her body and another around her head, leaving a trail of water from the living room to her bedroom.

She changed into a pair of biker shorts and a T-shirt, then went to the attic to exercise as she waited for Sebastian to come over.

Tiffany chose to ride the exercise bike first. As she looked out the window, she thought *Dad was right to suggest I move the bike by the window. What a beautiful view. I'm still angry at him though.*

She had a view of the backyard. Keisha was on the porch, crying from the altercation she had moments ago with Steven. Tiffany's heart broke for her mom.

Tiffany wiped her face and neck with a towel she had around her neck while she continued cycling.

Her cellphone rang; it was Sebastian. She answered the call and placed it on speaker, so she could exercise and talk.

Tiffany asked. "Are you on your way over?"

"Soon," Sebastian replied, chewing into the phone. He swallowed his mouthful of food, then said, "Is your dad still mad at me?"

"No, he's not. He wants to tell you he's sorry. He felt terrible about the way he behaved towards you during dinner. But he and my mom had an argument a little bit ago."

"Sorry to hear that. You won't—"

Tiffany's phone instantly turned off and completely shut down, terminating the call with Sebastian. She powered her phone back on and called Sebastian back while pedaling as if her life depended on it. Again, she placed the phone on speakerphone.

"What happened?" Sebastian asked, then placed something in his mouth and crunched it up.

"My phone was being gay. It turned off," she said, wiping sweat from her head and neck again without interrupting her cycling.

"Oh. Should have bought an Android. iPhones suck."

"Shut up," she said, playfully. "They do not. What are you eating?"

"Crackers. Vegetable flavored. Yum." Munching away on vegetable–flavored crackers and grunting in between words, he spoke. "I talked to a friend of mine [grunt]. He still wants [grunt] to investigate [grunt] your house with his team [grunt] when he has some time."

"You did?" she shouted, her tone happy but concerned about his grunting. "I do appreciate it. Are you okay? It sounds like you're trying to push out a baby."

"I'm fine, and no problem. I hope your dad will allow it. I think it will be an interesting experiment. Your house is quite active."

"It is. I had the strangest encounter with the man in the black suit." She wiped her face and neck with the towel again. "Sometimes this house scares me. Sometimes the man in the black suit scares me. He didn't hurt me though."

Sebastian talked in a French accent, grunting occasionally. "Come with me, my [grunt] love. We shall run away [grunt] together and live happily ever after. I will wine and dine you. You will live in the lap of [grunt] luxury. We're made for each other, mon amour," then kissed into the phone several times.

Tiffany laughed, then responded. "I wish. What are you doing? What's with the grunting? Are you choking your chicken or something? Do you want me to let you go?"

Sebastian didn't answer. Her phone display was not illuminated; it turned off and powered down again.

"This is ridiculous," she mumbled, powering the device back on.

While the device was powering on, she looked out her window and saw her dad and Keisha talking. She opened the window slightly to get a listen to what they were saying. Before Tiffany could say hi, Sebastian said, "Did I scare you or something?"

"No, not at all. You heard me laughing, right? It's my phone. It's being gay again."

"It's cool. Ouch! Mother fluffer! That hurt."

"What's with you? What happened?" Tiffany asked. She stopped cycling and wiped the sweat from her head, neck, and arms with the towel again, parts of it now damp from previous wipe–downs. She laid down on the weight bench with the cellphone on her stomach. She wanted to take a rest before pumping some iron.

"I stubbed my toe walking out of the bathroom."

"Ewwwww. You talk to people when you're on the toilet?"

"Sure," he said, then crunched on another cracker. "Don't you?"

"You're disgusting. No. That is so nasty," she said, aghast. "That explains the grunting. And you were eating in the bathroom? And, come to think of it, I didn't hear a flush."

A few seconds passed. The sound of footsteps crept through the phone into Tiffany's ear. "Whoops." Then a loud flush erupted followed by the sound of flowing water streamed into Tiffany's ear.

Tiffany said nothing. Sebastian eventually said, "Hello? Are you still there?"

"Wow," she said, her tone shocked and surprised. "I can't believe you flushed the toilet with me on the phone. I can't believe you would use the toilet while talking on the phone with me. Just...wow."

"I would prove to it you with a picture, but alas, I already flushed."

"Ewwww. Stop it. That is nasty." Several seconds passed. "Sebastian? Dimple Butt?"

There was no answer. She picked the phone up off her stomach. Once again, the phone was powered off. She stood to stretch a little and pushed the button on the side of the device start it up. No response. She tried again. Nothing. She held the button down for several seconds. Nothing. Out of frustration, she smacked the side of the phone with her hand a few times. No change. She tapped once more, this time a little harder. A white screen appeared coupled with loud static, and for a second the man in the black suit appeared on the screen only to vanish a second later. She dropped the phone and when it hit the floor, the white display screen disappeared. The phone was off.

She stared at the phone for several seconds, unsure what to do. She bent down to pick the phone up. Just before her hand was about to contact the phone, the white screen and static returned. She screamed and recoiled. Over the static, an ominous voice said, "GET OUT... OR DIIIIIIE." Then the phone died.

She sat on the floor and sobbed, but not for long. Someone knocked over two fifty–pound weights that rested in a pile on her shelf. She picked up her cellphone, which was like a block of dry ice, burning her fingertips. She dropped the phone. Using the towel, she picked it back up and ran down the attic and main stairs, and peeked into the living room. Nobody was in there. Just as she was about to turn around to go to the kitchen, the T.V. turned on with no sound. Only a white screen with a minuscule black disc about the size of a quarter in the center. The disc expanded and morphed into the man in the black suit, who appeared for a split second and then flashed out of sight. Then the T.V. exploded.

"God, please help me," she whispered. Then the man in the black suit appeared directly in front of her and a second later vanished. She released a lengthy scream, louder than her previous one in the attic, causing Jeffrey to stop practicing his cello and rush to her aid.

"What happened?" he asked.

She had volumes to speak but the words couldn't escape her. Her face had a pale appearance to it. She was breathing heavily.

"Okay, relax," he said.

And she did. Perhaps the comfort of not being alone was just the medicine she needed. Tiffany said, "I can't be near the living room. Let's talk in the kitchen."

And they did. Tiffany sat at the bar counter while Jeffrey prepared a small salad for himself. He offered to fix something for Tiffany, but she was in no mood to eat. She explained the terrifying encounter to him.

When she was finished, Jeffrey said, "Maybe the ghost is smitten with you."

"Shit–ten? Shit ten what?"

"Not shitten, smitten. Smit... ten," emphasizing the *m* in smit, like s*mm*itten.

She sighed and threw her hands up. "Oh, my God. Here we go again with the big words. What does s*mm*itten mean?" echoing his pronunciation of the word smitten.

"Basically, it means to be in love with."

She grimaced. "You are something else, you know that. You see how terrified I am and I tell you what happened and all you can do is make jokes? This isn't funny, okay? I'm convinced this entity is dangerous and it wants us out of the house. Mom was right all along. This damn entity needs to be forced out. I want the damn thing—"

Jeffrey's cello began to play the *Dies Irae* theme. They looked at each other. Their jaws were on the counter.

Jeffrey faintly whispered, "Oh my, God," shaking his head in disbelief. "I need to record this for Dad. He'd love it."

"I'm out of here. I'm not sticking around for the encore," Tiffany said, walking out of the kitchen to the laundry room to go outside into the backyard.

Then one of the kitchen stools flew up and landed in the kitchen sink.

Tiffany swung open the back door and shrieked, "Mom! Dad! You won't believe this!"

"Lord have mercy," Keisha said. "What's wrong?"

Jeffrey walked out onto the porch and sat at the patio table.

Tiffany explained what happened while Steven went back inside to get Brittany. She was in her room playing with Scruffles.

When Steven returned to the porch, he apologized for letting his obsession with the paranormal and the ghost in their house blind his better judgment.

Steven said, "I'm going to check us into a hotel for a few days. All of you deserve some time away from this house. I'll call Father Thompson from St. Matthews and see if he can come here and bless the house for us. We'll accompany one another into the house. Pack one bag and include your bathing suits."

And they did. Each packed a bag, then they drove to the Holiday Inn Express. Steven and Brittany drove in Steven's car; Tiffany and Jeffrey drove in Keisha's S.U.V.

Later that evening, Steven received a call from Father Matthews. He wouldn't be available to bless the house for two weeks because he was out of town. He said he would be happy to bless the house when he returns.

Over dinner, Steven said, "Father Matthews won't be available for two weeks. We can't stay in a hotel that long but we can't stay in that house with the ghost either.

"What are we going to do?" Keisha asked.

"We'll force the ghost out ourselves," he said.

"Do you know how to do that?" Tiffany asked.

Steven said, "No, but I know someone who does. I'll explain later. For now, there's another order of business I wish to discuss."

"What's that, babe?" Keisha asked.

Steven took a big drink of orange juice. Then he said, "Before we force the spirit out, I would like for Sebastian's ghost hunters to conduct an investigation. I've concluded the ghost never intended to share his story with me. I've finally accepted that. I wish I would have done that sooner... Anyway, maybe it will open up to someone different."

"Oh, babe, it sounds like you're obsessing again. You need to let go. Please." Keisha said.

Steven said, "No. I'm not. I promise. If the ghost chooses not to share its story, I can live with that. At least I'll have peace of mind knowing I gave it an opportunity to share its story."

CHAPTER THIRTEEN
John's Scrapbook

Steven knocked on John's door early in the afternoon. He wasn't sure if John was even up, but he hoped he was. John frequently stayed up late, well past midnight, and slept until noon or one in the afternoon on days he didn't have to work.

"Good afternoon, my friend," John said. He opened his door and invited Steven in. "You're just in time. I have some lunch for us to enjoy as we have some conversation."

"Did you want to eat outside?" Steven asked.

"I wouldn't be caught dead eating outside in this heat," John responded, closing the front door. "Make yourself comfortable. I'll get the lunch plated for us. Be back shortly."

This was the first time Steven was inside John's home. Steven sat on the couch that was in front of the large picture window in the living room. In front of the couch was a large walnut–stained coffee table. It had several dings and dents. Pieces of the coffee table were missing, exposing the pure wood from which the table was made. The table had a long history, no doubt.

The table was cluttered. On it were several envelopes fanned out, most of which were from businesses, but some were from friends or family. A stack of handwritten letters also laid on the table. The main object on the table that caught Steven's attention was a maroon–colored scrapbook that was closed. The front cover was personalized in gold lettering with the word GYPSUM, INC. Underneath the title was John's contact information. Property of John Haber, 6733 Jefferson Ave., Whitmond, IN 46324. 219.773.1206. Cash reward offered if returned. A few sticky notes stuck out of the scrapbook, all different colors.

The scrapbook intrigued Steven. He was also mildly bored and wanted something to look at while he waited for John to serve lunch. He called out to John in the kitchen. "Do you mind if I look at this scrapbook—the one on your coffee table?"

"Knock yourself out my, friend," John said. "In fact, there's a page marked with a yellow sticky note. When you get a chance, check that page out. I think it's important you see it. Lunch served in fifteen minutes."

"Great, thanks. My mouth is watering and my stomach is rumbling and grumbling."

"Well, after this meal, it might be doing that, but in a different way. It's Indian food. I'm trying something new. I've got antacids on standby just in case."

Steven chuckled. Then he turned his attention to the scrapbook. He carefully turned the front cover of the scrapbook over, treating it as if it were a fragile antique. The first page of the scrapbook contained a piece of yellow legal pad paper, which served as a title page. On the title page was:

GYPSUM, INC.
John Haber
4/22/2011-

April twenty-second must be his first day on the job at the company, Steven thought.

The next page contained the reference letter Mr. Pistone wrote for John. The page after that contained John's notice of hire letter.

He continued thumbing through the scrapbook. Many of the items in the scrapbook were pictures of John operating a forklift, loading palettes of drywall onto flatbed trucks. Under each picture was a date and an inscription John had handwritten. Other pictures included those from company picnics, holiday parties, and company trainings.

There were also some newspaper clippings scattered throughout the scrapbook. One article was a feature article commending Gypsum for being a reliable provider of drywall and other construction needs. The picture included in the article was of John operating a forklift.

On some of the pages of the scrapbook were John's performance reviews, all of which consisted of the highest ratings. He was a model employee. Arrived early, if not on time, put in an honest day's work, did his job without any incidents, and never left early. His attendance record was commendable, also.

He continued thumbing through the scrapbook, one page at a time. More pictures, more newspaper clippings. Another article pasted in the scrapbook Steven read while waiting for lunch was:

Gypsum's Chief Accountant Missing

Dominic Facchini, 47, Gypsum's Chief Accountant, has been missing for two days now. On or around April 6, Facchini contacted his wife and said he would be home after he ran some errands, but he never returned. Facchini's wife contact police the following morning when Facchini didn't return home or return her calls.

Gypsum's Chief Executive Officer, Mr. Emiliano Pistone, stated, "All of us at Gypsum are deeply saddened by the news of Mr. Facchini missing. We will continue to keep the Facchini family in our thoughts and prayers. Mr. Facchini was an excellent accountant and one hell of a guy. I hope wherever he is, he is safe."

Facchini is a married man with two children, ages 14 and 9. He graduated from Cornell University with a Master of Accounting degree and Indiana University with a bachelor's degree, double majoring in accounting and economics. He has been employed at Gypsum for 12 years.

Gypsum, Inc., Gypsum City's biggest supplier of drywall and other construction needs. If anyone has information about the whereabouts of Mr. Facchini, please contact police at 219.773.1000.

"My, my, my. That's interesting," Steven said.

He continued thumbing through the scrapbook. More pictures of parties, more newspaper clippings about Gypsum's success. Several pages after the chief accountant article was one discussing the C.E.O.'s departure:

Gypsum's C.E.O. Sells Company, Plans to Move Abroad

Emiliano Pistone, Chief Executive Officer of Gypsum, Inc., has sold his company for 2.5 million dollars to Gypsum's current Chief Financial Officer, Vladislav Umberto.

Mr. Pistone's grandfather, Nazzereno Pistone, founded the company in 1917, and quickly became Gypsum City's largest supplier of drywall. When Nazzereno retired, the business was passed to his son, Salvatore Pistone, until his death, at which time Emiliano Pistone took over.

During Emiliano's tenure, he expanded the operation to supply not only high–quality drywall, but also other construction materials. Emiliano also invested money to start a construction company as part of the services Gypsum offers.

Emiliano Pistone said, "I've enjoyed my time serving as Chief Executive Officer, but the time has come to start the next phase of my life. My wife and family are moving to Vienna where we will spend our time traveling and relaxing for six months of the year while the other six months will be spent in our new home that is currently being constructed."

When asked about his successor, Emiliano said, "Mr. Umberto has been a valuable and invaluable asset to the Gypsum company, and I am confident he will continue Gypsum's long–standing legacy of providing top–notch drywall and other construction needs."

Mr. Pistone's last day at Gypsum is March 12, 2017.

Steven continued thumbing through the scrapbook, reading the articles and looking at the numerous pictures of John operating the forklift, sometimes wearing crazy costumes, likely for Halloween, or of him at company get-togethers. Some pictures were taken inside Mr. Pistone's old home. One picture had four gentlemen in it. The inscription underneath the picture: Christmas 2014. Underneath the date were the names of the people in the photo: Anthony Favelle, Emiliano Pistone, John Haber, Vladislav Umberto, George Haber.

As Steven flipped further and further through the book, nothing could have possibly prepared him for the next article he stopped to read. This was the article John marked with the yellow sticky note.

Gypsum Electrician Killed in Work–Related Accident

A tragic accident occurred at 6729 Jefferson Ave., when a Gypsum employee was electrocuted to death. The accident occurred around 1:47 p.m. when an employee of Gypsum, Inc., Timothy Vance, an electrician, was installing a chandelier inside the new home Mr. Pistone was building for himself and his family.

Once paramedics arrived, Vance was immediately transported to Whitmond Memorial

Hospital, where he was pronounced dead on arrival.

A preliminary investigation showed Vance failed to properly ensure power was cut to the area of the house in which he was installing the chandelier.

Gypsum's C.E.O., Mr. Vladislav Umberto, said, "We are deeply saddened we have lost one of our employees, and in such a horrific manner. Mr. Vance was a first–rate employee and was known for his by–the–book approach and commitment to safety and quality. His family is in our thoughts and prayers as they deal with this tragic loss."

Mr. Timothy Vance will be interred at Whitmond Cemetery. Funeral services are scheduled for May 12. In lieu of flowers, the family is asking for donations.

"That's the ghost haunting my house," Steven mumbled, his voice quavering. "God in Heaven." Steven called into the kitchen. He said, "John, I'm not upset with you, but why didn't you tell me someone died in my house?"

John walked into the room and handed Steven a plate. "I hope you enjoy this. It's Indian food."

"Thanks," Steven said. "This looks... different."

"I think you'll like it, my friend," John said, "and save room for dessert: barfi." John sat in his recliner and pulled the lever on the side to release the foot rest. "To answer your question, I didn't want to alarm you. I'm sorry."

"That's the ghost that's been haunting my house," Steven replied.

"I'm sorry, my friend. I didn't tell you because I wasn't sure how you would react to the idea of someone being killed in your home. I tried to tell you to cleanse your house. I wish you would have listened to me. This way, you wouldn't have needed to know about this tragic accident."

Steven looked at the food on his plate and began to wonder how he was going to ask about not eating the alien–looking food without being rude.

"Be adventurous. Dig in, my friend. And my rabbit ears are perked up waiting to hear about the hauntings."

"Before I begin, can you tell me what's on the menu, please?"

John chuckled. "I'm sorry. Of course. What you're looking at there is dhokla, date tamarind chutney, keema, and naan."

Knowing the names of the food weren't helpful to Steven. He needed to know specific details of each food. John gladly explained.

As they ate, Steven told John about the multitude of hauntings that occurred in the house. Steven told him about being pushed down the stairs, the live speaker connected to no source, the strangulation incident.

John said, "I'm your friend, and I don't mean to be rude, but you should be ashamed of yourself for turning a blind eye to these occurrences. You have children and you put them at risk by not forcing the ghost out sooner."

Steven accepted this. He told John he recognized the error of his ways.

"This food is a wonderful change from what I typically eat," Steven admitted. "Amazing burst of flavor. My palette is in shock."

"I'm glad you're enjoying, my friend. I like trying new foods from different ethnic cuisines," John said. He took a drink of wine, swished, and swallowed. Then said, "I have a story I'd like to tell you. Since we've opened this box of bones, I figure you need to hear this story. I think you'll like it though; it is a ghost story."

"I'm excited," Steven said, before placing the keema on his fork in his mouth.

"I wasn't when I experienced it. You'll understand what I mean by that after you hear this story. Are you ready?"

Steven swallowed his mouthful of keema, then replied. "Yep."

John took a deep breath and cleared his throat. "Well, after the house— your house— was built, nobody wanted to buy it from Tony, especially since many people in Whitmond and its neighboring cities read about the tragic death in the papers."

"Makes sense," Steven said, then sipped, swished, and swallowed some merlot. "That explains why Tony offered it to me at such a reduced price."

"Bingo!" John quipped. "One night, before you and your lovely family moved in, around three in the morning, I woke up to flashing lights, and not from an emergency vehicle, either. The lights were from your house. Several rooms randomly would light up. Your house seemed as if it was possessed. Even the porch light flickered at random. On, then off fifteen seconds or so, then back on with other lights within in the house. It was a sight straight out of a horror movie."

"Oh, my," Steven said. "When did it stop?"

"Good question. I slipped into my bathrobe and wandered over to the house. I stood on the lawn, just gazing at the sight. I've never seen a house so angry. Anyway, I started to get angry myself. I walked onto the front porch and yelled, 'Fucking stop it!'"

Steven choked a little on his food. He said, his voice strained, "Sorry. Food went down the wrong tube."

"Have some wine to wash it down."

Steven shook his head and, while choking, started to go through the six s–es.

John berated him. "Really? You're choking to death, but you're going to go through the motions of proper wine drinking? Just drink!"

And he did. After he swallowed the wine, he said, "Thanks. That helped a lot." Steven took a deep breath, then said, "So, when you said that, what happened?"

"Darkness. It was as if the main power switch had been flipped. Every light that was on turned off in an instant."

"Wow, you're a powerful guy if you can order a ghost around like that and it obeyed your command."

John put a finger up and then said, "Not so fast." After eating a forkful of the food on his plate, he said, "I thought that was the end of it, but it wasn't."

Steven swallowed hard, fearing what happened next, though realizing it must not be too bad since John is alive and well to tell the tale. "I'm bubbling over with suspense."

"So I was standing on the front porch. After I said, 'fucking stop it,' all the lights turned off in an instant. About five seconds or so later, the porch light turned on. Seconds later, it exploded, sending shrapnel in every which way, including towards me."

"My, my, my. Were you injured?"

"A laceration across my face and another one across my neck. Just one of many battle scars I've received over the years, my friend. Now, I think most people would have run off the porch screaming like a banshee. Not me though. I didn't care that my face and neck were bleeding. I was more concerned about the unrested spirit in the house. Before I left, I said a prayer. I prayed the electrician, Mr. Vance, I believe his name was if I remember correctly—"

"That's right."

"I prayed his spirit would rest. I'm sorry my prayer didn't work."

Steven was moved by John's altruism. He said, "You needn't apologize. You tried, and that's commendable."

John poured himself and Steven some more wine. Then he said, "Wait until you hear the kicker."

Steven was shocked already with what he heard, but there was even more to the story? Part of Steven didn't want to know since what he heard was frightening enough, but then there was the part of him that was curious and probably couldn't sleep soundly at night if he didn't know. That wouldn't have mattered. He wasn't sleeping well anyway.

"I'm on tenterhooks. Lay it on me."

John said he would tell Steven after he tried to guess. He gave Steven three chances to guess. Steven's first guess was the spirit started to haunt John's house. That was incorrect. The second guess was John dreamed the entire thing. That, too, was incorrect. Steven's third and final guess was it was a prank Tony played on John. Wrong, not to mention an awful guess. After all, Tony's a gangster, not a prankster.

John pushed the leg rest back into his recliner and poured himself a little more wine. Then he said, "Let me bring out dessert and then I'll tell you. Feel free to look at my other scrapbooks. They're in that cabinet," he said, motioning where the cabinet was with his hand.

The cabinet had two doors. They didn't open outward; they slid back and forth.

Steven wanted to take his mind off the ghost story for the time being, so he walked over to the cabinet and slid one of the two white doors open. He stood in awe and wonder at the sight before him. John had numerous— not ten or twenty, but hundreds— of scrapbooks along both shelves in this five–foot by four–foot cabinet. Each shelf had two rows of scrapbooks, one row on top of the other. The colors of the scrapbooks varied, but the color occurring most often was dark blue. The spine and front cover of each scrapbook was labeled.

The first scrapbook in the collection— a blue one with white lettering— was titled: *John Haber, 4/12/1956, Book 1 of 2*. The content of the scrapbook included his birth certificate, hand prints, foot prints, and even an imprint of his buttocks. It seemed John's entire first year of life was contained in that scrapbook along with its sister book, titled *John Haber, 4/12/1956, Book 2 of 2*.

Another scrapbook that caught Steven's eye was one titled *John Haber, First Job, 6/8/1965*. In the scrapbook were various pictures of John working in a wheat field on his uncle's farm. Other pictures showed John milking cows and feeding chickens. A wrinkly, faded dollar bill was on the last page of the scrapbook. It was the first pay John received for a week's work. Out of curiosity, Steven used his cellphone to calculate how much money one dollar would be worth in 1965 in terms of 2018 numbers. Turns out one dollar in 1965 would be approximately seven dollars in today's money.

John entered his living room carrying two plates. He said, "So, what do you think?"

"Impressive, to say the least."

"Well, thanks, my friend. My entire life is contained in those scrapbooks. Birthdays, graduations, weddings, the birth of my children, divorces, hospital stays. I could continue but you get the idea. I'm ready to dive into this barfi."

"You're going to vomit?"

John shook his head and pointed to the plates he had set on the cluttered coffee table. "Barfi. It's a dessert."

Steven snickered, then said, "I'm not going to lie. 'Barfi' is what I nearly did when you first handed me the plate."

In turn, John smiled, then laughed. "Well, I'm glad you didn't my friend. That's specifically pista barfi."

On the plate were two cake–looking, square pieces of pista barfi. The squares were light green.

"Made with pistachios?"

"Ding, ding, ding! Give the man one thousand dollars."

They both had a few bites of the pista barfi. Then John said, as he looked at his scrapbook collection, "It's an amazing collection." He took another bite of the barfi, then stood and walked over to the scrapbooks. He pulled one out and walked over to Steven. "Flip to the last several pages that have pictures on them."

And he did. Steven said, "Wow, John. So, that's why you wanted pictures of us when we had you over for dinner for the first time. You wanted to add them to your scrapbook collection. This is touching."

Other pictures included the few occasions Steven and John hung out together on John's porch.

"You have a passion for documenting your life's events. It's inspirational."

"Thank you. I don't take life for granted. Every experience has merit and often contains a lesson or two to make us wiser."

Steven closed the scrapbook and handed it back to John. Then he resumed finishing his barfi while John placed the scrapbook in his collection.

Standing in front of the scrapbooks, he reminisced about the many experiences he'd had over the years, the wonderful and the terrible, the joyous and the heart–wrenching.

John pulled out another scrapbook he had in a drawer underneath the cabinet of scrapbooks and stepped over to Steven with it. He presented the scrapbook to Steven and said, "Check this out."

Steven put the last piece of barfi on his plate in his mouth. While chewing it, he took the scrapbook from John.

"I can see it on your face. You'd like some more pista barfi. I'll be back, my friend."

The scrapbook was a silver one. The spine and front cover were titled *John's Death and Beyond: The Legacy Continues*. The scrapbook had tabs, each with a label, some of which included 'Death Scene', 'Autopsy', 'Morgue Storage Drawer', 'Death Makeup', 'Showtime: Funeral', 'Burial', and 'Visitations After Internment'.

"Pretty nifty, huh?" John asked as he entered the room with more pista barfi for the two of them to enjoy. "I bet you've never anything like that before."

"You'd be right on the money with that one."

With a wide smile on his face, John sat in his recliner and pulled out the leg rest to prop up his feet. "I have it delineated in my will how that scrapbook is to be handled. I want my life to continue after death."

"Not trying to be rude, but isn't this morbid?"

After swallowing the barfi he was chewing, he said, "No. It's subjective. You said morbid, not me. You might think it's morbid. I think it's fucking wonderful."

"Good point. Fair enough. Will you tell me the kicker now?"

"Kicker?" John asked, confused.

"Right. Remember? You were telling me about the light show at my house."

John thought for a moment with a perplexed expression on his face. Then he said, "Oh, right. I remember now. Sorry, I got sidetracked showing off my scrapbooks."

"No problem."

"The next morning, I contacted the electric company, NIPSCO. Damn bloodsuckers. Anyway, I reported the incident to them thinking maybe— just maybe— there was an electrical issue that needed to be fixed on their end. I was put on hold with this horrendous elevator music. Christ, every time I think of this story I can still hear it. Yanni or Kenny G or someone like that."

"Right. Horrible elevator music. I feel your pain. What happened? What did they say?"

John took a drink from his glass of merlot, swallowed, then answered. "Well, when the service representative got back on the line, she said I must have the wrong address because service wasn't being provided at the address I stated."

"I thought maybe I gave her the wrong address. I told her again the address and she confirmed there wasn't any service being provided."

"Jesus. Now that's frightening."

"That's why I tried to convince you to cleanse the house. If you would have done that, I don't think we'd be having this conversation right now. I didn't want you to find out someone died inside your house."

"Do you think the ghost you prayed for was the one who scratched you?"

"Probably, but who knows."

"I need to rid my house of this spirit. Keisha is right. It's not proper to keep the spirit in the house. It needs to be released."

John nodded.

"John, the reason I came here is to ask you for help. Will you lead our family in blessing the house, please? You mentioned you've done this before. I haven't. It's important to me that this be done right. Plus, I think there's strength in numbers. Instead of five people participating in the blessing, there'd be six."

John went through the motions of proper wine drinking. After he relished in the orgasmic sexiness of the wine's body, he answered. "I'd be happy to lead the blessing."

"Thank you so much, John. You're a true friend."

The blessing would occur three days from now. Steven explained to John he had a ghost investigation team visiting the house two days from now. He, Keisha, and the children would remain at the hotel while the team conducted the investigation.

The two men conversed for another hour, then Steven left and returned to the hotel.

CHAPTER FOURTEEN

The Investigation

The investigation crew consisted of four people, all of whom were Sebastian's friends. Jason Mills was the lead investigator; his girlfriend, Christina Anderson, was an investigator, and her specialty was E.V.P. analysis; Zach Joseph, an investigator and tech equipment specialist; and his girlfriend, Heather Kegley, whose area of expertise was video analysis. The foursome called their paranormal investigation group Whitmond Paranormal Investigation Society, W.P.I.S. for short, pronounced 'we piss'.

Because the Dobrowski house had three floors, two additional people were invited to join the investigation: Amy Sanders and Sara Mitchells. These two would be assigned to investigate the smallest area of the house, which was the attic.

Jason put his hair into a ponytail and placed a hair tie around it. He looked like Steve Tyler from Aerosmith. He said, "Alright, so let's get our equipment set up in the hot spots of the house that were discussed on the way here."

"Yes, drill sergeant! Too easy, drill sergeant!" Zack said with an overzealous voice while saluting Jason. He had a military cut. After finishing high school, he aspired to join the Marines.

Once their equipment was set up, Jason once again went over assignments. "Alright, Christina, Sebastian, and myself will investigate the first floor. Zach and—"

"Yes, sir!" Zach hollered, standing at attention and saluting Jason. "Ready for my mission, sir!"

"At ease, solider, at ease," Jason said, returning a sloppy salute. "You and Heather will investigate the second floor."

Even though Jason told Zach several times he didn't need to salute and shout, Zach said he liked to do it. Sure, it was annoying as hell to Jason, but this minor annoyance was nothing compared to the loyalty and compassion Zach had for Jason and their friendship.

"Sounds good, boss," Heather said, saluting Jason, but not standing. "I'm ready for combat, sir."

She, too, wanted to join the Marines after high school. Her and Zach planned to go through basic training together. She was one grade level ahead of Zach; she was a senior this school year at Whitmond High School.

Zach removed the hair tie in his hair. "Okay, so Amy and Sara, that leaves you two in the attic," he said while tying the hair tie around his ponytail.

The investigation officially started at nine–fourteen at night and was concluded at six–twenty–two the next morning.

After the investigation concluded, W.P.I.S. had a standard procedure to summarize preliminary findings of their investigation in a written report. Around nine–thirty in the morning the investigation was concluded, Steven received an email from W.P.I.S.

W.P.I.S. Preliminary Report

First Floor: Some pictures knocked off fireplace mantel and wall; chandelier would sway wildly sometimes; bar stools in kitchen shifted position; placemats in dining room knocked off table (provocation); T.V. turned on and off twice; kitchen cabinet door opened and closed (provocation); Two Class A E.V.Ps.

Second Floor: An apparition was observed around eleven–fifty–two walking up the attic stairs; swivel chair in home office spun on its own on a few occasions; chair was pushed from desk to near the office door (provocation); One Class A E.V.P.

Attic Floor: Bicycle pedals moved on their own; the rope hanging from the ceiling would sway back and forth and then stop when commanded (provocation); towel on weight bench pulled off; camera knocked over once; stack of weights on floor knocked over; marker on marker board thrown across the room; Six Class A E.V.Ps.

NOTE: Other E.V.Ps. (Classes B and/or C) and paranormal activity may be discovered after we review all evidence collected.

The next morning, Steven received an email from W.P.I.S. indicating that they had reviewed all the video and audio evidence and they were ready to meet with Steven and Keisha to go over it.

Each of the four members of W.P.I.S. presented their individual findings. All four W.P.I.S. members reviewed the video and audio evidence separately and shared their findings. As they presented their findings of possible paranormal activity, they also offered alternative explanations. For instance, the towel falling off the weight bench may have occurred because of how it was positioned, not necessarily because of a ghost pulling it off.

W.P.I.S. provided a summary report listing the message heard from all the E.V.Ps. They also played all of them for the Dobrowski's.

E.V.P. Transcript
(Timestamps are approximate)

First Floor

Class A

(12:13:47) Q: Are there any spirits who wish to communicate?

(12:13:50) A: Yes. (airy; drawn out short 'e' sound; 'yeeeees')

(02:43:42) Q: Did you die here or somewhere else?

(02:44:01) A: Here. (loud, fast; punctuated articulation)

Class B: None.

Class C: None.

Second Floor

Class A

(11:18:58) Q: Do you want the Dobrowski's to leave the house?
A: Yes. (emphatic)

Class B
(04:02:54) Q: Are you a demon?
(04:02:58) A: No. (airy; drawn out long 'o' sound; 'noooooo')

Class C
(--:--:--)Q: (none)
(02:17:22) A: Gonna kill... you. ('you' was high–pitched)

Attic
Class A
(11:06:48) Q: Why are you here?
(11:06:50) A: Murder. (fast; high-pitched)

(11:10:52) Q: How did you die?
(11:10:58) A: Couldn't... breathe. (slow; strained)

(04:22:39) Q: Do you want to hurt us?
(04:22:44) A: I will. (emphatic; fast)

(05:01:22) Q: What happens if the Dobrowski's stay?
(05:01:26) A: Die. (airy; long 'I' drawn out; 'diiiiie')

(02:11:54) Q: Are you an angry spirit?
(02:11:57) A: Yes. (loud; punctuated articulation; fast)

(--:--:--)Q: (none)
(03:17:12) A: GET OUT! (loud; angry voice)

Class B None.
Class C
(--:--:--)Q: (none)
(01:03:29) A: In the wall (airy; slow; short 'a' sound drawn out; 'waaaall')

Additional Paranormal Findings:
First floor: Kitchen cabinets and drawers open and closed; mail on kitchen counter moved; camera in living room turned slightly;

Second Floor: [hallway camera] Bedroom door opened and closed; office door open, light turned on, then off, door closed.

Attic: shadowy apparition caught; video camera stopped recording around three in the morning for approximately forty minutes.

W.P.I.S. supplied all video and audio evidence after making copies for their records.

After the meeting, Steven and the rest of the family discussed the findings.

Steven said, "It's obvious this spirit is angry and wants us out of the house, but my position is that it's our house and I am not backing down."

"What if the spirit doesn't leave, babe," Keisha asked.

"I don't know. Let's try and get rid of it first. We'll cross over that bridge if and when the time comes."

He did know, but he kept it to himself for now.

"Daddy," Brittany said, "I'm scared, and so is Mr. Quacks."

"Nothing to be afraid of, sweet pea. Mommy and Daddy and your sister and brother and Scruffles won't let that happen."

That was an empty promise and Steven knew it. He said it anyway because he didn't want to scare her.

"And Mr. Quacks!" she said, her voice chipper.

"You bet, sweet pea," Steven said. "And Mr. Quacks."

"Some of those E.V.Ps. were scary, Dad," Jeffrey said. "If we can't force the spirit out, would we sell the house?"

"Son, that's not going to happen. That's the house I intend to die in. That's the last house your mother and I planned to buy."

Stick around long enough in that house, Dad, and you just might find yourself dead, Jeffrey thought.

He didn't say anything to Steven about his firm position to stay in that house until his demise. He just nodded ever so slightly.

"Sometimes plans change, babe," Keisha said. "We have to think about the safety of our children... Seriously, don't give me that look. If the spirit doesn't leave the house, then what choice do we have? Continue to live in fear and angst until we kick the bucket? I'm not doing that, Steven."

Steven's face turned red and his fists clenched. He took a breath, recoiled, and said, "So what you're basically saying is if we can't get rid of the spirit and I demand we stay and fight this thing, you'd leave me? You'd take the kids away from me?"

She was on the hot seat now. She had to choose between keeping the family together or breaking it apart.

"I love you, babe, but I'm not going to let my kids live in a house where their safety is at risk. A house is supposed to be a place of safety and refuge. So, yes, I would leave you in that house all by yourself, but if you're as smart as I know you are, you would choose your family over a house."

And with that, Keisha stood and left the hotel room.

"Nice work, Dad," Tiffany said, then left the room to chase after her mom.

Jeffrey put his hand on his dad's shoulders. "Women, right Dad?"

That evening, Steven and Keisha reconciled. He told Keisha he would always choose family over any material object, including a house. He explained he wanted to make the children think staying in that house was their only option because it would add more power to the blessing and force the spirit out. She understood where he was coming from and felt relieved that Steven would ditch the house— if it came down to it.

While forcing himself to fall asleep, Steven played the different E.V.Ps. in his mind, but one seemed to be on a loop: In the wall. What does that mean? What's in the wall?

CHAPTER FIFTEEN
Blessings

John was sitting on his porch when the Dobrowski's pulled into their driveway. He stepped off his porch and walked over to their house.

Keisha and the children walked Scruffles to the backyard.

Steven approached John. He said, "Good morning, John. I hope this works. My family and I are depending on it."

"We're going to send Mr. Vance to where he is wanted and where he belongs," John said, shaking Steven's hand. "What's in the bag?"

"Bottles of holy water. I stopped at St. Matthews this morning and the church secretary gave them to me. Father Thompson told me to make the sign of the cross above each doorway."

John nodded. "That's the way to do it. Do you have the other items needed for the smudging? If not, I've got stuff in my house. I ran out to the store last night and purchased the things. It'd be no trouble for me to run and grab them."

He purchased the items in the event Steven forgot the items needed for the blessing. If Steven forgot, the family was covered; if he remembered, John intended to use the items to smudge his house.

"We're all set," Steven said. He rubbed the mole on his face. "I've got the items in another bag in the car. I forgot to grab it. I'll be right back." *I'm not sure I want to do this. The ghost still needs to tell me his story. Stop! Family first.*

Internally, Steven was conflicted. On the one hand, to keep his family together, he needed to play ball and release the spirit to Heaven, or, at the very least, force it out of the home. On the other hand, he wanted to continue to reach the spirit and find out its story. In his mind, by forcing it out, he was kicking out a close friend.

Because Steven didn't accomplish his goal of finding out the spirit's story, there was an emptiness within him. Once the spirit was banished or released, the opportunity to know its story would be lost.

"Steven," Keisha said, standing in front of the garage, "we're ready. Are you?"

Steven stood at his car, staring at the ground in contemplative thought. He snapped out of the trance–like state he was in. He said with a flat, stoic tone, "Let's do this."

John, along with the Dobrowski's, stood on the front porch and Steven unlocked the front door.

"The key won't turn," Steven said. "I can't unlock the door."

"Let me try, babe," Keisha offered. She removed the key, reinserted it, and tried to turn the key. It wouldn't turn.

She said a silent prayer as she continued trying to turn the key. Eventually, the tumbler gave way, and the door was unlocked.

"Good work, honey," Steven said. "Did you want to open the door now?"

"Thanks, babe. I'd like you to open the door."

She moved out of the way and Steven approached the door. He placed his hand around the curved bronze handle and placed his thumb on the lever to unlatch the door.

Keisha sensed the hesitation and offered some words of encouragement.

"You can do it, babe. I know this isn't easy for you, but we need to do this," Keisha said, rubbing his back.

John said, "It's the right thing to do, my friend. Mr. Vance deserves to be released, be that wherever. He doesn't belong in your house though. You're doing the right thing."

Steven nodded and pushed down on the lever to unlatch the door. He lightly pushed on the door to open it, but something was blocking it. He pushed harder, and then a little more. He peeked his head around the door when there was enough space to do so.

"The coffee table from the living room is blocking the door," Steven said, pushing even harder now to open the door.

John said, "Now that's a sign the spirit never wanted to tell his story to you, my friend. He wanted you all out of the house. You were invading his space. We'll fix that with this blessing though."

Steven nodded. "I think you're right. Alternatively, maybe the spirit is trying to keep us out because he knows we're about to conduct a blessing and it doesn't want to leave until its story is told. It has unfinished business."

"Listen, my friend. I need you to get your head screwed on straight. This spirit never had any intention of telling you its story. Now, let's get started. The sooner we get this over with, the better everyone will feel."

When they stepped inside the house, they were greeted with a mess. The kitchen drawers and cabinets were open. All the kitchen utensils were scattered all over the kitchen counters and floor. Two kitchen stools were sitting legs up in the kitchen sink. The remaining kitchen stools were atop the utensils on the kitchen counter. The crucifix along with all the pictures on the wall were on the floor. All the pictures that were on the mantel were on the floor.

"Looks like this spirit enjoyed himself while we were away," Tiffany said, shaking her head in disbelief. "This is one angry spirit."

"Should we clean up first, then do the blessing?" Keisha asked John.

"I don't think it matters either way. For everyone's sake, however, I wouldn't waste any time conducting the blessing of the house. We'll save the living room for last because I think that's where it's most powerful. Gut instinct."

Before the blessing started, John pulled Steven aside. He placed a hand on Steven's shoulder, then spoke. "Listen to me, my friend," he said. "You keep spouting remarks about the spirit's story. What story is there for it to tell? We know its story, don't we? The man was fried installing a chandelier in your living room. You already know the spirit's story. It doesn't want to talk to you, my friend. What it wants is your house without any of you in it. The spirit is angry. He's angry because he lost his life, and in a horrific way."

"I understand what you're saying, John," Steven said. "Thank you. I needed to hear that."

"Well, okay. I'm glad to hear that. Because if you have doubts about this blessing, the effect is weakened. Focus on your family, not the spirit. This spirit, for everyone's sake, needs to be released from the house."

John cleared a space by pushing the kitchen stools and utensils further up the counter. He laid out the items for the blessing: the blessing bowl, a tightly–bound bundle of sage, a candle, a long white–tipped gray feather, a lighter, and several bottles of holy water.

As he did this, the kitchen stools and utensils on the kitchen counter were knocked off by some unseen force.

"Stop the hissy fit, Mr. Vance," John said. "It's not going to scare me. I've been in live combat before and seen far scarier things. The time has come for you to be released and to enter the gates of Heaven."

The open cabinet doors slammed shut, opened again, then slammed shut. Lights throughout the house flickered. A rushing, howling wind traveled throughout the house.

"Wait. How do you know the spirit's name?" Keisha asked.

John went into damage control mode. He was so concerned with starting the blessing, he slipped up and said the name of the spirit. This was to their advantage, though, because now John could use the spirit's name to call it out and send it to where it belonged. He said, "I listened to some of Steven's recordings. He missed a few E.V.P.s I was able to catch."

"Oh, okay. That makes sense," Keisha replied.

"Write your names on this sticky note, and quickly, please," John said.

"What's this—" Jeffrey asked.

"No time to explain. Trust me and do it," John said. He handed Jeffrey a pen, then lit the candle. "Ouch!"

"What happened?" Tiffany asked.

John grabbed the back of his neck and said, "Something scratched me on my neck." He looked at his hand. "The damn spirit drew a little blood, too."

Keisha said, "Oh, my. That's a nasty scratch." Then she tore off a long piece of toilet paper from the roll in the downstairs hallway bathroom, folded it, and placed it on John's neck.

"That's a bad man. Right, Mr. Quacks?" Brittany said.

"A very bad man. An angry man," John said to her, patting Mr. Quacks on its head. "It'll be over soon though. Where's the slip of paper with your names on it?"

Tiffany handed it to him. He folded it twice, then placed it in the blessing bowl. Using the candle flame, he lit the sage smudge stick and placed it in the bowl.

John said, "Steven, my friend, you carry this candle and stay by my side, please. Keisha, as we bless each room, place the sign of the cross using the holy water. Everyone please follow behind Steven and me and remain in constant prayer as we move from room to room. We'll begin in the sitting room and go from there."

Entering the sitting room, John wafted smoke rising out of the bowl throughout the room while repeating an incantation. "Bless this house and all those in it. Banish any and all evil or demonic forces from it. Cleanse this house and make it clear. Only positive energy is welcome here."

John was machine–like. He tirelessly motioned his arm, wafting smoke from the smudge stick. He didn't waste any time. Once the final word from the incantation left his lips, he started the incantation over again.

While smudging the sitting room, John could see through the double doors that led from the sitting room to the living room that the chandelier light was flickering wildly and swinging erratically.

This isn't going to be easy, John thought. *Please let this work.* "Alright," he said as he walked to the next area to smudge, "dining room next. Then kitchen and laundry room. From there, upstairs. Then attic. Finally, living room."

All of the bedrooms were a mess. Drawers open and items tossed all over the place. Fortunately, Brittany brought the Michael statue, Granana's personalized dinner plate, and crucifix with her to the hotel. Had she not, the statue and plate would be in pieces.

In the attic, all the exercise equipment was toppled over. The weights were scattered across the room. There were a few dents and dings in the wall from a few weights that struck it. Around the dents and dings was a crimson–colored residue.

Finally, they reached the living room, the last room that needed smudging. The chandelier was swinging violently and flickering equally so. Some of the light bulbs exploded as John read the incantation and smudged the room.

John smudged from corner to corner and in between a few times. This was the last room the spirit had the chance to overpower the blessing, but John was steadfast.

As John recited the incantation the third time, the chandelier started to strike the ceiling as it swung furiously. Glass shattered from it, littering the living room.

Several times, the T.V. flickered on with a blank white screen and loud static, and at times when it did, the man in the black suit appeared for a second or so, then disappeared.

John continued smudging the living room and reciting the incantation while everyone else constantly prayed.

Finally, Steven screamed with a voice as loud and powerful tantamount to the angry spirit's, "Leave this house now! Leeeeeeeave noooooow!"

And then the paranormal activity instantly stopped, as if a switch was pulled, cutting off power to it.

The family embraced and cried. John continued to smudge and quietly recite the incantation.

After the house was cleaned and pieced back together as best it could be, given the damage, Steven prepared dinner for the family. Using Granana's recipes with some added twists of his own, the items prepared included meatloaf, homemade scalloped potatoes with cheddar cheese, steamed broccoli, buttermilk biscuits. For dessert, peach cobbler.

Everyone was emotional from the blessing, even though several hours passed. Keisha was particularly moved by Steven's order to the spirit to leave their house. The faith she lost in him was now restored and strengthened.

Steven removed the pan of scalloped potatoes from the oven and placed it on a cooling rack. Then he took a big gulp of coffee from his World's Greatest Dad coffee mug.

A sound came from the living room. It sounded like the family picture fell onto the hearth. How could that be? The house was blessed and the spirit was released.

Steven was on–guard. He walked into the living room.

"Sweet pea, what are you doing?" Steven asked.

"Mr. Quacks wanted to see the pretty picture, Daddy," Brittany said. "He likes to see himself in the picture." She placed the picture on the couch and then climbed onto it.

Steven sat down next to her. "It is a beautiful picture. How are you feeling?"

"Great, Daddy. How about you?"

"I feel wonderful, sweet pea. How's Mr. Quack's leg?"

"Just fine, Daddy. You fixed him good."

Scruffles started barking.

"What's wrong, Scruffles? Come here, boy."

But he didn't. He continued barking, so Steven got off the couch and looked for Scruffles. He found Scruffles in the dining room behind the curtains barking at someone walking their dog outside.

He knelt down and petted Scruffles. "You're a silly doggy, Scruffs. Yes, you are."

Once the dog and its walker were out of Scruffles' view, he stopped barking and sniffed and licked Steven's face.

Jeffrey came down the stairs and said, "I'll set the table, Dad."

"Thanks. John should be over soon."

Steven and Keisha invited John over for dinner as a thank you for the help he gave the family by leading the family in the blessing of the house.

Steven returned to the kitchen to finish preparing the steamed broccoli. He added a little garlic, butter, salt and pepper, and a touch of oregano.

Ding-dong.

Scruffles started barking.

"I'll get it," Steven announced. He wiped his hands and opened the front door. It was John.

"I thought you might like to have some of this over dinner, my friend," John said, presenting a bottle of wine.

"John, that's an expensive wine."

And it was. The wine was a bottle of 1961 Chateau Palmer Margaux, which was priced over two thousand dollars.

John believed the wine was appropriate. To him, this dinner was special. It marked a turning point for the family and he insisted the Dobrowski's accept it.

Steven graciously thanked John for his unexpected and generous offering.

While Steven finished preparing dinner, John sat in the living room. Brittany was still on the couch with Mr. Quacks. Scruffles was asleep next to Brittany.

Ten minutes later, Steven announced dinner was ready. Shortly after, everyone was seated at the table.

Steven and Keisha sat at the heads of the table. To Steven's right was John; to his left was Brittany. To Keisha's right was Jeffrey; to her left was Tiffany.

Because John was the guest of honor, Steven had him choose his slice of meatloaf first. As the food was rotated, the family talked about how the rest of their day went after the blessing was finished.

Steven said, "Here's some irony. Today, we liberated the spirit. But, I, too, feel as if I've been liberated."

John nodded. "That spirit had you in its grip."

"The house has a different atmosphere," Keisha chimed in as she used her fork to cut a piece of meatloaf from her slice. "There's a new shimmering brightness to the house it didn't have before."

"I feel the same way," Tiffany said. She reached for the gravy bowl and poured a heaping amount of it on her two pieces of meatloaf, one stacked on the other.

Jeffrey said, "Yeah, the air alone feels different. It feels light. Even right now I feel a difference in the air."

"I'm relieved you sense a difference in the house," John said. "That's a sign the blessing worked and has continued to work."

"Mr. Quacks and I love how the house feels now," Brittany said. "So does Scruffles. I'm glad the scary bad man is out of here."

"You like the house better now, little one?" John asked.

"Yeah!" she shouted with exuberance. "And if he comes back Granana will bend him over her knee and bust his butt raw."

Everyone laughed. The mood was cheerful and light. This was a feeling the Dobrowski's hadn't experienced since moving into the house. It was a nice feeling to have again.

Steven opened the bottle of wine and poured John a glass first. Then Keisha, and last, himself. Next, he poured grape juice out of a wine–looking bottle into the children's wine glasses.

As he rose his wine glass, Steven said, "Everyone raise your glasses. I have a toast."

Everyone raised their glasses and waited in anticipation for Steven's toast. He didn't speak immediately. He simply gazed at everyone at the table, thinking about how profoundly blessed he was.

"First, thank you to my wife and children for putting up with my insanity the past several weeks. I'm sorry for what I may have caused. Secondly, thank you to you, John. You've been a true friend and in a lot of ways a surrogate father to me. I love all of you." Steven raised his glass a little higher and said, "Here's to a new beginning and a bright future."

Then a door violently slammed shut.

"What the— " John said. "That was loud."

"I'll go check it out," Steven said. He wiped his mouth with a cloth napkin. "Be right back."

When he reached the top of the stairs, he checked to his left, and saw none of the doors were shut. Then he looked to his right, and Jeffrey's door was the only one shut.

From the top of the stairwell, he called to the downstairs. "Jeffrey, did you leave your door open or closed when you came down for dinner?"

"Open, Dad," he said, "I wanted to air it out a little."

"Okay," Steven said, walking towards Jeffrey's door.

Once again, Steven's senses were heightened. He didn't want to deal with a ghost in the house again. He was on board with Keisha's idea of teaming up to investigate haunted places together and communicate with spirits. He was no longer keen on the idea of living with one.

He opened Jeffrey's door, slowly. Something was pushing against the door, but it was a light force.

Steven returned to the dining room and said, "Hey, son, why did you have your window opened? We have the air conditioning running."

"Sorry, Dad," Jeffrey replied, "but I wanted to air the room out a little."

Steven sat down and said, "Oh. Alright. Well, I closed your window. A gust of wind blew your door shut."

"Ah, that makes sense," John said. "I read we may get a nasty thunderstorm later this evening."

The evening continued without a hitch. The conversation was lively and entertaining.

Keisha used her fork to tap her wine glass. She said, "I have an announcement to make. Earlier today I received a call from Portage Middle School. I've been offered conditional employment as a social studies teacher."

Everyone cheered and congratulated Keisha.

"They don't start their school year until September, so I have time to get a little more rest and relaxation in before I start."

"Lucky," Jeffrey said. "We start school soon. I can't believe how fast summer vacation flew by. Here one day, gone the next."

"It did, but I'm kind of excited to go back to school. I miss being on a team. I've decided I need to limit how many sports I play though, because I want to improve academically. Sebastian has been teaching me some study skills. He's super smart."

After dinner, Keisha had another announcement to make to the family. She stood and asked everyone to close their eyes. And they did. Keisha placed a ring pop in front of everyone at the table.

"Okay," Keisha said. "Open your eyes."

Everyone was confused at the ring pop. What did it mean?

Eventually, John said, "Congratulations, Steven and Keisha. Whether it’s a boy or girl, I hope it’s healthy."

"What?" Steven said. "Wait... You’re... No... Are you..."

Keisha rubbed her belly and said, "Yes, babe. We're pregnant."

Steven stood and shouted, "Yes!" He sprinted over to her and embraced her.

Everyone at the table clapped and said congratulations.

Shortly after, Steven had a surprise for his family. He told Keisha to make sure the children stayed in the dining room while he prepared the surprise.

While outside, John helped Steven prepare the surprise. Once it was ready, John summoned everyone out to the backyard on Steven's behalf.

Everyone gathered around the tarp-covered surprise.

Steven said, "To my family, I had this specially made. I love all of you." He lifted the tarp and said, "Tada!"

"That's amazing, Dad," Tiffany said.

"Yeah, it's so pretty, Daddy," Brittany added.

Everyone else stated their admiration for the lovely gift Steven bestowed.

"Babe, that is incredibly thoughtful," Keisha said.

Steven had a birdbath specially made. It was white and in the center of the bath was a Mt. Rushmore–looking thing. Steven had Keisha and the children's faces etched into stone. His face was included, also. From left to right: Steven, Keisha, Jeffrey, Tiffany, Brittany, and lastly, Mr. Quacks.

After filling the birdbath with water, everyone returned to the dining room for dessert. Steven's peach cobbler received rave reviews from his family and John.

After dessert, John and Steven sat on Steven's front porch, drinking wine and talking about past experiences and future plans.

That night, Steven and the rest of family had their best night of sleep since they moved into their new house.

CHAPTER SIXTEEN
An Unexpected Visitor

Two weeks had passed, and the house experienced nothing out of the ordinary. The children would be starting school in week.

Steven was in good spirits, also, but work started to eat at him. His supervisor, Melania Jordan, was loading him up with work and taking more and more risks to get into bed with him, no matter how assertive he was when declining and explaining he was a married man with children. Not only that, he cherished the relationship between him and Keisha, and he wasn't willing to throw it away on some two–bit skank, regardless of how appealing the idea seemed.

Steven's temperament was fairly level, but because of the stress at work, sometimes he was short–fused. Immediately after the outburst, he was apologetic. More recently, however, the outbursts were becoming more frequent and with greater intensity.

He pulled into the garage after and slammed his car door. While at work, someone threw a brick at the back window of Steven's car. There was a note wrapped around it. The note had the same characteristics as the other notes: the message was constructed using cutout letters and numbers from newspapers and magazines. The note this time presented the following message:

TIME IS RUNNING OUT. GET YOUR AUNT JEMIMA WIFE AND YOUR COOKIES N' CREME KIDS THE FUCK OUT OF THIS COMMUNITY. NO MORE WARNINGS.

When Steven noticed the damage to the car, he immediately called the police and filed a report. Once again, he informed the responding officers this wasn't the first race–related incident. He requested the detective working on the other cases related to he and his family should be assigned this case, also.

While sitting at the dining room table, Steven called the Whitmond Police Department and asked for the detective assigned to the incidents tied to his address. He couldn't remember the detective's name.

Stupid god damn elevator music, he thought, as he waited for the detective to take his call.

Ten minutes later, Steven was rerouted back to the main line of the police department and had to ask to be connected to the Detective Bureau all over again, then ask for the detective working the incidents that occurred at his address.

Someone with a masculine voice spoke. "Detective Auckland. What can I assist you with?"

"Yes sir, Detective Auckland. Good evening," Steven said. "This is Steven Dobrowski. Address is 6729 Jefferson Ave. I was calling to see if you had any updates for me."

"Yes, Mr. Dobrowski. Nice to hear from you. Sorry about your car window, by the way. The report was forwarded to me about twenty minutes ago. Same M.O. as the other letters as far as format goes. The note is at the crime lab as we speak being processed for prints."

"Well, that's good news, but I doubt there will be any prints on it, not even mine. I didn't touch the note with my bare hands this time. I wore a pair of winter gloves I had in the trunk. Anyway, what about the other cases? Any leads that forward the investigations?"

Detective Auckland scattered some things around his desk, then said, "Unfortunately, no, Mr. Dobrowski. We'll continue to pursue any leads we can. Is there anything else I can assist you with tonight?"

"No. That's all. Thank you."

Using his arms as a pillow, he laid his head down on the dining room table. The worry was wearing on him. He feared his family were in danger.

"Hey, babe," Keisha said, "I didn't hear you come in." She kissed him on his cheek. "The electrician is coming over tomorrow to install the new chandelier."

"Sounds good," Steven mumbled. What he said was slightly muffled.

"Oh, babe. What's wrong?"

"Just tired. Work is stressing me out. It's becoming too much, but I don't want to say anything to my boss. I don't want to risk being labeled weak. That boss of mine is riding me in more ways than I care to share. I'm on the brink of quitting, but I need to find a new job first."

Keisha rubbed his back and head. "I'm sorry work is hectic. Maybe in a few weeks you can take a vacation."

"Maybe."

"You also talked about starting your own advertising company, right? That's an option."

"Not anymore. It would be financially distressing to not know how much money I would be bringing in from one month to the next. With us being pregnant, I'm not willing to roll the dice and venture out on my own just yet. At least my current job guarantees a fixed amount of money every month since I'm on a contract."

"But the cost, babe. Is it worth it?"

"Cost?"

"Look at what the job is doing to you. You're exhausted. You're not sleeping well either. And, I'm sorry to say, your temper flares up from time to time. I'm not blaming you for it. I know work is stressful for you."

"Is it ever. I can't take it."

"Then quit. We'll make it work."

Steven sprang up and spoke with a caustic tone. "How? How can we make it work? We can't live off my salary alone, and we definitely can't live off of yours alone."

Steven had a valid point, but he didn't present it in the best way. It was true Keisha's salary was less than one–third than what his was, and because she moved from one district to another, she wasn't eligible for a raise this school year, assuming a raise was even available to the district. Even then, the salary increase wouldn't amount to much. Steven was disgusted at the lack of proper compensation for teachers given all the stupid–ass kids, bullshit, and dumbass administrators they had to deal with day in and day out. If he ever became President of the United States, he vowed to fix that.

"Excuse me? I don't think I like your tone of voice. My contributions have merit. Where do you get off acting all high and mighty?"

He stood. "I'm not. I'm stating a fact. I make more money." He walked into the kitchen to get some more coffee.

Keisha followed him and responded. "Right, but you say it like, because you bring home more money, you're better than me. Is that what you're saying?"

He slammed his World's Greatest Dad coffee mug on the counter. "Can we please have this discussion another time? I worked all god damn day. I had to deal with vandalism to my car. On top of that, the officers who arrived on the scene were Ofcs. McDumb and Smiling Dumbass. I came home and called the detective for an update and he had nothing for me. I'm exhausted and agitated and angry, and I don't think now is a good time to be picking at this scab. So, please, will you go away and leave me alone?"

Keisha pointed her finger at him. "Now, listen, sucker. I've been putting up with your bad attitude for weeks now, but it ends here. I'm sorry things didn't turn out the way you wanted them to, but you will not use that as an excuse to beat on me like I'm Tiffany's boxing bag."

He grabbed his World's Greatest Dad coffee mug and brought his arm back to throw it against the kitchen wall— the one adjacent to the living room, but he didn't. He stopped at the end of his back swing before the follow through. He stood there, breathing heavily. His eyes glazed. After several seconds, he placed the cup on the counter with a slight but forceful slam, then said, "Fine! I'll leave then!" He walked out of the kitchen, down the hallway, and to the front door, which he violently slammed shut when he walked out.

Keisha opened the front door and offered a suggestion. "Don't come back in until you're calm!"

He whipped around and ran after her while shouting. "You god damn overbearing rude bitch! I'll slice your neck ear to ear!"

She slammed the door— nearly as hard as he did when he exited moments before— and locked it. He didn't pursue her.

He muttered walking down the driveway to check the mailbox. "God damn ruthless, useless bitch. I can't believe this is how my life turned out. Suicide sounds attractive right about now."

Terry witnessed the exchange. As Steven was walking back up the driveway, he commented. "That–a–boy, Steven! I've got some noosed rope and a tall tree in my backyard if you're interested. We'll have ourselves a good old-fashioned lynching!" Then he chuckled like a jackass.

Steven threw the stack of mail in his hand to the ground and sped towards Terry.

"Steven! Stop!" John shouted in a fatherly tone.

And he did. Whatever spell cloaked him seemed to instantly lift like a once–grounded feather in a strong wind. He stood looking at Terry, who had his hand on his sidearm. He cackled like some demon from Hell.

John put his hand on Steven's back, which caused Steven to jump. He said, "I'm sorry, my friend. I didn't mean to startle you. Please come over to my place for a little bit. It'll help, I think."

Steven complied. While John's touch startled him it paradoxically comforted him at the same time.

They walked together to John's house. When they entered the living room John instructed Steven to make himself comfortable, then went to the kitchen to make a fresh pot of coffee.

From the kitchen, John spoke. "So, what's got your knickers all in a twist?"

Steven lightly snickered. "Work. What else?"

"Oh, I see. Well, my friend, I've been where you are. I can relate. I heard the way you talked to you Keisha. That was a little frightening to hear. And the way you approached her made me wonder if you were going to make good on your threat."

"I don't even remember what I said, to be honest. I was so mad. It was like something overtook my mind and body. I hate that feeling."

John walked out of the kitchen with a plastic brown serving tray. It had a freshly–brewed pot of coffee, a sugar bowl, cream, and some coffee stirrers. John didn't put granulated sugar in his coffee; instead, he used sugar cubes.

He handed Steven a coffee cup. Steven added two sugar cubes to his coffee, but no cream. John added one sugar cube and a little cream.

John sat in his recliner and took a small sip of the hot, steamy coffee. Then he said, "Well, like I said, I can relate to your circumstances. I'm still working after forty–some years, and I can positively tell you every job has stress. It's how you handle it that matters. Believe me, nobody knows better as to what you're dealing with than me. I was constantly stressed out as a hospital administrator. After so many years, it became too stressful. I'm still on blood pressure meds. Not gonna lie.

The money was nice, but in hindsight the years shaved off my life from the stress and bullshit wasn't worth it."

"I want to quit my job. I hate it. Keisha gets me so worked up though. Why did she have to become a teacher? They don't make shit and they're treated like shit, too." He sipped his coffee and placed it on the table in front of him; it was still messy like before, but not to the extent it was the last time Steven was there.

John took another sip of his coffee, then reached to his left and set the cup down on the coffee table in front of Steven. He pulled the lever to extend the leg rest and placed his legs on it. "So, you're mad at Keisha for becoming a teacher? Why?"

"She's always talking with joy and exuberance about her job. It's work. It's not supposed to be fun. She's always talking about how she can't wait to try some new idea out in the classroom or she can't wait for her students to learn a new topic using a different teaching approach. It makes me sick the way teachers are treated— the abuse, the demands, the lack of respect, appreciation, and pay, the clueless and ass–backwards thinking of the administrators from the lowest echelons up. I don't see how she can be happy being a teacher."

"But she is, and that's all that should matter, my friend."

"It pisses me off. When we both decided to go to college we were in our late–twenties. It took us seven years to get our bachelor's degrees, attending college on a part–time basis. I switched my major so many times over the years that, finally, I settled on marketing because it was the fastest way to finish. Not Keisha though. She knew what she wanted and she did it."

John nodded and said, "So, basically you resent your wife because in your eyes she made all the right choices and you didn't."

"What do you mean?" Steven said, scratching his head.

"You're upset because she knew what she wanted to do, she did it, and now she's happy. You, however, are saying you had to settle for marketing, which to me implies you didn't really want to do that. If that's the case, what's stopping you from doing something else? You're still young. Make a change. Hell, even if you were my age, I'd still tell you to make a change."

Steven was silent for a moment. Then he sipped his coffee. After he set his cup down, he said, "Maybe. I don't know if it's feasible though. I wish she were as miserable as I, then I'd feel better. She's content with her job and it gets me so mad at her."

"My friend, your anger is misdirected. You're not mad at Keisha, you're mad at you. You're mad at yourself because you settled. Now you feel trapped, helpless, and alone. It doesn't have be like that forever though. Start making changes to steer your ship back on course, but don't alienate your family because you're mad at yourself for choices you made. I guarantee you it will make matters worse, and I don't think you want your kids resenting you."

Steven shook his head. "No, I don't. I love my kids. I would rather be dead than not be around my kids. My kids are everything to me. They're the reason I am still schlepping to this stressful job each day."

"And that's another act that makes you World's Greatest Dad. So, tell me, if not marketing, then what?"

Steven smiled, but then stopped. "It's stupid. You'd laugh."

"C'mon, now," John said, picking his coffee cup off the table. "Do you honestly believe I would do that? Let's hear your ambitions, your dreams."

"I've always wanted to be a composer. Write some string quartets, maybe a symphony. It's dumb, right?"

John coughed, then cleared his throat. "Not at all. I'd say do it. And, while you're working your way to becoming a commissioned composer, in the meantime composing will help relieve some of the stress you're carrying, speaking of which, I'd recommend you see a doctor and get on some anxiety meds to help take the edge off. I can tell by your eyes you're not sleeping well. Am I right?"

Steven nodded. "You're right. I lay in bed stressing about work and it leads me to not sleep. In turn, I become stressed about not sleeping."

"Ah, yes, a classical vicious cycle. The two feed each other. Take my advice. See a physician and get some meds. I can recommend my doctor to you, if you're interested."

"Thanks, John. Yes, I'm interested. I've never been good with taking pill though. I have a nasty gag reflex."

"You'll adapt, my friend."

Steven and John conversed for another hour. Then Steven returned home and profusely apologized to Keisha for his unacceptable, belligerent behavior. That night, they fell asleep in each other's arms.

Following John's advice, Steven did see a physician who prescribed Steven Lexapro. The instruction told him to take one pill daily. The dosage was ten milligrams.

At first, Steven had difficulty swallowing a single pill, even with the aid of water because of his gag reflex, but soon he adapted, just like John said he would.

Today was the first day of school for Jeffrey, Tiffany, and Brittany. Keisha woke up early to make breakfast and see them off to school. Sebastian picked up Jeffrey and Tiffany since Sebastian had his license and a car, which his parents— both medical doctors— purchased for him. Although his parents purchased the car for him as a gift, he made token payments on it over the summer, working at his uncle's sporting goods store.

Keisha and Scruffles were alone in the house. She sat at the dining room table preparing some creative ideas to teach about the Civil War, which would be the first unit she taught at Portage Middle School, an urban school on academic probation and in its last year to improve or the state would step in and clean house.

Her interview at Whitmond Middle School never happened. When she signed in and sat waiting for the principal, the secretary called to the principal and mumbled to him about Keisha's color. The principal stepped out of his office, took one look at her, then called the secretary back and told her to tell Keisha the position had already been filled.

Scruffles started barking at the stairwell. Keisha tried to calm him down from her seat, but it didn't work. She stood and walked over to the stairwell. Scruffles was at the foot of the stairs, barking and snarling. Then he lunged up four steps, and continued to snarl and bark. Keisha told him there wasn't anyone there. He finally whimpered down the stairs, jumped on the living room couch, and took a nap. Meanwhile, Keisha resumed her creative thinking to reach young, ignorant minds.

An hour passed, and her stomach started to rumble and grumble. She said in a soft voice, "I'm a little peckish." She went into the kitchen and made a grilled cheese, using Steven's recipe. It consisted of Texas Toast bread and the cheeses included cheddar and Parmesan.

After lunch, she took Scruffles to the backyard. After his lengthy squat, he chased critters.

Their backyard was expansive. It was roughly the size of a football field.

She walked around the house to the front to check the mail. While standing at the mailbox, she flipped through the different letters received, one of which was from her employer, School City of Portage.

As she walked up the driveway, John waved at her. He was sitting on his porch. He stepped off of it to say hello to her face to face.

Keisha asked, "What's with the binoculars? Some sweet, young thing across the street catching your fancy?"

John laughed. "Now that's funny. No, I'm a birder."

"A birder? What's that?"

"A person who watches birds. Being semi–retired leaves a lot time to try new things. Anyway, how has the house been since the blessing? Still good?"

Keisha scratched her leg, then said, "It's wonderful, John, and we can't thank you enough. Even after all the weeks that have went by, the house still feels warm and inviting. The air is lighter. Colors are sharper. Smells are stronger."

"Well, I'm happy to hear that. I'm a little nosy, but how did Brittany take to her first day in a new school?" John removed a handkerchief from his back pocket and wiped the sweat from his forehead.

"She did well. She's excited about her new school. I stayed in the class for an hour, then left. She's already met a friend. They seem to be feathers of the same bird."

"I'm glad to hear that. It was nice chatting with you. I'll see you around."

John returned to his porch and resumed his birdwatching. Keisha went inside and sat at the dining room table. Scruffles remain outside and played until he became tired. Then he laid in his doghouse after drinking some water.

Keisha stared at the letter with a smile on her face. She was excited to start her new teaching job in a couple of weeks from now. Her stomach had butterflies in it and she was on cloud nine.

The principal told her to watch the mail because the district would be sending her a welcome letter and information about new teacher orientation, a mandatory unpaid requirement for all first–year teachers to the building.

She flipped the letter over and tore a small portion of the envelope flap at the end. She ran her thumb through the inside of the envelope to open the envelope. When she did, the smell of the copy ink was palpable.

She removed the letter and unfolded it. Reading it aloud, she said, "Dear Mrs. Keisha Dobrowksi. We regret to inform you the Board was unable to approve your recommendation for employment due to an unexpected decrease in enrollment. Thank you for your interest in a position with the School City of Portage. Respectfully Mr. Terrance Watson, Director of Human Resources."

The teaching position she was eager and ambitious about was now gone. Her heart sank and she cried for several minutes. Her eyes hurt from so much crying. She picked up her cellphone a few times to call Steven, but always stopped herself. He was going to be beyond angry when he found out she no longer was employed.

She continued crying and inadvertently fell asleep at the dining room table. The pain was too much. A short nap helped a little, but when she awoke, her mind immediately raced, thinking about the financial danger they were headed for if she didn't find a job, and fast. She had one more paycheck on her last contract and then that was it.

She placed the letter in the envelope and tucked it away at the bottom of a box in the laundry room storage closet. She didn't want Steven to find it; instead, she wanted to break the news to him when she was good and ready.

In the meantime, she decided to go upstairs and take a hot bubble bath in the bathroom of her bedroom. She believed it wouldn't make her feel much better, but that didn't matter to her. If anything, it might help take her mind off being unemployed.

She ran hot— nearly scalding— water and dropped a pineapple–shaped bath bomb in the water. The mirror was slowly fogging up from condensation as steam rose from the bath water, and the bath water was changing color from the bath bomb.

After undressing, she stepped into the hot, soapy pineapple–scented water and slipped her body into the water. She closed her eyes and eventually fell asleep as the water continued to run. The overflow drain prevented the bathroom from flooding.

Twenty minutes later she woke up and shut the water off. Using the shirt she was wearing before she stepped into the tub, she wiped the screen of her cellphone down and started to look for a new position in another neighboring city, but that was fruitless. She started to look for other positions, such as retail or fast food. She'd do anything, as long as it meant she and Steven could provide adequately for their children.

She pulled the plug to drain the water in the tub and stood until the water was completely drained. She grabbed her pink housecoat, threw it around herself, and tied the belt.

Standing at the sink, Keisha wiped down the mirror with a hand towel that hung on a rung to her right. She wrapped a towel around her hair and stood looking at herself in the mirror.

A dime–sized black dot was in the middle of the mirror. She tried to rub it with her finger but it didn't budge. She moved her head closer and closer to it while rubbing trying to figure out what this black dot was and why it wasn't going away.

Within a second or two, the dot expanded and morphed into the man in the black suit, who lunged out of the mirror after Keisha with his hands in a strangling position and growling.

Startled and terrified, Keisha rapidly took several steps back, tripped backwards into the tub, and cracked the back of her skull on the bathroom wall. She was immediately rendered unconscious.

CHAPTER SEVENTEEN

The Hospital Visit

The doctors deduced Keisha suffered a concussion. She was in the hospital for two more days, during which time doctors ran additional tests.

Her symptoms included headaches, blurred vision, and nausea. She also had no recollection of the event that caused her fall nor any of the events that lead to the event causing her fall.

Steven rushed into her hospital room and said, "Is she okay?"

"Shhh, Dad," Tiffany whispered. "Mom is sleeping right now."

"How did this happen?" Steven asked. He gently sat down on her bed.

Jeffrey said, "Mom doesn't seem to remember, Dad."

"This is awful," Steven said as he sat next to Keisha on her hospital bed. "I hope this isn't a sign of something serious like a brain tumor or something like that."

Jeffrey shook his head. "Oh, I hope not, too, Dad."

"Tiffany and Jeffrey, thank you for your quick thinking. You called 911 right away. It must have been hard seeing mom incapacitated like that in the bathroom."

"It was, Dad. We were frightened. I think she tripped based on the way she was positioned in the tub," Tiffany said.

Steven loosened his tie and unbuttoned the button of his dress shirt. "How was she positioned?"

Tiffany opened a Reese's package and popped one of the four cups in her mouth. After chewing and swallowing, she said, "Well, let me describe it like this. Picture your bathroom, okay?"

"Right," he said as he leaned forward towards Tiffany.

"Well, to me it seems she fell backwards into the tub. Like she was standing in front of the sink and slipped on the wet floor."

Steven released a long sigh and stood. "Well, thank goodness she's here now. The doctors will take good care of her. What about Scruffles? Where is he?"

Jeffrey said, "I brought him inside, Dad. When he left, he was in the living room sound asleep on the couch. We filled his water and food dish up before Sebastian drove us here."

"Okay, good," Steven replied as he stood and stretched. "I'm going to use the bathroom and then hit the vending machines. Anybody want anything?"

Tiffany asked for some more Reese's, Jeffrey wanted Skittles, and Brittany wanted Starburst. He used the restroom down the hall and then went to the vending machines.

When he returned, there was an unexpected visitor in the room.

"Honky ass piece of shit is here," someone with an abrasive feminine voice said.

It was Denise, Keisha's mother and Steven's mother–in–law.

"Wow, Denise," Steven asked as he handed the children their treats. "You're really going to come at me like that right out of the gate? No hello. No how are you. No nice to see you. Is that why you don't like me? Because I'm white?"

"No," she said, with one hand on her hip. She continued to speak as she bobbled her head. "I don't like you because you're ugly. Speaking of which, while we're here in the hospital, why don't you get that thing soldered off your face?"

When it came to Steven, she was a never-empty pistol. And she never fired blanks. Even when she sometimes shot from the hip, she always hit her mark right between the eyes.

Steven swallowed hard and tried to mask how humiliated he felt. His face turned red and he felt flushed. "Nevermind my mole. I'm more worried about my wife."

She put her hand up as if to say ‘don't speak to me anymore’, and he didn't. He left the room and asked someone at the nurse's station if he could have a few more chairs brought into Keisha's room. This also provided him an opportunity to regain his composure. The remark about his mole was hurtful. His heart was made of candy–glass and her remark about his mole was the flying hammer that shattered it.

Steven sat in one of the extra chairs hospital staff brought into the room. Denise on and off mean–mugged Steven as if he were dressed in KKK garb holding a cross he was about to burn in her yard. The three children were doing their own things on their cellphones, with the exception of Brittany, who was reading parts of the newspaper Denise had bought on her way up to visit Keisha.

Keisha slept for two more hours before waking up. When she did, the first thing she asked for was a glass of water. Jeffrey sprang into action and filled a plastic cup with water for her.

Meanwhile, Steven rushed to her and gently kissed her.

Denise immediately came in for the kill. "Honky! Get your spotty lips off my daughter!" She tried to stand to go after him, but she couldn't get out the chair fast enough.

Keisha said, "Mom, don't start, please."

Denise snapped. "Fuck that cracker ass gargoyle–looking motherfucker! Wonder bread piece of shit."

"Mother!" Keisha shouted in a strained voice. "Please. I'm not feeling well. Put your feelings about my husband aside for right now. I'm not in the mood for this."

Denise turned her head and bobbled it a few seconds. "Fine." Then she walked out the hospital room while extending both middle fingers in Steven's direction.

When Denise was out of the room, Steven offered his opinion about Denise. "That woman embodies hate and evil. What a shame. We should all pray for that woman."

He was shocked at the level of contempt and disgust Denise had for him. All because he was white.

He never did anything to insult her or her family. He wished he could do something to change her views about him. His heart crumbled when she insulted him. After all these years, her hatred for him seemed to exponentially increase at a fast rate.

He sat on Keisha's bed and held her hand. "I can't wait until she leaves for good." He pulled out a twenty and a ten from his wallet and said, "Kids, please take this money and get yourselves some dinner from the hospital cafeteria." After they left the room, he asked Keisha, "How are you feeling, honey?"

"Still a little discombobulated," she said as she tried to sit up on her bed.

"I'm sorry, honey," he said, fighting back tears. "I know it might be too early to ask this, but do you know what happened?"

She didn't answer immediately. She tried to retrace her steps. Then she said, "I don't know what happened. I don't recall."

"That's okay. I understand. It's not your fault. What's the last thing you remember?"

"Watching birds with John," she said after some hesitation.

Keisha and Steven continued to talk about different topics. She talked about her excitement to start teaching. He talked about how stressful work was.

Keisha said, "I appreciate you letting Mom stay with us."

"What?" he shouted as he lunged off the bed.

"I told you about this. We discussed her staying with us. We need someone to be around to take Brittany to and from school. We both work. Mom agreed to pay some rent to help us with the added costs of her staying with us."

"Right. Our food bill has just quadrupled."

Keisha gasped. "Steven. That's a horrible thing to say about my mother. And, it's an exaggeration."

"Damn it, honey. I don't like the idea of her being around my— I mean, our— children. She'll corrupt their minds into hating me. She's always ragging on me and in the most hurtful ways, too. She makes fun of my mole and hair and other imperfections. She should examine herself in a full–body mirror and study what she sees closely. She's got the face of King Kong and the ass of a hippo."

Again, Keisha gasped. "Steven. What's gotten into you? I've never heard you speak that way about my mother. That was terrible what you just said."

"Well, I've had it with her. Year after year when she visits, I get the same hateful treatment. I need to start standing up to her. Otherwise, she's going to continue to do it."

Keisha shook her head and sighed. She adjusted the pillow behind her, then laid on it. "Please, babe, for me don't fight with her. She's had a rough life."

"Oh, I see. So, if you have a rough life you can treat people with hate and disdain."

"I didn't mean it quite like that. I don't want to argue right now. I'm too weak."

"Well, I think she can stay in a motel. I'm sure there are some truck drivers who could use a pair of warm lips. It would be good for her to put those double–breasted lips of hers to use for the good of someone else."

Keisha was about to cry. "Steven, please stop talking this way about my mother. It's hurtful and hateful. When you get home tonight please put some sheets and a blanket in her room. She's staying in the spare bedroom. That's why I bought the air mattress."

"Are you crazy? An air mattress can't support her gelatinous ass. The damn thing will explode on impact! And, we need to back it up a few steps. You and I never agreed your mother would stay in our house. We talked about the idea and I vehemently protested it. I don't even want her taking Brittany to and from school. She's not staying under my roof, I'll tell you that right now."

Keisha was angry but was too weak to express it. She released a growly exhale. Then she said, "Listen, sucker. That house isn't only yours. Now, we need someone to be at the house while you and I are at work. She's going to be a big help. She's going to cook meals, she's going to take Brittany to and from school, she's going to take care of Scruffles."

Steven started to pace back and forth in front of Keisha's bed. His face was beet red from anger. He pulled out his Lexapro bottle and popped two pills in his mouth and swallowed them without anything to help wash them down.

"Babe?" she said after he said nothing for a minute or so.

"I'm thinking," he said. The pacing continued with his arms behind his back.

"Okay."

Nearly five minutes passed. Steven stopped pacing and sat on Keisha's bed. "What about John?"

"What about him?"

"Why don't we see if he can take Brittany to and from school? That way, King Kong can go back to the jungle."

She pointed at him. "Steven! Stop talking that way about my mother. You don't have any idea how racist you sound right now. I'm about to slap the shine out of your teeth."

He had recently had a teeth whitening treatment done. His teeth were a radiant white now.

He slowly exhaled. "I'm sorry. I shouldn't stoop to your mother's level. Now, what do you think about John helping with Brittany?"

"No."

"Why?"

"Because he can't do it."

"What do you mean he can't do it? He's raised two children. He's fit to take care of children."

She shook her head and again released a growly sigh. "That's not what I mean. The man works. His schedule fluctuates."

"Well, yeah, but maybe we can ask him to adjust his schedule to accommodate us."

"You're an inconsiderate fool. We're not asking John. We already have someone who willingly offered to rearrange their life around to help us out. I'm sorry, Steven, but this matter is no longer open to debate. She's staying at our house and she's going to be a big asset to us."

Steven stood. When he did, his feet stomped the floor. "Excuse me? You don't get to close debates any more than I do. We don't resolve things like that. We go back and forth until a consensus is reached."

"I'm so tired, babe. Please let her stay. She'll take so much burden off of us. And, besides, it provides an opportunity for you and her to become closer."

"I don't want her close to me or the children. She's a dangerous influence on the children. She'll turn them against me. She's... not... staying... Got that?"

They discussed the matter further for another ten minutes. Finally, Steven relented and agreed Denise could stay at the house just until they found someone else to replace her.

Keisha agreed, knowing full well she would not allow anyone to replace her though.

When the children returned from the cafeteria with Denise, he kissed Keisha goodbye. Then the children did the same. It was time to leave.

As Steven and the children drove home, Denise called Tiffany and told her she would be at the house in an hour. She needed to stop at the store and pick up some odds and ends for herself. Fig Newtons, Oreo cookies, Ding Dongs, Pork Rinds and Slim Fast.

Steven shook his head in disbelief with his teeth clenched. He muttered, "I can't believe that ungodly woman is sleeping under my roof."

He used the time with all three children in the car to discuss his concerns about Denise. They reassured him that they weren't going to let her thoughts and actions change their perceptions of Steven. This brought a little comfort to him, but he was still angry and frustrated that Denise would be around constantly. Going to work was more attractive now than it ever was before.

When they pulled into the garage, all three children went upstairs. After a quick drink of cold coffee, Steven went to the living room to take Scruffles outside.

He stood at the entryway to the living room. "Scruffs? Come on. Let's go outside."

Normally Scruffles would jump off the couch and come right to Steven. But he didn't this time.

He said a little louder, "Scuffles, let's go outside. You need to go potty?"

Still, Scruffles did not jump off the couch and walk over to Steven.

Out of concern, Steven walked to the couch. Scruffles wasn't there.

"Scruffles?" he shouted. "Where are you, boy?"

Steven looked in all the downstairs rooms for Scruffles. He couldn't find his beloved new pet though.

Calling from the stairwell, Steven said, "Son? Where did you say you put Scruffles before you left?"

"He was in the living room, Dad."

"No, he's not. I can't find that furball anywhere. Check up there, please. I'll look around down here again."

Steven checked all the rooms again, but his search didn't find Scruffles. Once more, he checked the living room to see if Scruffles was on the longer couch— Scruffles favorite couch of the two in their living room— but he wasn't.

As he stood behind the couch, the sound of nails scratching glass caught his attention. The sound was coming from the sunroom. Using his hand, Steven pushed the vertical blinds to look into the sunroom.

"There you are, boy," Steven said, his tone joyful. His tone shifted from joyous to frustrated. "My, my, my. Damn it, Jeffrey. Poor dog."

When Steven opened the sunroom sliding door, Scruffles ran to his water and food dishes. He drank most of his water first, then started to eat.

Meanwhile, Steven summoned Jeffrey downstairs. He said, "Why did you put Scruffles in the sunroom? You told me he was in the living room when you left."

"Dad, he was in the living room. That's where I last saw him before I locked the house up."

Steven sarcastically shook his head. "I see. Scruffles opened the sliding door to the sunroom, let himself in, then closed the sliding door."

"Dad, I swear. He was asleep on the couch before I left."

"I got it. Scruffles wanted to darken his coat a little bit. He needed some sun. So, he let himself in the sunroom. It makes perfect sense. Stupid me for thinking you put him in the sunroom."

Jeffrey didn't like this new side of his dad. Short–fused, curt, rude, and sarcastic. He didn't want to be around him.

"Dad, I don't know—"

"Never mind. Go to bed. You have school in the morning."

"Fine. Is it okay if practice my cello for another thirty minutes though? I lost practice time today."

Steven nodded. His agitation over Jeffrey leaving Scruffles in the sunroom ended. He figured Jeffrey placed Scruffles in the sunroom when paramedics arrived to tend to Keisha. It was an honest mistake, assuming Jeffrey was the one who did it.

After Scruffles ate, Steven took him outside. He wanted to get upstairs and get some work done before morning. Just as Jeffrey lost time to practice his cello, Steven lost time to accomplish tasks for work.

As a courtesy to Keisha, he blew up the air mattress for Denise and covered it with two sheets and a blanket. Then he resumed work in his office.

When Denise went to bed and walked past his office, she muttered, "Jive ass honky." He ignored it. He decided to make the best of the situation and take the abuse. And, a small part of him believed Denise and him could become closer over time.

He worked at his iMac computer for an hour, then turned in for the night. He entered his bedroom and closed the door. He took a quick shower, brushed his teeth, and went to bed. He cuddled Keisha' pillow and laid down. The sound of his ceiling fan created a relaxing whooshing sound. He was asleep moments after his head hit the pillow.

A creaking sound woke him up though. Directly across from his bed was his bedroom door, and it was open. Standing in the doorway, was the man in the black suit. Steven couldn't move; he was paralyzed. While his arms were at his side, his legs were spread eagle. It was as if he was strapped to an execution table. The man in the black suit walked into the room and reached upwards towards the fan, which was not a fan anymore, but a circular saw blade. A handle morphed out of the casing that covered the mechanism that spun the fan blades. The man in the black suit grabbed the handle and positioned the saw so the blade was right–side up. Then he sawed into Steven, starting at his groin and working his way up to his head. When the saw blade reached his neck, pillow feathers flew into the air and scattered in all directions.

Steven screamed and sprang up from his waist in his bed. *It was only a dream. It was only an awful dream.*

He thrust himself backwards and when his head hit his pillow, several feathers shot up into the air and rained down on him.

CHAPTER EIGHTEEN

Keisha's Return

The doctors ascertained Keisha had no tumors or lesions on her brain. She was fully recovered and released from the hospital. Steven was elated that she had a clean bill of health, even though she still had no recollection of the fall.

On the drive home from the hospital, Keisha asked Steven if they could stop at Portage Middle School so she could pick up her keys to her classroom and view her room. She also wanted to get a sense of where things were in the building so she could help direct students on the first day of classes.

Steven agreed. While she went inside, he waited in the car and did whatever he could to pass the time away.

Waiting for Keisha proved to be a chore. Steven was running out things to do on his phone. He didn't care much for sitting in the car and regretted not tagging along with her. The boredom was causing his eyes to become heavy. He needed to get out the car and do something other than sit. He decided to go into the school and look for her. It would also provide him another opportunity to be supportive of her career. At least it was a job that brought in enough additional income to cover the household expenses.

The school was not well–maintained. The outside had all sorts of vegetation growing on the faces of the building. Large fissures ran up and down the front of the building. This school needed to be raised and rebuilt.

The inside wasn't much better. The hallways were carpeted with no padding underneath. The scent of musty linens permeated the building. The walls needed a fresh coat of paint. This building had seen better days.

Steven stepped into the main office. Sitting at the front desk was an elderly woman. She said, "Hello. How may I help you, sir?"

She looks so much like my mother. "I'm looking for my wife. Her name is Keisha."

"Oh, right," the lady said. "She went with the principal to her classroom. The room number is...135."

"Thanks," he said, and then turned to exit the main office door.

"Excuse me, sir, but you'll need a visitor's pass. Just wait a moment and I'll write one out for you. Sign in." She tossed a clipboard onto the counter and slammed a pen down on top of it.

"Fuck this school," he muttered as he turned around. He signed the discolored sign–in sheet. *Old, pushy bitch. She sounds like my mother, too.*

"What did you say?"

"Love this school, is what I said. It has a very 'Tales from the Crypt' vibe to it, don't you think?"

She gave him a look of contempt as she handed him the visitor's pass. "You need to wear this at all times in the building. When you finish doing what you need to do, you return here to sign out. Got it?"

He snatched the visitor's pass out of her prune–skinned hand without responding.

"That's okay, son. I forgive you," she said. Then she mumbled, "Killer."

He walked down a long, narrow hallway, passing the library along the way. Only a few lights within it were on, which gave the library a dungeon–like look.

After passing the library, he stopped at a corner where a school map was located. He studied it to locate what twists and turns he would need to take.

The next hallway he turned into had every third light illuminated along its stretch of ceiling. All the classroom doors were closed except one. He walked down the hall, stopping at a few classrooms here and there to take a peek inside of them.

When he passed the classroom door that was open, a voice from within said, "Excuse me, come back."

Steven turned around and peeked his head in the classroom. Sitting at the desk was a young woman in her mid–twenties with golden hair and ruby red lips. She was wearing a summer dress that clearly accentuated her upper womanly features. She was more stacked than a double–decker bus.

He was becoming sexually aroused.

Think cold shower. Cold shower. Cold shower. Fuck! Who am I kidding! That never worked before!

She stood up and slowly walked towards Steven, looking in his eyes. Her heels produced a beautiful strident sound on the tile floor. *Click... clack... click... clack...*

"Can I help you with something?" he asked, bewildered.

No response. She continued walking towards him. *Click... clack... click... clack...*

"What is it?"

No response. Her eyes were firmly locked with his.

Does this bitch ever blink? "You're not much of a talker, are you?" Then he lightly chucked at his own remark.

No response.

Now she was standing in front of Steven. She leaned forward a little. He was standing with his arms relaxed at his sides. His hands desperately wanted to reach out and grope her ample–sized breasts. He lightly clenched both hands into a fist to harness his primal instincts from running loose like a wild dog.

She grabbed both his arms. The grip was firm. "Kill 'em, Steven," she whispered, in a deep growly inhuman voice. "Kill them slowly. Either you kill them or I'll do it myself, and then I'll kill you."

This wasn't the first time he heard this voice. Two days ago, he was in the shower and heard it, also. The voice told him to bash his family's skulls in with a meat tenderizer then decapitate them with a meat cleaver.

He tried to pull away, but her bear–like grip tightened. His bones slightly cracked. "Do it," she said. "Don't you wanna please me? Kill those fuckers."

She lifted Steven up and turned him in the direction of the door. He was airborne. Out the door and against the hallway wall. When he struck the wall, a large imprint formed from the impact.

He sat up, placing his back against the concrete wall. She stood in her classroom staring at him momentarily, then the classroom door slammed on its own. The instant the classroom door slammed, the lights in her classroom turned off and she was nowhere to be seen.

Now someone was calling Steven's name.

"What?" he said, startled and dazed.

"You fell asleep, honey," Keisha said.

It was nothing but a dream? Oh, thank Go— goodness.

He rubbed in the corners of his eyes, removing the small amount of rheum within them. The pain in his back was intense and his arms were sore.

Keisha turned to him and spoke. "Babe, I have some bad news."

"Oh, really?" he asked, concerned. "What?"

She pursed her lips but said nothing. Her palms began to sweat. Her heart rapidly palpitated.

"I lost my job," she said, then sobbed. She wrapped her arms around Steven.

He didn't reciprocate though. He delicately pushed her away. "What? I think I didn't hear you correctly. I'm a little out of sorts at the moment. I thought you said you lost your job."

"I did say that. I was involuntarily terminated. Waves of parents withdrew their children from the district recently and unexpectedly. I'll find— "

He pounded a fist on the dashboard. "What the fuck did you do to get fired before your first day of work?"

She screamed. "I'm sorry. It wasn't my fault."

"The fuck it wasn't your fault. You've been wanting to push out of that house since we moved in it."

"It wasn't my fault. I swear. The district had to RIF. Enrollment nosedived. Teaching positions had to be cut, and not just mine. Last one in, first one out."

The inhuman voice crept in again. *(Just kill her. Kill the entire lot of them. Problems solved.)*

He pounded his fist several times on the dashboard. "So now what? What the fuck happens now? We can't survive on my salary alone."

"I'll find another job. Even if it means donating blood or a kidney."

He stepped outside of the car and with a ferocious thrust slammed the car door. The window cracked. He unscrewed the lid off his Lexapro bottle and tapped it against his palm. Three pills down the hatch. The fire in his belly extinguished almost instantly. It was likely more psychological than physiological.

He took a few steps away from the car. His mouth and throat were parched. He took a few deep breaths. The inhuman voice returned. *(Kill her. Do it! Do it now! Or I'll kill you!)*

Leave me the fuck alone! I won't do it!

He strode to the passenger side door and grabbed Keisha by the arm, pulling her out of the car. He pushed the power lock button and slammed the door closed. No cracked window this time.

As he walked to the driver's side door, he confessed his mental state. "I'm dangerous right now. You shouldn't be around me."

He unlocked his side of the door with the key. He sat inside and closed the door. He was terrified of the thoughts creeping into his head. He hoped the Lexapro would take its full effect soon.

She ran to the driver's side door and pounded on the window. She said, "Babe, don't do this. Wait."

He started the car and thrust the gear shifter into drive. The inhumane voice in his head returned with another threatening directive. *(Run the bitch over! Do it!)*

SHUT THE FUCK UP! He pounded himself in the head several times with closed palm–up fists. His second knuckle joints bled. He placed his head in the steering wheel and cried. *What's happening to me?*

With caution, Keisha opened the driver's side door (he forgot to lock it), an inch at a time. She put her arms around him and said, "Everything is going to be okay."

"I'm sorry," he said. "I don't know why I snapped like that. My emotions got away from me." With a trembling hand, he put the car in park and turned it off, leaving the keys in the ignition. His forehead glistened with sweat. "You better drive."

And she did. The drive home was quiet. Steven was in a quasi-catatonic state from the three Lexapro he took before they left the middle school parking lot and the additional two he took during the drive home. The additional two Lexapro he took were from a breath mints tin.

Once the car was parked in the garage, Keisha woke Steven up. She said, "Babe, I promise you I'll find another job. I don't care what it is. I'll fix this."

"It's okay, honey. And, hey! There is a silver lining to all this. I get to throw your mother out of the house now."

"Excuse me? No, I don't think so."

"Oh, but I do," he said, then flashed a wicked smile. "We don't need the likes of her anymore, my love. With you being out of work, you can take Brittany to and from school."

"Listen, babe. She's going to be a source of income for us. I don't want her to leave. And, besides, I may have a job within a week or two. Then we'll be screwed without her there."

"Why? How? Huh?! I want her gone!" he said as he pounded the dashboard with his fist.

She placed a hand on his shoulder, but he pulled away. "Calm yourself, babe. You're getting all worked up for nothing."

"Nothing? You think the way your mother treats me is nothing? I'm telling you I'm going to end up hurting her and I don't want that to happen, because if it does I go to jail. And if I go to jail, I lose my job. I lose my job, I lose this house. I lose this house, I'll kill myself."

Keisha gasped. "You're scaring me. You need to go upstairs and take a nap because you are not in your right mind." She exited the car and headed towards the garage door that led into the laundry room. Steven exited and followed her.

When they entered the kitchen, Denise was cooking some lunch for everyone. She waddled as fast as she could to her daughter and hugged her. She said, "I'm so glad you're home, darlin'."

Steven walked over to the stove to see what was cooking. There were two saucepans on the stove. One had boiling water in it with elbow macaroni in it; the other had a molten cheese. A plate of freshly–cooked bacon sat on the counter next to the stove. The grease on it was still sizzling.

"Smells good, Mom," Steven said, stirring the cheese sauce with the wooden spoon that rested on top of the saucepan lid. "Jeffrey can't eat this stuff though. He's a vegan."

"Fuck you, cream cheese," Denise snarled back.

The warm embrace turned frigid. "Alright, Mom," Keisha said as she pulled away from her mother. "We need to talk about some things."

"Sure, darlin'," Denise said. "Anything you want."

Steven walked upstairs to rest. Keisha and Denise remained in the kitchen. Keisha took a seat on one of the stools at the bar counter while Denise stirred the cheese sauce.

"First, I'm delighted you're here, Mom. It means so much to me."

"No problem, darlin'. It's gonna be mighty nice bein' around here. And this house is just amazin'. Though I heard some scratchin' in the middle of the night. Maybe you gots rodents or somethin'," She cringed a little.

Keisha stood and walked to a cabinet and pulled out a glass. As she walked to the fridge, she spoke. "I'll have to look into that. Anyway, Mom, I'd like you to ease up a little on Steven. Would you, please?" She placed the pitcher of tea back in the fridge.

Denise shook her head as she placed the lid back on the saucepan containing cheese. "I don't know if I can, darlin'." While stirring the macaroni, she said, "I'm still sore you married a white dude. Your biggest mistake, child."

"Why, Mom? He's made me so happy and has always done right by me and the children. That's what should count. And after all these years, you're still upset he's white?"

"That's right."

"So, do you detest your grandkids then? You know they're part white. Have you thought of that?"

"Yes, darlin', I have, and that's not their fault. They had no control over you and pasty-face slappin' skins."

After Keisha gasped, she responded. "Mother. I can't believe those words left your mouth. I'm shocked. Would you please kick it down a few notches with Steven. For me? Please. If we're all living under the same roof, we need to all make an effort to get along. Please."

Denise sighed. "I will try, but it's not going to be easy. It might take me a few days to adjust. By the way, I know I've said this before but I feel the urge to say it again. I hope and pray that when you and flour face have relations, you use protection. The thought of you bearing another zebra child makes me sick to my stomach."

And that's exactly why Keisha hadn't told Denise she was pregnant yet. She also instructed the kids to not say a word about the pregnancy either.

"Mom, please. Stop with the racist name calling."

"Alright, child. I'm sorry. Anyways, now that we're alone, I have something important I need to tell you before I forget. As I enter my declining years, I've started to make arrangements for myself. I've decided to make you the executor of my will and the beneficiary of two of three life insurance policies since your daddy died four years ago and can no longer collect on them. He was the original beneficiary."

In a flash, several horrific memories of her father flooded her mind. She regrouped. "Mom, this is morbid to discuss."

"It's not morbid, child. It's life. We live and we die. I think you should know what my wishes are so they aren't sprung on you when you're distraught over my demise. And something else just sprang into my brain. How is talking about death morbid when you and Paleface and the Oreo cookie children watch all those ghost shows? Or when you and vanilla–icing–skinned honky would go to cemeteries and try and communicate with the dead. Now that's morbid, child."

"Okay, Mom. Thank you. I get it. I'll be sure to handle your affairs as you wish when that time comes but it's not going to be for a long time."

"I hope so, darlin'" She waddled around the counter and hugged Keisha again. "I love you so much. Are you hungry?"

"Yes. Very," Keisha said.

"Well, not to worry. We'll squash that appetite fast, quick, and in a rushed hurry." She walked over to the stove as Scruffles barked. "Lord, child, what's that dog barkin' at now? That's the third time already today."

"He probably sees someone walking down the street with their dog. I'll check."

But Scruffles wasn't barking at someone outside. He was at the foot of the stairs barking.

"Come on, Scruffles," Keisha said. "Let's go outside." She gently pulled him from the collar and he followed her lead. After she put Scruffles outside she returned to the kitchen.

Denise was plating her a big helping of bacon macaroni and cheese. She added a dollop of sour cream on top of the pile. She turned around to place the plate in front of Keisha, but she dropped the plate. "Who is that?" she screamed as she pointed to the living room.

Keisha turned around and saw no one. "Who is who, Mom?"

"There was a man wearing black who walked into the living room."

"What?" Keisha leapt off the stool and walked into the living room. Nobody was there though. She returned to the kitchen. Denise had already fixed Keisha a new plate. It was resting on the counter in front of the stool on which she was sitting. She sat on the stool. "I didn't see anyone, Mom."

Steven stormed down the stairs and entered the kitchen. "Is everything okay? I heard glass shatter."

"Yeah, babe," Keisha responded. "Everything is fine. Just a little accident. Right, Mom?"

At this point, Denise was cleaning the macaroni mess. "Yeah, sorry, darlin'. Maybe I need new glasses. These ones are messin' with my mind."

"That's good. I'm relieved everyone and everything is fine," Steven said. He stepped into the garage for a few minutes then returned to the kitchen. "May I have some of your macaroni, Mom," he asked Denise.

Denise rolled her eyes. She was about to make another snide remark, but Keisha gave her a look that stopped her. Denise took a breath. "Sure, Steven. Have a seat. I'll fix you a plate."

"No, Mom," Steven said. "You've been working hard around here for the past several days, I'll get it. I'll fix you a plate, also. Why don't you two go into the dining room? We can sit, eat, and a have a chat."

And they did. Steven and Denise made a sincere effort to become friends. Keisha was pleased.

CHAPTER NINETEEN
A Terrifying Encounter

Two weeks passed since Denise moved into the house. Steven and her were getting along better than anyone expected, though occasionally she slipped and called Steven a racist name. Ironically, it didn't bother Steven when she did it since it was so infrequent, and when it did happen, she would immediately apologize and both would relish in a laugh. In a strange way, he liked it when she slipped once in a while.

Steven and Denise sat in the living room most evenings and chatted for hours. They discovered they had a lot more in common than they thought.

Much to Keisha's surprise, Steven admitted to her that it was a joy to have Denise living in the house, and she was a tremendous help, just as Keisha told him she would be. Denise prepared meals, she cleaned the house, and she drove Brittany to and from school. Financially, she provided money to Steven to help pay for bills, though even with her contributions money was still tight.

Denise was appalled at how racist the community was. Over dinner one evening, she told the family a story wherein, as she walked out of the house to go to the store, Terry called her a tree–swinging ape. He told her she needs to return to the jungle. When at the supermarket, the customers gawked at her like she was a museum exhibit. Finally, the cashier rudely said to her, if she returned to the store, to pick a different cashier to check her out. Steven asked Denise if she reported the cashier to management and she said yes. Management assured Denise they'd deal with the situation. Steven asked her if she intended to sue and Denise said she didn't. It was already forgiven and forgotten. She did leave a nasty review on Yelp though.

In terms of the house, Denise noticed strange things happening, but she always managed to attach a logical explanation to the events. One example was knocks in the middle of the night, which sometimes woke her up. She thought it was one of the children kicking their wall as they tossed and turned in bed. A few times she thought she saw shadows in the corner of her eye, but she attributed this to her glaucoma. And, most recently, she was poked in the back while walking back to her room from the bathroom, but nobody was around her when this happened. She rationalized this as an insect crashing into her back. She did have an experience that she was unable to explain using logical means, and she intended to tell Keisha about this as soon as she had the chance.

The three children assimilated well in their new schools. Most students didn't care they were of mixed race, but there were a few who did. The children did the best they could to ignore those people though.

Tiffany recommended she and Sebastian hang out together away from her house. She was afraid of what Denise would think when she met Sebastian and saw he was white. Tiffany wanted to do nothing that would jeopardize her friendship with Sebastian. After school each day, Sebastian and Tiffany drove to the local library where they completed their homework and studied. This impacted Tiffany's exercise regimen, but she didn't care. She preferred Sebastian's company over exercising, and he helped her develop better study skills.

Because Keisha was still out of work, Jeffrey wasn't able to start his cello lessons with the teacher he wanted yet. In the meantime, he made arrangements with his former cello teacher in North Haven to have lessons over Skype. Eventually, however, Jeffrey wanted to take lessons with the retired virtuoso, even if only for a year or two.

One afternoon, Keisha and Denise sat in the living room, drinking tea and talking about various topics. Keisha was using a laptop to fill out job applications while Denise read the newspaper.

"Darlin', I need to talk to you about something," Denise said. "I heard these awful noises coming from the attic a few nights ago and then again last night when I stepped out to empty my colon. Pardon my crassness."

"Noises? What sort of noises?" Keisha asked.

"I heard a few men arguing. Then it sounded like one of them was dying— murdered by the other two men. I didn't stick around though. I went straight to my bedroom and said a prayer for this family. Actually, I pray a lot when I'm in this house. I think your house has unrested spirits in it."

"Oh, Mom, it's probably a residual haunting. I think Tiffany heard that same thing several weeks back. We don't have any unrested spirits in this house."

She curled her lip. "Don't be usin' all sorts of fancy ghost terms with me. What's that anyways?"

"A residual haunting is one in which a past event repeats. Those types of hauntings are the most common and the least to worry about."

"I beg to differ, darlin'. I sense somethin' sinister lurking around the house. Sometimes, when I'm alone, I feels like somethin' is watching me from behind. And no matter how I turns my body to see what it is, it shifts with me to prevent me from doing so. This house needs some Jesus."

Keisha shook her head. After a few keystrokes on her laptop, she said without taking her eyes off the screen, "You're paranoid. That's all. I thought by now you would have adjusted to the house."

"Excuse me, darlin'. I have adjusted. Anyways, I think we should bless the house again. I know the neighbor came in here and played priest wearing a stole and all, but I strongly feel you should have a real priest go over your neighbor's shoddy work. Just to be on the safe side. By the way, on that note, you need to get your behind back in church."

"Mom, I don't want to go to church," Keisha said as she added some sugar to her tea. "I have too much to worry about right now. Once I secure a job, maybe I'll start attending church again. I've applied to all sorts of openings within Whitmond, but I've gotten no calls back yet. I feel like I've been blacklisted."

"Oooh, darlin', I hate that term. Blacklisted. It's sounds so racist to my ears." She shuddered her body. "And what do you mean you don't wanna go to church? That's the devil speakin' through you, child. I think once you start attendin' church again the good Lord will make money rain upon you. You'll receive blessin' after blessin'."

"I'm still grieving over the loss of Granana. It wasn't her time to go."

"Well, I knew Granana well myself, and she would tear up one side of you and then down the other if she heard the way you're talking right now about church. Now you know god damn well she would want your baboon ass to be in a pew shouting praises to the Lord. So what churches are around here? And how do you know it wasn't her time to go? You don't make that call."

Keisha's frustration with her mother was mounting. She tried to contain it. "I have a church in mind already, Mom. I don't feel like going at this time though. I have too many other things pressing on my mind."

Denise blew across the top of her cup, then took a sip of tea. After placing her cup down, she responded. "Darlin', please. Let's go to church together. You'll feel better once you do. It'll give us somethin' to do. The children need to come with, also. I know Steven is still in his I–no–longer–believe phase, but I think he'll snap out of that soon."

"I'll think about it."

Denise's face lit up with excitement. "Well, that's a start. In the meantime, we need to get a priest in this house and force the evil that's coming out of its dormant state out of here. What church were you thinking of attending?"

Keisha did a few neck rolls to release some building tension. "St. Matthews on Columbus. Father Thompson is the priest."

"Perfect. Get him on the phone and schedule a blessin' with him."

"I don't know if he'll come, Mom. We had a blessing scheduled with him, but Steven and I forgot about it. When he came to the house, nobody was home. Father Thompson tried calling us, but we were so ashamed we couldn't answer the calls."

Denise gasped in shock. "How could you do that to a priest, darlin'? No wonder this house has evil lurkin' about. You snubbed the priest. How could you forget something as important as a house blessin' by a member of the clergy?"

Keisha sighed. "Everyone in the house did. It was as if that entry in our brains had been deleted. It wasn't until Father Thompson called we remembered."

"He'll still bless the house. Please, darlin'. Call him."

"Fine. I'll call him, Mom."

"That's wonderful, darlin'. Would you like some more tea?"

"Yeah, Mom, but I'll get it. I need to stretch anyway. I'll also check on the lasagna while I'm in the kitchen." She stood and picked up the coffee mugs.

Truthfully, the main reason she wanted to get the coffee was because she wanted a little breather from her mom. Keisha felt she was being nagged and harassed.

As Denise sat in the living room, the reflection of the man in the black suit appeared on the T.V. She turned around, but he was gone. She rubbed the back of her neck for several seconds.

Keisha walked into the living room with two cups of steaming coffee. "What's wrong, Mom?" Keisha asked as she placed the cups of coffee on the glass table in front of the couches.

"My neck is burnin'," she replied. "It burns bad."

"Let me see. Oh, my! Mom! You have two scratches on the back of your neck. I'll get you some antiseptic and gauze."

"Thank you, darlin'." She prayed as Keisha stepped out of the room. *I knew there was something angry here.*

When Keisha returned, she treated her mother's wound. The two scratches were bleeding a little.

"Say, darlin'. I think I should tell you, I saw in the reflection of the T.V. a man in a black suit. Does that ring any bells? Was that the same spirit living in the house?"

"As a matter of fact, yes. You saw him?"

"I did, but only for a second or two. When I turned around, he was gone."

"Thank you. I'm going to call Father Thompson right now. You're right. This house needs to be properly blessed." She pulled out her cellphone and searched in her contacts for Father Thompson.

"That's good to hear."

Keisha walked towards the kitchen to speak to Father Thompson. Denise picked up her cup of tea and brought it to her lips. Just before her lips touched the cup, it shattered, raining tea and pieces of glass onto her dress. She was left holding only the cup handle. The scalding hot tea burned her legs. She hollered in pain.

"Mom! Mom! Are you alright?" Keisha ran to her.

"I'll be okay," she said, crying. "Please get me a towel."

Keisha dropped her cellphone to the floor and rushed to the laundry to get a towel. She was furious the spirit was back. She wondered if the spirit would ever leave. If Father Thompson couldn't clear the house of the spirit, the only option would be to surrender the house to it and move somewhere else.

The towel was one from a laundry basket of dirty clothes. Keisha handed it to her mother. Denise used it to pat dry her dress where the coffee spilled. She also rubbed the carpet to try and minimize the stain.

Keisha asked, "Are you better? What do you need? Anything?"

"I'm better now. I'm gonna take myself upstairs and soak in some cool bath water. You call Father Thompson and tell him to get his cute little holy heinie here to rid this house of the evil. Somethin' tells me this is only the beginnin' of what's to come."

Keisha called Father Thompson and profusely apologized for not being present when he came over to bless the house and for ignoring his calls, and he forgave her. He explained it's quite possible the entity in the house manipulated everyone's mind as a way to prevent itself from being removed. Unfortunately, he was once again out of town, delivering a presentation as a guest lecturer at a university, and he would not be returning for two weeks. A date for him to bless the home was scheduled. In the meantime, he suggested the family once again do a blessing on their own.

Father Thompson also assured her the spirit inside the house was unlikely to be anything demonic in nature. He explained to her demons are rare and more likely than not it was an angry spirit competing for territory.

Lastly, Father Thompson told her, when the spirit begins manipulating the environment, to assertively confront it. Ignoring or running away from the spirit's rants only strengthens its power. The spirit needed to know everyone in the house was not going to be bullied into submission by the spirit.

After ending the call with Father Thompson, she called Steven, who was at work. She said, "The man in the black suit is back. Mom was scalded with hot tea minutes ago. He's back and he's angry."

"Excuse me? What?" Steven replied, confused.

"I guess our blessing of the home wasn't as effective as we thought. Father Thompson said to bless the house once more. I scheduled a date for him to perform a blessing himself. He's out of town right now delivering a lecture at a bible college."

"Alright. I'll ask John to assist again. I want that damn spirit out of our house once and for all. He's going to foil my plans."

Keisha didn't understand what Steven meant by his remark 'foil my plans,' but she didn't give that much thought. She did remind him of something. She said, "I'm glad you feel that way, because if we can't force it out, we'll have to leave the house."

"Steven?" she said when he didn't answer within a few seconds.

"Yeah. I'm still here."

"What's wrong?"

"Nothing. I don't want to think about leaving the house. I want to focus on forcing the spirit out. That's our house and the thought of having to walk away from it angers me to my core."

"I know, babe," she said as she pat–dried the stain on the carpet.

"We're going to beat it. Please call the electricians and reschedule the installation of the new chandelier. There's no point in having them install it yet. Remember the last time we blessed the house? Our chandelier was destroyed."

"I do. I'll call them right away."

They said goodbye to each other. She immediately called the Efficient Electricians— the company through which Steven and Keisha contracted with for their new chandelier and the installation. Steven called John and explained to him what happened. John couldn't talk long because he was at work, but he agreed to do another blessing, and this time they would do a more powerful one.

As Keisha talked with a representative at Efficient Electricians, the family picture slid off the mantel and fell onto the hearth and the crucifix fell to the floor. The viscous substance bled from the orifice where the nail was in down the wall.

The laundry room door slammed shut, opened, then slammed shut a few times. Simultaneously, cabinet door and kitchen drawers opened and slammed shut.

"Stop! Stop! Stop! I command you to stop!"

And the activity subsided, eventually dying to a stop.

The following day— a Saturday— the house was blessed with John leading it. Denise was impressed at how thorough John was, and felt a little bad for referring to his previous work as shoddy. They blessed every single room in the house.

The blessing was lengthy and intense, and everyone had a more participatory role in terms of speaking. For example, when the family blessed the sitting room, John said, "See what a good and joyous thing it is," then everyone else said, "For everyone to live together as one." After that, John said, "Lord God Almighty, we implore you to bless this room so that all who live together in this house are united in true fellowship on earth, they may hereafter be united with all your saints in heaven. Through Jesus Christ our Lord," then everyone else said, "Amen. Glory be to God."

Every room in the house was blessed three consecutive times using different smudge sticks. Everyone felt confident the blessing this time was foolproof.

After the blessing, Steven and John went over to John's. They sat on his porch and drank some wine in a celebratory fashion. As Steven walked with John to his house, he asked "John, I hope you don't take offense to this question, but why don't you have a garage? Did it burn down or something?"

John stopped in his tracks and looked at Steven. "Perceptive of you to ask. I had my garage demolished." John started walking, which signaled to Steven to do the same.

"Why?"

Since John had grown admiration for Steven over the months, he confided in him. "I don't like discussing this, but you've become my best friend, so I'll tell you. My son committed suicide in the garage. He hanged himself."

(*Good! I hope that fucker suffered a slow, agonizing death! Ask Old Man Johnny if he has any photos of the hanging in his scrapbooks he can share with you!)*

SHUT UP! FUCK OFF! Leave me alone! "I'm sorry to hear that," Steven said. "May I ask what possessed him to do that?" Steven pulled out an Altoids tin containing Lexapro and popped three of them in his mouth. *I need to find a back-alley pharmacist to get more Lexapro.*

It took John a few minutes to decide whether or not to tell Steven the circumstances surrounding his son's death. "My son became involved with a cult," he said. "Devil worshippers. Satanists. Need I say more, my friend?"

The pain on John's face tore through Steven's heart. A part of Steven regretted asking John about his son's death. Based on John's last remark, it seemed he didn't want to discuss his son's death any further. Ironically, after John had a few swigs of wine, he told Steven in detail about the events leading up to his son's suicide.

CHAPTER TWENTY

Denise's Birthday Surprise

Two weeks passed since John and the family blessed the house. Initially, there was no activity, but recently the chandelier lightly swung at random times throughout the day. The family picture on the mantel would be oriented askew, but it hadn't been knocked off the mantel.

The entire family— except Steven— was seated at the dining room table. Steven prepared dinner for the family.

"Happy Birthday, Mom!" Steven said as he entered the dining room with a long, rectangular birthday cake.

Denise was taken by surprise. The entire day she was led to believe everyone forgot it was her birthday, but that was all part of Steven's plan.

"Oh my!" Denise shouted with joy "You all fooled me good! That was a cruel joke to play on an old woman, but I have to give you credit. You all were terrific actors. I sensed there was somethin' going on behind the scenes."

The top of the cake read *Happy Birthday, Grams, And Many More to Come.* There weren't any candles in the cake yet. Dinner was to be eaten first, then the cake would have the candle lit and the family would sing Happy Birthday to her.

Steven prepared a special meal on account of Denise's birthday. The special meal consisted of Denise's favorite foods. Dinner consisted of pot roast, homemade mashed potatoes, corn on the cob, and Hawaiian rolls.

After the family dinner but before the cake was cut, Denise received presents from the family. Steven and Keisha gave her a one hundred dollar gift certificate for a spa day. The gift they gave her costed them no money since Steven received it from one of his clients as a thank you to him from work. Jeffrey composed his first piece for cello: a sonata for solo cello. He dedicated it and performed it for her and the family. Her heart was forever touched. Tiffany made Denise a vase in an art course she was enrolled in at school and Brittany constructed a wooden wagon with Steven's supervision and guidance for her, which Denise said she would place in her living room when she got her next apartment. For now, Denise insisted the wagon be placed on the front porch as decoration.

"Alright, y'all," Denise said. "From the bottom of my heart, thank you for the lovely gifts. Shall we have some cake now?"

"Indeed. But before that, there's one more thing for you," Steven confessed. "I hope you like it. I'll be right back." He left the room and returned with a gift–wrapped box. "This is a gift from all of us."

"Oh, you guys. You've given me more than I could even ask or hope for," Denise said as she slowly ripped off the solid red gift wrap. She opened the box and pulled out a plate. "Mercy, this is beautiful. It's glorious."

The plate was solid black with *Grams* written in large gold cursive lettering in the center of it. Underneath *Grams* was *We Love You.* Around the circumference of the plate were the names of everyone in the Dobrowksi household: Steven, Keisha, Jeffrey, Tiffany, Brittany, and Mr. Quacks.

Denise broke down in tears. She was rendered speechless. The plate touched her heart in more than one way. She said, "This plate isn't meant to be eaten off of. I'll be placin' it on my nightstand, just like Brittany did with Granana's plate."

"What?" Steven snapped. "You still have Granana's plate?"

"Yeah, Daddy," Brittany replied with a trembling lip. "Is that wrong?"

"Did Daddy say you could take the plate to your room?" he asked.

"No, Daddy. I'm sorry," Brittany said.

"Go get the plate," he demanded.

Keisha intervened. "Babe, let her keep the plate. All this time she's had it and you never said anything. You've been in her room several times to say hi and check on her and you never noticed the plate resting against her lamp?"

"No, I didn't. I've been too tired to notice," he said, popping two Lexapro in his mouth.

Keisha wiped Brittany's tears with a napkin. "It's okay, baby doll."

Several seconds passed. Brittany finally mustered the courage to ask her dad for his approval. "So, Daddy, may I keep the plate, please? I'm taking good care of it," Brittany asked.

Steven's eyebrows furrowed for a few moments, then relaxed. "Yes. Fine. I'll go get the cake. Mom, may I have your plate to place your cake on, please?"

"Oh, no, Steven. This plate is too special to be eating off of. Uh-uh. I'll have my cake on a regular plate like everyone else," Denise said.

Steven clenched and released his fists a few times. "Very well. It is, after all, your plate. Who am I to tell you what to do with it?"

Denise smiled. "It's okay. You had the best intentions. I just think this plate is too beautiful a work of art to eat off of. Also, I don't want any of the beautiful writin' on it to get damaged from food being plopped all over it and forks and spoons scrapin' across it."

(You fuck up! You can't do anything right!)

Leave me alone! Piss off! God fucking damn you!

(That's right, Steve-O! You get angry! That's exactly how I want you!)

"I'll be right back." Steven went to the kitchen to bring the cake into the dining room. He decided to order another personalized plate for Grams. One for her to have on her nightstand; the other for eating meals. He wanted her to feel extra special while sharing meals with the family.

When Steven entered the dining room with the cake, he brought five small red and orange plates and one larger red one. He lit the candle, which was in the shape of Denise's age: 74.

"Make a wish and blow out the candle, Mom," Keisha said.

And Denise did. Then she sliced her piece and Steven served it on the larger red plate. Before she ate though, he asked her if she wanted some chocolate sprinkles on top of it, and she did.

Denise cut into her slice and had a bite of cake. "Oh, this is wonderful. My favorite kind of cake. Banana with vanilla frosting."

(What do you know! The bitch actually likes something white, Steven!)

Will you shut the fuck up! I'm tired of you! Steven said, "Enjoy it, Mom. We all love you."

For the next hour, the family sat around the dining room table eating cake and conversing. Jeffrey finished his slice of cake fast and he didn't want seconds. He remained at the table and proofed his manuscript. Brittany toggled between eating her cake and petting Scruffles and Mr. Quacks.

Denise said, "Tiffany, princess. Why don't you tell me more about this Sebastian fella. Why don't you bring him over so I can meet him?"

"Well, he's a super genius. He wants to be a medical scientist. We spend a lot of time after school at the library studying, and some days he still works at his uncle's sporting goods store. He's... sapient. I think that's the correct word. Right, Dad?"

Steven eyebrows raised. He was surprised to hear Tiffany use such an esoteric word. He said, "Yes. I would say he's sapient."

"Well, that's lovely to hear, princess," Denise said, "but what's it mean? I've never been book smart."

Tiffany wanted to see if her dad knew what sapient meant, so she passed the ball to him. "Dad, you're good at explaining what words mean. Will you indulge Grams?"

Steven cleared his throat. "It basically means... Well, he's a smart chap."

Tiffany smiled. "Close enough, Dad."

"Why don't you bring this fella over for me to meet? Are you ashamed of your Grams?" Denise asked, then placed another bite of cake in her mouth.

"No, it's not that at all," Tiffany replied.

But she was, and what's more is she still was hesitant to bring Sebastian over to the house while Denise was living there.

Brittany chimed into the discussion. "Hey, sissy, why don't you show Grams a picture of Sebastian?"

"Yes, that's a terrific idea. Thank you, angel," Denise said. "Let me see a picture of this genius of yours."

A brief surge of anger ran through Tiffany towards her younger sister, but she knew Brittany wasn't intentionally trying to create problems for her. Tiffany flashed a forced smile. "Sure, Grams. I'll show you a picture of him." While searching on her phone for a picture to show Denise, she inquired about a subject she brought up with Denise a week ago. She asked, "So, Grams, have you made a decision about getting a Facebook account?"

After Denise swallowed her bite of cake, she replied. "Oh, please, child. I don't need to be messin' with all that mess'. That's for you young folk. I've said that countless time to you already."

"Here you go," Tiffany said as she handed Denise her cellphone.

Denise looked at the picture and said, "Oh, Lord. You, too? You're dating a bird turd? I swear it's becomin' a disease in this family. First my daughter, now my granddaughter."

Keisha gave her mother a look as a signal to stop talking like that. Denise felt bad after saying what she did.

Steven stood and picked the uneaten cake off the table. As Steven moved the cake into the kitchen, Denise spoke to him. "Oh! Steven, please bring that cake back on in here. I want me another slice."

Steven ignored her, but he did return to the dining room and retrieved her plate. "I'll get you a slice, Mom," Steven said, to which she thanked him for his willingness to do so. He sliced her big piece of cake, added some chocolate sprinkles, and brought it to her. She was once again appreciative.

Meanwhile, Tiffany responded to Denise's remarks. "Grams, first of all, Sebastian is only a friend. We're not dating. Second of all, why are you so hung up on color of skin? You're a woman of God. You're supposed to love everyone."

Denise conceded. "Yes, princess. You're right. Thank you."

Tiffany went to the kitchen to get another slice of cake. This would be her fourth slice. When she returned to the dining room, Denise said, "Princess, I have a question for you. How can you eat like a horse but look so thin?" She knew the answer, but Denise wanted to talk a little more with Tiffany to smooth things over with her.

"Well, I exercise every day," Tiffany said.

"Oh, that's right. My mind keeps slippin'. I forgot you have all that fancy exercise equipment up in the attic. Do you think I could join you and exercise? I'd like to lose some weight. Lord, have mercy. There's that God awful rotten egg smell again."

Tiffany said, "Yeah, that would be nice. You can even use my exercise equipment when I'm at school. After I finish this slice of cake, I'm going to the attic to exercise some more."

"Tell you what," Denise said, then started coughing heavily and excessively. She'd been having these sorts of coughing spells shortly after she moved into the house. She took a big drink of her coffee. "Sorry. Somethin' up in these parts is making my allergies act up like somethin' wicked. Anyways, why don't I join you tonight? You can be my personal trainer."

"Okay. It would be nice to have you up there. Honestly, sometimes I think I'm not alone in there even when I am. I know we blessed the house good, but lately I've been feeling apprehensive up there."

"Don't worry, child. We'll fix that. And, Jeffrey? I'd like to hear that cello sonata you composed later tonight, if you're willing to perform it again."

Jeffrey was thrilled Denise loved the piece of music he composed for her so much she wanted to hear it again. He thought she was throwing him warm fuzzies earlier when she raved about the piece of music. "Sure, Grams. I'd love to."

"Fabulous. You really need to publish that piece. You could make a little extra money through sales and that would help you pay for that fancy–pants cello cat you were trumpetin' about to me a few days ago."

"Mom, that's an excellent idea," Keisha said.

"Well, don't look so surprised now, darlin'. Those are the only kinds of ideas I have to offer," Denise replied. She smiled widely afterwards.

Jeffrey was proofing his manuscript of the sonata he composed for Denise. Brittany was eating her cake. Keisha and Steven were talking quietly among themselves about Keisha's progress with finding a job while Grams talked to the children.

"And, Brittany, my special angel. I have experience buildin' things. When I was in my twenties working two jobs to help support my bum of a husband and my six kids, I made little knick-knacks for people to buy. As I got better, I started to make benches and windmills and things like that. Maybe this weekend you and I can build something together."

"Yay! Thanks, Grams!" Brittany said. She held Mr. Quacks up. He was on her lap. "What about Mr. Quacks?"

"Mr. Quacks is more than welcome to join us," Denise said.

"Do you want any more cake, Mom?" Keisha asked.

"No, darlin', but thank you. I'm actually startin' to feel a little nauseous." Her eyes became heavy and started to close.

The dining room light flickered, but only briefly. Keisha figured the light bulbs were on their last legs.

"Mom?" Keisha asked, walking over to Denise.

"Grams?" Tiffany and Jeffrey said, nearly in sync.

"Yes, darlin'. I'm still here. Tiffany, let's get up to that gym of yours and get to sweatin' up a storm."

Tiffany didn't think Denise was in a condition to be exercising. "Grams, are you sure you're up to exercising right now?"

"Child, yes. I think it's just what I need," Denise replied.

"Alright. Great. You'll want to change into something more comfortable. And wear tennis shoes, too." Tiffany said as she stood to place her plate in the kitchen.

"I'll change into something more comfortable and meet you up there in ten minutes." She took her gifts upstairs.

Tiffany and Denise exercised for an hour together. Denise spent ten minutes stretching and warming up, thirty minutes on the exercise bike, and fifteen minutes on the elliptical. That's all Denise could handle and quite frankly Tiffany thought that was more than enough. She told her grandmother they would build a little each day and cap their exercise time initially to an hour at a time.

While they exercised, the rope that hung from the attic ceiling would sway on its own. Denise felt an ominous presence a few times, but silently prayed, which made the feeling dissipate.

Like Sebastian, Denise was concerned about Tiffany weighing and measuring herself constantly. Tiffany denied being obsessed though. Denise didn't argue with her.

After exercising with Tiffany, she asked Jeffrey to perform his cello sonata for her again. He said he was going to talk to the department chair of the music department at his school. He wanted to record it for

Denise using the music department's recording studio. She was delighted to hear that he intended to record it.

Her next stop was in Brittany's room. Scruffles was laying on Brittany's bed. Brittany was working on a new jigsaw puzzle. This one was one thousand pieces. Denise sat on her bed. They talked about different things, mostly focused on Brittany. School. Her goals.

Scruffles leapt off the bed and sniffed the Michael statue and plate on her nightstand. Denise said, "What's with your dog? He's actin' all kinds of crazy."

Brittany looked over at Scruffles. "Oh, he does that sometimes." She stood and walked over to her nightstand. She picked up her Michael statue and climbed on her bed. Scruffles jumped back onto the bed. "See, Grams. This used to be my Granana's, but Mommy let me have it."

"May I hold it, please?" Denise asked. She held the statue in front of her with it resting on her palm. "This is a lovely statue. Michael the Archangel. I need to get a statue like this."

"Yeah. It's great. He protects us from the man in the black suit."

"Oh, you've seen him, too, huh?"

"Yeah." While making sword–fighting gestures, she spoke about all her protectors. She said, "Michael will use his sword and slice him to ribbons. And Mr. Quacks will use his bill to bite his nose and Scruffles will bite him in his privates. Then Granana will bend the man in the black suit over her knee and bust his butt."

Denise broke out in a fit of laughter. "I bet Granana would do that!" She couldn't stop laughing. When she finally did though, she spoke. "This is a beautiful statue. I am going to buy me one and put it on my nightstand along with my plate."

"That sounds good, Grams. Are you going to get a statue like mine or one like my daddy used to have where Michael had his sword extended out to slay some demons?"

Denise was amazed at Brittany's intelligence and wit. She said, "I don't know, my angel. Tell you what. Tomorrow morning, after breakfast you and me can use your mommy's laptop to find me the perfect Michael statue. How does that sound?"

"Yay!"

"Alright, child. It's a date. Now, why don't you get into bed. I'll lay here with you for a whiles." Denise started to heavily cough again and Brittany's lamps flickered a few times, but subtlety.

"Are you okay, Grams?" Brittany asked.

"Yeah, I'll be fine. Go on to sleep now, my angel. Sweet dreams."

Brittany fell asleep holding her Granana's crucifix in one hand and Mr. Quacks in the other.

After Brittany fell asleep, Denise retired to her room and went to bed herself.

CHAPTER TWENTY-ONE

Father Thompson

Denise laid in bed sick. For the past few days she was constantly nauseous. She vomited a few times, which seemed to decrease the intensity of the nausea. One time, she vomited a little blood. Keisha said, if she wasn't better within one more day, she wasn't backing down any longer. She would take Denise to the hospital.

Steven fixed her breakfast every morning and brought it to her bedside. She was moved by his kind gesture to have a duplicate personalized plate made for her, on which he served her most of her meals.

Keisha finally confessed to her mom she was pregnant. When Denise heard this news she was ecstatic, which was a complete turnaround from Keisha's previous three pregnancy announcements where Denise would ridicule and chastise Keisha for marrying a white man and bearing children with him.

Father Thompson was scheduled to bless the house at ten o'clock. Keisha and Denise were the only ones home. The children were at school and Steven was at work. Father Thompson would have preferred everyone residing in the house be present for the blessing, but he was willing to bless it anyway.

When the doorbell rang, Keisha was indisposed in the bathroom and Denise was too ill to get out of bed.

A few minutes later, the doorbell rang again, but Keisha was still preoccupied. She kicked herself for not having her cellphone with her, but she read in an article it was unsanitary to bring cellphones into bathrooms.

When she opened the front door, Father Thompson was getting into his car. She hollered, "Father! I'm sorry! I was in the bathroom! Please come in!"

He smiled at her and waved. As he walked up the walkway to the front door, he said, "Good morning, and God be with you always, my child."

Father Thompson was wearing a clerical shirt with the tab collar. Black slacks, socks, and shoes. In his hand he carried a black briefcase containing everything he would need for the blessing.

"Thank you. Please come in. I have a fresh pot of coffee brewing for you. Would you like a cup before blessing the house?"

"Yes, thank you. That sounds fine."

She led the way to the living room. Father Thompson couldn't resist the urge to ask. "Not intending to put any pressure on you, but have you considered attending service? We'd love to have you and your family join our congregation."

Keisha smiled. She believed Granana had something to do with Father Thompson asking that question. "I think I will. Once my mother is feeling better, she and I, along with the children, will attend."

Father Thompson looked concerned. "Ill? Your mother is ill?" He sat on the smaller couch in the living room.

She sat on the larger couch. She nodded. "Unfortunately. She's come down with something out of the blue. She's upstairs resting as we speak. I've never seen her this ill before."

Father Thompson felt bad about the next question he was going to ask Keisha. He was after all there to bless the house. "If she's up and willing to see me, may I visit with her for a few minutes? I'd like to pray with her. I feel the Lord compelling me to do this. Afterwards, we can proceed with the blessing."

"Father, I think that's a wonderful idea," she said as she stood. "I think my mom would like that very much. Tell you what. Let me get you a cup of coffee first. While you're enjoying that, I'll pop up to her room and see if she's up. I know if she is she'd be delighted to fellowship and pray with you." She went into the kitchen and prepared Father Thompson a cup of coffee.

She was moved by Father Thompson's concern for her mother. She hoped his prayer with Denise would help her recover at a faster rate. Keisha's faith in God and religion was shaken when Granana died. Granana was in her sixties when she passed. She didn't smoke or drink. She didn't abuse prescription drugs and she never tried street drugs. She lived a healthy lifestyle and exercised regularly. And, she was one of the kindest, sweetest ladies anyone would ever meet. It made no sense to Keisha why God would take Granana when he did.

Secretively, Denise contacted Father Thompson about a week ago and explained to him why Keisha's faith was shaken. She begged him to not reveal to Keisha she contacted him about her.

Keisha walked into the living room with a serving tray. She poured him a cup of coffee and handed it to Father Thompson. Steam billowed from the cup.

"Thank you," he said. He blew a few times across the top of the cup.

Keisha was slightly on guard. She didn't know if the angry spirit was in the house or not. If he was, he hadn't made his presence known, but now would be an opportunity for the spirit to strike by breaking Father Thompson's coffee cup and spilling its contents all over him.

She nervously stood as he brought the cup to his lips. He took a drink and set the cup down on the coffee table. She said, "I'll be right back. I'll go check to see if Mom is up. Be back in a few minutes."

Father Thompson replied. "Sounds good to me." He opened his briefcase and removed a thin book from it.

Keisha walked upstairs. A cold breeze passed by her, causing her to stop on the stairs momentarily. She continued up the stairs and knocked on her mother's door, but Denise didn't answer.

She knocked again— a little harder and longer this time. Still no answer. This didn't concern Keisha too much. She figured Denise was asleep. Regardless, she still wanted her mother to converse and pray with the priest, so she entered the bedroom.

Denise was laying on her back with the sheets covering her chest. From her neck up was exposed. Keisha said, "Mom?"

No answer.

"Mom? Mom?" she said. Her voice was a little louder this time.

No answer.

Is she breathing? Keisha tapped her mom on the shoulder a few times. "Mom?"

"What?" Denise asked, mildly irritated, though her voice was faint and weak.

"Father Thompson is here to bless the house, but when I told him you were sick, he asked if it would be okay if he came up and prayed with you for a speedy recovery." She placed her hand on top of the bed sheet to touch her mom's hand.

Her breathing was labored. "Yes. Please. Send him on up, darlin'."

Keisha forced herself not break down. The strong–willed woman she once knew seemed to be near death. The physical pain Denise recently experienced seemed to parallel the emotional pain Keisha felt seeing her mother's deteriorating condition.

She went downstairs and escorted Father Thompson to Denise's bedside. Father Thompson knelt down, then spoke to Denise. "How are you feeling?"

Denise opened her eyes slightly to see Father Thompson. "Hello, Father." For a moment, when she laid eyes on Father Thompson her pain seemed to fade. With her eyes closed, Denise said, "Deathly ill. Stomach pains. The room is spinning. I see angels flying all around my room. They have black wings."

Father Thompson feared the worst. He asked Denise if she wanted final rites to be read. She declined. She insisted this sickness would pass. She did, however, request he prayed with her, and he did.

Father Thompson pulled Keisha aside. "She's very sick, but she's going to pull through. The power of prayer can move mountains."

Keisha wanted to believe what the priest was touting, and she hoped divine intervention would cure her mother.

He said a final goodbye to Denise. He held her hand and spoke. "God be with you always, my child."

Next on the agenda was the house blessing. Father Thompson placed his briefcase on the coffee table and laid the items needed for the blessing.

He removed a stole from the briefcase— a purple one with gold trim. Each side of the stole had the sign of the cross. "We'll start in this room and bless this floor. Then we will work our way to the second floor and attic."

"Let's begin. Let us pray." He made the sign of the cross as he spoke. "In the name of the Father, the Son, and the Holy Spirit. Amen." Then he said, "Peace be with all those who dwell here always in the name of the Lord. Amen."

"Father. Your nose," Keisha said. "I'll get you some tissue." She ran to the hallway bathroom near the kitchen and handed him a few sheets of tissue.

"Thank you," he said. He wrapped the tissue around his nose, pinched, and tilted his head slightly back. Within a minute, the tissue was saturated with blood. Keisha ran to the bathroom to get some more tissue to stop the bleeding. This time she brought twice as much toilet paper. Minutes later, that toilet paper was saturated with blood. Once more, she ran to the bathroom, but this time she brought the box back with her. She handed him several more sheets of tissue, but within minutes they were satiated with blood.

"Father, please sit down. Right this way." She took him by the arm and sat him on the couch. She handed him several more sheets of tissue, which were saturated within a minute. "I'll get you a towel." She was sickened— both emotionally and physically— at the amount of blood falling from Father Thompson's nose. It was making her stomach queasy.

She handed Father Thompson a towel. His face and neck were painted in red. He coughed several times, spraying blood onto the items on the coffee table that were to be used for the blessing: a crucifix, a holy water shaker, and a book of scriptures.

The bleeding didn't stop. Father Thompson coughed more violently than he did the last time. Blood spewed not only on the coffee table but also the carpet on the side of the table opposite him. "Please call an ambulance." More coughing. More blood spraying. A few of the coughs expelled long, thick blood clots.

Then his stole crossed over his shoulders and strangled him. Keisha tried to unloosen the stole, but the force pulling back on the stole was too great. She ran into the kitchen and grabbed a pair of scissors out of the desk drawer. She ran back to the priest and cut his stole, freeing him from the death grip.

Paramedics arrived on the scene within five minutes after she had called. He was transported to Whitmond Community Hospital. As he was wheeled out of the living room on a stretcher, Keisha's cellphone rang. The caller's name on the display read: BABE'S WORK. It was Steven calling her using his office phone. She answered the call. She said, "Oh my, God! Babe! You won't believe— "

"How's the priest?" he asked in a sinister tone. Then he wickedly laughed. His voice wasn't his own; his laughter wasn't his own.

Keisha shrieked and threw her phone. When it hit the floor, it skidded a little ways, stopping in some of the priest's blood. The phone died, then turned on, displaying a white screen with loud, cacophonic static. The man in the black suit appeared for a second, then disappeared, and with him the phone shut off. She picked up the phone and it was blazing cold to the touch. Her fingertips turned a little discolored.

Using the bloody towel, she attempted to turn the phone back on, but it would not turn on— it was completely dead.

Then a voice seeped into her brain; it was Steven's, but distorted. An invisible hand grabbed her by the neck and applied a little pressure. *(That was fun, wasn't it? We need to have Father Thompson over more often, don't you think? You dumb bitch! Fuck with me and I'll kill you! Don't ever let him in our house again!)*

Later in the evening the same day, Father Thompson visited the Dobrowski house, he returned to the house again for a special dinner as a thank you.

Steven was pleased he agreed to come over on such short notice, especially since this would be Father Thompson's third visit to the house in the same day. He was looking forward to speaking to Father Thompson personally.

Because Denise was still ill and asleep in her room, Steven prepared dinner. He prepared Father Thompson's favorite meal: lamb shank with potatoes with carrots and rye bread lightly spread with butter. For dessert, key lime pie, also a favorite of Father Thompson's.

Jeffrey was in the living room practicing his cello. He didn't want to the noise to bother Denise even though she said it didn't.

"Jeffrey?" Steven said, basting the lamb in the oven. "Set the table, please."

"Daddy?" Brittany said with a sad tone in her voice while holding Mr. Quacks. "Mr. Quacks needs surgery again."

Steven closed the oven door. "No problem. Dr. Dad is here to help." The threading that attached the leg to Mr. Quacks' body was giving way. The same repair he made before would need to be made again, just on a different leg.

He quickly threaded a needle and repaired the limb. It took less than ten minutes. He handed Mr. Quacks back to her after kissing Mr. Quacks on the head. Then he kissed her on the cheek. She said, "Thanks, Daddy!"

Keisha entered the kitchen and put her arms around Steven's waist as he stood at the stove stirring the sauce for the lamb. "I love you, babe."

He turned around and kissed her. "I love you, too."

"It was a tremendously thoughtful gesture of you to offer dinner to Father Thompson."

"Well, it's the least I could do after what he did. I hope he likes the food I prepared for him." He turned around again to check the lamb and baste it one final time. "And, it's done." He pulled it from the oven and removed the lamb from the pan and placed it on a cooling rack to rest.

When Father Thompson arrived and rang the doorbell, Steven answered it. "There's the man of the hour!" Steven said. "Please, Father Thompson, come on in. I guess you don't need the grand tour after today. Am I right?"

Father Thompson chuckled. "Quite right, my son. Quite right."

"Please step into the dining room and make yourself at home. Keisha will show you to your seat. Dinner will be served in about five minutes or so."

When Steven brought the platter of meat and the bowl of potatoes and carrots, he was delighted to see Denise sitting at the table. "Mom! You're feeling better! I guess Father Thompson's prayer is more powerful than we presumed. You truly are a man of healing powers, Father."

She nodded. "You is right about that, Steven. I feel like a million dollars. And, I'm starved so let's dish up the dinner. Steven, where's my special plate?"

While Father Thompson was shocked and amazed Steven cooked his favorite foods, he was also perplexed. He said, "Steven, this is most unexpected. How on God's green earth did you know my favorite meal?" When Steven didn't answer, Father Thompson said, "Ah, it doesn't matter. The Lord works in mysterious ways."

"Yeah, he sure does, Father Thompson. That he does," Denise affirmed, nodding her head. Irritated Steven didn't respond to her question, she asked again. "Steven, god damn it— Whoa!" With a quick reflex, she placed her hand over her mouth for a few seconds then retracted it. "Excuse me, Father Thompson. It won't happen again. Steven! Where is my special plate?"

"I'll get the plate for you, Mom," he said. When he returned to the dining room, he plated her a nice slice of lamb and hardy helping of potatoes and carrots and handed it to her.

"Steven, where's my Mrs. Dash. Now you know I can't eat any food without a dash of that bitch's spice—whoa!" Again, she covered her mouth for a few seconds, then uncovered it. "Sorry about that Father Thompson. Sometimes the words slip out."

Steven took her plate to the kitchen to sprinkle some Mrs. Dash on her food while Father Thompson provided some words of comfort to diffuse the social gaffe. "Not to worry. Happens to me sometimes, too. None of us are free of sin, are we?"

Everyone at the table nodded in agreement.

"Here you are, Mom," Steven said. He placed the plate in front of her.

"Thank you, son. Next time please try to remember to set my shi— I mean, my Mrs. Dash— on the table. I don't like people handling my food."

Steven walked up to the attic and told Tiffany dinner was ready. She told her dad she'd be done in about ten minutes. She wanted to change into something more presentable since Father Thompson was joining the family for dinner. Steven agreed. He said, "That's good. And please wear your bra as tight as possible. I love that bastard of a man Father Thompson, but sometimes he has a tendency to let his eyes wander where they shouldn't be." Tiffany thanked her dad for the tidbit, though she was also repulsed.

Once everyone was seated at the table, the family ate and conversed about various topics. Weather. Sports. Politics. Life in general.

Father Thompson asked Denise, "So, what do you think your illness was?"

Denise used her fork to stab another piece of lamb in the casserole dish. "I think it was stomach flu, perhaps. I've gotten it maybe two times before this time. I wouldn't wish that on my worst enemy, right Steven?" Then she chuckled.

"Good one, Mom!" Steven quipped as he chewed a piece of lamb in his mouth. He high–fived her.

Father Thompson said, "So, Keisha. I am delighted you'll be attending mass this Sunday with your family and your mom. It's a joy to have you as part of our congregation."

"I'll be sure to make a big breakfast for everyone on Sundays and Wednesdays, just like before," Steven said as he put a few more vegetables on Brittany's plate. "Do you remember that, sweet pea?"

"Yeah! Like when Granana was alive and we would go to church on Sunday mornings and Wednesday nights," Brittany said. "Mr. Quacks remembers, too!" She presented him to the family and Father Thompson.

"That's a beautiful duck," Father Thompson remarked.

"Thanks. My daddy and I won it some time ago. And, today, my daddy operated on Mr. Quacks. He made Mr. Quacks all better."

"He's a good man, your dad. I hope all you realize how fortunate you are to have him looking after you," Father Thompson said, then he finished the rest of his wine in a final gulp.

Nothing but nods from the family.

"More wine, Father Thompson?" Steven asked while grasping the neck of the bottle like he was strangling a Thanksgiving turkey.

Father Thompson thought for a few moments, then said, "What the hell! Why— Whoa!" He covered his mouth with his hand for a second or two, then retracted it. "I'm sorry. I hope you'll all ignore that minor transgression."

Keisha said, "It's already forgotten." She made the sign of the cross in the air.

The rest of the family members agreed as they laughed at Keisha's gesturing. Steven poured the priest some more wine and then a little more after that glass.

After dessert, the family thanked Father Thompson for spending the evening with them. Steven walked him to his car As Father Thompson opened his driver's side door, Steven said, "I'm just checking for my own edification. Are you sure you're alright after what took place today?"

In a soft-spoken voice, Father Thompson responded. "Yes, why, of course. Things happen. Life goes on. There's nothing more to say, my son."

Steven wanted to tell Father Thompson an issue of Playgirl was visible on the floorboard in his back seat, but he kept his mouth shut. He didn't want to embarrass the priest, especially after all he had done for family. To each their own was Steven's motto in that situation.

They shook hands and said good night. Steven stood on the driveway until Father Thompson's taillights were out of sight.

(You need to kill your family! Don't you wanna see 'em bleed? Do it! Or I will! And then you'll be next you mole–faced fuck! [evil maniacal laughter])

No! I won't do it! I'll kill myself before I hurt my family! Leave me alone! Go back to Hell! GO BACK TO HELL! GO BACK TO HELL! GO BACK TO HEEEEEEEEEEEELL!!!!

CHAPTER TWENTY-TWO

The Die is Cast

Brittany was in her room assembling another K'Nex kit Steven and Keisha purchased for her a few days ago. She worked on it a little each day after school— once her homework was completed, if she had any.

"Hey, sweet pea," Steven said. He walked over to her desk where she was working. "You're doing a great job on that. Need any help?"

"Not right now, Daddy. Thank you, though," she said.

"How's Mr. Quacks doing?"

"Fine, Daddy."

"Alright. I've got work in the morning. I'm going to bed. You should do the same, also."

"Okay, Daddy."

"I have a surprise for you kids tomorrow. Shhh, don't tell your brother or sister. It's our secret." He petted Scruffles a few times who was on Brittany's bed. "Good boy, Scruffs!"

Scruffles jumped off the bed and started sniffing the objects on Brittany's nightstand. She walked over to Scruffles and admonished him. "Oh, no, Scruffles, don't sniff that. It's dangerous." She picked up the Michael statue and explained why. "See that point. It's dangerous.

His sword is pointing in the air. I don't want you to get cut, Scruffs." He sniffed her cheek, then licked a few times.

Brittany went into the hallway bathroom across from her room and brushed her teeth. Scruffles accompanied her. Then she slipped into bed. She was asleep within minutes. After Scruffles sniffed the nightstand objects again, he leapt onto the bed and nestled his body against Brittany's leg, facing her bedroom door. Moments later he was asleep.

Brittany was fortunate to still have Scruffles. Last week a man saw one of Steven's LOST DOG flyers on a billboard. He contacted Steven and demanded Scruffles be returned to him. The next day, Steven met with the man and confirmed he was the owner of Scruffles. Steven offered the man two thousand dollars for Scruffles. The man put up a fight; he demanded three thousand dollars. Eventually, the two men settled on a price set at two thousand six hundred dollars. He never told Brittany about this— or anyone else for that matter.

Brittany's bedroom door slowly opened. Scruffles lifted his head to see who had opened the door, but nobody was there. He jumped off the bed and walked into the hallway. Her bedroom door closed. Scruffles started scratching Brittany's door to be let back in her room. At first, she didn't hear the scratches. When she did, she opened her eyes. Someone was standing at the foot of her bed; it was the man in the black suit. He swish panned his hand up near his face; it was holding a meat cleaver. He repeatedly struck the front of his neck. It was a strike–stop motion, which he did five or six times. A waterfall of blood flowed from his neck to his chest, turning his white dress shirt a wet red.

Brittany screamed at the top of her lungs. The man in the black suit flickered three times. Flicker–flicker... flicker— disappear.

Denise's room was closer to Brittany's than Steven's. She ran into her room and turned on the light. "What is it, child? A bad dream?"

Brittany was hysterical, crying her eyes out. She couldn't talk no matter how hard she tried. Brittany wrapped her arms around Denise when she tried to walk away to get Steven and Keisha. She wondered why those two weren't out of their room yet.

While carrying Brittany, Denise pounded on Steven and Keisha's door. "Wake up in there! Get up now!" She opened their door. Both Keisha and Steven were dead to the world. Not even the hysterical crying woke either of them up. She flipped their bedroom light on and shouted at them. "Damn it! Get up! Get up! Get up! God damn it!"

"What? What's going on?" Steven stammered, his voice soft and lethargic.

"Look at your daughter! She's filled with terror. That damn honky in the black suit is back again, with a vengeance I bet! Some job Father Lush did blessin' the house!"

Denise rubbed Brittany's back. Now Tiffany and Jeffrey were up. "What happened?" Jeffrey asked.

"I don't know, but whatever did happen has your sister scared out of her mind. Lord have mercy!" Denise was rocking Brittany back and forth on the floor while rubbing her back. "Well, Steven! What are you going to do about this? This house doesn't seem to be safe."

"She'll be fine, Mom. She can sleep in our bed," Steven said.

"God damn it! Is my daughter still asleep? Get her Rip Van Winkle black ass up! She needs to see this!" Denise was furious, and she was sick again with what she believed was stomach flu, though this time her symptoms weren't as severe.

Keisha swung herself out of bed and took Brittany from Denise, but Brittany still couldn't stop crying. Denise went to the bathroom to vomit. She didn't know if it was from her illness or the excitement.

It took more than an hour to calm Brittany down to where she could explain what she witnessed. After she finished explaining, Steven stood on the bed and shouted, "Leave my family alone! Stay away from my family, you dead motherfucker!" Then an invisible force slugged Steven in his gut. The impact knocked him into the wall behind him. Keisha and Brittany screamed in fear for Steven. A few minutes later he was on his feet.

They comforted Brittany, and soon she was asleep. Keisha and Steven couldn't sleep, so they went downstairs to make some coffee. Steven called off for the day. Since he was staying home, he decided to make breakfast.

"Steven, we need to find a new house. This house is too dangerous. We tried. We put up a good fight. Now it's time to leave before someone gets seriously injured or killed," Keisha insisted.

He approached her and pointed at her face. "No! We are not fucking leaving this house ever! You hear me! This is our house and I'm not backing down. I'll hang in this house until I take my last dying breath."

She was afraid he was going to hit her, but he didn't. He wanted to though. He wanted to see her suffer; he wanted to see her bleed.

She cried. "We can't do this anymore, Steven. If I have to, I'll take the kids somewhere myself. My mom and I will leave." She started to talk away from him.

He grabbed her arm and stopped her. "You listen to me. I have one more idea that might help us rid the house of the spirit once and for all."

She didn't want to hear what he had to say, but asked him to explain anyway. He said, "We'll bring in a medium who can communicate directly with this spirit and find out what he wants. We've seen this happen on paranormal shows before. Mediums can help unrested spirits cross over."

She was tired of contending with this unrested, volatile spirit. She broke down and cried again. "Fine. Let's try it. But this is it, Steven. If this doesn't work, we leave this house. I'll leave with the children and my mom— with or without you."

He didn't respond, but he released her arm. She went upstairs. The inhuman voice told Steven: *(Just kill the bitch! Kill her with pain! Then kill that bitch mother-in-law! Then kill the children! Save the best for last!)*

Will you go back to Hell! Get the fuck out of my mind and out of my house! I won't hurt my family! You can't force me! He popped two Lexapro pills into his mouth. These were bootleg from a back-alley pharmacist.

(We'll see about that, Steve-O.)

During breakfast, he explained to the family what the plan of attack was to permanently rid the house of the spirit. He instructed the family to not exhibit fear if the man in the black suit revealed himself to anyone because that increased its power.

After breakfast, Denise asked Steven if he would plate her some more eggs and grits, which he did. On her personalized plate— her favorite plate.

Denise said, "Shouldn't we bring in a different priest? This sounds like a job for the church."

Keisha replied, "No, Mom. I'm sorry. We've tried that and it didn't work."

"Right, but the last time the priest blessed the house not everyone residing in the house was present. Maybe you should try to bless the house when everyone can attend."

"Thanks, Mom," Keisha said. "That's a good idea, but we're going to try a medium first. Maybe she can get this angry spirit out of here once and for all. Then we'll have a priest properly bless the house with all of us here."

(Did you hear that, Steve-O? You better kill that piggly-wiggly bitch mother-in-law of yours! Then your monkey-faced wife! Then those mongrel mutt fuck children of yours! Kill 'em, Stevie-Steve! Or I'll do it myself and then kill you!)

Fuck off! Leave me alone, you fucker from Hell!
"Here you go, Mom," Steven said as he placed her personalized plate in front of her.

"Steven, you know, you should be attending church with us."

"Sorry, Mom," he said. "I'm not ready yet." He attempted to leave the dining room.

"Alright. Well, son, I do appreciate you preparing breakfast and dinner on Sundays for us," Denise said, causing Steven to stop. "And dinner on Wednesdays, too. You should quit your stressful executive job and open your own restaurant."

"Thank you, Mom. That's sweet," Steven said, then left the dining room.

She started violently coughing after eating a few bites of her eggs Steven brought to her. The last cough produced blood.

Denise believed Steven not attending church with the family was giving the angry spirit more power, but she kept her tongue knotted. She was too sick to her stomach to argue anyhow.

"Oh, Mom! You're coughing so hard it's making your throat bleed. Drink some water." She did and it helped.

Steven returned to the dining room with a white plastic bag. "As a thank you to you kids for dealing with the insanity in this house, we— me, your mom, and your grandmother— have some tokens of appreciation," Steven pulled out the large white plastic bag from underneath his chair. "I have something for all of you."

Everyone was appreciative and excited with Steven's surprise. He distributed the gifts to each of the children first, then to Keisha and Denise.

"Okay, open them," Steven said.

And they did. Jeffrey's gift was a card with a check inside for his cello lessons with the virtuoso cellist. Tiffany's envelope contained a card and a manual for a new treadmill. Brittany's gift was a new model skyscraper kit.

Steven recently received a salary increase and a bonus from his new boss and he used the bonus money to purchase the gifts.

After the children had a chance to read their cards to themselves and see their gift, Steven asked each of his three children to read their cards aloud in birth order: Jeffrey, Tiffany, then Brittany.

"This is your bridge to the start of a successful career as the virtuoso cellist you *wish* you could be. Here's a check for your first three months of lessons. No strings attached. Love Mom, Dad, and Grams."

Keisha and Denise shook their head in bewilderment. They couldn't believe Steven's passive–aggressive behavior.

"Ah, yes, words of pure truth," Steven said, nodding his head. "Do you like the use of the cello terms? Bridge, strings."

"Yeah, Dad, it's... clever," Jeffrey said, shocked at the veiled cruelty of the message.

He snapped. "You're god damn right it's clever. Don't sass me!" He took a breath. "Tiffany, read your card's inscription I wrote, then I will read Brittany's since she's too du— I mean, young— to read."

"I can so read, Daddy!" Brittany protested. "I will read it myself."

Steven laughed, but it wasn't his normal laugh. This sounded sinister. "Okay, you can read, sweet pea. Tiffany, please read. Let me know if you need any help sounding out any of the words."

"You're strong in terms of brawn, beauty, and brains. Well, okay, two out of three ain't bad. Love Mom, Dad, and Grams."

"I don't get it," Tiffany said.

Steven snickered, shaking his head. "The prosecution rests," he said. "The treadmill is already in the attic waiting for you. That's why I didn't want you in it yesterday. It would have spoiled the god damn fucking surprise. By the way, I want you to be safe with Sebastian" He handed her a box.

"Dad! What the hell? Condoms? Are you serious?" Tiffany shouted.

Steven ignored her. "Okay, sweet pea, read yours," Steven said.

"Keep on trying to be the man you want to become. We're all proud of you. Love Mom, Dad, and Grams."

Brittany shook her head and said, "Oh, Daddy, that's not nice."

Steven slammed his hand down on the dining room table. "Now, listen up, you ungrateful little fuckers! I have the electricians coming over here today to install the chandelier." He took a deep breath and exhaled. Then he shook his head as if an insect had flown into it. "I'm sorry. I'm so sorry." He cried for a minute. "I don't know where that came from. Please forgive me. Excuse me" He stood and walked to the living room to be alone to cry a little more.

(You fucking cry baby, Steve-O! I should kill you right now! You better kill your family or I will. Tick-tock!)

As Steven sat on the couch, the crucifix on the wall tapped against the wall as it shook. It fell to the floor. Then the family picture fell onto the hearth. The sound of shattered glass resonated.

Steven walked to the picture and picked it up. The glass was shattered, but it was a plexiglass kind of shatter. It looked as though someone had punched the picture. Everyone's face was encompassed in the shattered portion of the picture.

Steven placed the picture back on the mantel. When he turned to replace the crucifix the man in the black suit was standing in front of the picture wall. Steven lunged towards him with his fist cocked back. When he reached the suited man, the man disappeared. His fist hit the wall, leaving a large indentation in it. The crimson–colored viscous liquid oozed out. Steven looked at the wound with scrutiny. *Maybe it's time to leave this house after all.*

Denise and Keisha rushed to the living room to see what the ruckus was. Steven stood near the picture wall with his head down.

(You can forget it! You're stuck here, Amicus. You're going to die here. And so is your family, you bald big–nosed mole–faced piece of worthless shit! I should kill you right now!)

Steven started pounding himself in the head. *FUUUUUUUUUUUUUCK OOOOOOOOOOOOFF! Fuck off! Fuck off!*

"Steven, stop!" Keisha demanded. "Stop!"

And he did. He laid on the couch and eventually fell asleep after taking three Lexapro pills.

Later in the afternoon, electricians installed the chandelier, but not without difficulty. The switch cutting power to the living room toggled back to ON several times while the men tried to install the chandelier. Denise suggested the switch be duct taped as well as the panel. That didn't work though. Someone still tampered with the switch because the electricians could see power indicator lights on to various electronic devices in the living room. When the electrician checked out the fuse box, the tape had been ripped off the outside and the tape holding the switch in place was on the floor. Denise said she would stay at the fuse box and ensure it didn't switch to an ON position. That did the trick. Had she not stepped in and intervened, there could have been more accidental deaths at the Dobrowski house.

After the chandelier was installed, Steven decided to take Scruffles for a walk. Scruffles was laying on the longer living room couch. Steven said, "Walk, boy? Wanna go for a walk?" Scruffles jumped off the couch with his tail wagging. "Let's go."

As Steven and Scruffles were about to reach the front door, Scruffles ran towards the stairs, stopped at the foot of it, and started snarling and growling.

"There's nothing there, boy," Steven said. "Come on. Let's go."

Scruffles didn't listen. He lunged up four stairs, then stopped and continued to snarl and bark.

"Scruffles, there's nothing there. Let's go."

He lunged up three more stairs, abruptly stopped, and whimpered. He slowly walked down the stairs back to Steven. They went for a long walk and returned an hour later.

Steven made dinner for the family and asked for a status report regarding the man in the black suit. Nobody had any encounters with him, fortunately.

As dinner continued, Steven said he would start investigating credible mediums that night. Once a few were chosen, he, Keisha, and Denise would collectively choose one to bring to the house.

CHAPTER TWENTY-THREE

The Big Christmas Gift

Three months passed and there was no sign of the man in the black suit. Steven, Keisha, and Denise chose a credible medium and paranormal investigation team to attempt to make contact and release the angry spirit— which right now was likely in a state of dormancy. The team was so credible and highly–recommended that the team wouldn't be able to investigate the house until April because they were backed up with cases.

Unknown to Steven, Keisha asked John to perform another blessing about two months ago, which he did. John expressed his concern about Steven. He noticed drastic changes in his behavior and temperament. Even his eyes looked different— glazed over. Lights on but nobody home sort of look.

Denise was on and off sick, but most recently she seemed to be on an upswing. She continued to provide support to the family, both financial and emotional. She also continued to help around the house.

Although the money Denise provided on a monthly basis helped, it wasn't enough for Steven to pay all the expenses on time. To his credit, he always paid the mortgage and utilities first. Then food. Whatever was left went to whatever creditor he felt like paying at that time.

He regretted spending his bonus money on gifts for the children, Keisha, and Denise, but he did it as a way to butter them up and keep them happy in the house.

The children loved having Denise around. She helped Brittany construct her K'Nex kits. Denise also exercised with Tiffany most days, provided Denise wasn't sick to her stomach. She helped Jeffrey with his music by critiquing his expression in his playing. Denise knew the basics of music, but never mastered an instrument.

Tiffany and Sebastian were dating, even though his parents adamantly disapprove since she was of mixed–raced. He told Tiffany he would risk being thrown out his parents' house for her. They were taking the relationship slow; it was their first boyfriend–girlfriend relationship.

The weather was brutally cold. The ground was frozen solid. Several wind chill advisories were in effect the past two weeks.

Steven cleared the snow from a large area in their backyard. Now he was digging. Brittany bundled up and walked outside to her dad. She said, "Dad, what are you doing?"

Holding the shovel with in one hand, he stabbed it into the concrete–like ground. Only a small portion of the shovel stuck above the ground. He wasn't wearing any winter clothing. No gloves, not hat, no coat. He knelt down and looked into her eyes. He talked slowly with a matter–of–fact tone. "I'm working on the big Christmas present for everyone— for you, your siblings, your mom, and Grams. Now, if I tell you what it is, will you promise not to tell anyone? Because if you tell anyone, Daddy will get mad, and if Daddy gets mad, Daddy will hurt you. Do you want Daddy to hurt you?"

Brittany believed her dad was acting a part. She was game and was willing to play. She whispered in her dad's ear, "I won't tell anyone. Not even Mr. Quacks. I promise. It'll be our secret." She pulled away from his ear, smiled and nodded.

He slowly smiled. Using a slow and matter–of–fact voice, he said, "Okay... Then I'll tell you... I'm digging a large rectangular trench because I want to install an in–ground swimming pool for the summer. Isn't that a nice Christmas gift?"

Brittany nodded. "Yeah, Daddy. It's nice. Thank you. Mr. Quacks is going to love the water."

"I bet he will." He stood and spoke. "It's awfully cold out here. Why don't you go back inside and warm up."

And she did. Steven resumed his digging.

(The day is approaching Stevie! We're going to slaughter us some lambs, aren't we, boy! I'm trying to hibernate in the shadows, but it's becoming too difficult! I got to come out of my cave for some action! Get ready!)

Steven seemed to be a machine— never stopping to rest— as he dug the trench. Several hours passed. Day became night. Around nine–thirty, he finally stopped and lumbered— not walked— inside the house. Sebastian was sitting on the longer couch in the living room. As he lumbered through the kitchen to get to the living room, Tiffany greeted him, but he didn't respond to her. She was in the kitchen making sandwiches.

He sat next to Sebastian on the couch who was watching *Autopsy* on T.V., and Sebastian properly greeted him. Steven placed his cellphone face–down on the coffee table. "Have you hit that yet?" he asked, gesturing towards the kitchen.

Sebastian gasped. "What?! No, sir. No, Mr. D. I would never hurt your daughter. Not ever."

Steven shook his head. "No, not hit like that. Have you hit that," he asked, this time rapidly raising his eyebrows up and down with a sinister smile.

After processing Steven's intent, Sebastian gasped again. "No way, Mr. D. No! I would never take advantage of your daughter like that."

He firmly placed his hand on Sebastian's shoulder. He looked into Sebastian's eyes for a few seconds, then he spoke. "Try it before you buy it." Then he lumbered out of the living room.

Sebastian was mortified. This was not the Mr. Dobrowski he met several months ago, and quite frankly, he didn't want to get to know this new Mr. Dobrowski.

As Steven walked in a heavy–footed fashion down the second–floor hallway, he knocked on Jeffrey's door. Jeffrey was inside practicing his cello. Jeffrey opened his door and Steven said, "Sounds good. Keep up the good work." He looked at his cello. *You know, I bet that wood would make good kindling. Note to self.* "Good night."

Ungrateful son. Always leaving this fucking bathroom light on. I'm tired of it.

(Just kill him! Kill 'em all! DO IT!)

He took out his Lexapro bottle and popped three into his mouth and swallowed. He stood at his dresser and opened the top drawer for a clean pair of boxers. When he whipped a pair of boxers out, an object flew out of the drawer. He watched it hit a wall, bounce back, and land at his feet. It was a ring— the ring that unexpectedly landed in his lap his second day in the house.

He picked the ring up and squeezed it in the palm of his hand. In his mind, he was being transported somewhere. He couldn't see any faces, but he could hear what was being said. There was a dispute about money and some threats were exchanged. He put the ring back in his drawer; he wasn't much interested in the story behind the ring anyway. He had too much other stuff on his mind.

He showered, changed, and laid in bed until he was startled by a loud thud and then one more in the attic and Denise screaming at the top of her lungs. He heard her say, "That honky mayonnaise–faced man in the black suit is back! And he nearly shattered my foot!"

Steven was not in the mood for the man in the black suit. He was sick of that spirit wreaking havoc on his family, on him. April couldn't come soon enough.

He begrudgingly left the warmth of his bed and oafishly walked up to the attic to see what happened. Denise said, "I wanted to exercise on the treadmill. I stepped on it and I pushed nothing, but I was fixin' to. Then the treadmill started all by itself and I fell. The belt pushed me off the treadmill. I crawled alongside of the treadmill, heading for Tiffany's weight bench to stands myself up. Then two fifty–pound weights rattled on the shelf. I looked and saw them about to be knocked off. I moved my legs just in time. A second or two later, my feet would be crushed to dust."

He said nothing. He picked one of the two weights up and put it back on the shelf. Then he picked up the other. He held in his hands for a few seconds.

(Now's your chance, Stevie, my boy! Crack her skull open like a coconut with that weight! Use that weight and part her skull just like Moses did to the Red fucking Sea! Kill her and the rest of your no–good ungrateful family and I'll leave! I'll leave you alone!)

"Son?" Denise said. "Are you alright?"

He sighed, placed the weight on the shelf, and lumbered towards the attic stairs. "Night."

(Did you see how weak she looked! Shouldn't be much longer now! Keep it up!)

When Steven returned to his room, Keisha wasn't in bed. She was in the shower. *Please let me sleep peacefully for once. I haven't had decent sleep in months.*

(Fuck your sleep, cry baby! You'll sleep well when you're dead after I kill you for not killing these people! DO IT! I'll leave once you do it!... Stop ignoring me!... I'll get your attention!)

The sound of someone slipping on linoleum and busting their head open broke Steven's slumber. He jumped out of bed and stepped into the bathroom. She was laying in the tub— unconscious.

(She looks good, right, Steve-O! Imagine how she'll look postmortem! Do it now! Send her on her way, and that demon fuck of a fetus, too! Go ahead and kill them both! Then we can say she has postmortem prepartum depression! Those pictures will look great on your Facebook and Twitter feed!)

Other family members were about to enter the bathroom, but Steven slammed the door. "She's naked."

He lightly slapped her on the face a few times, and she woke up. Steven asked her what happened and a few minutes later, she said, "I was washing my hair. I looked up and the shower head morphed into a king cobra snake. It lunged at me, causing me to slip and fall. I need to go to the hospital. I'm having bad stomach pains. I think the baby is in trouble."

(Fucking kill that Satan spawn of a baby! Cut it out of her, Steve-O! Your wife fucked Satan and got pregnant! Kill the bitch and that evil seed of a demon growing in her before I do!)

"The baby is fine. You're shaken up at the moment. You had a scary event happen."

Keisha was fuming now. She wasn't before, but for some reason listening to Steven talk sparked a rage inside of her. She started slapping him. "You miserable fuck! You ruined our lives by moving us to this house! God damn you to Hell! Get away from me! Get out!"

And he did. He lumbered back outside and resumed work on the trench for the in–ground pool. Denise rushed Keisha to the hospital. The baby was fine, fortunately. Denise helped Keisha come to her senses about Steven though. It wasn't Steven's fault she slipped in the tub— at least not directly.

Keisha was still infuriated with Steven. He helped make the ghost feel welcome by trying to communicate with it.

As Denise and Keisha drove home, Keisha proposed a plan to leave Steven; that is, if he didn't want to leave the house. Keisha didn't know if she could last until April waiting for the medium and her paranormal team. Denise listened and was supportive of Keisha's plan, but she also encouraged her to do her best to hold out as best she could.

While Steven was outside digging in the backyard, Steven glanced at the house a few times. All the lights were off except for those in the kitchen. About an hour later, Jeffrey's light was on, and someone stood staring at Steven from Jeffrey's bedroom window. It was the man in the black suit. Steven stabbed the ground with the shovel and ran into the house and up the stairs to Jeffrey's room, which was locked. Using his shoulder, he busted the door down and entered Jeffrey's room, which was pitch black.

"Dad!" a panic–stricken Jeffrey asked. "What's going on?" Jeffrey was asleep before his dad entered the bedroom and had been for some time.

"Where are you, you cowardly motherfucker?! I'll kill you! Leave my house! Leave! Leave! Leave!" He pressed his back against the wall near Jeffrey's door and slid to the floor. His breathing was labored. *I can't deal with this anymore.*

(Kill the boy! Do it! Look what he did! He left the bathroom light on again! You better do it soon or I will!)

"What's wrong, Dad?" Tiffany said standing in Jeffrey's doorway, squinting her eyes.

Steven shook his head. "That man in the black suit needs to go." He lumbered out of Jeffrey's room and went back outside to continue digging the trench for the swimming pool.

He was near the end of his rope. Time was running out to get rid of this persistent spirit. He knew if the man in the black suit didn't leave and continued to terrorize the family, Keisha would leave him and take the children with her. Nothing would tear him up more if that happened. At the same time, he didn't want to leave the house either. It was too nice of a house to walk away. And, because he'd had difficulty paying bills on time, his credit was shot to shit. He wouldn't be able to secure a mortgage to pay for a nice house like the one he had now.

Around one in the morning, Steven oafishly walked into his bedroom, stripped to his boxers and T-shirt, and slipped into bed. He laid awake and his thoughts raced. Eventually, mental exhaustion from the racing thoughts led to him falling asleep, but it didn't last long. The sound of shattered glass followed by the house alarm interrupted his— and everyone else's— slumber.

"What the—" he said leaping out of bed and running down the hallway. "Everyone stay in your rooms! Where's my nine! Where's my nine!"

"You don't have a nine! Quit saying that!" Keisha yelled from their bedroom.

He ran down the stairs and opened the front door. A luxury car— maybe a Lincoln town car— sped away. The smell of burnt rubber made Steven's nose hairs twitch. He ran down the lawn and into the street but there was no sign of the car.

He lumbered back inside the house to assess the damage. The sitting room window was busted for a second time and shattered glass littered the floor. In the sitting room, he found a brick with a note attached to it with rubber bands. The note said: TIME'S UP.

He called the police, but this time Keisha dealt with them. Steven couldn't handle Officers McDuff and Davies again. While she dealt with the police, Steven resumed digging in the backyard.

As the early morning hours passed, Steven decided to go inside and sleep. He did for about an hour, then woke up to get ready for work. As he slipped the knot of his tie to his collar, something registered in his brain. An E.V.P. *In the walls. Maybe the spirit left something behind the in the walls and wants it... Nah, that's too far–fetched. Go to your stressful job and get shit on by that pervert of a boss. Hopefully the boss will be out of the office today.*

One thing that always seemed to help minimize the stressors in his life was coffee. He poured some coffee into his World's Greatest Dad mug and walked into the living room. He picked the family picture up and set it on the mantel. He looked at the picture as he sipped his coffee.

He checked his combover a few times in the mirror above the fireplace. On his final check, someone was standing in the doorway of the kitchen. It was the man in the black suit. Steven turned around, but the man in the black suit was no longer there.

It was time for a refill. One more cup, then off to work. He walked towards the kitchen.

(World's Greatest Dad! Ha! You aren't shit!)

Then his favorite coffee mug was airborne. It struck the mirror above the mantel, causing an explosion of sound and shattering the glass.

(Do I have your attention now, Steve-O? Time's a–wastin', mole face! Kill 'em before she leaves with the kids and that weeble–people walkin' bitch Denise! Kill them, my boy!)

CHAPTER TWENTY-FOUR

Denise Departs

"I called the medium and asked if there is any way she and her team can get out here sooner. No luck," Steven said to Keisha and Denise. They were sitting at the dining room table, drinking coffee and eating breakfast. Steven cooked scrambled eggs this morning for everyone— including the children, all of whom were at school at this point.

Keisha was tired. She wanted to cut their losses and move somewhere else, but Steven persistently told her they needed to stay and fight for their house. Regardless, she tried to convince him otherwise. "I've said it before. It's time to leave, Steven. I'm sick of this house. I'm tired of fighting whatever is here. Let's leave." Keisha said.

Steven hesitated to speak. Then he said, "When I first met John he told me you can't run away from your problems. There's no guarantee if we do move we'd be any safer. Also, the next place we move into could be just as haunted or worse. We know the devil we have. If we move, we may not like the devil we get."

Keisha cried. "I'm tired, Steven. I can't do it anymore. Please, let's walk away from this house."

Steven said, "The spirit that's here may follow us to the new house. We need to stay and fight that fucker."

"Darlin', I think Steven's right," Denise said to Keisha. "And it's only a few more months until April. This spirit— this man in the black suit— seems to be passive–aggressive. He tries to scare us, but he's not trying to hurt us. Just hang in there a little longer and you'll see it will work out in the end."

(Is that a challenge Steve-O? That bitch should be dead by now! You're getting cold feet! Finish the job! Kill all of 'em!)

"I also called the chief of police yesterday and told him Detective Auckland needs to be removed from the cases. When Terry and I had the altercation, he revealed to me his brother was a cop. After some sleuthing, I confirmed that the lead detective handling the harassment and vandalism cases is in fact Terry's brother. The chief spit loudly into the phone and said, 'Mr. Dobrowski, there are some things that are better left alone.' Then he hung up on me."

"Shit, I'm not surprised. This whole city is racist. The cops are clearly coverin' for whoever the perpetrator is, and if you want my opinion, I think it's Terry." Denise said. She took a sip of her coffee. "The racist people in this city would be of a reason to move somewhere else than that fruity fuckin' spirit livin' in this house. Black–suit–wearin' bitch."

(She's going to pay for that Steve-O! Break that fucking coffee mug she's drinking from over her nappy ass head!)

Steven swallowed hard, then spoke. He said, "I think it's Terry, too. I think his brother has been covering for him. I left several more messages for the chief and he finally relented after I threatened to go to the mayor, the

D.A., and the F.B.I. There's a new lead detective on the case now. Terry better be careful."

Keisha said, "I still can't believe you pulled a gun on him. Where did you get that gun from anyway?"

"From the sporting goods store Sebastian works at. By the way, the gun is in a lock box in our closet, just in case you need it."

(Gut shoot them, Stevie! Let them bleed out slowly! Shoot them, then gut them like a pig! Especially that fat foul-mouthed cunt bitch mother–in–law of yours! Then your ass ugly wife! You better get it done soon, my boy! Tick-tock! Kill those chocolate milk children of yours, also!)

"Say what now? What happened? And why isn't your criminal ass in jail?" Denise asked.

"Criminal? I'm not a criminal," Steven said.

"You can't be pullin' guns on people, you fool. You should be in jail," Denise snapped back.

(You're going to let her talk to you like that, Steve-O? Slit that bitch's throat! Get that electric knife you used last night to slice the turkey and slice that bitch's turkey neck!)

Steven sighed, "It was self–defense."

"What the hell are you talking about," Denise said. "What happened? Why am I hearing this now?"

"Mom, you were sick in bed the past three days with abdominal pain and nausea. I'm sorry I didn't tell you." Keisha proceeded to tell the story. "Steven came home early from work to get some documents he left in his office. I was up there with him searching for stamps in one of his desk drawers. I came across a letter belonging to Terry that Steven chose to not return. Can you believe that?"

"Shit, I can see why. Terry is one rotten motherfucker," Denise said as she added some more sugar to her coffee and stirred it.

Denise wanted to see Terry suffer. He was always nasty to her, and to Keisha and the kids. He also constantly taunted Steven about lynching them.

Keisha continued. "Anyway, Mom. I went over to Terry's to return it. As I was walking up Terry's driveway, he stepped out of his house and started saying all sorts of racist things to me. When I told him I was there to return a letter, he said, 'Why would I want it now after your nasty ass fingers touched it. Leave it in the mailbox, you tree–swinging ape.' So I did. As I walked back to the house, he pushed me to the ground. Steven ran towards Terry and slammed his flour face against his car. Steven yelled, 'Where's my nine? Where's my nine?' I, of course, said my usual reply to his stupid remark. I said, 'You don't have a nine!' Then to my surprise, Steven pulled out a nine-millimeter handgun and pressed it against Terry's fine–lined forehead."

"Oh, my. Lord have mercy," Denise said as she placed her hands to the sides of her face.

"Steven made it clear to Terry that if he ever touched me again, he'd kill him. I have to admit, it was scary and exciting at the same time."

"Damn, Steven. I didn't know you had that in you. Good for you," Denise said. "Still, you both could be in jail right now."

"Thanks, Mom. I know I wouldn't have been in jail, though," Steven replied.

"While we're on the subject of neighbors, how's John been?"

Steven took a sip of coffee. "He's fine. He's in Wisconsin visiting his daughter and grandchildren. He'll be back in a month or so. He took all his vacation time."

Denise said, "He works at the drywall place? Gypsy, right?"

"Gypsum," Keisha replied.

"Well, I'm pleased to hear that portly, jolly Santa–Claus–lookin' man is doing fine. Don't you two agree he looks so much like Santa Claus?"

"Yeah," Keisha and Steven replied, then chuckled.

"Except for his dirty beard. He needs to dye that sucker one color. Pick a color and stick with it." Denise's coffee cup was nearly empty. "Son, I'm circling the drain with coffee. Would you please get me some more?"

He stood and replied to her request. "Sure, Mom. I need a refill, also." Looking at Keisha, he said, "Let me get you some more coffee, too." He took the cups to the kitchen and refilled their cups. When he set their cups in front of them, he said, "Oh, I talked to the credit card companies and they gave us a forbearance."

Keisha said, "I'm sorry I've been unable to secure a job, babe. I think I have three strikes against me. I'm a woman, I'm black, and I'm pregnant. I've gone to several interviews and haven't been offered a thing."

"Well, shit, darlin'. You shouldn't be workin' anyway. You're pregnant," Denise insisted.

Keisha took a sip of her coffee. "Mom, lots of pregnant women work."

(God damn you, Stevie! I told you to snuff that demonic fetus out like a lit cigarette! DO IT SOON OR I WILL!)

Steven took out his Lexapro bottle and popped three pills into his mouth and swallowed. "I had that nightmare again."

Denise replied, "Lord, no. You mean the one about your mother blowin' your mole face— whoa, excuse me, I mean your face— off at her grave."

"Yeah," Steven confirmed as he set his cup of coffee down. "That one." His eyes welled up with tears.

"Oh, babe. I wish you could stop having that dream," Keisha said. A small part of her was delighted Steven was being tortured. Before, everyone in the house was suffering except for him.

"Then I had another one, but not about my mother. This one involved the man in the black suit. There was no audio in the dream and I wasn't sure where I was, but three men were talking. I tried to read their lips, but couldn't. Then one of the three men wrapped a cord around another man's neck and strangled him."

"That's an awful dream, son," Denise said as she rubbed his back. "Start prayin'. It'll help."

(Fuck praying! Don't you dare pray, Stevie! I'll kill you if you do!)

Keisha said, "Tiffany's school counselor called me earlier today. She's passing all her subjects with flying colors and made the honor roll."

"Lord, that's amazin'," Denise said as she stood and picked up her personalized plate.

"I'll take care of that for you, Mom," Steven said. "Did you want some more eggs?" And she did, so Steven plated her some eggs and sprinkled some Mrs. Dash on it for her.

Although Denise cooked many of the meals, Steven insisted on serving them to the family. He plated everyone's food and, like a restaurant waiter, served everyone. It helped take his mind off things. Denise found it odd, though. Why would he work long hours trying to prove himself so he could get a promotion and make more money to sustain the household only to come home and work even more. Neither Denise or Keisha worked. Denise felt they should be serving the meals. Regardless, though, Denise let Steven do what he wanted; it wasn't her house, after all, and it made Steven happy to do it.

Keisha, Denise, and the children continued to attend church every Wednesday and Sunday. Those days Steven did a lot of the cooking, namely breakfast and dinner. He made arrangements with his boss so he could have Wednesdays as one of his off days, which allowed him to cook both breakfast and dinner on that day.

He returned to the dining room with Denise's plate.

Thank you, son," she said. After she swallowed a mouthful of eggs, she said, "I saw the man in the black suit near the foot of my bed last night. He placed a noose around his neck and hanged himself in front of me."

Keisha excused herself to use the bathroom.

"Is that why you were cheering last night?" Steven asked.

"Fuck right, now. I want that fucker dead."

"He is dead; he's a ghost."

"Well, I mean I want his marshmallow ass the hell out of here. Come on, now, don't be playin' with me. That son of a bitch scared the hell out of me bad last week." She took another bite of eggs. "Steven, son, did you put any of my bitch's spice on these here eggs? They taste somewhat bland."

(She's ridiculing your cooking, you ugly bald mole–faced fuck! Take her fork and stab her over and over again in the neck! Her blood will be a nice substitute for ketchup on those eggs! Then cram the fucking bloody eggs down her throat as she chokes on her own blood! DO IT! DO IT! DO IT!)

Steven rapidly shook his head a few times as if to reset his mind. "I did, Mom. Not enough?"

"Son, please get me my Mrs. Dash."

"I put plenty on there. Isn't that enough?"

"No, it's not. Now, please got get my bitch's spice. I'm not feeling well at all. I threw up blood again this morning. Go get it."

And he did. She generously sprinkled Mrs. Dash on her eggs and took a bite. "Mmmm! Now that's some good eats."

"How did the man in the black suit scare you?" Steven asked, twisting the cap back on the Mrs. Dash bottle.

"I went into the livin' room to watch me a little T.V. Family Feud. Oh! I just love that bald–headed tall glass of mocha host! Anyways, I turned the T.V. on and flip to my Family Feud. Moments later, the T.V. shut off. So I turn it back on, and moments later, the motherfucker turns off once again."

Steven chuckled. "Are you sure it wasn't Jeffrey pranking you?"

"No, because I told him if he ever pranked me again, I'd tear his ass up. He don't play with me no more. So, I tries the remote, and it wouldn't work at all. I pushed the power button several times, but the T.V. wouldn't turn on. So I gets up and moseys on over to the T.V. and try to turn it back on, but it doesn't respond. I turn my back to go to the kitchen to get me some Jon Daly, and out of the clear blue the T.V. turns on with volume at full blast and someone says, 'Are you ready to die?' At first, I thought it was the man in the black suit speaking from his grave."

"Oh, wow. That must have scared you." Steven said.

"Damn right, it did. My Shamu–sized ass nearly fell onto the motherfuckin' coffee table. Anyways, the T.V. turned off and I went to the kitchen and fixed me a little afternoon delight: iced tea with a little vodka added to it. I brought fresh batteries with me into the living room and replaced the old batteries in the remote with them."

"Oh, that makes sense. I'm dumb. It didn't enter my mind maybe the batteries were dead."

"Well, that wasn't it anyways. The T.V. wouldn't turn back on. I tossed the remote on the couch and the instant it hit it, the T.V. turned on with a white screen and ungodly loud static. The man in the black suit appeared in a flash and then disappeared. After that, I took my Jon Daly beverage and sat on the front porch." She took a few more bites of her eggs. Her eyes became heavy. She started to cough and couldn't stop.

"Mom?" Steven asked. "Mom? Mom? Drink some water."

She coughed and choked and gagged. Steven performed the Heimlich, but it was useless. She continued to cough, choke, gag, and vomit.

"Jesus Christ! Steven! What the hell is wrong with Mom?" Keisha asked.

"I don't know! I tried to stop her from choking!"

"Call an ambulance!"

(Don't you do it! Let that rotund bitch choke to death! Then call for a hearse!)

Denise was transported to the local hospital where she was pronounced dead on arrival. The primary cause of death was not by choking; it was a heart attack.

At the hospital, Steven and Keisha sat in a waiting area. They were asked if they wanted to view the body and they did. Keisha said, "That was frightening, Steven. She died a horrible death. How are you holding up?"

(No it wasn't! It was a great show! Right, Steve-O! Fuck that dead bitch!)

"Me? I'm shaken up, but I'm keeping it together. Why do you ask?" Steven replied.

Keisha shook her head. "Never mind."

"No, please."

"Well, seeing my mom choke the way she did brought back memories of Granana's death. She died in our dining room at our old house and in a similar manner. I didn't want to mention it because I didn't want you to be flooded with the awful memory."

Steven had to stand. "I remember. My mom died in my arms."

"There's something else I wanted to ask you about your mom. I know you don't like me asking this, but I feel the need to do so. Have you cried yet for your mom?"

"We've been over this. I don't want to talk about it."

Keisha had her answer without him saying a word. "I think once you cry, you'll stop having that recurring dream of your mother blowing your head clean off your shoulders." She approached him and held his hand. He didn't look at her though.

He fought back tears. He wanted to change the subject. "I don't understand why the man in the black suit continues to return. We banish him, he returns. We banish him, he returns. All those paranormal shows we watched, I think, are not grounded in reality."

"What do you mean?"

"I've seen episodes where a priest blesses the house, and POOF! The spirit or demon is gone for good. Or a medium frees the spirit. It must not be reality."

"No, that's not true. I've seen some episodes where the spirit does return, but the family doesn't stay and fight. It packs up and leaves."

He turned to her. "Is that what you want to do? Do you want to leave?"

She didn't answer right away. Part of her wanted him to sweat a little waiting for her answer. "Not anymore. And, I think now that my mom is in Heaven, she's going to be a guardian angel for us. She'll watch over us and make sure the man in the black suit stays in line. She told me she would a few weeks ago when she was bedridden and seemed deathly ill."

(Oh, is that so! You better kill your due–to–deliver–a–demon–baby wife and that demon fuck of a baby she's carrying! Then kill those ungrateful children of yours! Or I will! I think I've already proven I can kill!)

"She said she'd watch over us?" Steven asked.

"Yes. Steven, what's with your eyes? They look... different. It's frightening me."

"Nothing is wrong with them. They're fine." He turned away from her and violently shook his head a few times.

(You can't shake me off, Steve-O! We're inseparable! Kill your ugly wife and children and I'll leave you in peace! If you don't, I'll leave you in pieces instead! Kill those motherfuckers slowly and painfully! Until then, I'm going to continue to fuck your mind more times than a two–dollar whore!)

He removed an Altoids tin from his pocket and placed three Lexapro pills from the tin into his mouth. Keisha asked for a couple of his mints and he obliged.

Keisha said, "Your eyes are blackened. Maybe while we're here at the hospital you can see a doctor."

"No!" he shouted, then walked away from her.

The wake was two days later and the funeral was two days thereafter. Denise's wishes were to be cremated. Keisha had her mother's ashes placed in the vase she gave her months ago, when Steven and Keisha first moved into the house.

Among the three children, Brittany was hit the hardest. To her, it was like losing Granana all over again.

Over the next two months, Steven exhibited violent and unpredictable mood swings. At times he was his normal self while at others he turned into someone nobody in the house recognized. He wavered between happiness and anger.

Even his walking had its own extremes. Sometimes he would walk like the average person while at others he would lumber.

Through prayer and support from friends at church, Keisha stood by her husband, though at times she wanted to pack up and leave.

It seemed Grams was keeping the man in the black suit at bay, though he still popped up once in a while. On one occasion, he ransacked the kitchen from top to bottom. Anything glass in the kitchen was destroyed, including doors to the microwave and bagel toaster.

As a promise to Grams, Keisha continued to attend church with the children on Wednesdays and Sundays. St. Matthews was under new leadership. Father Matthews was removed when he was arrested for solicitation of sex to a minor— a sixth–grade boy.

Sadly, a few weeks after Denise's passing, Keisha had a premature delivery and gave birth to a stillborn. Steven seemed unaffected by this tragic event, and in some respects, he was happy. Keisha attributed this to his addiction to Lexapro. She looked forward to the day she could admit him to a mental facility to receive the treatment he desperately needed.

CHAPTER TWENTY-FIVE
Granana Visits

Keisha was intensely angry with Steven, and intended to leave him if his demeanor and behavior didn't change. She believed his behavior was a manifestation of stress from work coupled with his abuse of Lexapro.

John suggested she admit him to a mental health facility to detox, but she couldn't. It would be a financial disaster if he was in detox and not working. Once the estate of her mom was out of probate and she received her inheritance, she planned to admit Steven to a mental health facility to become clean. In the meantime, she replaced some of his Lexapro meds with aspirin tablets. Interestingly, this diminished some of his symptoms, and he was never the wiser because he never checked the pills before ingesting them.

Brittany's bedroom opened and Scruffles jumped off the bed. When he was out in the hallway, the door closed. Uncharacteristically, he didn't scratch at the door for some strange reason.

"Brittany?... Brittany?" an angelic voice said.

"Granana?" Brittany replied, her voice lethargic.

"Yes, angel. It's Granana."

Brittany woke up and turned the light on her nightstand on. Standing at the foot of her bed was

Granana. She wore the same dress in which she was buried— a white dress with lavender flowers.

"My special angel," Granana said. "I got your card. It's good to be able to visit with you again— just like old times."

"I miss you, Granana. How's Heaven been?"

"It's been wonderful. Soon, you and I will be there together. I'm excited about that. Aren't you?"

"It would be nice for us to be together again."

"Yes, it would, and you can join me in Heaven whenever you're ready. All you have to do is die, and once you do that, I'll be at the gates of Heaven waiting to greet you."

"But, Granana, I won't be dying for a long time. I'm still a little girl."

Granana snickered. "I know that, my special angel, but you can choose when you die, too. You don't have to wait for the Grim Reaper to take your hand. Oh, my special, special angel, how I miss us spending time together. I want us to be able to do all the things we used to do. If you truly love me, you'll come to Heaven soon."

"How can I do that?"

"End your life, angel. Let me give you some options on how to do that. You ready to hear how you can get to Heaven?"

Brittany swallowed hard. "Yes, Granana. I'm ready."

Granana smiled. "That's good. The important thing to remember is you have to choose a way you're comfortable with, and you should think carefully before you decide. Now, here are some ways. You could open your window and jump out. You won't feel a thing. I promise you, my angel. Or you could hang yourself in the attic using Tiffany's rope. Or you could sneak some of your daddy's pills and swallow them all down with some of his wine. I'll unlock the liquor cabinet for you if you decide to end your life this way. You could use your dad's gun and shoot yourself in the head. You could cut your wrists and neck using the blade of one of your sister's cheap razors. I already took the liberty of taking one of them out for you. The blade is tucked away in the back of the bathroom drawer where the cotton balls are. Now, if you're scared, that's understandable, but know that when you end your life, I'll be there by your side to take you to Heaven. If you truly love me, you'll join me in Heaven now. Do you want— "

Another apparition of Granana appeared at the foot of Brittany's bed. "Brittany, my special angel, don't listen to her. She's not me. She's an impostor. She's misleading you. It's evil. Ignore her."

The first apparition countered. "I'm your Granana, Brittany. She's lying to you. She doesn't want you to be happy in Heaven with me."

"Brittany, ignore her. This person is trying to send you to Hell. Don't listen to her. Don't do a thing she's said. You listen to your— "

The first apparition of Granana grabbed the second apparition by the hair and threw her backwards and she disappeared.

"Granana!" Brittany shrieked. "What did you do with my Granana?"

Then the apparition of Granana morphed into a solid black humanoid figure with red eyes and snarled at Brittany.

She screamed at the top of her lungs and the apparition faded away. Keisha ran into her bedroom. "What's wrong, baby doll. Are you okay?"

"No! The mean man hurt Granana!"

"How? Baby doll, Granana is in Heaven."

Brittany wanted to explain what she meant, but she couldn't find the words. "I don't know how to explain it."

"It's okay, baby doll," Keisha said as she embraced Brittany. As she hugged Brittany, she had her eyes closed. When she opened them, she screamed. "Oh, my God!"

Jeffrey and Tiffany stood at the doorway to Brittany's room.

"Mom! What's wrong?" Jeffrey asked

"Brittany, your Michael statue. Don't look, baby doll."

"God in Heaven," Tiffany said.

"Tiffany, take Brittany," Keisha insisted. She walked over to the Michael statue. The sword Michael once leaned on and touched ground now impaled him though the abdomen. Both of Michael's hands clutched the handle of the sword as if it were self–inflicted. A trail of blood exuded from the wound onto the base of the statue and from there onto Brittany's nightstand. Additionally, Michael's eyes wept blood.

Keisha was afraid to touch the statue. She didn't know what would happen if she did. She left it where it was.

"I need to get my children out of this house," she whispered. "We need to leave." As she turned around to go to tell the children to pack some things, Steven was standing in the doorway of Brittany's room.

"What's going on?" he asked, his tone stoic.

"I'm leaving. I'm taking the children somewhere safe. You can stay here or you can go with, but my mind is made up. This house is too dangerous. Please move out of my way. There's nothing more to discuss."

Steven's blank expression slowly changed to a smile. Then he said, "No one is going anywhere... We're staying here and we're going to fight this man in the black suit, this unrested spirit. This is our house, not his. Not any other entity. Ours." He smiled again and continued to smile as Keisha responded.

Her anger and frustration were firing on all cylinders now, and she held nothing back. She shouted, "The man in the black suit is not a spirit, you fucking stoned idiot! You're too drugged up with Lexapro to see and comprehend reality! The man in the black suit isn't an unrested spirit! It's a demon from Hell! Look at Brittany's statue! We're dealing with something we can't contend with, you fucker! You can stay here and fight this demon yourself or you can come with us, but I'm taking my children the hell out of here! Now move the fuck out of my way!"

He was still wearing the smile from before. "Sure," he said, moving out of the doorway.

She ran to the Tiffany's room. Brittany and Tiffany were on the bed. Jeffrey was sitting on the floor. Keisha said, "Pack some clothes as quickly as possible. We're getting out of here. Pack your bag and wait outside on the porch."

They started to pack and Keisha went to her bedroom to pack a bag for herself. Steven was not in their bedroom. Keisha's neck was grabbed and she was catapulted onto the bed. The grip never loosened while she was airborne and now it was even tighter. Then Steven started talking as Keisha struggled and gasped for air. "Now, you listen to me, you bitch. You will never leave me. Because if you do, I'll find you... You don't believe me? How can I be strangling you and talking to you but not even be in the same room as you? I'll find you and I'll kill you... And I'll kill the children... Until death do we part, baby. Don't fuck with me." After Keisha lost consciousness, the invisible grip clutching her neck released.

Brittany walked into her mom's bedroom wearing a nice T-shirt and a pair of short pink overalls. On her back was her backpack. Her hair was in pigtails. Brittany tapped her mom on the shoulder a few times and said, "Mom? Mom? Can you take me to school now?"

Keisha was startled and woke up. Still lying on her back, she turned her head towards Brittany. "What time is it?"

"Eight-thirty-something, Mommy. I let you sleep. You looked so tired this morning. I made breakfast myself."

"You did? What did you make?"

"Cereal. Apple Squares." Brittany smiled at her.

"I feel weird, baby doll. Something isn't right."

"Are you sick, Mommy?"

"A little bit, but my sick is more up here in my head than anywhere else. Did you have a bad dream last night?"

"No, not at all, Mommy. I dreamed about Granana again. She gave me all sorts of good advice." Brittany walked towards the closet, then opened it. She looked up at the top shelf. "I can't wait for Daddy to teach me how to shoot a gun. Then I fill the man in the black suit full of holes." Brittany giggled.

"Shut Mommy's closet door, baby doll. We need to leave now. Meet me downstairs, okay? Take Scruffles outside, please."

"Okay, Mommy." Brittany hightailed it out of her mom's room.

Keisha dressed herself and stepped into the hallway to go downstairs. As she walked down the hallway, Brittany's door opened of its own accord, but Keisha didn't have an ominous feeling overtake her like she did lately when unexplained things happened in the house. This was different. She stood in the doorway to Brittany's room and peeked around. Everything seemed in place. Bed was made. Room was neat. *What a lovely little memoriam she's created for Granana. Nightstand. Plate. Crucifix on the bed.*

"Mommy? Can we go now, please?" Brittany asked, calling from downstairs in the living room.

"On my way," she said. As she walked away from Brittany's room, the door slammed shut, startling her. *Your time is almost over in my house, man in the black suit,* she thought. *You'll be on your way to Heaven soon.*

The drive to school was short. Brittany could have walked there, but she didn't want to take a chance having her walk in a racist community and then become six o'clock news. That fear was a reality given the bricks thrown through their window and the harassing notes left in their mailbox. A few days ago, another letter was slipped in the mailbox threatening to burn their house to the ground.

When Keisha pulled into the elementary school parking lot, Brittany asked a question that had been on her mind since she had her dream about Granana. "Would you be mad at me if I visited Granana in Heaven?"

"Baby doll, why are you asking that question?"

Brittany lowered her head. "I miss her that much, Mommy."

Keisha rubbed Brittany's head. She said, "I know you do, baby doll, but your Granana will have an eternity to see you when your time comes. She would want you to experience a long and full life just as she did. We'll talk more about this when you get home from school."

They hugged, and Brittany went into the school. Keisha drove home. *I feel like I had an out–of–body experience. My mind is scrambled.*

In Keisha's mind, Granana's voice said, "Where's the Michael statue?"

When Keisha returned home, she walked upstairs and opened Brittany's door. She stood in the doorway, focusing on the nightstand. The Michael statue was missing. Thinking about the Michael statue helped jog her memory about last night's events, but she remembered only in bits and pieces, not events or a continuous stream.

The ring of her cellphone shattered her concentration. The call was from Bryan Kaldenbach, the lead investigator from the paranormal group that would be investigating the house in April. He wanted to contact Keisha to see if there had been any activity from the man in the black suit recently since Keisha hadn't sent him any recent updates.

Keisha said, "The man in the black suit hasn't made too many appearances recently. I think my mom is keeping him on a tight leash. I do feel her presence in this house more so than I do the man in the black suit's."

"That's good news. We'll be there in April to conduct a full–scale investigation and rid the house of the man in the black suit. In the meantime, hang in there. April isn't too far off."

CHAPTER TWENTY-SIX

Mr. Quacks Sleeps with the Fishes

Sebastian and Tiffany were sitting on the larger couch in the living room, watching T.V. They had spent the morning exercising and studying together. She was going to make some lunch for them in a little bit. After lunch, they had plans to drive to a university to check out a campus Sebastian was interested in attending after graduation.

She sat on the couch, staring at Sebastian. She was enamored with him. Her sexual attraction to him was growing, also. She leaned over and kissed him on his freckled cheek. He said, "Thanks, but what was that for?"

"No reason, other than I wanted to," she said, smiling widely.

"Well, two can play that game." He kissed her on the cheek in response, not once or twice, but three times.

"So, it's a game, now, huh? I see your three pecks on the cheek and raise you a kiss on the lips." Then she followed through. "How was that? Did you like it?"

"Very much," he said, placing the newspaper sitting on the coffee table over his shorts.

She giggled. "You know, Sebastian, we can take things to the next level. We have been going together for quite some time now."

"What do you mean?" he asked her, trying to focus his mind on redirecting the blood flow to other parts of his body.

"I'll show you." She took his hand and placed it on her neck. He gently massaged it. She said, "You can go lower, if you want." And he did. She was becoming as aroused as he was. He pulled his hand away, but she brought it back, placing it on the exposed part of her cleavage. He continued to rub the upper part of her breasts. She said, "You can go lower if you want."

"I don't know if we should. We're in the living room and your dad is outside in the backyard digging. He could walk in at any time."

He wanted to go lower, but he also didn't want to suffer the wrath of Steven, whose behavior and temperament were about as predictable as knowing when and where lightning was going to strike.

"Okay," she said, discouraged he didn't want to go any further. He continued to caress the exposed part of her cleavage though. A few moments later, he started to rub the lower parts of her breasts. She moaned in pleasure. Then she said, "You can even squeeze them if you want."

"Really?... When?" he asked, as his hand continued to caress her curves.

"Whenever."

A few more laps around the track, and then it happened. He grasped her breast as if squeezing remnant juice from a lemon. "Ow!" she exclaimed, slapping him on his arm.

"Ouch! What the fluff? What happened? I did what you said." He was honestly bewildered.

"Not like that. They're sensitive."

"Well, I'm sorry. This is all new to me. I've never done this stuff before."

She rubbed her assaulted breast. "It's okay. I'm sorry, too. We're both new to this. A little at a time." Both heard the back door open and close. "I'll go make us some lunch."

Steven lumbered into the living room and sat next to Sebastian. He leaned over and spoke. "Trying it before buying it, huh? Good for you, son."

Sebastian didn't respond. His mind was scrambled. He didn't hear Steven right; he heard Steven say, "Trying it before buying it is good for you, son." His mind wondered if Steven saw what he and his daughter did, or was he psychic, or was Steven in the dark and simply making another suggestion. Finally, he said, "How are you, Mr. D?"

Speaking slowly in a dry tone, he said, "Not well, son. Not well. The man in the black suit ruined me. He won. Last night, he scared the hell out of my wife." As Steven spoke, Sebastian turned his head towards the T.V. but was still listening. Steven snapped, "Do you want to hear the god damn story or am I fucking boring you to death?"

Sebastian was startled by the abrupt change in Steven's attitude. He turned the T.V. off. He said, "Yes, I'd like to hear the story."

Steven swallowed hard and took a deep breath. "Good. That's better. I'll tell you the fucking story then." He started wickedly laughing, then continued to tell the story. "Keisha was trying to nap in our bedroom. I was at work— I mean, where the fuck else would I be, right? Got to work to pay the bills, son. I work and have nothing. Always fucking broke. Can't pay my fucking bills because that bitch wife can't get herself a job. Oh, that bitch... She's going to pay... At least her dead mom's insurance money will be funneling in soon... My wife and kids have insurance pol— Anyway, the kids were at school and Scruffles was lying in the bed next to her, so nobody else could have been in the house. Now— " Steven shouted, "Are you fucking paying attention to my god damn story?"

"Dad!" Tiffany said from the kitchen. "Take it easy!"

"Fuck yourself! I pay the fucking god damn bills in this evil haunted house, you tramp. Shut the fuck up before I nail you to a cross!" He resumed talking to Sebastian. "Anyhow, Keisha woke up to these sounds coming from the attic. She got up and walked up the attic stairs. When she reached the top, she saw no one. Not a soul. Still, she's one curious bitch, so she inspected all around the attic, and couldn't find a motherfucking thing. She was as far back in the attic as you could go. Are you with me, boy?"

"Ye— "

"Don't fucking interrupt me when I'm storytelling! It's rude, son!" He took a breath, then proceeded telling his story. "So, as I was saying, she was clear on the other side of the attic. Her back was to the stairs. When she turned around, she saw the man in the black suit hanging from Tiffany's rope." Steven remained silent for several seconds. Then he continued using his slow–paced dry tone. "It took me four hours of begging and pleading and ass kissing and boot licking to convince that fat–with–child bitch to stay with me— for the sake of the family and for the sake of keeping this marvelous house of ours. I'd kill that bitch before I'd let her leave me. I love her that much." Steven stood and lumbered to the hearth. He placed the picture on the mantel— the glass still shattered. He knelt down to pick up the crucifix. Right before his fingers touched the wood, he relented. "Fuck it. Let it sit there. I'm getting a vibe I shouldn't touch it." As he lumbered to the kitchen, the family picture slid and landed on the hearth. He approached Tiffany who was slicing the sandwiches but he said nothing. He stared at her until she left the kitchen.

He made a fresh pot of coffee. As it brewed, Brittany ran into the kitchen, crying, and said, "Daddy! Mr. Quacks is sick. Look at his legs. They're coming off again. Please fix Mr. Quacks. Please!"

He knelt down to be at eye–level with her. "I promise you I'll take care of Mr. Quacks for you. You can stop crying."

"Thank you, Daddy! I love you! I hope you feel better."

Keisha walked in the kitchen. "We're going to the store. You need anything?" she asked Steven.

He stood and looked into her eyes. "Just for you to come back." He knew she was plotting to leave him and take the children with her. He was waiting for her to tell him. It was coming. Maybe not today or tomorrow, but it was imminent.

"I will."

(You fucking wimp! You know she's lying to your ugly face! She's going to leave you and find another man

to fuck! Kill her now! And then kill that little mini–bitch daughter! I'm about done telling you!)

"Good... Thank you... The thought of us— you, me, the kids— not being together hurts me more than you'll ever know."

"Okay. See you later," Keisha said. "Come on, baby doll. Let's go."

(Kill her now! She gets away, she'll never return! Slit her throat! Then kill the children!)

After tending to Mr. Quacks, he did some additional work on the swimming pool trench. The dimensions of the trench were eight–and–a–half feet long by twelve feet wide. The depth of the trench was approximately six feet.

Next to the trench was a pile of tombstones he had created in the past week. Each tombstone had a wooden stake nailed to the back of it. Along the longer side of the deep, rectangular trench, Steven planted six wooden black–painted tombstones— all equally spaced apart— into the ground. They were shaped like a Norman window, a seamless fusion of a rectangle and semicircle. From left to right: STEVEN DOBROWSKI, 1981-; KEISHA DOBROWKSI, 1980-; JEFFREY DOBROWSKI, 2002-; TIFFANY DOBROWSKI, 2004-; BRITTANY DOBROWSKI, 2012-; DEMON BABY, 2017-2018.

(You better kill them slowly and painfully, you ugly ogre fuck! I want to hear bones breaking! I want to hear the sounds of a knife piercing their organs! Let's make the pain last as long as possible! Once it's over, I'll leave!)

He covered the tombstones with a large blue tarp, then resumed preparing dinner for the family he loved. Tonight's dinner menu was out of the ordinary. He was eager to try it, and he couldn't wait to see the faces of how tasty the meal was once they tried it also.

When Brittany and Keisha returned home, Brittany ran from the car to her dad, who was in the kitchen. She said, "Daddy! How's Mr. Quacks? Is he all better?"

Keisha walked in carrying plastic bags of groceries in both hands and placed them on the counter.

Steven smiled, and in that slow, dry voice, he responded to her question. He was excited to provide her with an update about her beloved Mr. Quacks. "I'm so glad you asked me that. Let me check on dinner first." Brittany took a seat on one of the kitchen stools. He lumbered over to the oven and pulled out a pan without using an oven mitt. He placed what he cooked in the oven on a cooling rack and moved the cooling rack in front of Brittany and Keisha. "I hope you're all hungry for duck."

In the pan was a smoldering, blackened stuffed animal, the beloved Mr. Quacks.

"Daddy! Brittany screamed. "You killed Mr. Quacks! How could you?" She dropped to the floor and started wailing. "You killed Mr. Quacks! How could you?"

"God damn you, Steven! This was the last straw! I'm done with you! You're too far out of your mind to be around! I'm leaving you!" She rushed Brittany out of the room.

As Keisha headed up the stairs, Steven's voice faintly said, "No, you won't." Then grinned.

Steven slammed the pan containing Mr. Quacks several times on the counter and shouted. "Mr. Quacks is fucking dead! Mr. Quacks is fucking dead! You all will be joining him soon! Mr. Quacks is fucking deaaaaaad! Mr. Quacks sleeps with the fishes! And you all will soon be sleeping with the fishes, too!" Then he laughed maniacally and wickedly.

Steven removed a plate from the kitchen cabinet and placed it on the counter, next to the cooling rack. With an electric carving knife, he bisected Mr. Quacks, then opened his chest up using a two-pronged serving fork and the knife blade. He removed several pieces of Mr. Quacks' insides and placed them on his dinner plate.

Simmering on the stove was an orange sauce. Using a small spoon, he stirred it and then sampled the sauce. He said, "Needs a little more sugar." After adding sugar, stirring, and sampling the sauce, he was content with it, and poured some of the sauce onto his plate.

Afterwards, he moved to the dining room table and enjoyed his meal. He elegantly placed some of the duck stuffing on his fork and lightly dipped it in the orange sauce, then ate it, slowly— relishing each bite. After swallowing the duck stuffing, he swished the merlot in his glass, sniffed it, took a swig and swished it around, then swallowed and savored it.

The screams and cries of Brittany added to the macabre ambiance of the meal. The meal was far more enjoyable to Steven with the screams and cries. Keisha toggled between cursing Steven and comforting Brittany.

Steven found the meal so delectable, he had seconds, during which time Sebastian and Tiffany returned. He said, "Would you two like to join me? I prepared stuffed duck tonight with a delicious orange sauce."

Tiffany said, "Yeah, Dad. Thanks. That sounds good."

"Thanks, Mr. D," Sebastian added.

"Great. That's fucking wonderful," Steven said, "You two soon–to–be–departed souls have a seat and pour yourselves some wine and drink it. I'll be right back."

When Steven left the room to plate their food, Sebastian said, "What does he mean soon–to–be–departed? That sounds like a threat."

"It's not a threat, son. Relax," Steven said from the kitchen. "Be right there. I need to heat this son of a bitch up for you." In the meantime, he returned to the dining room and placed a plate in front of Sebastian, then Tiffany. "How was the wine?"

"We didn't have any," Tiffany answered.

He was enraged that they disobeyed his order to have some wine. He poured each of them a glass and slammed the wine bottle on the table. He raised his glass to them and spoke. "Please drink with me. Here's to your health. Now drink!" And they did. Then the microwave chimed. In his slowly–spoken dry voice, he said, "It's ready." He returned moments later and placed the smoldering duck in front of them.

Tiffany wretched and vomited onto the dining room table. Sebastian nearly did the same, but he managed to stop himself.

"You're sick!" Tiffany said.

Tiffany and Sebastian went upstairs and found Keisha in Brittany's room. By this time, Brittany was asleep.

Throughout the evening and early morning hours, Steven consumed the stuffed duck and orange sauce. By daybreak, there was nothing left of Mr. Quacks.

CHAPTER TWENTY-SEVEN

The Last Supper, The Last Straw

Keisha searched high and low for a duck that was a replica of Mr. Quacks. She traveled from store to store the day after Steven turned Mr. Quacks into a gourmet meal, but she eventually found one. She felt Grams or Granana leading her to the right spot.

When she presented the duck to Brittany, she told her Steven was playing a mean joke on her. She told her Steven didn't cook Mr. Quacks at all— it was a different duck he cooked.

Brittany knew the truth, but she accepted the duck and didn't call her mom out on the carpet.

Brittany wasn't the only child to suffer at the hands of Steven. Back in January, Steven bound Jeffrey to a chair, moved him to the living room, smashed his cello to pieces using a sledgehammer, and threw the pieces in the lit fireplace.

About a month later, while Tiffany was at school, he annihilated the majority of Tiffany's exercise equipment with an ax. He videotaped the entire incident and sent it to her.

Finally, about two weeks after Tiffany's exercise equipment was destroyed, Steven threw Keisha's vase containing her mother's ashes onto the living room floor and rolled around in them like a pig in mud.

The time was approaching for Keisha to set her plan in motion to murder Steven. She was going to threaten to leave him once again to start an argument. Once it turned physical, she would shoot him and claim self–defense. She prayed to God her murderous plan would work; she never prayed for something as intensely as she did this.

The primary reason she waited this long was because she didn't want the insurance company to become suspicious. She took out a one–million–dollar life insurance policy out on Steven. She figured, if she's going to murder him, she may as well collect some money so his death wasn't completely in vain.

Keisha opened the back door to let Scruffles back in the house. The month was April and the weather was pleasant, which was a nice change from the bitterly cold and snowy winter.

She knelt down and petted him. "Good boy, Scruffs. Soon you, me, Brittany, Tiffany, and Jeffrey will be out of this house. You'll be in a better place soon."

She entered the kitchen to start dinner. Scruffles started barking and snarling. When Scruffles continued longer than usual, she stopped mixing her meat mix for meatloaf, wiped her hands, and walked to where Scruffles was barking. He was standing at the foot of the stairs, looking towards the top of the stairwell. She said, "There's nothing there, Scruffs. It's okay."

He continued snarling and barking, his intensity growing. "Scruffles, take it easy. Come on." She tried reached for his collar, but he lunged up four stairs, snarling and barking. He stood on the step for several seconds, incessantly snarling and barking. Then he lunged up four more steps. A black translucent mass passed through and around Scruffles, causing him to tumble down the stairs. He landed at Keisha's feet, eyes open and static.

"Scruffles! Scruffles!" she shrieked. She felt for a pulse; there was none. She laid next to him and cried for several minutes.

Out of desperation, she called Steven. When he answered, she said, "Steven, Scruffles is dead. He fell down the stairs."

He said, "What? No! Not Scruffles! Brittany is going to be crushed! I'm on my way home." And he was home within fifteen minutes.

Steven entered the living room and embraced Keisha. "I'm sorry this happened. I'll take care of Scruffles. We'll have a nice memorial service this weekend. We'll lay him to rest in the backyard, behind the garage." He removed his Altoids tin from his pants pocket and popped three pills into his mouth and swallowed, then exhaled a sigh of relief.

"That would be nice," Keisha said, wiping tears from her eyes. "I don't understand it. It was like something bum–rushed him.

From the garage, he brought in a wooden box to serve as a makeshift coffin. He gently placed Scruffles in it and placed a sheet over him. Then he placed a wooden lid on top of the box and moved the coffin to the garage, placing it inside the chest freezer.

When all three children arrived home from school, Steven and Keisha broke the unfortunate news to them. Brittany cried for hours, stopping only because she fell asleep from emotional exhaustion.

Around two in the morning, Granana— the real spirit of her— visited Brittany and told her Scruffles was with her in Heaven. She told Brittany to stay strong because soon a wonderful change would happen. She told Brittany she wouldn't be in that house much longer. She also told her Scruffles was looking for a special dog to send to her. Before leaving, Granana hugged Brittany, and told her she would bring Scruffles with her next she visited.

The next morning, the family dressed in all black and stood near the empty grave of Scruffles. Steven struggled to carry the coffin on his own, so Jeffrey sprang into action and offered his dad a hand. The coffin was gently placed into the grave and then each person said a few words, starting with Brittany and ending with Steven. Then each person placed a shovelful of dirt onto the coffin of Scruffles.

To conclude the ceremony, Steven presented a wooden tombstone— Norman–window shaped— painted in black. The front of it bore a name and birth and death dates, one under the other, respectively. SCRUFFLES DOBROWSKI ca. 2012-4/2018. A family picture with Scruffles was glued underneath the name and dates. Nailed to the back of the tombstone was a wooden stake. Steven hammered the tombstone into the ground.

After the ceremony, Steven continued to fill the grave of Scruffles with dirt. John unexpectedly offered to help, and Steven welcomed it. Steven went to the garage to get John a shovel. When he returned, he handed John the shovel, then popped two Lexapros in his mouth and swallowed.

John shook his head as he started to drop dirt into the partially–filled grave. "My friend, you don't look so well. I know you're fighting tragedy right now, but I think you should get some treatment for your addiction to Lexapro."

(Listen to that fat motherfucker playing dad with you! Crack his skull the fuck open with your shovel! You can bury him in the swimming pool trench! Surprisingly, there's plenty of room, even for his behemoth ass!)

Steven cleared his throat, then coughed. "I know. I'm so doggone stressed I continue to pill pop without even knowing it. It's become an involuntary motion. Keisha is going to admit me to a facility once we get the estate with her mother's inheritance settled. Her brothers are fighting over the distribution of assets. Sick."

"Sorry to hear that, my friend. How's the house been? Mr. Vance still lingering in there? We can conduct another blessing if you want. It'd be no trouble."

(Don't you dare let that unholy fuck bless the house! Fucking slice his throat with the shovel! Or I'll take care of him myself!)

"Thanks, John. Things have been mellow. The spirit is still around, but it is not as active. Keisha's mom watches over the house from time to time, I think. The medium will be here next week to help Mr. Vance— the man in the black suit— cross over to the other side where he belongs."

John continued to shovel dirt and tenderly pour it into Scruffles' grave. "I hope it works. He's a persistent spirit."

(Fuck you! Kill him now, Steve-O! He's trying to split us apart!)

"Would you like to come over for dinner tomorrow? I'm making hamburgers and hot dogs, two of Scruffles' favorite foods. We're celebrating Scruffles' life today and tomorrow. You and him had a lot of good times. Shit, come to think of it, I should have invited you to the ceremony we had. I'm sorry."

"It's no big deal. I'd love to join you and yours for dinner and participate in immortalizing the memories of Scruffles. Why is the dinner tomorrow, if you don't mind me asking?"

"Great. We'd love to have you," Steven said, frantically pushing dirt into the grave. "Today is a bereavement day, tomorrow is a celebration day."

Once the grave was filled, the two men shook hands. John said, "I'm sorry for your loss, my friend."

Steven replied, "Thanks, John. You've been one hell of a friend. Well, I'll just say it. You're family to me."

"Same here, my friend."

"Do you think dogs go to Heaven?"

"I hope not," John said, with a wide grin on his face. "I'm allergic."

"Allergic?" Steven said, then chuckled. "You watched Scruffles at your house a few times. How can you be allergic?"

"I'm not blowing smoke here, my friend. I truthfully am allergic to pet dander. I took some allergy meds though. It was no problem to watch Scruffles. And my allergies were nothing compared to the distress you and your family endured. Friends sometimes put themselves in situations they usually avoid to help another friend out. It was no big shakes." John pulled a folded piece of paper from out of his pocket. "I've got a little gift for you." He handed it to Steven.

"What's this?" Steven asked.

"Open it and see, my friend."

"It's a picture of a man opening my mailbox."

"Mmhmm," John said as he nodded his head.

"Wait. Are you telling me this is the guy who has been leaving the notes in my mailbox and likely the same person who sent me and my family messages via Brickmail?"

"Mmhmm," John said as he nodded. He had a huge see–how–smart–I–am grin on his face. "You see, when I was in the Marines, I was in special ops, covert ops. I decided to put those skills to good use. You know I'm a night owl, so I used my binoculars I usually use for birdwatching to stake out your mailbox. I used one of my high–powered cameras to snap several photos of the man. When he left, I did inspect your mailbox and he did leave a letter. I removed it from your box. I'm not even going to tell you what the letter said. What do you think of the photo?"

"John, this is amazing, but I don't think the police are taking the cases seriously."

"Funny you mention police. Look closely at the man's waistline."

Steven did, but needed additional guidance. "I'm sorry. I don't know what it is you want me to see."

John pointed to the man's waist above the right leg. "See that pointy thing? That's a badge. Your perpetrator is likely a cop. He looks a lot like Terry—probably one of his relatives. I'd turn this information over to the F.B.I. Let them handle it."

"Thank you, John. I appreciate this more than you know."

The two men shook hands and parted ways.

Ding-dong.

"I'll get it," Steven announced as he walked to the front door.

It was John, holding a bottle of merlot with a ribbon around its neck. Steven invited John in and they shook hands.

Steven said, "Well, dog my cats, you're a sight for sore eyes. Did you have a whitening recently? Your canines are pearly white."

John had a perplexed look on his face. He shook his head slightly as he said, "No... No, my friend, I haven't, but thanks for the compliment." John added a moment later, "If it makes you feel better, I did switch toothpastes though."

Steven asked John if he wanted to sit in the living room while he worked in the kitchen preparing the meal. He declined. He wanted to hang around Steven and shoot the breeze. Steven poured John a tall glass of iced tea. Steven got to work adding ingredients to the meat for hamburgers.

The smell of barbecue sauce burned John's nostrils. "Wow, you weren't kidding. You do like to add barbecue sauce to your hamburger meat, lots of it, too. Wow. Holy moley." He lightly chuckled.

(Listen to him, Stevie-son! He's mocking you! He made fun of your mole! Place that meat cleaver in his skull! Do it! Then you can kill your ass ugly wife and kids! It's going to be a blast today!)

Steven stepped into the laundry room and popped three Lexapro tablets into his mouth. John knew what he was doing. He heard the lid of the Altoids tin close. Steven returned to the kitchen. "Sorry about that," he said to John.

John shook his head and heavily sighed. He didn't say anything to Steven about his drug misuse since Keisha would be placing him in rehab not too long from now. "How's work been going?"

"Fine. No problem. My boss has been reducing my workload though. She said my mental faculties are too impaired to be meeting with clients. So she's had me doing more behind–the–scenes tasks."

"You mean you're unfit to do your job to its fullest and you're still employed? How is that possible?" John regretted asking such a pointed question, but sometimes he couldn't help it.

"Ouch, John. I felt the sting on that one. I guess the kid gloves are off."

"Well, I'm sorry for going between the eyes. I wish I worded my question a little better. Don't get me wrong. It's not that I want to see you out of job, but I can't help but wonder why a company would keep you on if you're unable to meet the demands of the job."

Steven stopped mixing the meat. With his elbows on the counter, he put his face in his hands. He nearly cried, but didn't. "John, I'm going to trust in you not to say a word to anyone."

"Fine. I don't kiss and tell. Lay it on me."

After a heavy sigh, Steven said, "My boss has been covering for me. I do bare minimal work. The work I can't do gets shuffled to other people in the department. In exchange, I work for my boss as a personal assistant."

John took a big drink of his iced tea. "Is that so? And, tell me, my friend, what services do you personally assist with?"

Steven didn't answer immediately. John gestured his hands as if to say 'let's hear what it is'. Eventually, Steven said, "You name it, I probably do it."

John shook his head in disbelief. "Are you telling me you and your boss engage in sexual relations on the job?"

"Yes," Steven nodded. "I'm not proud of it. Please don't tell my wife. If this ever leaked out, I'd lose my job. Then I'd lose my wife and the children."

"I won't tell. You can trust me. I'm repulsed your harridan of a boss would stoop to this level. Is she aware—"

"He." Steven resumed stirring his meat for the hamburgers.

John's mouth was in his lap. He was rendered speechless for several seconds. "Let's change the subject. Do you mind if I read that newspaper? We'll talk current events."

Steven nodded and John stood and reached for the paper that was strewn about the far end of the kitchen bar counter near the wall. John said, "Thanks, my friend. I didn't get a chance to read the paper today. I woke up around noon. Showered. Shaved. Then wandered over here." He didn't grab the main section of the paper. He muttered, "Damn it, this is sports. I want the breaking news part of the paper." He sat back down and said, "Wow. Now this is something for my Gypsum scrapbook."

Steven added some garlic salt and bread crumbs to the bowl of meat. "What's that?"

"The former chief accountant was sighted in Barbados. Authorities are now on the prowl trying to find him."

"Hmmph... That's interesting," Steven said. He started to make patties to be cooked on the grill. "Say, John, there's something I wanted to ask you."

"Sure, my friend. I'm like one of those balls you shake to get answers. Lay it on me." John continued to peruse the paper for other news that tickled his fancy.

"It's kind of morbid, but it's a question that's been on my mind for a while. Do you think your former C.E.O. ever whacked anybody here? Well, I mean, the old house that was here before this one."

John shook his head immediately. "Absolutely not. The man had a wife and kids who loved it here. If he wanted somebody whacked, it wouldn't happen in his home. He wasn't a psychopath— sociopath, yes, but not a psychopath. Come to think of it, I'm not even sure he could have anyone whacked. He was a counterpart to the Sorrentino family, but not a member."

"Thanks. That's helpful," Steven said, continuing to shape the meat into patties.

"Why do you ask though. Now my curiosity is peaked."

Steven finished shaping the final patty. He picked up the plate and walked to the laundry room entrance. "Do you want to continue this conversation outside? I need to get the food on the grill."

"Alright, my friend. I'll tag along."

The wind was calm and the temperature was mild. The sky was partly cloudy. John said, "What a lovely day."

"It is," Steven replied.

"Not to change the subject, but what's under that blue tarp? You hiding some bodies under there?"

(Kill him, Stevie! Kill that fat, bald son of a bitch! You keep ignoring me, I'm going to have to do some damage!)

"I'm installing a swimming pool for the summer. It was my Christmas gift to the family."

"That's nice of you. Let me know if you need any help. I'd be glad to lend hand. So, tell me. Why did you ask me about mafia whackings?"

Steven placed some patties on the grill. The sizzle the meat made was a sexy sound to John, and Steven loved it. Smoke billowed from the grill. As he added patties to the grill, Steven told John about an experience he had. "A few nights ago, I woke up in the middle of the night and I heard three men in the attic. It was a verbal altercation that soon turned to a physical one. It sounded like someone was strangled. To me, it sounded like a mafia hit. Every so often I hear this residual haunting. Keisha and the kids have heard it, also. When Denise was alive, she did, too. I thought maybe it was a Mafia hit."

"Mr. Pistone, the former C.E.O. of Gypsum, wouldn't be that callous to have somebody whacked in his own house. He wouldn't want to risk his children or wife accidentally stumbling in on the murder. Anyway, like I said, I don't think he had that sort of pull in the mafia anyway."

"What could it be then?" Steven asked, placing some hot dogs on the grill.

John walked over to the patio table, set his glass of iced tea on it, and sat. He rubbed his beard for a few moments. "Well, Mr. Pistone wasn't the only person to own that house. Maybe when Mr. Pistone had his house torn down and this one built, it stirred some things from decades ago with older spirits. Maybe a murder did happen in the house a long time ago, well before Pistone bought the house."

Steven turned over the burgers. "That makes sense. I didn't consider the possibility the destruction of his house and construction of this new one may have woken dormant spirits. Did Mr. Pistone ever mention anything about his house being haunted— the old one, not this one."

"Nope. He never did, though I rarely associated with him. Every once in a while, I'd wander over for a birthday party or a holiday get–together. You saw the pictures in my scrapbook."

The food was done and John and Steven returned to the kitchen. John asked, "Do you need any help?"

"Thanks, but I've got this. Why don't you make yourself comfortable in the dining room."

And he did. When John entered the dining room, he said, "Hey, Steven. You have some water damage on one of your walls in here." Steven walked into the dining room, then walked out. He returned with a hair dryer, plugged it in, and started to dry the large circular wet area. After several minutes, John said, "It's turning red."

"I see that. Odd," Steven said, turning down the heat setting on the hair dryer. "It looks sunburned. That should be good enough for now."

"It does look sunburned. I've never seen a wall do that before. I was gone for over a month. Did you replace the drywall in this house?"

"No, I didn't."

"Well, you should. That's some defective drywall you've got there."

Steven called the family down to the table. When everyone was seated, Steven said, "We gather here to commemorate Scruffles, our beloved dearly–departed pet. I've worked like a dog today preparing this food and I hope everyone enjoys it. I'm sure you all are panting to dig in and eat. I think the meat is cooked perfectly, though I've never used this sort of meat before. I hope I didn't screw the pooch cooking it. If I did, please feel free to hound and bitch at me. It would be a fair bone of contention. I can handle your barks and bites, and I won't bark or bite back. On the other hand, if you like the food, I have some doggie bags I made for everyone. Enjoy."

Keisha said, "It looks wonderful. You did a great job."

(Fuck that bitch, Steve-O! She's plotting against you! We need to cut that bitch up into little pieces!)

"Yeah, Daddy," Brittany said. "It smells good. And me and Mr. Quackson are hungry."

"Why'd you change Mr. Quacks' name?" Steven asked, bewildered.

Keisha wanted to change the subject. "Is there ketchup?"

Jeffrey replied, "Yeah, Mom. It's right in front of you."

"I think once you all bite into my hamburgers and hot dogs, you'll be like a pup with two tails," Steven said, placing some mustard on his hamburger. "Excuse me, it sounds like the T.V. turned on. I hear some barking heads talking." Steven stood and was about to leave the room.

"Please stay. It's not bothering anyone," Keisha said.

"I wasn't going to dog trot to the T.V. I was going to sprint to it. But I'll stay," Steven said, then sat.

"I'm thinking about attending Indiana University for psychology. I think I'd like to be a clinical psychologist and help treat teenagers with weight issues," Tiffany said. "My psychology teacher said she'd write me a letter of recommendation to the colleges to which I apply as long as I continue to do well in her class. I have an A+ in her class right now. I hope I can maintain it. Sebastian has been super helpful teaching me how to study."

"Every dog has its day. I guess today is yours," Steven said.

"What happened to the wall?" Jeffrey asked. "It looks like it has a rash. Weird."

John shook his head. "I have no explanation for that. That's something I've never seen in my life. I've worked with drywall for the past seven years or so and I've never seen drywall do that before."

"I'll fix it later. Does everyone have food?" Steven asked. Everyone nodded or said yes. "Excellent. Let's say a few words."

Brittany offered to say some words about Scruffles. She talked about the different nuances of Scruffles. For example, how he'd take one piece of his dog food out of his bowl, step into the living room, eat it, then go back to his bowl and repeat the process. After four or five trips, he'd stay at his bowl and finish eating. She talked about how Scruffles would lick his lips after being given a bite of food. The small things about Scruffles were the focus of her elegy.

Everyone praised Brittany for the speech she delivered about Scruffles. John said, "That was one of the most touching soliloquies I've ever heard, and I've been around for a long time."

Steven said, "Jeffrey, you're eating a hamburger?"

"Yeah, I think I want to try it," Jeffrey replied as he squirted some ketchup on his burger.

"Hot diggity dog!" Steven shouted. In a calmer tone, he said, "You're going to be head over paws when you try my tasty foods. Dig in, everyone. If it sucks, you can pooch kick me in the balls."

Jeffrey, John, and Tiffany bit into their hamburger while Brittany and Keisha bit into their hot dog. "Dad, this is delicious!" Jeffrey said. "I can't believe I waited this long to try meat." He took another big bite of the burger.

"I'm glad you like it," Steven replied. "My, my, my. You're going to town on that burger. Like quick as a dog can lick a dish."

"Aren't you going to eat, Steven?" John asked, then took another bite of his burger.

Steven nodded. "Yes, in a moment. Right now, I'm enjoying the sight of all of you sinking your canines into the food I prepared from scratch."

Jeffrey took another bite of his burger and chewed a little. Then he opened his mouth, reached in, and pulled out a large tuft of golden–colored hair. "Gross."

Then Tiffany and Brittany did the same thing followed by John and Keisha. Jeffrey and Keisha were retching. Brittany and Tiffany were covering their mouths to stop from vomiting.

"What kind of sick joke are you playing here, Steven? This is supposed to be a meal to remember Scruffles and you mixed in fake hair into the hamburgers and hot dogs?"

"It's not fake," Steven said, then laughed. "Excuse me. I need to get something for the wall. It's screaming. That wall is in pain, and it's bothering me," he said, his tone not garnished with any flavor of emotion.

Everyone at the table nearly threw up. When Steven returned, he stood in front of the wall with the rash on it. He popped the lid off a tube of aloe vera. He squirted a generous amount of the gelatinous substance in his hand and rubbed it onto the circular sunburned–looking patch.

"Is everyone done eating?" he asked.

Nobody could answer because they were still retching. Steven said, "Speak up. Dog got your tongues or something?" Then he wickedly laughed.

John stood and spoke. "You need help. Goodbye."

"Would you like a doggie bag?" Steven asked, causing everyone at the table to throw up. John stopped in his tracks.

"God damn it, you nasty fucks! That's disgusting! We're at the dinner table! How dare you bite the hand that feeds. You ruined my beautiful Scruffles meal. You've disgraced the memory of our beloved and most–recent dearly–departed member of this family. Scruffles would be crushed. Here I do something wonderful for all of you. I helped you become one with Scruffles. The hamburgers were made from his flesh. The hot dogs, too. The casings for the hot dogs were his intestines. Weren't the hot dogs and burgers the dogs bollocks?" Then he laughed wildly and wickedly again. "The bones? What did I do with the bones, you wonder? I pulverized them and used them as seasoning for the meat to make the hamburgers and hot dogs. Ruff!" He resumed his insane–sounding laughing. He regained his composure and spoke. "You'll be delighted to know I drained Scruffles' blood and mixed it in some of the Ray's Barbecue sauce. I added that delicious goodness to the meat, then used the meat to make the hot dogs and hamburgers. Now, as a commemorative token, I used the majority of Scruffles' coat to make winter gloves for all of you. The Farmer's Almanac predicts a "ruff" winter this year." He picked up the bag from under his chair and passed out a pair of Scruffles gloves to everyone while uncontrollably laughing.

John wanted to leave, but he feared for the safety of Steven's family. He took his seat.

When Steven stopped laughing, he spoke to his family and John. "We're in this together until the last dog dies. And, on that note, I'd like all of you to join me outside. I've something I think you all need to see." He looked at Brittany. "Did you tell them my surprise?"

"No, Daddy," she replied, "I didn't say anything about your gift. I swear. I didn't even tell Mr. Quacks or Mr. Quackson."

Steven slammed his fist on the table and said, "Stop with the retching and vomiting! We have a guest at the table, for dog's sake!" He left the room and lumbered outside. He stood next to the blue tarp near where the tombstones were lined. He waited for his family and John to join him, but they never did. They stood at the kitchen window, watching him. He then unveiled what was under the tarp. "There's room for all of you," he said.

John said, "I think you better call the police."

"That's okay, John. I assure I can handle this myself. This was the last straw."

CHAPTER TWENTY-EIGHT

Grams Visits

Two days after Steven's abominable meal, Keisha laid in bed for several hours, finalizing when she'd set up Steven to assault her so she could kill him and claim self–defense.

Steven told Keisha and the children that the tombstones were a gag, and he wouldn't ever do a thing to hurt his family. The trench he dug, however, was a far cry from the usual size of a typical in–ground pool.

The time was two–forty–seven. Keisha and Steven were fast asleep in their beds. Their bedroom door slowly opened. The hallway light illuminated more and more of their faces as it opened.

"Darlin'," a raspy voice said. "Darlin', wake up."

"Mom?" Keisha said, nearly inaudibly.

"Over here, darlin'. Come on, now. Take a look."

Keisha sat up and looked towards her bedroom door with squinted eyes. "Mom? Is that you?"

"Of course, it's me, darlin'. Now get out of that bed and follow me."

Denise was wearing a solid purple dress with a big purple flower puffing out of it near her left breastbone. The flower was part of the dress design. Her shoes were purple and the hue matched the dress. She looked twenty years younger and she was considerably thinner than she was at the time of her passing.

Keisha stood and put on her housecoat. She followed Denise downstairs to the living room. They sat next to each other on the larger of the two couches.

"How's Heaven, Mom?" Keisha asked.

"Darlin', it is absolutely amazing. Words can't express the radiant, shimmering beauty Heaven is."

"You look so youthful. Healthier."

"Thanks, darlin'. Oh, it's so nice to see you. Now, listen. I didn't drop by to make idle chitter–chatter about the hereafter. I came here to warn you, child."

"Warn me? About what?"

"Steven. You see, you think he's fucked up—Whoa!" Denise placed her hands over her mouth. "I need to be careful with the profanity. If I curse one more time, I'll be sent to purgatory. Now, what I— " A few seconds later, she gestured towards the sky. "Oh, thanks, J.C.! You're the man!" She looked at Keisha with a smile. "He said he'd give me a pass for that bad word I said since I'm here doing a good deed."

Keisha laughed. "I must be in a dream." She pinched herself, thinking she'd wake up in her bed.

"Not a dream, darlin', but we are in a different dimension right now. A different plane. Steven or one of the children could sit right where you are right now and they'd be none the wiser you and I are sittin' here talkin'. They can't hear or see us."

"I believe you, Mom. I do."

"Good, child. Now, I'm here to warn you that the way you're fixin' to handle this Steven situation is all wrong. Do you realize you're riskin' not ascending into Heaven by plottin' to murder your husband in cold blood? We're talkin' you bein' sent to the depths of Hell, child. And, nobody is goin' to believe your story he provoked you to shoot him. There's no paper trail to corroborate that, not to mention the fact you'd be a black woman accused of killin' a white man in one of the most racist cities in the nation. The D.A. would nail you to a cross and the all–white jury would return a unanimous verdict of guilty. Then you'd be locked up for life."

Keisha disagreed. "The trial could be moved to different location, Mom. I've thought of that."

"Darlin', you can't continue this way. You can't murder Steven. You see, you think he's messed up in his mind because of the Lexapro, but that's not the entirety of it. It's the demon. The demon is controllin' his thoughts and actions. And, at times, yours and everyone else's in this house."

"Really, Mom? A demon?"

"Think about it, child. Do you remember Easter dinner? You and Tiffany set out all that fancy china. Plates, saucers, cups, all sorts of unnecessary silverware? You and Tiffany stepped into the kitchen for a few moments. When you returned to the dining room all the silverware and plates and cups and such were whipping around all over the place, like they were in some sort of violent tornado. Steven walked from the kitchen to the dining room to the sitting room and didn't bat an eye. Now how can that be? He's under the influence of the demon. The Lexapro is part of it, yes, but the primary influence is the demon, child. Do you remember what I'm talking about?"

"I remember, and who could forget that. I became so enraged at what was happening I screamed, 'Stop it!' Then the plates and cups and silverware returned in an instant to where they belonged—everything was back in place. I thought it was over, and then a plate flew in my direction. I moved just in time before it struck my head. Then another plate came flying at me and Tiffany as we ran into the kitchen. Oh, that was terrifying."

Keisha swallowed hard. "What am I to do, Mom?"

"Have the medium and paranormal team do their little scavenger hunt. It'll help bring out a lot of answers to questions you've had in the past, and it will help give you peace of mind. Aside from that, you need to meet with Father Desdemona. He's a demonologist and exorcist. Have him come to the house and perform an exorcism on Steven."

"What happens after Steven is exorcised? Do we live happily ever after?"

"I'm sorry, darlin'. I can only reveal a finite amount of information to you, and I have to discriminate among the information to decide what to tell you. I've chosen the most important pieces you need to know. I'm sorry, my child, but it's the rules. Heaven is an indescribable place, and once you're there, it's not a place you want to be kicked out of. I must abide by the rules. I'll tell you somethin' else, darlin'. I shouldn't even be doin' this here with you, but I persistently begged and was granted permission."

Keisha's eyes welled up with tears. "I'm scared, Mom."

Denise placed her hand on Keisha's and said, "Put your trust in God, child. Heed my advice. You do those things and everything will work itself out better than you could have ever imagined." Denise hugged

Keisha. They embraced for a minute or so. "I must leave now, darlin'."

"Mom, please don't go. I don't want you to go."

"Oh, my baby. I won't be far from you. I'm in your heart, darlin'. You must always remember that. Now, before I leave I must tell you that you and me, right now, are communicatin' spirit to spirit. Your physical body is still in your bed. Now, when your spirit enters your body in a moment, you're going to abruptly wake up. Your legs and arms and their extremities will feel intensely tingly— almost a painful kind of tingly. Don't worry, though, child. Just stay put for a few minutes and the feeling will die away. It's caused by the electrical matter and energy from our spirits, but it's nothing to fear."

Denise and Keisha hugged for several minutes. Then Denise walked Keisha back upstairs to her bedroom. Before Keisha's spirit entered her body, Denise blew her a kiss and said, "I love you, my child. Go on, now. Don't be afraid. I'm right here." Then Keisha's spirit reentered its body and just as Denise said, she abruptly woke up with a tingling sensation radiating throughout her body, but most prominently in the extremities.

She whispered, "Thank you, Mom," then went back to sleep.

"Do you remember what to do, baby doll?" Keisha asked Brittany.

"Yeah! We're making Daddy all better! Yay! Daddy! Daddy! Daddy!"

"Good girl." She hugged Brittany.

Tiffany said, "Mom, the table is all set. Do you need me to do anything else?"

"No, my angel. That's all I needed help with."

Jeffrey said, "I've got the food ready. Are you sure you want to do this, Mom?"

"Absolutely. I need to be sure. I don't want to proceed any further without some sort of confirmation."

When Steven entered the house through the garage, he slammed the door behind him.

(You better kill them today! Hang them upside down and slit their throats! You fuckin' mole–faced faggot! DO IT! Or I'm going to kill your family myself! Then I'll kill you! Kill 'em, Steve-O!)

Steven took out his Altoids tin and popped four Lexapro into his mouth. Then he walked into the kitchen.

"Surprise!" everyone shouted with exuberance.

"What's all this?" he asked.

Keisha approached him and grabbed his hands. She kissed him on the cheek. "God loves you, and so do we."

Steven pulled away. "Fuck off with that shit, bitch!"

The family started singing "Amazing Grace." Steven pounded his fists on the counter and repeatedly shouted. "Shut the fuck up!" But they didn't. He opened the cabinet doors and started smashing plates and glasses in an attempt to drown out the sound.

Keisha signaled the family to stop. "We're sorry. Come into the dining room and eat something. It's obvious you've had a hard day."

"Don't say hard, bitch! I've had nothing hard in me all day! Fuck you!" Steven complied and sat at the table.

"Let me get you some wine," Keisha said, walking to the kitchen. "John brought over another bottle of merlot for you. He said he accepts your apology and he apologized for some of the harsh words he said to you. He's still sick from the meat you served though." She entered the dining room with a glass of wine. He gulped the wine down in one drink. "Want some more?" she asked.

He slammed the glass down on the table. "Yes."

As Keisha left the room, Steven plated himself some of the food that was on the table. Meatloaf, using Granana's recipe, and fried chicken, using Gram's recipe, with homemade mashed potatoes, corn on the cob, and homemade biscuits.

The children sat at the table and made themselves a plate, also. Tiffany kindly made a plate for her mom. Keisha returned to the dining room with a glass of wine in one hand and another bowl of mashed potatoes. She didn't hand Steven his glass of wine immediately. She sat down first, then asked Tiffany to pass it to Brittany, who would then hand it to her dad. Keisha had a motive behind doing this.

Steven grabbed the glass and once again gulped the wine down in one drink. When he slammed the glass down, he exhaled, and with his breath traveled streams of smoke. He exhaled a few more times, and with those exhales was wisps of smoke. Then he said, "What the fuck did you put in my wine, bitch? You plotting on me? You trying to kill me?" When she didn't answer he slammed his hand down on the table. "Bitch! Answer me when I talk to you!"

She smiled, then spoke. "Why, Steven, I'm shocked you think I would even consider doing such a thing."

"Yeah, well you better keep it that way, bitch. I'll kill every one of you here at this table and still sleep well tonight," Steven said, then wickedly laughed. Seconds later, he shouted, "More wine!"

"Right away," Keisha said. She returned within a minute and once again she sat first, then had the glass passed to Steven. He drank it and more smoke trailed out of his mouth. He slammed the glass down on the table and squeezed it slightly, though it still broke. "God damn it."

"I'll get you a new glass," Keisha said.

And she did. When she returned, everyone was eager to eat.

"Shall we say grace, mom? We haven't done that since Granana passed," Tiffany asked.

"No grace! No grace is ever to be spoken in my presence," Steven shouted.

"Everyone, bow your heads," Keisha said.

And everyone did, except Steven, who repeatedly shouted. "No!" as he vigorously slammed his hand on the table.

Brittany warned she was about to say grace. Steven tried to make a preemptive strike. He placed both his hands in the mashed potatoes and scooped out a large helping. Then he shoved the mashed potatoes into his ear canal. As Brittany said grace, he could still hear it, which caused him to gyrate his head and body uncontrollably, as if he were convulsing.

"Enjoy dinner, everyone," Keisha said.

Everyone started to eat, including Steven. After everyone had a chance to ingest a couple of bites, Keisha said, "Brittany, do you want to give your dad the surprise now?"

"Yeah!" she said, "and Mr. Quackson does, too."

"Surprise?" Steven said.

"Yes, babe. It's time to give you what you deserve. I hope you like it. Baby doll, go and get the surprise."

"Okay, Mommy!" Brittany said, leaping off the chair with Mr. Quackson. "Yay! Daddy! Daddy! Daddy!"

"Steven? Babe?" Keisha said. "Close your eyes. It's a surprise, and no peeking." He complied.

Brittany returned with an object in her hand. It was covered with a white cloth. "Okay, Daddy, hold out your hand." Keisha approached Brittany. Tiffany and Jeffrey moved to their assigned positions, also.

"Why?" Steven barked.

"Because, Daddy. It's your surprise," Brittany said, then giggled. She made sure his eyes were closed, then removed the object from the cloth concealing its identity.

Steven held out his hand and when Brittany placed the object in his hand, it produced a sound similar to raw meat hitting a hot griddle. Smoke billowed from his hand. The smell of sulfur was pernicious. The portion of the object that burned his hand left an imprint, and skin and blood transferred from Steven's hand to the object, which was a stainless-steel crucifix, Granana's crucifix. Tiffany and Jeffrey grabbed their dad’s hands and placed them behind the chair. Keisha bound them.

Then they wrapped thick rope around his torso, looping it through the chair and around his legs. They further secured Steven to the chair using handcuffs and zip ties.

The entire time Steven was being secured to the chair, he cursed and kicked and snarled and growled. He fought as hard as he could, but he was overpowered as Keisha and the children recited scriptures they rehearsed, which weakened the demon inhabiting Steven's body.

Keisha made a call. "John? We have Steven secured and he's ready to be transported."

"I'll be right over," he replied. He was at the Dobrowski's house within a minute.

John, Keisha, and the children covered Steven up with the blue tarp he used to conceal the gravestones and placed a necklace over his head on the tarp. It was a rosary. After Steven was asleep, John, Keisha, and the children— except Brittany— lifted Steven and placed him on a flatbed with wheels. John and Jeffrey transported him to his house, placing him in his wine cellar. Steven asked for some of his Lexapro, and Jeffrey placed four tablets in his mouth, unbeknown to John, who was out of the wine cellar at that time.

After Steven was secure, John called her and asked how long she predicted Steven would need to be in captivity, and she hoped it wouldn't be longer than forty–eight hours.

Steven's menu for the next forty–eight hours would be chicken broth to eat and water to drink, all delivered through a straw placed in containers from a separate room. John cut a hole in the blue tarp while Steven was asleep to allow Steven to gain access to the straw, which were directly in front of Steven.

Tomorrow evening, the medium and paranormal investigation team would investigate the Dobrowski home. Then Keisha would make arrangements for Father Desdemona to perform an exorcism on Steven.

Jeffrey was unable to sleep. He couldn't believe what he witnessed at the dinner table several hours before with his dad. He wavered between crying for his dad to shaking his fists at God for not protecting his dad. Eventually, Jeffrey wised up and realized it was his dad who allowed the demon inside of him, not God or the Devil.

He needed to use the bathroom. He swung his legs from underneath the covers and walked down the hallway towards the bathroom. His dad's office door was shut and Jeffrey was able to see the light was off, because, had it been on, the small crevice between the door and the floor would be illuminated. The light that trickled through the crevice was even more prominent if the hallway light was off. With the exception of his own bedroom door, every other bedroom door on the second floor was closed and the lights inside of them were off.

He stood in the dark hallway, looking towards his dad's office door. He thought about the times he would leave his room to go get something to drink or use the bathroom and would hear his dad typing away on the keyboard, preparing reports for work or transcribing one of several E.V.P. sessions. He also chuckled at how his dad would sometimes chicken–peck at the keys when he became overly tired from typing too much or just didn't feel like typing efficiently.

Jeffrey said in a soft voice, "Dad, I love you, and I hope you're safe. Soon, it will all be over." Then he entered the bathroom, used it, and washed up. He opened the bathroom door and turned off the light. As he was about to step into the hallway, he heard the sound of typing. Rapid typing.

He stepped into the hallway. His dad's office door was open and the light was on. Jeffrey shook his head in disbelief. He looked around the second floor. All the other doors, except his, were still closed and all the lights within the rooms were off.

He slowly walked down the hallway towards his dad's office door. When he reached his dad's office, he stood in the doorway. "Dad?" And at that instant, he knew it couldn't be his dad. Not because his dad was being held hostage at John's, but because, had his dad been in the chair, his head, shoulders, and portion of his back would have been visible above the chair. Jeffrey couldn't see any feet either. Whoever was sitting in the chair typing was short.

Leave or die? Why is someone typing that over and over?

The rapid typing continued. "Hello?" he said again.

The chair backed up about six inches and spun around and faced Jeffrey, but there was nobody in it. Then Jeffrey was knocked backwards. His feet left the ground. He struck the wall behind him, leaving a large imprint. The sanguine-colored substance pooled from the imprint and onto Jeffrey and the carpet.

Jeffrey was nearly unconscious. Jeffrey's eyes were wide open, and standing in the doorway of his dad's office was the man in the black suit, who stepped into the hallway and walked towards the attic stairs. The man in the black suit started off a solid figure, but with each step he took down the hallway he became more and more translucent, eventually fading out completely. With each step the man in the black suit took, Jeffrey's eyes became heavier and heavier. The instant the man in the black suit vanished, Jeffrey passed out. Simultaneously, when the man in the black suit vanished, the computer and lights in Steven's office turned off and the office door slammed shut.

Keisha, Tiffany, and Brittany woke up when Jeffrey impacted the wall, but they were trapped in their rooms. It wasn't until the man in the black suit vanished that they were able to exit their rooms and rush to Jeffrey's aide.

CHAPTER TWENTY-NINE

The Medium

Ding dong.

Keisha answered the door. The woman standing in front of her was a short, middle–aged woman. She was Hispanic. She had long, black hair and a flawless complexion. A small dark birthmark was on her right cheek.

"Good evening, Mrs. Dobrowski," the woman said. "I'm Sara Warlock and the gentlemen behind me are part of our paranormal investigation team. This is George Hartford, Chris Sanchez, and Jesus Morando."

Keisha invited them in and the medium entered first. She took two steps inside the home and stopped slightly past the front door. She placed her hand on the wall and caressed it slightly. Then she said, "These walls have a story to tell."

"Getting something already?" George asked.

"Yes. I need to see more of the home though. The energy I'm getting is negative. I feel pain, sorrow, and grief."

"Yeah, that's what we've all been feeling here," Keisha said. "Would any of you like some coffee?"

And they did. Keisha made a fresh pot and invited the investigation team to sit in the living room.

The chandelier was swaying and the family picture and crucifix were out of place again.

Brittany, Jeffrey, and Tiffany were with Sebastian at a twenty–four-hour diner. Sebastian and Tiffany studied for upcoming exams. Brittany read a children's book that introduced her to the fundamentals of engineering. Jeffrey added corrections to his manuscripts; he recently composed two new pieces for cello.

"Watch this," Keisha said, walking over to the hearth. She placed the family picture on the mantel. As she walked to the crucifix on the floor— that had been left there for weeks— the family picture slid and fell onto the hearth. She picked up the crucifix and tried to place it on its nail. "What's going on?" a frustrated Keisha said. It was as if the crucifix and the wall were the same pole on a magnet. The harder Keisha pushed the crucifix towards the wall, the harder the force repelling the crucifix was. Finally, she pushed the crucifix with all her might and it flew out of her hand and crashed through one of the sunroom sliding doors. "Oh my!" she screamed. "I don't know why that happened. The entity in the house loved when we'd hang it up because he would knock it right back down."

The investigation team believed Keisha somehow staged the event. One of the investigators retrieved the crucifix from the sunroom and tried to place the crucifix on its nail, but he had the same problem. The medium and remaining investigators tried, also, and all were equally unsuccessful.

"There's something demonic here," Chris said, "and I have to admit I'm terrified."

Jesus said, "I am, too, but that's why we're paid so well. We have to stay brave and continue with the investigation. A family is depending on us."

While the team planned where to place the equipment, Sara went from floor to floor and room to room, trying to acquire as much information as she could about the house and any spirits in it.

When she entered the attic, the negative energy she experienced upon first entering the house intensified. She felt threatened, but remained resolute. She continued further in the attic. The light flickered intermittently. Then she saw an apparition. "Who are you?" she asked the spirit. Then she explained who she was and why she was there. The spirit broke off communication for the time being, and she returned to the living room.

"I made contact with one spirit. He wears a black suit. He has a prominent scar on his forehead," Sara reported to her team members.

"The demon, right?" Keisha asked. "It's a demon."

"No," Sara contended. "It's not a demon. It's an intensely angry spirit. As the night progresses, I'll try to communicate with him more. I introduced myself to him, told him I was there to help him, and advised him if he wanted help crossing over to the other side, I could provide it to him. He didn't respond to me, but I think I established a good rapport with him. I sensed he was a good man in his life who became entangled in a web of deceit."

"I'm confused. I thought he was a demon," Keisha confessed. "Does this mean there are two entities in my house?"

"You've got more than two. There were several others I saw but they didn't come forward when I asked them to. I saw one spirit— a white woman wearing a white dress with purple flowers on it. Another woman— a black woman wearing a solid purple dress."

"Granana and Grams," Keisha whispered, fighting back tears. "They're here." Then she smiled.

Sara stood and analyzed the streak of dried sanguine substance originating from the nail. The streak was about two inches long. She placed her hand over it and closed her eyes. Moments later, she said, "He's showing me something."

"Who is?" George asked.

"The man in the black suit," she replied. Moments later, she continued. "Three men. He's one of them... There was an argument. A dispute over money. One of the men strangled this man in the black suit with an extension cord... That's it. That's all he's shown me so far."

"Strangled? I thought the man in the black suit was electrocuted, right here in this living room installing a chandelier. That's what Steven— my estranged husband— told me several months ago," Keisha said.

"No... He wasn't electrocuted," Sara said, feeling around on the walls in the living room. "These walls... it's almost like they're alive, like tissue. Weird, yet fascinating."

"It's funny you mention that," Keisha said. "In our dining room, the wall developed a rash. My husband rubbed some cream on it and the next day the rash was gone."

"I've heard it all now," George muttered to Jesus. They both snickered.

Sara walked over the hearth and picked up the family picture. As she held it in her hands and closed her eyes, she said, "He's showing me something else now... He was a family man. Two kids. A wife. A dog. An adorable little dark brown dachshund... He's gone again— that's all he's shown me." She opened her eyes. "That's why he knocks this picture off the mantel. He's angry about what he lost. He no longer has his family, his wife, his kids, his dog." She didn't set the picture back on the mantel; instead, she set it face down on the hearth.

Everyone in the living room was amazed at the details Sara shared with them. Keisha was not only amazed, but also confused. She hoped, by the end of the evening, all her questions would be answered.

The investigation team set up their equipment and started conducting E.V.P. sessions. George took the first floor, Chris took the second floor, Jesus took the attic.

Sara remained in the living room for the next hour, which allowed the team to complete some of their tasks, collecting audio and video evidence. She'd return to the attic after an hour passed.

While waiting in the living room, she reached over and picked up the crucifix that was on the end table, next to the couch on which she sat. She held it in her hands and closed her eyes. *Why are you showing me you knocking this down?... Okay, I've figured it out. That's why you knock the crucifix down. You're angry at God for not protecting you. You blame him for your murder.*

George sat on the couch next to Sara and said, "Shall we do an E.V.P. session together?"

"Sure," she said, still clutching the crucifix with her eyes closed. "Do you smell that? Is someone smoking?"

"Maybe someone outside is. That's one hell of a strong cigar though." He took a big whiff. "I smell expensive cologne, too."

"Yeah, me, too. Weird, huh?"

"The cigar smoke I could do without, but the cologne is pretty nice." He placed his digital recorder on the coffee table.

"He's showing me something else. A picture of him on a yacht with the same men who were at his murder. He's smiling while holding a cigar... We're smelling scents of the man in the black suit. He loved to smoke cigars. And, while he wasn't materialistic, he did fancy expensive cologne."

"You're amazing, Sara."

"Naturally. That is, after all, why you married me."

They both had a little chuckle and conducted an E.V.P. session together. Afterwards, Sara journeyed up to the attic to see if she could make contact with the man in the black suit.

"Anything interesting?" Sara asked Jesus.

"Yeah. There were several spikes on the E.M.F meter as I scanned the attic with it. Several colds spots, too. Two Class A E.V.Ps. And I was scratched."

Sara gasped. "You were? Let me see." And he did. "That's a telltale sign of a demonic entity."

"That was one of the spoken words one of the Class A E.V.Ps."

"Demon?"

"Yeah."

She listened to the E.V.Ps. "That voice sounds like the man in the black suit's voice."

Jesus joined Chris on the second floor while Sara remained in the attic. While in the attic, she felt disoriented and terrified, but was undeterred. "Is there a demon up here with me? You like to scratch people? Come and scratch me then." But the demon didn't. Instead, the man in the black suit appeared and she conversed with him for several minutes, during which time he supplied her with a wealth of information.

The investigation concluded and the team sat with Keisha and reported to her their findings. Chris, Jesus, and George left Sara alone with Keisha to break down their investigation equipment. After a quick sip of coffee, Sara said, "The man in the black suit was overall a good, decent man. He did what he had to do to take care of his family. He took pride in taking care of his family. He was active in his church. He was a youth pastor. A devout Catholic."

"If he's such a good, decent man why did he terrorize the hell out of me and my family?" Keisha asked.

"He was incredibly angry. He lost his life. He was murdered. He wanted the house to himself. He was also jealous of you and your family."

"I see, because he no longer had his family, right?"

"That's right."

"Why didn't he go to his family and watch over them instead of sticking around here terrorizing us?"

"That's a good question. There are two reasons. The first: he was ashamed to return to his family. The second: he didn't want to terrify his children. You see, this man is presumed alive."

"I am thoroughly confused now."

"Let me start from the beginning. He was an accountant at a drywall company. Gypsum, Inc. He was a co–conspirator with other executives of the company. They cooked their books to make their company seem like it was worth more than it was. Similar to HealthSouth."

Keisha took a drink of her coffee. "He was a decent Catholic man who became corrupted by the love of money."

"Basically, yes. He regrets it. Anyhow, this company also had ties to organized crime. As an accountant, he discovered he wasn't getting his fair share and he threatened the C.E.O. that he'd expose the fraud if he didn't get what was due to him."

"This is crazy."

Sara nodded. "Yes, it is. The C.E.O. said he would pay him. He instructed the accountant— the man in the black suit— to meet him at his new house that was under construction late at night. Midnight or so."

"I think I know where this is headed, but please indulge me."

"The C.E.O. lured the accountant up to the top level of the house being built under the guise he wanted to show the accountant the new house. There wasn't much to see. Only the skeletal structure of the house was built at that time. Once in the attic, one of the C.E.O.'s henchman murdered the accountant. The house where he was murdered is your house. He was murdered here, Mrs. Dobrowski. Upstairs in the attic."

Keisha swallowed hard. After a few breaths, she asked, "What happened to his body? Is he buried on the property?"

"No, he's not. The C.E.O. along with his henchman took the body of the accountant back to the Gypsum plant and essentially pulverized his body. The remains were added to the ingredients to make drywall. The slabs of drywall produced using his remains were installed throughout this house. Floors and ceilings."

"I guess that explains the bleeding walls."

"In a sense, yes."

"Does this accountant— this man in the black suit— have a name?"

"Yes. Dominic Facchini. Other than the murderer and the C.E.O., nobody else knows he's dead. Media reports say he's been sighted in Barbados, but it's not him at all. It's someone who closely resembles Mr. Facchini and is masquerading as him to make people think Mr. Facchini is alive and well."

"What about the electrician? Is his spirit here at all?"

"Not that I'm aware of."

"I don't understand why the chandelier swayed if the man who was taunting our family was murdered in the attic."

"Mr. Facchini witnessed the electrician killed. The chandelier shaking, however, was merely a scare tactic he tried to use to get you and your family out of the house."

"Did he kill the electrician?"

"I don't know about that, but I doubt it. If he did, I don't think he would have crossed over to the other side."

"He's crossed over?"

"Yes. I helped him. He's no longer in your house. Did his activity diminish recently?"

"Yes, it did. After the house blessings it did. And after my mother passed it did, also."

"Yes, Grams. She's a nice lady. Here's some irony. The demon also kept Mr. Facchini in line, preventing him from wreaking havoc on the house. As Mr. Facchini's power as a spirit grew, he intended to increase his scare tactics. Throw objects at your heads, for instance. The demon took control and stopped him. That's why you've seen a drastic decrease in activity in the house. The demon was policing his behavior."

"Why would the demon do something altruistic? It doesn't make sense."

"You're right. All Mr. Facchini would tell me is there was a reason the demon wanted you all to stay in the house. He wouldn't tell me why though. He said he'd risk entry into Heaven if he divulged too much information."

"I can believe that," Keisha said.

"It's strange, isn't it?" Sara questioned. "Mr. Facchini wanted you all to leave the house but the demon wanted you to stay. Anyway, Mr. Facchini is no longer attached to this house. He's come to terms with his death and is no longer earthbound. I also had to convince him the demon couldn't prevent him from crossing over. I hope Mr. Facchini can now rest in peace. There is another matter I need to discuss with you though."

"Excuse me a moment." Keisha made the sign of the cross and said a quick silent prayer for Mr. Facchini. "Yes? What is it?"

"Time is of the essence, so I must be blunt. Is anybody in your household a Satanist?"

"Absolutely not."

"Has anybody in your house ever used a Ouija board?"

Keisha was beside herself. She didn't understand why Sara was asking her these questions. "I don't mean to be rude, but why are you asking me these questions?"

"Because you have a demon in your house and I am trying to find out how it got here in the first place."

"Nobody in this house has used a Ouija board nor is any of my children practitioners of Satanism. I can guarantee you that."

"When I was in the attic, I had a vision of two teenage girls— both of whom were white— using a Ouija board. I don't mean to sound racist, but I say they're both white because it excludes your daughters. With that said, does your son or daughter have friends who may have used a Ouija board in your house?"

She didn't answer right away. "The ghost investigators. W.P.I.S." Keisha pulled out her cellphone and called Tiffany. She told her the vision the medium had and asked her to ask Sebastian to ask the lead investigator of W.P.I.S. to ask the two teenage girls who participated in the investigation if they used a Ouija board. Several minutes later, Tiffany called her mom. Keisha placed the call on speakerphone. Tiffany said, "The two girls admitted to using a Ouija board."

Sara asked, "Where is the Ouija board?"

"I don't know," Tiffany said.

"Can you call or text your friends and ask them where it is?" Sara inquired.

Tiffany said, "Not being rude, but they're not my friends. Yes, I'll call them and find out where the board is."

And she did. Minutes later, Tiffany called her mom back and said, "The Ouija board is in the attic closet under the file cabinet."

"God damn it," Keisha hollered.

Sara stood and said, "We need to get the board and bury it. It was the Ouija board session that invited the demon into your home," Sara said. "Burying it ensures no other negative spirits can come through the board. The planchette needs to be buried separately from the board."

"Will you come with me to get it?" Keisha asked.

"Absolutely. I wouldn't want to go alone either."

They walked to the attic and opened the closet door. Keisha lifted the file cabinet up while Sara knelt and pulled it out. Sara asked, "Where's the planchette? I don't see the planchette."

Keisha instinctively opened the file cabinet drawers. Both were empty. Then she checked behind the file cabinet. "Here it is," she said, reaching behind the file cabinet.

"Good. Let's get outside and bury the board and planchette. I've got some holy water we can sprinkle over these things once they're buried."

They turned towards the attic stairs and directly in front of them was an all–black figure with red eyes. His skin was reptilian. They dropped the board and planchette and ran towards the stairs. The planchette shot towards them like an arrow from a crossbow and struck the attic wall next to the stairwell, piercing it like a bulls–eye. The Ouija board whipped towards their heads like a Chinese star. They ducked, and the board missed their heads. About one–third of the board penetrated the wall in the stairwell.

"We have to get the board and the planchette," Sara pleaded. "I'll get the planchette. You get the board." As Sara walked up the attic stairs, George stopped her. He didn't want her going alone. She said, "We need to get the planchette. We saw a demon in the attic. We need to be careful."

When George and Sara reached the attic, the planchette was no longer in the wall. It was near Tiffany's rope that hung from the ceiling. They approached the planchette with caution even though there was no sign of the demon. She knelt to pick it up. As she stood with the planchette in her hand, the rope coiled around her neck like an anaconda— but incredibly faster— and rapidly hoisted her towards the ceiling. Her head struck the ceiling, nearly rendering her unconscious. She tried to pull the rope away from her neck, but the grip was too tight. George tried to pull her down, but he wasn't strong enough to counteract the force hoisting Sara in the air. When Sara lost consciousness, the rope untangled from around her neck and she fell to the floor. Moments later, she regained consciousness and George carried her in his arms down to the first floor. He laid her on the longer couch in the living room and said, "You rest. Jesus and I will take care of the board and planchette."

"Bury them separately," she mumbled, rubbing the rope burns on her neck.

Once George and Jesus returned from outside, the team loaded their equipment into their van and left.

CHAPTER THIRTY

Father v. Demon

Keisha placed the steaming pot of hot coffee on the serving tray and brought it out to the living room. Father Desdemona was sitting on the smaller couch taking in his surroundings. When Keisha entered the living room, he said, "You have a lovely home. These are nice pictures."

"Thank you, Father," Keisha said. "Do you take cream in your coffee? I forgot to place it on the tray."

"I'll take some cream if it's no trouble." He placed a few spoon–fulls of sugar in his coffee and stirred it while Keisha went to the kitchen.

She handed the creamer to Father Desdemona. "What did you think of the video I showed you?"

"Terrifying. I'm more inclined than not to believe your husband is possessed by an extremely powerful demon. Still, I need to do some preliminaries of my own before I say for certain. You put holy water in his wine, huh?

"Yeah. I thought that would be subtler than having Jeffrey fill up one of his squirt guns with holy water and shoot Steven."

"I see. Where is he? Your husband, I mean."

"He's been staying with my neighbor next door for the past few days. I had a medium come to the home and she indicated a demonic presence. Does that mean it is possible for the demon to pick and choose when it inhabits Steven?"

He took a sip of coffee. "Yes. The demon doesn't have to be inside Steven all the time. That's why it's possible for Steven to be happy–go–lucky one minute and mad at the world the next. It often will inhabit a body when it's convenient for the demon."

"I'll be glad when this is over with and Steven and the children and I can get on with our lives."

"I can't guarantee the exorcism will be a success. Steven must want the demon to be expunged from his body."

"I see. I understand."

When they finished their coffee, Father Desdemona stood and spoke. "Let's go ahead and debrief your children on their roles and what we'll need from them."

After debriefing the children, Keisha called John and told him the priest was ready to conduct the exorcism. It would take place in the living room. The priest and Keisha moved the larger living room couch all the way to the back, placing it against the wall separating the living room from the kitchen.

While waiting for Steven to be brought over from John's house, the priest opened his satchel and pulled out a purple stole and placed it around his neck. Each side of the stole had a gold cross on it. He laid out a crucifix, a ritual book, and a bottle of holy water onto the end table next to the smaller couch. Before setting the crucifix down, he kissed it.

When Steven was carried into the living room, Father Desdemona was greeted with a foul odor; it was a combination of urine, feces, and sulfur. "Why is he soiled in his own waste?" Father Desdemona inquired with an agitated tone.

Keisha replied, "We've kept him out of the house and restrained for the past several days. We weren't sure how dangerous he was. I'm sorry."

"You've denied him his human dignity," Father Desdemona said. "He's filthy."

Steven said, "Father, please let me use the bathroom. I promise I'll come right back."

"Not going to happen, Steven," Father Desdemona said. "Not right now. We need to talk first." He looked at Keisha. "Please get him some water."

"How are you feeling, Steven?"

"Not good, Father. Please let me go to my room and rest. Let's talk another day."

"Today is the day we talk, my son. Drink this," he said, handing Steven a plastic cup of water. After Steven finished the water, streams of smoke danced out of his mouth. The odor of the smoke was a cross between sulfur and rotting flesh.

"You deceived me, Father. That was holy water."

Making the sign of the cross midair, Father Desdemona spoke. "In the name of the Father, the Son, and the Holy Spirit," during which time Steven snarled and fought his restraints. He placed the crucifix on Steven's forehead, which produced a sound akin to steak searing on a grill. Smoke rose from his forehead.

"Ouch!" Steven cried. "You're hurting me. Stop! It burns!" Father Desdemona pushed the crucifix harder onto Steven's forehead.

"Father, please stop," Keisha demanded. "It's hurting my husband,"

"What is your name?" Father Desdemona asked.

"I'll never tell," Steven said in a low, growly voice.

"Tell me your name!"

This back and forth went on for several minutes. Finally Steven said, "Samael!"

"Samael, I command you and whatever other unholy, ungodly entities are in this creature of God to leave at once." Father Desdemona removed the crucifix from Steven's forehead. The crucifix left a burned imprint on his forehead.

"Nooooooo," Steven said, in a low, growly voice. "I'll never leave." Then he talked in a foreign dialect as he thrashed against the restraints.

"Leave this body and never return!" Father Desdemona commanded. He spritzed holy water onto Steven. Steven flinched each time it hit his body. When the water contacted bare skin, smoke rose from it.

"I don't wanna go," Steven drawled in the low, growly voice.

"You must leave now!" Father Desdemona insisted.

"I'll kill you!" Steven said, then laughed wickedly.

"In the name of Jesus Christ, I command you to leave this body!" Father Desdemona shouted, placing the crucifix back onto Steven's forehead, causing Steven to snarl and growl. His face contorted uncontrollably.

"Daddy! Please get the bad man out of you!" Brittany demanded. She disobeyed Father Desdemona; she was to remain silent in prayer.

Father Desdemona placed his hand on Steven's forehead and started to read prayers from his ritual book. One of the priest's assistants placed the crucifix in front of Steven. "I hate you!" Steven said.

After three hours of battling the demon inhabiting Steven, Father Desdemona commanded the demon to leave. "Samael and any other diabolical influences must leave this creature of God now!" He placed the crucifix on Steven's chest and repeated the command several times.

"Daddy! Please get rid of that bad man!" Brittany shouted.

Steven looked at Brittany and silently commanded the demon to leave. Moments later, it was over. He returned to his normal, happy self— the man everyone knew and missed. "I'm sorry for all of this," he said to everyone.

"Don't be sorry, my son. There's nothing to be sorry about."

Father Desdemona directed Steven to kiss the cross of Christ, and he did. The restraints were removed and Steven and Keisha embraced. Jeffrey, Tiffany, and Brittany joined in the hug, also.

Afterwards, Steven showered and napped. Later that evening, Steven and his family enjoyed dinner and pleasant conversation together.

The house had a different atmosphere. Colors were more vivid; smells were more pungent. The feeling of love and warmth permeated every inch of the house.

The next morning after the exorcism Keisha awoke to her bedroom filled with radiant light. She turned to her left to hug and kiss her husband, but he wasn't in bed.

She put on her housecoat and went downstairs to the kitchen, thinking he'd be there cooking breakfast, but he wasn't. She peeked out the kitchen window to see if he was working out in the backyard, but he wasn't there either.

She was beside herself. She wanted nothing more than to feel the warm embrace of her husband and she couldn't. She walked to the laundry room and opened the door that led to the garage. His car was still parked inside of it.

She checked the living room, but he wasn't there. She was pleased to see the family picture and crucifix were in their proper places. That gave her some peace of mind that the man in the black suit— Mr. Facchini— did cross over to the other side, where he belonged. She said a quick prayer for him again.

He wasn't anywhere on the first floor nor was he outside in the front or backyard. Her next stop was his office on the second floor. As she walked up the stairs, she thought she heard typing, but it was in her mind. Perhaps she so desperately wanted to see Steven, she fooled herself into thinking he was typing on his computer in his office. She opened his office door, but he wasn't in there.

Before checking the attic, which would be the most unlikely place he'd be, she checked her bedroom and bathroom once more, but he wasn't there.

She walked up the spiral staircase to the attic and as she got closer to the top stair, she found Steven hanged from the ceiling. He was wearing a black suit.

He used Tiffany's rope and the table on which she kept her weight/height/BMI journal.

From both of his partially open eyes were dried tear streams. He finally cried.

He left behind a suicide note.

Dear Family:
You all mean more to me than you could possibly know. My reasons to commit suicide had nothing to do with you or were caused by any of you. I systematically murdered my mother and my mother–in–law for profit by sprinkling poison in their food. I regret my crimes and cannot live with myself. I hope in time you can forgive me. Before I tightened the noose, I asked my maker for forgiveness. I hope to see you all in Heaven, but given my sins, I likely won't be there when you arrive. I love you always.

And that was the reason he committed suicide: he was a cold–blooded murderer. He hanged himself because he finally came to terms with the evil son of a bitch he was...

CHAPTER THIRTY-ONE

New Beginnings, Bright Futures

After Steven's funeral, cremation, and burial, Keisha and the children moved into a new house, located in Chesterton, Indiana, a city near Whitmond. Keisha was hired as a social studies teacher at an urban high school where she successfully helped the school be removed from academic probation. The inheritance money she received from her mother's death along with Steven's suicide had essentially secured her and her family's financial future.

Jeffrey continued his lessons with the renowned cello virtuoso and composed several short pieces and large–scale works for cello. He also started sketches for his first symphony.

Tiffany excelled in school and scored within the tenth percentile on the S.A.T. She still aspires to become a clinical psychologist as a career, though part of her wants to conduct paranormal investigations and help families rid their homes of unwanted, unrested spirits. She and Sebastian continue to date.

Brittany built several prototypes for a spirit communication device. Granana and Grams have visited her on and off. She placed Mr. Quackson in the ground with her father's urn. At a park near her house, she found another stray puppy, and Keisha agreed to let her have it. She named it Scruff, Jr.

John retired from Gypsum and spent most of his time birdwatching and sailing.

The F.B.I. investigated the harassment the Dobrowski's endured and evidence eventually led to Detective Auckland, Terry's brother. He plead guilty and was sentenced to seven years. He was fired from his position with the Whitmond Police Department.

CHAPTER THIRTY-TWO

Epilogue

Holly unlocked the front door of the house at 6729 Jefferson Ave., the former Dobrowski house. Her seven–year old son, Nathan, ran in the house. "I can't wait to pick my room!" he announced.

"Okay, champ," she said. "Go ahead upstairs and pick one out for yourself."

Her husband, Mark, kissed and hugged her, then picked her up and carried her across the threshold. "You are such a romantic, it makes me sick," she said, with a jesting tone.

"You know you love it," he remarked. He kissed her and set her down. "I'll start bringing more of the boxes in." A few moments later, he entered the living room with a banker's box marked LIVING ROOM PICTURES written in blue marker.

"Thanks, hubby. I'll start putting the pictures on the mantel."

"I can't wait to see how it looks. I'll be back in a few minutes. The neighbor next door wants to talk to me."

"Okay," she said, opening the box of pictures. She pulled out a picture from the box; it was a family picture. In the picture, Mark, Holly, and Nathan were dressed in their Sunday best. Nathan and Mark in matching gray suits and Holly in a solid maroon dress.

She momentarily gazed at the picture and walked over to the fireplace. "Yikes. That's dusty," she said. She placed the picture on the hearth. In the picture box, she had glass cleaner, wood cleaner, and all–purpose cleaner. Using the wood cleaner and rag, she wiped the dust from the mantel, which now had a sheen to it. Then she placed the family picture on the far right–side of mantel and stood back. "Looks good," she said.

She turned around to choose more pictures from the box to place on the mantel, but the sound of something sliding and falling caught her attention. She turned around. The family picture was on the hearth. She swallowed hard and walked towards the hearth. Once there, she knelt and turned the picture over. She stared at it for a few seconds, trying to make sense of what happened. Someone was staring at her from behind. She slowly stood and turned around. Standing near the picture box was a man in a black suit with a balding head and a dime–sized mole under his left eye. She broke the silence with a lengthy screamed and the man in the black suit flickered three times, the first two in rapid succession, followed by a small gap between the second and third. On the third flicker, the man in the black suit vanished...

<<<<>>>>

CPSIA information can be obtained
at www.ICGtesting.com
Printed in the USA
LVHW110842150819
627750LV00002B/133/P

9 781949 472790